"I can always trust Lexi Blake's Dominants to leave me breathless...and in love. If you want sensual, exciting BDSM wrapped in an awesome love story, then look for a Lexi Blake book."
~Cherise Sinclair USA Today Bestselling author

"Lexi Blake's MASTERS AND MERCENARIES series is beautifully written and deliciously hot. She's got a real way with both action and sex. I also love the way Blake writes her gorgeous Dom heroes--they make me want to do bad, bad things. Her heroines are intelligent and gutsy ladies whose taste for submission definitely does not make them dish rags. Can't wait for the next book!"
~Angela Knight, New York Times bestselling author

"A Dom is Forever is action packed, both in the bedroom and out. Expect agents, spies, guns, killing and lots of kink as Liam goes after the mysterious Mr. Black and finds his past and his future… The action and espionage keep this story moving along quickly while the sex and kink provides a totally different type of interest. Everything is very well balanced and flows together wonderfully."
~A Night Owl "Top Pick", Terri, Night Owl Erotica

"A Dom Is Forever is everything that is good in erotic romance. The story was fast-paced and suspenseful, the characters were flawed but made me root for them every step of the way, and the hotness factor was off the charts mostly due to a bad boy Dom with a penchant for dirty talk."

~Rho, The Romance Reviews

"A good read that kept me on my toes, guessing until the big reveal, and thinking survival skills should be a must for all men."

~Chris, Night Owl Reviews

Love and Let Die

Masters and Mercenaries, Book 5

Lexi Blake

Love and Let Die
Masters and Mercenaries, Book 5
Lexi Blake

Published by DLZ Entertainment LLC

Copyright 2013 DLZ Entertainment LLC
Edited by Chloe Vale and Kasi Alexander
ISBN: 978-1-937608-18-7

Acknowledgements

I would like to thank a few people without whom nothing in my life works. Thanks to my family—my amazing husband of twenty years, my three kids, and my wonderful mom who always helps out where needed.

Thanks to the best beta readers in the world—Riane Holt and Stormy Pate. And to my dear friends, Liz Berry and Kris Cook, who listen to my every worry and help to lift me up. Special thanks to Shayla Black because we've seen some of the places I describe in this book. It's so much better to see the world with a beloved friend at your side.

But this book is dedicated to the woman who has been there all along, who started Sophie with me and then followed me here.

This book is lovingly dedicated to Chloe Vale.

Prologue

"Mr. Taggart?"

Ian Taggart heard the doctor speaking, but all he could do was stare at the sight in front of him. She'd been alive when he'd left this morning, and now he was standing in the morgue of a London hospital looking at her body laid out on a metal table, covered by the thinnest of sheets. He wanted to smash the glass between them. How was it possible?

Charlotte couldn't be dead. Not his Charlie. She couldn't be in that cold exam room while he was standing in the hall staring at her body.

"Mr. Taggart?" The man's voice grew more agitated, his accent losing its clipped sounds and betraying the fact that the medical examiner was likely from somewhere in the country. "The authorities will need to have a word with you."

He fucking bet they did. They would want more than a word. They would want to arrest him. They would want to set him in a cell and leave him with absolutely no

7

defenses and then someone would very quietly and calmly end him because this was a setup and he knew it. This was about making sure he was vulnerable.

Someone knew about the Irish mission. It was set to take place in a few hours. He was supposed to be on his way to Dublin to meet with the G2 team he had in place, some kid named Liam and his brother, Rory.

Charlotte couldn't be dead. He'd made love to her hours before, driving into her body again and again while she clung to him. She was the strongest woman he'd ever met, and he'd managed to tame her. He'd managed to get a ring on her finger and a collar around her neck. He'd known the minute he'd laid eyes on her that she would belong to him.

Mine. His whole fucking being still called out to her. Mine.

"Are you listening, Mr. Taggart?" Ian could hear the voice, but it seemed far away, like someone was talking to him from a great distance.

His vision had narrowed to one thing, blocking out everything else.

God, Sean didn't even know he'd gotten married. He hadn't told his brother about the wedding and now his wife was dead. His life was in shambles and he couldn't even reach out to his brother. Sean was somewhere in Afghanistan. Sean thought Ian was with a team in Iraq. Sean had no idea he worked for the CIA. None of them did. Alex might suspect it, but he would never ask.

Would they even tell his brother that he died in prison or would the US government cover it all up? Would he even die or would he be renditioned somewhere by god only knew who?

Why was he fucking thinking this way? He needed to move. He needed to get the fuck out of here. He needed…

He needed to be with her.

One of the technicians moved in and started to close the drawer that held Charlotte's body. They would autopsy her later in an attempt to prove that Ian Taggart killed his wife. Ian had no doubt that they would come up with all types of evidence against him.

"Don't you fucking close that!" He slammed his fist against the glass but it didn't shatter like he wanted it to. It held firm. The tech guy looked like he was about to pee himself though.

And Charlotte was still dead.

"She doesn't like closed spaces." She was terrified of really tight places. Something about her childhood. Her father had been a controlling asshole who had tortured his daughters, and one of the ways he'd abused them was by locking them in small spaces. Charlotte hated even being in elevators.

Until he'd wrapped his arms around her and let her hide her eyes against his chest. At first he'd wondered if it had all been a game, a way to seduce him. She seemed to figure him out so easily, but there had been genuine fear in her eyes and her pulse had sped up.

It's different with you, Master. I'm safe with you. Tell me I'm safe with you, Ian.

Charlotte was dead. He'd brought her into his life and now she was dead. She hadn't been safe with him at all.

"Mr. Taggart, the police are here. You have to go with them now."

The police had escorted him to the hospital, a couple of bobbies who had treated him with some respect, but he had no doubt he would get a visit from the detectives of New Scotland Yard. They wouldn't be so careful with him. Or someone else would show up, the type of men who didn't have restrictions on the way they treated a suspect. Men like Ian himself.

God, she was still so fucking gorgeous. Her skin was pale, but it was always pale. It didn't make sense. She had to get up. She had to walk out of here with him.

He loved her.

If he went with the police, he might be able to be with her again. Maybe all that shit about heaven was right and he would be able to see Charlie. Maybe he could leave everything behind—all the lies and manipulation.

He'd been a different man with Charlotte, a softer man, a man who might have had a future.

God, he'd even thought about children in a vague, undefined way. Just a little fleeting vision of how sweet his Charlie would look with a baby in her arms.

Something touched his right shoulder and he reacted without thought, his elbow coming up and back. He felt the impact, heard the cracking sound of cartilage giving way, and then a flurry of curse words as the nightsticks made their first appearance.

He put his hands in the air, giving up this particular fight. He sure as fuck wasn't going to get taken down in a goddamn morgue.

Oh, god, he was leaving his wife in a morgue.

He forced the pain down. Someone had killed Charlotte, and it likely had something to do with the operation he was working. He was tracking a Russian national who was attempting to buy nuclear material. Charlotte had ties to the Russian mafia. She hadn't tried to hide it. She'd shown up at the club he was playing at while he worked in Paris, and he'd thought she would be a pleasant way to spend a couple of weeks and gather intelligence. It was only supposed to be some short-term sex, but somehow it had become more. Then he'd brought her to London with him and she'd been his lover, his wife, his submissive.

Now she was his mistake and someone was going to pay.

He got to the ground because there was nothing else for him to do but comply for the moment. The hall was too crowded for him to move. Once they got him in cuffs, he would only have his legs to work with, but he'd been in worse situations before. He couldn't let them put him in a cell. The minute he was in a cell, he was a sitting duck.

A million scenarios ran through his head, but at the end of the day, he was alone. This was his operation, and he'd fucked it up.

Cold metal circled his wrists, and he let his body go limp. The cops struggled to get his six-and-a-half-foot frame upright, but he wasn't going to help. No fucking way. A tired cop was a cop he could get away from. He would let the fuckers drag him the whole way.

A man in a suit and tie walked in. He was different from the cops, but there was no mistaking his authority. He had a partner with him, a slightly smaller male, still tall but leaner. They pulled badges out, showing off their credentials.

Ah, Scotland Yard had finally made their appearance. These men looked like they could handle themselves. These weren't paunchy, over-the-hill detectives just trying to make their way to retirement. No. These were predators.

Maybe they were really Scotland Yard and maybe they weren't. He was about to find out one way or the other.

The Agency would disavow any knowledge of him. He was utterly on his own. His brother had no idea where he was. His best friend was in Washington working at the FBI.

Ian Taggart would disappear into the system and

another operative would take his place.

After a few moments of arguing, the larger of the two men stepped forward, having won the right to the prize at hand—him.

"Come with me," the big man said with an elegant British accent. Ian bet he wouldn't lose his perfectly upper-crust sounds when he was angry. He had an aristocratic look about him.

He had to run. He had to find a way to get to his contacts.

Ian looked back at the window as they began to haul him along, but the little fucker technician had shut the drawer, sealing Charlotte away from him.

He was in a daze. His eyes didn't seem to want to function. His stomach was in knots. He didn't want to leave her. How could he fucking leave her?

He struggled, reason fleeing. He needed to hold her again. He needed to be sure. Things in his world could be false, manipulative.

"Just a little more, mate." The man he was walking beside never looked anywhere but toward the elevator. "And don't bloody well try anything. I've had a rather rough night and would like to get home in one piece. I believe my handler would prefer to be the one to take me apart."

His partner stepped up beside him, a smile on his face as he winked at one of the nurses. "Oh, aren't you a pretty little bird. Are you sure we don't have a minute, Damon? I won't take long, and the Yank there looks like he could use a rest."

One thing had gone right. One fucking thing. The elevator doors dinged open. "You're MI6."

The dark-haired one gave him a tip of his head. "Of course. Should have been here sooner, mate, but my partner insists on afternoon tea. The name's Damon Knight."

"And I'm Basil Champion the third, but obviously the third time's the charm. You can call me Baz. I think the three of us are about to spend a bit of time together. We've hit a snag with the Irish. Into the lift you go before the police figure out we're not really Scotland Yard and we all get fucked."

They all stepped into the elevator.

Damon Knight pushed the button to go up and turned to him. "What do you know about a man named Liam O'Donnell?"

O'Donnell was an Irish operative, the very one he'd hand selected to meet with the Russian. He felt numb, but compelled to ask the question. "What's gone wrong?"

"Everything."

The doors closed and despite the fact that he had two other men with him, Ian suddenly knew he would always be alone.

* * * *

Charlotte Dennis came awake in complete darkness. For just a moment she thought she'd gone blind. The drugs she'd taken could cause numerous horrific side effects. Maybe this was just one of them. But the pain in her shoulder was pure gunshot wound. *Fuck.* Had they taken the bullet out? She'd known they would have to leave it in for a while. If they had taken the fucking bullet out, they might have noticed she was still bleeding. Corpses didn't bleed. She was sure someone had given her a drug to stop the bleeding but removing the bullet would have started it again. Was she still bleeding? Still pierced by metal?

God, she was in so much pain, and the ache in her

heart was worse than the bullet wound.

"Hello?"

Someone was supposed to be here to take her to Chelsea. She and Chelsea were supposed to be free of their father now.

"Hello?" She felt weak, but then her body had been so close to death that no one would suspect she was alive.

Where was Ian now? Had they arrested him? She wasn't stupid. She knew what Eli Nelson was trying to do. He wanted to "distract" a CIA operative. What better way would there be to distract him than to kill him?

The trouble was, her husband was damn hard to kill.

God, if she found out he'd been arrested and killed while in custody, she would lie back down and she wouldn't need drugs. She would die, just fade away.

Why did Ian Taggart have to be the one man in the world for her?

Charlie took a breath, her head still groggy. She needed to get to her sister. She hadn't seen Chelsea for months. What if their father had hurt her again? What if he'd killed her? She had to see Chelsea, make sure she was alive.

And she had to save Ian. She had to find a way.

But first she had to find the light switch.

She tried to move her good arm and felt cold metal at her fingertips. Her hands began to shake in a way that had nothing to do with the drugs she'd taken.

The lights weren't off in the room. She wasn't in a room.

She sent her hand out, desperate to prove her instincts wrong, to prove she wasn't trapped in a box.

All she found was more metal. She wasn't trapped in a box. She was trapped in a coffin.

The scream that came from her throat nearly split her

ears. She was fourteen years old again and trapped in that box her father would lock her in when she rebelled. Sometimes, she wasn't alone in the box. Sometimes a rat or a snake had managed to find its way in and Charlie had to kill it with her hands or feet. She could still remember that snake biting her over and over and over before she'd found a way to kill it. Luckily it hadn't been venomous, but she hadn't known that.

She smashed her hands against the walls that held her and screamed the way she had when she was a kid.

No. Not the same because now she screamed a name.

Now she screamed for her husband. The husband she'd betrayed.

She felt her whole body jerk back and then light flooded her vision.

"Shut the fuck up, Charlotte, or you won't see your sister again. You can't see her if I have to kill you."

She went utterly silent. She'd given up everything for Chelsea. Everything. Because Ian Taggart had become her everything. Tears blurred her vision as she started to be able to make out shapes. A dark figure loomed over her.

She forced herself to sit up, every muscle achy and twitching. Her stomach rolled and suddenly there was a trash can in front of her as she began to heave.

There was a long sigh. "The drugs will do that to you. An unfortunate side effect."

Eli Nelson, the man who had promised to save her if only she would do this one little teeny tiny job for him, stood next to her in his suit designed to attract the minimum of attention. Everything about the man was calculated to make him look as bland and normal as possible. From his average height to his nondescript hair, he fit into the crowd.

She'd decided Eli Nelson was the devil.

She finished emptying her stomach and turned, her legs dangling. She looked at her left shoulder. A bandage was wrapped around her.

"Yes, dear, I rather thought I should have them take the bullet out before you woke up. I couldn't have you unable to run. The pain must be excruciating. I congratulate you on your fortitude."

"Who took it out? They suck." She now had one more scar on a body full of them.

Nelson's lips lifted in a ghastly imitation of a smile. "I took care of it. I didn't want to leave any pesky evidence behind. I have a man on the inside here who let me in after all the formalities were over. The sutures might not be perfect, but they did the job."

God, would she ever stop shaking? It was so cold. Had it really been hours ago that she'd been warm in Ian's arms? Now she was here. She recognized where she was.

A morgue.

She was in a morgue because she'd died and now she was alive again. Lazarus in high heels. Her clothes were covered in blood. What the hell was she going to do now? She couldn't think about the future. All that mattered was the answer to one question. "Where is Chelsea?"

Nelson gestured to someone behind him and the door opened.

"Charlotte." Her kid sister shuffled in, her braces scuffing across the floor.

Chelsea was all of twenty-two years old, but she seemed so much younger. She was thin and weak because their father kept her that way. To their father, Chelsea was nothing but a tool to get Charlie to do what he wanted. Despite the fact that they were technically adults, their father still ruled them with an iron fist. After he'd found them and kidnapped them from Mama, he'd made it

16

impossible for them to leave Russia. Until Eli Nelson had shown up with his devil's bargain. Now Chelsea was here and they could run. They could hide.

Would he find them?

"Your father is dead," Nelson said bluntly. "I kept up my end of the deal. MI6 will likely find his body in a couple of days and they'll believe that everything is over. Eventually they'll figure out that your dear papa wasn't the one trying to buy uranium, but for now they'll believe what I want them to believe. Thank you, dear. That little bit of chaos wouldn't have been possible without you."

With shaking hands, she clutched her sister, pulling her behind her body in case everything went to hell. "I don't understand."

Nelson shrugged a little. "You aren't supposed to. You did a halfway decent job leading Taggart around by his dick, and I appreciate that. You're looking at me like I'm going to kill you. If I had wanted to kill you, I wouldn't have faked your death. I would have made it real. Do you understand how complex this was? No, dear, I want you alive. You've proven to be very resourceful when it comes to information retrieval. I could use you in the future. In fact, I want you to start tracking a few key players, including your beloved."

Ian. Ian wasn't dead. She breathed a deep sigh of relief. If Ian had been dead, she might have crawled back into that coffin-like box and let the madness take her. "I thought this was a play to kill him."

Nelson chuckled. "Oh, no. I never sacrifice a pawn until I need to. Right now our mutual employers are working so hard to deal with Mr. Taggart's issues that they're not looking at me, and that's how I want it for a while. I have some plans for Mr. Taggart's operatives that require that his attention be aimed elsewhere. Not that you need to know what my plans are."

No. She was just another of his pawns, exactly like she'd been for her father.

Nelson handed her a set of keys. "There's a BMW in the parking lot with new passports, plane tickets, and a briefcase with fifty thousand dollars inside. Contact me when you settle in the States. I expect great things of you, Charlotte Dennis."

She almost said it, almost corrected him. Her name was Taggart. She'd been Charlotte Marie Taggart for thirty-two days, and she would never have another name because she would never take another man. She belonged to her Master and always would.

Nelson turned and started out the door. "You should hurry, dear. Your corpse will be missed soon. It's not every day one just goes missing. I'm leaving enough evidence behind to point to your husband or the family who so dearly loved you. I wouldn't want Taggart asking too many questions after all. Scotland Yard will suspect Taggart, and Taggart will suspect your recently deceased father and his men. My guess is I went easy on dear old dad. I just slit his throat. I bet Taggart would have done something worse."

He whistled a little as he let himself out of the morgue, his cronies following along behind. The door shut with a little swish and they were alone.

"Charlotte, are you okay?" She asked the question in the language of their childhood, the language of their mother—English. Their mother had baptized them with American names. She'd managed to run, to get away for years, before their father had found them again. For years all they had spoken was Russian. Except in their secret places. When they were alone, they had kept up their English. Their true language. When she'd heard it, she'd known she was safe.

Chelsea. She had to think of Chelsea. Chelsea was completely helpless, and her husband could take care of himself. "We have to go. He's right. I can't be found here."

"They drugged the night guard and apparently Nelson has some of the employees on his payroll. We have a few minutes. Is your arm okay?"

"I think it still works." They would be a pair. Chelsea with her limping walk and she with a bullet wound in her arm. Yes, they were real physical threats.

"Charlotte, do you think he's really dead?" Chelsea asked, the question ringing in the near-silent room.

Vladimir Denisovitch. Their father. Their abuser. The man who had beaten Chelsea so badly that her legs had never been the same again. The one who had turned Charlotte into a trained killer because no one would suspect such a soft girl. "I don't know."

She wouldn't believe it until she saw it. But her father's death would only solve one of her problems. It probably opened up a hundred more, including the fact that her husband would eventually suspect she'd been lying to him. She'd worked so hard to gain his trust, and it was all shattered now.

"Are we going back to the States? I want to go home, Charlotte. Not to where we lived, just back to America. But what if Dad's men find us?"

"Then we'll have to kill them."

Chelsea looked up at her, and for the first time Charlie saw the deep strength in her sister's eyes. For so long, Chelsea had been her burden. She loved her sister. She'd also sacrificed most of her life for her. But now, Chelsea reached for her hands and steadied them. "Did you really marry that man? Ian Taggart?"

"I love him." At least one person in the world should know the truth. "I didn't mean to. It was stupid, but I love him."

"Can we go to him?"

And risk Nelson taking them all out? God, would Ian even speak to her after everything she'd done? "I don't think so. I don't even know where he is. I'm not sure why Nelson thinks I'll be able to track him. Ian is an operative and a damn good one at that. I think I need time to figure everything out."

She needed to find a way to be worthy of him. If she walked back into his life now, he might actually kill her. Her husband was a dangerous man, and she'd placed him and his entire operation in peril. He would take that seriously. There would be no light spankings followed by a little withheld orgasm.

No, his sub had betrayed him. He wouldn't trust her again.

Unless she found a way to make it up to him.

Chelsea nodded. "Then we take our time and we get strong. I want to be strong now. I've figured a few things out. We've been trying to get out of this world, but we can't. It will always pull us back in. We will always be Denisovitch's daughters. We can shorten and Americanize our last name all we like. The men like Nelson will always know and they'll want to use us."

"We have to stay away." She'd been trying to get out for years, but she'd become known for everything her father had trained her to do. He'd found her again at the age of thirteen and hadn't waited long to start teaching her what it meant to be his daughter. He hadn't had any sons, so he'd treated Charlotte like one. She'd run her first long con at fourteen. She'd made her first kill at the age of fifteen. Robbed her first bank on her seventeenth birthday.

She'd done it all because her father would have killed her if she didn't, but the stains were on her soul all the same.

And when she was twenty-six, she'd finally figured out what love was when a man who looked like a Viking had taken her in his arms and shown her an entirely different world. A world where she could trust someone enough to submit to him.

"He won't let us. You heard what he said. He expects you to call him."

Charlie nodded. "Yes. Me. Not you. When we get back to the States, you're going to college, and I'll handle this."

Her sister held on to the table and looked her straight in the eyes. "I am done with letting you ruin your life. Hear me and hear me now. I know you think I'm just a cripple."

"Chelsea, no." Her sister was fragile, but she never meant to make her feel bad about it. Since their mother had been killed, Chelsea was her whole life.

She shook her head. "Yes, it's how you see me and until now, it's how I've acted. I've been a scared little mouse. I've let you give up everything for me. But not anymore. When we go home, I'm going to help you. I've learned a lot in the last few years. Papa made me learn how to hack into systems. I'm really good. I can write code, too. I can be helpful."

"I don't want that for you." She'd been trying to get out of this world for her sister's sake.

"And I don't want you to lose the man you love, but I have to deal with it now, don't I? No, if we can't run from this world, then there's one thing to do."

Her heart hardened slightly as she realized the truth of her sister's words. "We have to rule it."

Chelsea nodded. "This world runs on information. So

we become the center of it all. We use them the way they used us."

She found her feet, her sister steady against her. They were just two girls against a world of black operations and money-fueled crime.

Suddenly she knew that she would win. She would have her husband back and she would bring down everyone who tried to stop her. Optimism. She had to have it. She had to believe that she could do everything she needed to.

If there was one thing she'd learned in her lifetime, it was that the world was a game.

She would win or she would die.

Chapter One

Dallas, TX
Five Years Later

Ian Taggart looked across the table at his previously dead wife and took in the changes the last five years had brought.

She was older. There were fine lines around her eyes that had been previously absent. Her hair was a reddish blonde, but it looked oddly good on her. It went with her stark blue eyes.

Death had been damn good to her. She was still the most stunning woman he'd ever seen. Her return from the dead had stirred more than his curiosity.

His cock was rock hard, but he wasn't going to give in. Nope. Not this time.

"Tetraodontidae?" Ian asked after a very long, very tense few moments. He was curious about what she'd used to fake her death. Tetraodontidae was a good bet.

She'd shown up on his doorstep, all bright-eyed and

bushy-tailed and calling him Master. She'd gotten past his incredibly rigorous security system. His brother liked to call him paranoid, but Ian knew the truth. The world really was out to get him. That was what happened to spies. They rarely made it to old age, even the ones who got out.

He'd watched many of his colleagues die, some painfully and under torture. This was the first time one had come back from the other side. Of course, when he'd married her, he hadn't exactly realized she was a spy. He'd known something was wrong with her, but he'd thought she'd been in trouble. He'd been a fool.

He'd invited her in because it was only polite. And because he was going to figure out what the fuck she wanted from him.

And because he couldn't help himself. Fuck, he couldn't help himself at all. He didn't like the feeling any more now than he had back then. From the moment he'd seen her, he'd known he would have her no matter what it took, and that feeling was taking root in his gut again.

"The puffer fish neurotoxin?" She shook her head. "No. I mean I think it might be based on that, but it was a pill. I had to take a pill, and then it was mostly like going to sleep."

He nodded briefly. When he'd realized it was really Charlotte standing on his doorstep, he'd put it together. Too bad he'd been too stupid to back then. "I heard rumors that the Agency has been working on a zombie drug. I guess I got out before I really needed to use it. Lucky me."

A zombie drug was used to fake an agent's death. The puffer fish had a neurotoxin in its body that would render a human lifeless, seemingly breathless. The victim would appear dead. The victim would almost always end up dead, but apparently someone out there had perfected the mix.

She shuddered a little. "I wouldn't recommend it."

"What about the blood?" She'd been covered in it. He'd gotten covered in it. Sometimes he could still smell that coppery scent mingling with the lavender soap she used on her body. He'd loved the smell of lavender until that day.

"Oh, he really shot me. He gave me the drug and then he pulled the trigger." She pushed one side of her blouse toward her shoulder, showing off the puckered scar below her left clavicle. "It was close enough that I suppose the blood made you think it was my heart."

He wanted to shove that material off and take a look at every inch of her skin, looking for the new scars she would have, skimming his fingers across the ones she'd had when they'd gotten married.

Before she died. Before she came back.

The first time he made love to her he thought she had a bad Dom in her past. She had more scars than most of the men he knew, and they were all Special Forces.

For now, he would settle for having his questions answered. He wasn't going to give in to the heart-pounding adrenaline of having her back. His first instinct had been to wrap himself around her and never let her go. His second had been to drag her to the dungeon and take out all of his anger. But no. He would do neither of those things during this little interview. He would view it as a post-op debrief. It was the kind of thing he would do with his employees. He would sit them down and go through a million questions in an attempt to figure out just how the little fuckers had screwed things up.

This time he was the one who had completely gone off the rails, and he was deeply curious just how far it went.

"Who?"

Charlotte frowned as though the whole meeting wasn't going quite the way she'd planned. She'd no doubt expected him to give in to instinct number one. "What do you mean who?"

He liked the fact that she was off balance. She couldn't seem to get a handle on his calmness. He couldn't blame her. He'd always been a dipshit passionate idiot around her. She didn't know the real Ian Taggart, the one he'd been before he'd married her, the one he'd found his way back to after long years of mourning. He was cold, calm, collected. He was a professional. "Who shot you, Charlotte?"

She stilled. "You're not going to like it, Master."

"Ian, please. I'm not your Master, sweetheart. I would prefer you use my given name. I keep the honorary title for the submissives I top." He kept his voice at the same even keel, but the word "Master" did something to him when it came out of her mouth.

"You're always my Master," she said, her voice sweet and a little sad. "And I'm your submissive."

"We'll have to agree to disagree on that." Or he could shove her over his knee, work those jeans off her hips, and slap her ass silly. Charlotte could take it. Charlotte craved it.

Who had been smacking her cheeks and tying her up and fucking her until she screamed? Because there was no way she went without.

"Master, I need you to listen to me." Her blue eyes fairly pleaded with him. Those eyes were what had gotten him in the first place. Oh, he'd loved her breasts and her hips. She was solidly built, and that just did it for him. He wanted a woman he could fuck for hours and not worry about breaking, but her eyes were striking. Ocean blue, like the waters of the Caribbean reflecting a crystal sky. He'd been drawn into those eyes.

"I'm listening, Charlotte." A thought occurred to him. "Is that the name you're going by now or should I call you Kristen? I have no idea what your real name is."

Her hands made frustrated fists. Ah, she hadn't changed her little tells. Those fists always made an appearance when she thought he was being stubborn. Her hair might have changed, but he could still tell when he was getting to her.

"I'm Charlotte Dennis and you damn well know it. You checked me out the first time. I never lied about my background."

He raised a single brow.

She bit into her bottom lip, her eyes sliding submissively away. "I apologize, Master. I shouldn't have cursed."

He shook it off. It was just a habit. Disciplining her had been a habit, the same way her sinking to her knees at his feet and rubbing her cheek to his leg had been a habit. The way he'd been able to relax and think as he'd petted her hair and enjoyed the contact before he would inevitably pull her into his lap and start to make love to her.

Yep. Just a habit. He could break habits. He hadn't had her in five years and he'd survived perfectly well. "Curse all you like. I probably would if my boss had shot me and then dosed me up with puffer fish toxin. Do you think he expected you to live?"

He tamped down the panic that flared at the thought of someone shooting her and dosing her up and leaving her there on the floor of their flat like a sacrifice. The protectiveness was a habit, too. She wasn't his to protect, and she never had been. She hadn't really been his sub.

She'd been his opponent, and the first round had gone to her.

But she wasn't going to win this one.

"He wasn't my boss, babe. He had something I needed, and I thought he was the only one who could do the job. After I met you, I realized just how stupid I was." Her eyes were cloudy with tears, and she started to reach out for him. He moved his hands and leaned back out of her reach. "I should have talked to you but by then the man I was working for had Chelsea. After he killed my father, he took her as insurance that I would do the job. I couldn't risk Chelsea."

"Of course not." He had no idea who Chelsea was. Probably her dog. "I would like a name, Charlotte."

Her jaw tightened, and she looked down at her hands. "Chelsea is my sister's name. I know I didn't tell you about her, but she's younger than me. She's more…fragile. You remember how I told you about my father?"

Her Russian mobster dad. Yes, Vladimir Denisovitch. He had a rap sheet about twelve miles long in twenty-two different countries. If he'd followed the Russian mob practice of tattooing his crimes on his body, Ian was sure there hadn't been an inch of skin left on Vlad's flesh. But his crimes against Charlotte were even worse. However, Ian no longer cared. "I asked for a name. I don't need to know about your sister."

"You're going to be difficult."

He shook his head. "Not at all. If you don't want to talk, you should feel free to leave. There's nothing at all difficult about it."

She took a long breath before speaking. "I'll tell you, but I want you to stay calm."

Everything fell neatly into place. There was only one

name he could think of that would truly enrage him. Or would if he really gave a shit about her. "Then it's Eli Nelson. That makes sense. I thought I would find him at the bottom of this particular shit pile."

Nelson seemed to be at the bottom of all the nasty shit that happened to Ian these days.

At the time he'd met Charlotte, Ian had been working a complicated case involving the Irish G2 intelligence unit, MI6, and a purported Russian terrorist. Eli Nelson had been with the CIA, but the case was Ian's operation. Unfortunately, Ian had been distracted by the lovely Charlotte Dennis—as Nelson had planned. Nelson had gotten away with a couple of million in bearer bonds and set himself up as an arms dealer.

Ian had gotten the fuck out of the CIA.

"I didn't know you when I agreed to help him." Charlotte did nothing to stop the tears running down her cheeks. "I didn't love you."

"Yes, well, I figured that out a few moments ago when you showed up on my doorstep."

Her blonde and red hair shook. It actually suited her quite nicely. When he'd known her she'd had black hair. This warmed up her skin. "No, Master. I meant I didn't love you when I began the operation. That changed so quickly. Please believe me. I never meant you harm. Master, I love you so much. I've been working for five years to get back to you."

"A plane ticket would have done it. You should have tried the airport." He wasn't going to buy this line of bullshit. "I made it from London to Dallas quite nicely."

Of course he'd done it on a private jet because MI6 had to cover up his wife's death. At the time they believed her body disappeared in an attempt by the Russians to make Ian look guilty and throw the whole operation into chaos. Now he knew it had just been good old Eli Nelson, American-grown fuckwad and all-around criminal.

He was going to find Eli Nelson. He was going to rip Eli Nelson open and play with his entrails while the fucker was alive to watch it. He would go old school on his ass. No fancy schmancy waterboarding for Nelson. He wouldn't send the bastard to Guantanamo. Simple. He would keep it simple. Just him and a ball gag and one of Sean's filet knives. He would let his brother play, too. Sean would likely enjoy castrating Nelson, sautéing up his dick, and force-feeding it to him. It could be a family project. Maybe they could take a weekend.

"Why do you look so happy, Master?" Charlotte asked. "It actually frightens me."

He forced the smile off his face. Lately, his revenge fantasies made him far happier than the sexual ones.

Because the sexual ones all revolved around her.

"I'd ask for a detailed accounting of everything you know about Nelson, but I wouldn't be able to trust a word you have to say, would I? I can very likely toss that e-mail you sent in the trash bin." Just moments before he'd opened the door, he'd gotten an e-mail with all sorts of intelligence on Eli Nelson. Now it was useless because it came from her. He was ready to end this little interview. There was a bottle of fifty-year Scotch calling his name. Where was his phone? He needed some music.

"I'll tell you everything you want to know. I sent you the e-mail because I want to help you find Nelson." Charlotte stood, moving around the table and getting to her knees in front of him. "Master, I know I have so much to make up for, but I'm going to do it. I'm going to help you. I already did. I saved Alex. I did that for you."

He felt his eyes narrow. "That's right. You put yourself in front of a bullet for Alex."

She'd been playing a longer game than he'd given her credit for.

She nodded her head. "Yes, and I would do it again because you love Alex and I love you. I watched over them. I guided them back together. Do you think I don't remember how you talked about them? You wanted us to all live close together."

They had lain in bed the night they were married and talked about moving back to the States. He'd wanted to move to Virginia to be close to Alex and Eve. It had been pillow talk, nothing more. He hadn't meant a word he said. He hadn't intended to give up his career for her so he could be some schmo living in the suburbs and having backyard barbecues and going to his kids' soccer games.

"Well, I guess I got my wish, though we're in Dallas and not Virginia." A sudden thought occurred to him that had his hand practically twitching. "You brought my friends together all right, but that's not all you did is it, you little brat?"

She gave him a weak smile. "I had to keep you away, Master. I changed parts of my appearance, but I would never have been able to fool you. You would have shut everything down. You can be a bit of a bully when you want to be."

She'd pretended to be a reporter and offered to help Alex track down the man who had raped and terrorized Alex's wife, Eve. She'd brought most of the team to her condo in St. Augustine, Florida, but Ian had found himself in a series of clusterfucks. "You put me on a no-fly list."

Among other things. She'd wreaked havoc on his life.

"If I hadn't, you would have found out it was me and the whole op would have been blown."

"You tied up my banking accounts. You moved them to another name." He'd been so fucking stupid. He'd believed it was Nelson screwing with him. God, would he ever have a brain in his head when it came to this woman?

"I should get points for calling you Hottie McHot Pants. I meant it as a compliment. You look so good, Master. And actually it was Chelsea who handled all the computer stuff. I'm mostly just muscle compared to her. I'm good at finding information, but nothing like her. She's very smart, you see. If I had known better I would have changed it all over to Big Tag." The sexiest smile curled her lips up. "I got to know your brother a little on the Florida op. He is an excellent cook, but he thinks far too much of his own looks. He's attractive, but nothing compared to you."

Now his dick was right back to fighting strength. She was kneeling at his feet, her eyes all soft and sweet, that husky voice of hers calling to him. She always looked at him like she could eat him up and come back for more. He could reach out and wind his hands in her hair and tug on it. She fucking loved to have her hair pulled. He could be rough with Charlie because it just got her hot.

That was precisely why he couldn't touch her. She was his Achilles' heel. Nelson had always known it. "So I owe my recent body cavity search to this Chelsea person."

"Like I said, Chelsea is my sister, Master. I'd love to tell you all about her. Why don't you let me make you a drink and we can talk more? If you're hungry, I can fix you something." She placed her hand on his thigh. "I've become a much better cook over the years. I know how much you enjoy Italian, so I worked on that. I might not be as good as Sean, but I look better cooking naked than he does."

His cock twitched. His heart rate sped up. His whole central nervous system was attuned to her. Five years later and she had him on edge with a simple touch. No one ever got to him the way Charlie did. She was his sexual hot spot.

Or you just loved her, idiot. His inner voice was starting to sound an awful lot like Alex.

He carefully moved her hand off his leg. "I think I'll pass. I have a job to do. You should let your boss know that I'm going to kill him really slowly."

"He's not my boss, Ian." Her cheeks had flushed, her brows coming together in a frustrated *V*.

Finally he was getting to her. "I would totally believe you, sweetheart, if you weren't such an excellent liar."

"I'm not lying." She seemed to take control of herself again. Her face grew placid, her submissive look. She'd used it on him more than once, and it always got to him. "I've spent the last five years trying to be a better person for you, Master. How do I prove it to you?"

She couldn't. There was no possible way he could ever believe her again. He'd been a fool to believe her in the first place.

But her hand was right back on his leg, her breasts showcased in a scoop-necked shirt. He loved her breasts. They were just the right size and real. He loved how they looked outside of the punishing bras she wore. They would sag just slightly, but that proved how soft they were. Her nipples used to pucker up sweetly for him. Were they hard little pebbles now?

"Master…Ian, I know this is going to be difficult, but you should know that I'm not giving up. I love you. The only other people I've loved in my life are my sister and my mom, so I won't give up on you."

Or she had another agenda, and fucking him senseless had worked before. She wasn't being terribly creative, but then he'd given her no reason to think she had to be. She'd flashed him her love-me, save-me, fuck-me eyes and Ian let his whole career and a major operation go into the toilet. He'd almost cost Liam his life.

Of course, turnabout was always fair play. Not that it mattered. He didn't play fair.

"Did you miss me, Charlie?" He didn't fight his cock this time. Maybe he and his cock could get what they wanted. There was always a compromise. Charlie hadn't minded taking about a thousand orgasms from him without explaining her true intentions.

There was no way to miss the hitch in her voice. Her hand slid across his thigh. "You know I did. I missed you every minute of every day."

He'd certainly missed fucking her. He ignored that little voice that sounded way too much like Alex, that was kind of screaming at him that this was a horrible idea. If Alex was the angel on his shoulder, his cock was the devil, and the devil thought this was one of his more brilliant plans. "Show me."

He flexed his hips, demonstrating exactly what part of him needed her attention.

Charlotte's hands went straight to his pants, and Ian let the devil take firm control.

* * * *

He was up to something. She wasn't stupid. But she also wasn't willing to let the chance go. Sex had bonded them together all those years ago. It could do the same thing now.

It had to work. She'd come too far to give up. She wanted him too much.

She struggled a little with the button on his slacks. He was still dressed in his tuxedo pants. She'd watched him walk into Sanctum, his club, earlier this evening. Alex and

Eve's wedding ceremony had been held there. She'd wanted so much to join him. Alex and Eve and Adam and Sean had become her friends during the time they spent in Florida. Sure, they hadn't known her real name or anything, but she'd been honest about most things. She'd felt like she belonged in that little circle of friends—Ian's circle.

She'd been brutally jealous that Jesse the jerk had gotten an invitation and she hadn't. Jesse had been the one to shoot her. Oh, he'd thought he was aiming at Alex, but she'd taken that bullet, and Jesse had been all smiles and grins as he'd waltzed right into Sanctum like he owned the place. Shouldn't they have brutally murdered the little fucker?

"Is there a problem?" Ian's voice was positively arctic.

Sometimes she went the slightest bit ADD when she felt safe enough. She lived her life on the edge so often that when she had a chance to relax, she tended to take it. She could usually only relax in her well-secured apartment, high above the city, but just being in Ian's presence had an effect on her. "I apologize, Master. My mind wandered."

"Some things never change," he grumbled.

No they didn't. She sighed as Ian's cock pulsed against his slacks. It was a monster in his pants. Yes, her Master was hungry, but then he always was. This might be the only chance she had to put him in a reasonable frame of mind. He could really be an unconscionable prick when he wanted to be.

She worked the button free and eased down the zipper. She hadn't done this in years. Since that moment when she'd "died," she'd remained perfectly pure because while Ian might have thought their marriage was over,

Charlie knew damn well it wasn't. Couldn't ever be.

He wasn't wearing underwear. He often didn't when he was wearing slacks. She loved that, loved that he was one zipper away from taking her. Now that she was here in the same space with him, all she wanted to do was revel in everything about her husband—his scent, the way his skin felt against hers, and most of all she wanted to remind herself just how good he tasted.

"I saw you hired Jesse Murdoch."

"Don't talk," Ian commanded between gritted teeth. "I don't need a running commentary."

"But I can do both." She was good at multitasking, and there was really only one way to keep Ian on task or he would go off on one of his arctic, curse-filled rants that tended to make everyone around him dive for cover. "Jesse Murdoch shot me."

Ian grunted a little, his hips bucking slightly. "I knew there was a reason I liked the kid."

She rolled her eyes. "Nice."

She took his cock in hand and was deeply satisfied with the sigh that filled him. He leaned back in his chair, forcing his hips up, putting his cock on display. "It wasn't like I hired him. I don't fucking hire any of them. They show up for work and then Grace gets pissed when I won't pay them. PTSD Jesse followed Alex back from Florida like some lost puppy. I keep telling Alex not to feed strays. They never fucking go away. Not even after they die."

She couldn't help but smile. "I was a little bit of a stray, wasn't I?" She'd been lost and Ian had taken her in.

He growled a little. "I don't want to listen to you talk, Charlie. I definitely don't want to rehash our very pathetic past. Don't romanticize this. I've had a shit day and I want to come. That's all I'm willing to offer you. I want you to suck me off and then leave. If you won't do it, I can call someone in who will."

He'd always been honest about sex, but she was pretty sure she could convince him otherwise. Sex had always been incendiary between them. One kiss and she went up like a match. She planned to be riding her Master's cock before the night was through. She would be back in his bed, his arms wrapped around her. She would make him listen.

She definitely wasn't going to let his stubborn nature cause him to sleep with one of his little playmates. He was about to figure out that his time of playing with every sub who walked in the door was over.

"Well, if it's going to be so one-sided, Master, I think your poor sub should at least be able to plead her case." The head of his cock was already weeping, a drop of pearly goodness sitting on the tip. She couldn't help herself. She swiped at it, gathering the pre-come on her tongue. So long. It had been so long.

Ian hissed, his body tensing. "I won't listen, Charlie."

But he already was. He was simply too stubborn to admit it. He'd gone from calling her Charlotte in that icy tone of his to rumbling Charlie from deep in his chest, a low, sexy growl. Charlie was his nickname for her. He was the only person in the whole world who called her that.

"Probably not," she admitted, but her eyes were on his cock. He was bigger than any man she'd ever seen before, and he knew how to use it. "Do you know how much I've missed this, Master?"

Now his eyes opened and she could see a hint of the rage she'd expected. "I'm surprised you remember. I'm sure you've gone through a dozen Masters since me."

She shook her head quickly, attempting not to show him just how much the possessive tone he was using pleased her. She needed to make it very clear. "No, Ian.

There's been absolutely no one, though you likely can't say the same."

She knew the truth. She'd kept track of him. He took many women, but he hadn't been serious about any of them.

"I've had a hundred women since you, love. I barely remember you at all."

Such a liar. He was like a freaking lion with a thorn in his paw. He always had been. She'd gotten close enough to take it out once. She just had to do it again. And sex was the only way to Ian Taggart's cold heart. "Then I'll have to remind you, Master."

She gripped his cock by the stalk. He was so big and thick that she could barely get the whole of her palm around him. Her fingers couldn't quite close. She ran her hand from just below the plum-shaped bulb at the top to right above his dense balls. She would suck them one by one into her mouth when she had time. He would let her play for hours with his cock, licking and sucking and worshiping him. Cock worship, cock love, she'd done it all and wanted it again. His cock had been the first and only to bring her pleasure, to show her lovemaking could be something special.

She pumped his cock in her hand again and again before hovering over the head, giving him a hint of the heat in her mouth.

"I love you, Ian." She whispered the words over his flesh as though she could make them a part of his body. "I missed you every second of every day we were apart and every night I dreamed of you."

He pulled away, his face perfectly blank. "I won't listen to that shit, Charlie. I might be willing to ignore your ramblings about the past, but I won't listen to that."

Her heart ached a little, but she backed off. He wasn't

ready. She had to give him a little space. He was letting her in physically. The emotional part could take a while. She leaned over and lightly sucked at the head of his cock, satisfied when he relaxed again. There had to be some trust left between them. "Fine. Then let's talk about something more pleasant. I like your city. It's hot, but I like Dallas a lot."

"Good for you because it never really gets cold. Not like in Russia." He groaned. "Lick the underside."

So bossy. She let her tongue find the underside of his cock and laved the deep *V* there with affection. The skin of his dick was soft like silk. "I bought a condo in Victory Park. I can see the whole city."

His hands wound into her hair. "Those condos are fucking expensive, Charlie. What have you been up to, you little criminal?"

He might say he'd forgotten, but he still knew her pretty well. She let her tongue run down the long length of his cock, ignoring the pull to her hair. "I've made a little money in the information business."

He tugged on her hair again, a sharp little pull. She nearly closed her eyes at the way it lit up her scalp. "You're a broker?"

She shrugged a little. "It's a living. I try not to get involved in anything too nasty. You shouldn't judge me, Ian. My business found Michael Evans for Alex. I'm the one with a line on Eli Nelson. You haven't been able to find him."

He shook his head and let her go. "I don't want to hear about him, Charlie. He was your boss. I can't believe anything you say about him. For all I know he's sent you here. Cup my balls."

He was going to make her insane. "Don't be so stubborn, Master. I'm trying to give you what you need."

"Don't you give me orders, sub. What I need is to feel your hands on my balls."

Well, she'd wanted him thinking about sex. He got very bossy and unrelenting when his dick was hard. At least he wasn't using that cold tone on her anymore. She reached down and rolled his balls in her palm.

This was where she'd needed to be every day for the last five years. She sank into the submissive role Ian had taught her to cherish. Everything had been a fight before that day in a Paris club when she'd found her lover, her Master, her husband.

They just had to get over that one little horrific betrayal and everything would be fine.

"Just suck me, Charlie. Just fucking suck me." He wouldn't ask her for what he needed. She knew that. It wasn't in his nature. His needs and wants came out as demands, but long ago she'd figured out what he was really asking her for. He wanted to forget everything just for a few minutes. He found his peace in dominance and she sank into her submission.

Halves of a whole. Soul mates. Somewhere along the way, Ian had become the angel on her shoulder. Oh, he was a cranky angel, but it was his voice she heard when she was tempted to follow in her father's footsteps and burn the world down around her.

She'd only known violence and anger before Ian Taggart.

And she owed him more than her life. She settled in and prayed he could forgive her.

Chapter Two

Ian gritted his teeth and promised himself he wouldn't ever forgive his bitch goddess wife, but fuck, she knew how to suck his cock. He couldn't remember how many blow jobs he'd received over the course of his lifetime, but he knew how many he'd had from his Charlie.

Charlotte. Her fucking name was Charlotte Denisovitch, and she was an information broker and she was back here to use him the same way she'd done it before. It didn't matter that she'd given him fourteen blow jobs, each one a searing memory in his head because she'd done it with such sweet submission. She'd been hesitant at first, but then her enthusiasm had overwhelmed him. There had been joy in the act, not a simple exchange of pleasure.

She ran her tongue down his cock, lighting up every inch of his flesh. He watched her red and gold hair as it covered his thighs, and he wanted to shove his slacks away so he could feel how soft it was. He was utterly fascinated with it. It gleamed in the low light. He'd thought she was gorgeous before, but there was an odd confidence to the woman in front of him that was even sexier.

Most of the subs he'd fucked in the last couple of years would have cried if he'd used that tone of voice on them, but, no, Charlie just growled right back. There had been no scurrying away in the hopes of finding some kinder Master. Charlie knew what she wanted and she didn't back down.

It was what had attracted him to her in the first place. She was a mix of vulnerability and predator, and he just couldn't fucking resist her.

He let his head fall back.

"Do you want to make it last, Master?" Charlie asked between long swipes along his cock.

She was the only one who had to ask. He had control of himself. It was his stock-in-trade. He would come when he wanted to come. He always did. Except when Charlie went wild on him, and then he was in her world and she could take him places he'd never been.

He was going to have to show her that he wasn't the same idiot she'd duped before. He slid his hands into that heavenly strawberry blonde hair and fisted all that silk. "You stop talking."

Every word that came out of that lying mouth of hers brought him closer to the edge. He was not going to end up in bed with her. He wasn't. He was going to control this encounter, this little bit of revenge, before he dumped her back in the yard and got on with his life.

His heart felt like it was squeezing inside his chest. She was alive. Charlie was alive. She was here and warm and soft and willing.

He shut that shit down fast. There would be absolutely no heart issues or weird, twisty gut flip-flops. She'd lied to him. She'd used him. She'd damn near gotten Liam killed. She'd cost all of them years of their lives.

He hated her. He fucking hated her with every bit of

passion he'd once put into loving her.

"Take me. Take me deep." If he allowed her to control the scene, she would play with him for hours. He knew damn well what she was doing. She was attempting to reforge a bond with him, the one they had found in Europe, the one that had been made strong with hours and hours of sex, with days spent lazing in bed and learning every inch of the other's body.

He wasn't wasting that kind of time again.

She swallowed him down. Again, she wasn't a petite and delicate flower. No. When Charlotte decided to take a man deep, she forced him down. His eyes nearly rolled into the back of his head. The pleasure was so forceful. Charlotte closed her mouth around him and worked him down with a pointed deliberation. All the while, that hand of hers was cupping his balls softly, playing with him.

Her tongue worked the underside of his cock, laving it with affection. Ian guided her up and down, using her hair to force her to take more.

Charlie just moaned around his cock, not a sound of pain, but one of pleasure. She'd loved him pulling on her hair. She had the sweetest touch of masochist inside her. She got hot from hair pulling and spanking, and she would light up when he nipped at her skin.

His cock was swelling, getting ready to shoot off. The heat from her mouth was more than he could take. His skin was too tight, his heart beating too fast. She was too much. Always too much.

She didn't fight him, simply allowed him to fuck her mouth. She didn't complain or prevaricate. A low hum began in the back of her throat, the sound transferring to his cock.

He wouldn't be able to last. No matter how much he tried to control the scene.

Soft heat enveloped him, making his spine curl and balls draw up.

"Give it to me, Master," Charlie said against his cockhead before she moved back down his dick.

She didn't wait for him this time. She took him whole, working him to the silky place at the back of her throat. She held him there and then swallowed.

It took everything he had not to shout out as he came. It felt like it had been years since he'd shot off, like he'd been starving for this, dying for it.

He pressed into her mouth, giving her his come, what seemed like an endless stream.

Finally, he fell back against the chair. His body felt limp, drained, wrung out, but in the most pleasant of ways.

Charlie licked him clean. Her tongue didn't stop because the come had. She suckled him softly, and just like that he felt the pressure start to build again.

He was not going for round two.

Ian forced himself to sit up. "Thanks, sweetheart."

He called all the subs sweetheart because most of the time he couldn't remember their names. He was going to put Charlotte firmly in the same category as the other women he'd screwed and forgotten along the way.

Of course, there had been a contract in place with those other women. *Fuck.* He'd just had sex and he hadn't negotiated anything.

He needed to get her out of here.

"Master?" Charlie turned her eyes up when he stood and buttoned up his slacks.

There was no point in correcting her. She would just do it again. No. There was very little point in arguing or fighting with Charlotte. She was deeply stubborn, and he wasn't willing to discipline her. That was a very bad idea. He leaned over and scooped her up into his arms.

Charlotte gasped a little, but then her arms were around his neck and a soft look hit her eyes. "You won't regret it, babe. God, I missed you."

"I never regret anything, sweetheart." A blatant lie, but he was good at those. He was also going to enjoy the next couple of minutes. Charlie thought she had him right where she wanted him.

Instead of walking down the hallway to his private dungeon space or his bedroom, he turned back to the front door.

Charlie frowned. "Ian, don't do this. Talk to me."

He just kept walking. "I have nothing to say to you. Like I explained before, you tend to lie. You're a very accomplished liar. The only thing you're better at than lying is whoring."

Her face went red and despite the fact that she was in his arms, she managed to plant a fist firmly in his face.

Yeah, that kind of got him hot, too. Charlie wouldn't cry when she could lash out.

"You are a fucking asshole, Ian Taggart."

"You're just getting that?" He'd been called so much worse. He would take the decent right hook again because watching her get pissed was one of the few joys to come from this ill-conceived reunion. "I thought you were a big time information broker. Maybe you should rethink your career."

"Let me down now."

"Not until you're on the right side of the door, sweetheart." He managed to get the front door open even as she struggled against him.

The night was humid, heat slamming into him as he strode down his driveway.

"This is stupid, Ian. You have to listen to me."

His inner asshole was getting a serious workout

tonight. "If you wanted me to listen, you should have held out on the hummer. I have what I wanted. I see zero reason to help you out now. Really, Charlotte, you should know by now to get the money upfront."

He set her on her feet and immediately had to duck another flying fist. She feigned right and then came at him from the left. Luckily, he still remembered how to fight. He caught her fist in his palm and held her there. He didn't show it, but everything about her excited him. He was already rock hard not five minutes after he'd come.

"Don't you call me a whore again, Ian." Her body was practically vibrating with rage.

"I call it like I see it." She thought she was mad? He could give her mad. "How much did Nelson pay you to fuck me the first time? He's not going to get his money's worth this time because that was all the connection I intend to have with you. Been there, done that and all."

He let her go. If she tried it again, he would have her on the ground, but then she would know what a liar he was because his cock was painfully hard despite the blow job. If he got her on the ground, he might just fuck her right then and there.

She backed up slightly, giving him a little space. "You are going to regret every filthy word that is coming out of your mouth. Do you think you can scare me away by calling me a whore and saying the sex was meaningless? Try again. Because while I might be an excellent liar, you've lost your edge, Taggart. Do us both a favor and cut the bullshit. You know you're going to talk to me. You know you want to find out what happened."

The jibe about losing his edge hit too close to home. She was the reason he'd lost his edge. She was the reason he'd gotten out of the game in the first place. "I know what happened. I got led around by my dick and a two-year operation went up in flames. Do you know how many people you nearly got killed? Liam almost died because of you."

She softened. "I know. I can't tell you how sorry I am about that. Let's go inside, Master."

He turned and started back up the drive. He wasn't doing this with her. "Find your own ride home. I'm all out of charity for the night."

"Charity? You call me giving you the blow job of a lifetime charity?" She was on his heels, obviously not willing to give up.

He turned because she was right back in his trap. Despite what she said, he did know exactly how to hurt her. She could lie all day about her reasons, but she'd been honest when she submitted. She'd been honest about what hurt her as a woman. "Yes, it was charity. I'm not attracted to you. I was attracted to your innocence, well, to the lie of your innocence the first time around. Now I know just who and what you are, and I have no interest in fucking a criminal. Did you take over daddy's enterprise? Is that what Nelson promised you? Did he off your dear pops so you could be the queen? You cried about all the times daddy hurt you. I wonder now. Maybe you liked it."

He knew the moment he'd gone too far. Even in the moonlight he could see how she paled and her hands started to shake. She couldn't fake that reaction. When her hand came out to connect with his face, he let it, holding still for her.

He deserved it. Guilt gnawed in his gut, but he wouldn't apologize. He wouldn't back down. "Go home, Charlotte. There's absolutely nothing for you here."

He closed the door between them, locking it again. Tomorrow he would redesign his whole security system because he obviously wasn't paranoid enough. But for tonight, he had a bottle of Scotch calling his name.

And he knew just what he wanted to listen to.

* * * *

Charlie bit back a cry as she watched the door slam shut.

And then she forced herself not to walk right up to it, beat it down, find her asswipe husband, and tear the balls right off his body.

That would teach him not to call her a whore again.

Damn it. Except by definition she had been one before. She'd agreed to distract Ian Taggart in exchange for her and her sister's safety, and she'd taken the money Nelson had given her afterwards. She hadn't used it quite the way he'd wanted her to, but she'd used it all the same.

She didn't feel like a whore. She felt like a woman who had just had the world ripped out from under her.

How could he say those things about her father? Tears welled, a crushing sorrow drowning out the rage. Ian had been the only person on the planet she'd told about what her father had done to her. She'd hidden much of the truth even to her sister. She'd trusted him, and he'd thrown it right back in her face.

Could she have been wrong? She'd been so sure that once she'd helped out his friends and brought him good intelligence that he would sit down and listen to her.

Her phone trilled. She sniffled, trying to banish the tears. There would be time for them later. When she was safely in her room high above the city, she could cry and wail and let it out, but she wasn't safe now. She flipped the phone to answer. "Chelsea?"

"You've just had a mega shit ton of hits on your personal information. Someone is looking for Charlotte, not Kris."

Well, she'd known they would figure it out sooner or later. She'd left a few threads undone that a smart man could follow.

"I'm sure it's Adam." Adam Miles was Ian's computer guy and a very smart man. She knew it had only been a matter of time before he tracked her down. "He's the one who'll be looking."

"Then he's the one I'll be sending in circles. Again." There was a wealth of satisfaction in Chelsea's voice. She did enjoy a challenge. She and Adam had gone a couple of rounds during the Florida op.

"He's good." Adam had worked with her on the Michael Evans takedown. He didn't know it yet, but he'd already tangled with Chelsea.

For all the good it had done her.

"I'm better," Chelsea said.

Charlie sighed. "Let him in. It doesn't matter now. They've figured it out. I bet they finally found the recording of the night I downloaded their copy machine."

It was how she'd figured out everything about them. It had been an operation she'd been more than happy to complete.

"Why didn't you erase it?"

Because she'd always kind of hoped he would come looking for her. "It doesn't matter now. It looks like we won't use the new IDs the way I planned."

She'd had new identities crafted for both of them. Her uncle had been quiet for a while. She wouldn't have come after Ian if she'd thought there was a ton of heat on her. Her plan had been to come into town and try to work things through with Ian. Then she could hide here under a new identity and she would keep her nose clean and her uncle would lose interest in punishing her.

"What are you saying, Charlotte?"

She didn't want to go over all the ways she'd screwed up. "I have to hike back to my car and then I'll come home."

"Are you done stalking the big guy? Because we need to move on." Chelsea wasn't exactly on board with Charlie's plans to win Ian back. Since her sister had come into her own, Chelsea seemed to think they didn't need men.

Charlie looked back at the house. Ian had done well for himself. His house was big and sturdy, like the man himself. She'd expected him to be in a condo like hers. No fuss. No muss. But no, Ian Taggart's home had a big yard and trees. It looked like a family could live there.

But it wouldn't be her family.

She felt like he'd just ripped her heart out. Was this the way he'd felt when he'd discovered her betrayal? She'd worked so hard to become a woman who was worthy of him, but maybe there were some things she couldn't come back from.

"Charlotte? Shit. You saw him, didn't you? What did he do? Because I'm three keystrokes away from getting him institutionalized. I can have him put down like a rabid dog."

"Don't you dare." As mad as she was, she understood. If he'd done the same thing to her, she might have called him all sorts of names, too.

Chelsea's voice softened. "Charlotte, I know you loved the man, but we can't stay here forever."

"The condo is secure." She'd made sure of it.

"Nelson has eyes everywhere, and he would love to slit your throat, big sister. He isn't the only one. If Taggart isn't interested in a reunion, then we should head out. Why don't we sell the Florida condo and go to Europe for a while? Or the Caribbean. I could use a tan."

"No, don't sell the Palm Coast property. Put it in Alex's name. Alex and Eve McKay." They had fallen in love again at her condo on the beach. She'd watched them and they had given her so much hope. Just because she'd fucked up didn't mean they should lose out.

It was over. He was too stubborn, too brutally slavish to his own code of conduct. He'd broken his rules for her once, but he wouldn't again.

Maybe it was time to move on.

And then she heard it. A familiar wail of guitars and drums and Axl Rose's voice blaring from inside the house.

One single memory flared to life. Ian spreading her wide and taking her for the first time, his face so serious as he worked over her. She'd held on to him for dear life, and when he was done, she'd known that she'd been caught in her own trap. She'd lain in his arms, this one song echoing from the club below.

Sweet love of mine

He had forgotten nothing if he was listening to that song. Not a single moment. All these years had passed and he was still listening to their song the same damn way she did, as though it could connect them across the distances.

It was so not over.

"Chelsea, I will murder you horribly if you harm a hair on his head." She was the only one allowed to do that.

A low huff came over the line. "Way to talk to your baby sister."

Her baby sister had become a shark with six rows of teeth, perfectly capable of ruining a man's life without ever leaving her keyboard. "He's my husband. He might be a dipshit, but he's mine, and I will protect him so don't think you can manipulate this situation. We're not leaving. If that means I have to deal with a few assassins, then bring them on. Find Nelson for me. I need a full report on everything we have on him."

Because she was planning a little meeting for her new team. An unnatural optimism came over her. Her first plan hadn't gone gangbusters, but there was always another plan. The one she had in mind was absolutely certain to make her husband stand up and notice.

And potentially throttle her, but, hey, a girl had to take a few chances in life.

"I have to go. Get that report ready. I've got a meeting in the morning." She caught a glimpse of Ian through his curtains as she hung up on her sister. He had a bottle in his hand. Damn it. He was going to make a long night of it.

He probably needed backup. Charlie was in the mood to confess.

She dialed Sean Taggart and was happy when he immediately answered.

"Kris? Is this you? Because we need to talk. What the fuck is going on? Do you know what Adam is claiming?"

She was so glad she'd kept the number she'd given him. Typically she tossed a phone after an op, but she'd kept her Florida line. It made things easier. She was pretty sure she knew what Adam was telling everyone. "Hello, Little Tag. We definitely need to talk, but tonight Big Tag needs you more than me. He's getting drunk off his ass because his wife just returned from the dead. You should probably get over here. Oh, and tell Grace I said hi. She looked really beautiful tonight."

"What?" Sean's voice shouted over the line.

Family counseling might be in their future. Maybe Eve had an opening. "Yeah, Ian might not have told you about me, brother, but I would make a bet that Adam is hunting down all the facts even as we speak. But seriously, he needs you tonight. As for tomorrow, tell the team I'll see them bright and early. I have intel on Eli Nelson. I'll need a conference room and a copy machine. Don't worry, I know where they keep those."

She could practically hear Sean's frustration over the line. "Kris, you need to explain this to me right fucking now."

"No time. And the name's not Kris. It's Charlotte. Charlotte Taggart and I need to get my beauty rest because I'm going to have to run McKay-Taggart in the morning. Ian's going to be too drunk and Alex is on his honeymoon. Talk to you soon."

She hung up on her brother-in-law and turned the phone off just as it started ringing again.

Charlie began the long walk to her car thinking about how nice it was that Texas was a community property state. It was about time she laid claim to her half.

Chapter Three

Eli Nelson looked out over the Neva River. There was a fine mist over the water this early in the morning, but then Nelson had discovered that Saint Petersburg, Russia, stayed in a damn near perpetual gloom. Oh, they tried to brighten things up with red flowers and perfect green spaces, but Russia was just dark and dank most of the time no matter how much elegance the former czars shoved onto every street.

The sun was still hidden behind the never-ending clouds. There was a phrase he'd heard once about the hope for summer in Russia. The year was nine months of optimism and expectation followed by three months of disappointment.

Fuck, he hated Russia. One day he was going to have a little mansion on his own private fucking island where the days were hot and the nights were filled with some serious pussy—and by serious he meant some dumb bitch who was less than half his age and didn't know better.

He felt it the minute Denisovitch walked up behind him. The Hermitage was across the river, and there was already a long line of tourists waiting though it wouldn't open for hours. The Naval Museum was at his back. He was caught in the middle of tourist hell, and that was the only way he would meet with this snake. The Russian mob might rule, but they preferred to do their dirty work in the dark.

Mikhail Denisovitch stepped up to the wall, leaning forward in his immaculate suit as though the fog and mist couldn't touch him. Of course, he hadn't come alone. Nelson let his eyes drift back to the little park overlooking the Neva. It was lovely, with bright red begonias and those damn white and green park benches. But they were all empty as though even the intrepid tourists knew that the two men currently occupying the gravel inlaid paths were not something to be messed with. Denisovitch never went anywhere without his enforcer, a big scarred man who didn't really try to hide the fact that he was packing. He was an overgrown ape someone had stuffed into a suit, and he wasn't smart enough to hide the bulge his gun made. Or perhaps that was at Mikhail's request. Perhaps Mikhail wanted everyone around him to know that he was protected. It was a lesson Nelson was sure he'd learned from his brother.

It was a lesson Nelson had taught Mikhail Denisovitch, though the man had no idea he'd been the teacher.

Gulls squawked overhead, but Nelson ignored them. "I thought you were going to miss our appointment."

He spoke in flawless Russian. One of the perks of long-term training with the CIA was an intense study of languages. He could screw someone over in five different languages.

Denisovitch looked out over the water. "Our traffic can be a problem at this time of the morning. I had to come in from Moscow. The plane was delayed and then we fought through traffic."

"Yes, I was surprised you asked me to meet you here. I rather thought you stayed in Moscow." Saint Petersburg wasn't a hotbed of activity. It was a tourist town, a place for artists and intellectuals. The power was all in Moscow for now.

Denisovitch chuckled slightly, his eyes watching a boat as it sailed toward the Palace Bridge. The Venice of the North was awake and alive. He pointed toward the Hermitage. "There is much to do here. This is our port city. We might stay quiet here, but don't doubt we own all that's in sight. Do you see that building?"

It took everything Nelson had not to roll his eyes. The building was a baroque masterpiece. Anyone who understood museums knew what the Hermitage was. Three separate palaces that together housed all the treasures of Russia, some stolen from Germany after World War II. Russia understood the art of the deal. To the victor went the spoils. "It's the Hermitage. Do you want to give me a lesson in art?"

"No, just history. It was the summer palace of the czars. I am the czar now. I summer here like Peter the Great. It is more civilized here than in Moscow. Too many fucking politicians putting their hands in my pie. It's nice here, and I can worship in the cathedrals."

Saint Petersburg had more than its share of orthodox cathedrals. He'd heard Denisovitch was devout. It was good to know that hypocrisy was alive and well and living in Russia. "We all need to find a home."

"This is true. Now, I am finished with small talk. You will tell me the truth. Have you found her?"

Nelson almost sighed because this was the part of the job he so deeply enjoyed. He'd loved it when he'd been in the CIA. He loved it now. He was fucking over multiple people who believed or had believed him to be their partner. It was a little slice of heaven. "I have."

Charlotte Denisovitch could have been his queen. He'd been grooming her. Oh, she was nothing but a woman so he'd used her like one. Her beauty was her greatest asset, but then he'd never deeply prized purity. He didn't give a shit that Ian Taggart had her first. It had been necessary. Had she followed his plan, he would have forced his way into her bed and taken her luscious body and that devious brain for his own. He would have used her as he'd liked, but he also would have taken care of her in his own way.

She'd decided on another route, and it was going to cost her everything.

"Tell me where the little bitch is," Denisovitch ordered.

This was why he'd come all this way when he needed to be watching that fucking idiot playboy in India. "Yes. I believe you'll discover she's in Dallas, Texas."

Denisovitch tensed. "Then she's gone to him."

She'd gone to "him" a couple of weeks back, but Nelson had missed it. He'd been busy trying to clean up the mess that fuckwad Taggart had caused for him by blocking a shipment of arms to Africa. Those dictator warlords didn't like a working man to take their money and give them nothing.

Thank god he wasn't an ordinary arms dealer. Ian Taggart had no idea what he was dealing with and that was how Nelson planned on keeping it. If Taggart ever found out how deep the conspiracy went, they would all be fucked.

"She and that cunt of a sister of hers bought a place in Dallas a few days ago. I've had a man case it. Whatever you want to say about the bitch, she's thorough. She's installed a state-of-the-art security system, and she takes multiple exits when she leaves. She never follows a schedule. If you're trying to catch her coming out of her place, you'll need three assassins to be sure."

Charlotte Denisovitch was a problem. She'd proven to be too clever for Nelson's satisfaction. He'd tried to have her killed three times now, but she'd proven elusive. He'd lost three good men to her skills. He couldn't afford to look weak. His men tended to look down on any weakness.

"I will send them all then. I wouldn't want my dear niece to think that I've forgotten her." Mikhail leaned forward, his elbows on the concrete wall that kept them from falling in. "I had the same intelligence. I sent a few to America yesterday. It's good to know we can trust each other."

It was good that, for once, telling the truth got him somewhere. He was more enamored of lying out his ass. "I would never give you anything less."

Denisovitch tipped his head. "It is good to have friends. Perhaps we should help each other out again."

Yes. Yes. Yes. This was what he'd really come all this way for. A way to get rid of all of his problems. He schooled his expression to a polite blank. "What do you mean?"

Denosivitch laughed, but it was a harsh sound. "I mean you have a problem and so do I. Our problems are very likely screwing each other as we speak. It should be easy to take them out, no?"

So easy. Now Denisovitch could deal with this shit and he could get back to his real score—India and that fuckwad royal from nowhere Loa Mali. "Taggart has been an issue for a while, but if you kill him, the rest of that team will come after you."

Denisovitch snapped his fingers and the stoic-looking goon in a suit stepped forward, a file in his hand. "This is an issue I have already thought about. Will this do?"

Nelson took the folder and quickly flipped through it. Sean Taggart. Alexander McKay. Liam O'Donnell. Jacob Dean. Adam Miles. Eve St. James. "What about the Brit? He hired a Brit a couple of months back."

"Do you really think he's loyal?"

The bastard had been MI6 and given up his place to follow Taggart. Sure as fuck he would be loyal. Taggart commanded nothing if not a crazed sense of loyalty from his men. It had been that way during his Army years. Luckily the CIA discouraged loyalty to anyone but the Agency. "I think it's safe to say he could cause trouble. Kill him, too. Accidents would be best but assassinations are fine."

Denisovitch pointed to the picture of Eve St. James, who had recently changed her name back to McKay. "You really think the woman is a threat?"

He couldn't let the man back out now. "Don't underestimate the women. Didn't your brother make that mistake?"

Denisovitch grimaced as though he'd smelled something rotten. "I told my brother not to marry that American whore. When she ran off, I told him to let the cow's children go, but he had to punish her. All right then, I'll kill the woman, too."

"Grace Taggart," Nelson said. "Don't forget about Sean's wife and child. It's always best to take out the entire line. After all, your brother killed his disloyal wife only to be killed by a disloyal daughter."

Nelson had unfinished business with Grace and Sean. Oh, he wished he could see Sean's face when his wife and baby were gone and he realized he was next. That would be a lovely day, but he had better things to do. He would just have to imagine it.

"All right. But Charlotte is first. She will die and then her sister and then the rest will follow shortly after. I insist on this."

If the fucker didn't get Ian and Sean first, there would be a war on his hands. But then again, a war with the syndicate would keep Taggart occupied and allow Nelson to work freely. Not such a bad thing.

Nelson held out a hand. "I'll leave it all to you then."

"I will take these people down. Anyone who is involved with Charlotte and her sister will die. This I will swear when I pray today."

The Russian started talking about vengeance and God, but Nelson stared out into the city. Off in the distance were the high spires of the Church of the Spilled Blood. Nelson stared at them.

It was fitting since he was going to make Taggart bleed.

* * * *

Ian came awake to the smell of bacon frying. And promptly wanted to vomit. Oh, he joked about vomiting a lot, but today was the real thing. His stomach rolled and rumbled and threatened to blow.

How much fucking Scotch had he gone through last night? Enough to have had the craziest dream. Charlie had come back. She'd walked right up to his house and dropped to her knees and sucked his cock in that enthusiastic, crazy-hot way of hers.

And she'd had strawberry blonde hair and new scars.

And she'd punched him in the face.

He reached up and felt his nose. Yep. No dream.

"You might as well wake up. The sooner you give in, the quicker you can move through the hangover, brother."

Sean. This wasn't a dream. It was a nightmare. He forced his eyes open and sure enough, his brother was sitting across from him, one leg negligently crossed over the other. The sun was streaming in through one of his bedroom windows. It must have been courtesy of Sean because he never opened those blackout drapes. He liked it dark, but the sun shone in and practically gave his younger brother a halo. "What the fuck are you doing here? Come to think of it, how did you get in?"

Everyone was getting through his security these days.

"You let me in, Ian. I showed up at the gates. You buzzed me in after making me promise I was the pizza man."

It was worse than he thought. "I did not."

Sean nodded, his eyes wide and an amused grin flashing on his face. "Oh, yes, you did. You got the munchies somewhere around midnight. It's all right, man. You were very controlled and perfectly manly when you threatened to shoot me if I put anchovies on your pizza."

His stomach rolled at the thought, but he made sure his face was perfectly clear. "All right, I'll rephrase the question. Why are you here?"

"Because your wife said you needed me."

He was going to kill her. He was going to wrap his hands around her pretty throat and squeeze. Except the minute he had the vision of killing his back-from-the-dead wife, she was suddenly naked and he wasn't thinking about throttling her anymore. Maybe he could fuck her to death. That would be a better way to go.

"I was surprised to get that particular call," Sean continued. "Since I wasn't aware you had a wife."

"I don't." He needed to get up. He needed to take a

shower and get moving. He couldn't lie around in bed. He had to figure out if Charlie was lying about Eli Nelson. She was too smart to completely fabricate a story, so he was sure there was a kernel of truth somewhere in it. It was his job to pull the truth from the bullshit, to beat her at her own game this time.

"She seemed really clear about it." Sean leaned forward. "There's water and ibuprofen on the bedside table. What's with the Guns N' Roses overload? Seriously, you listened to that song three hundred times last night. I wanted to blow my own ears off after an hour."

He really hated her. How could she have brought Sean into this? "I like Axl Rose. Something about the hair just does it for me."

He downed the pills. If anyone else had been sitting across from him, he wouldn't have taken them. He would have assumed they were poison meant to horrifically liquefy his insides. Hell, he rarely drank a drink he didn't pour himself, but he trusted Sean. Even though Sean rarely talked to him anymore. Come to think of it, this was the closest he'd been to Sean in a year.

He trusted his team—Alex and Eve and Li and Jake, and even that fucker Adam. He trusted Grace and Serena and Avery because they loved his brothers, but that was the extent of it. He hadn't known Simon long enough, and he trusted Jesse as far as he could throw the little fucker.

Charlie was proof positive that he couldn't trust anyone outside his circle.

"Come on, man. I've never seen you the way you were last night."

He sent his brother a questioning look. "Did I behave in some way I shouldn't have?"

Sean ran a frustrated hand through his hair and sat back. "No. You sat. You drank. You yelled at me when I tried to turn off the music. You were utterly stoic and refused to talk about anything except your pizza. Which I'm honestly surprised you managed to keep down. I had to make that crust from scratch, you know. If you're going to force me to cook in the middle of the night, let's talk about stocking your kitchen. I had to call Alex in with supplies. How do you survive on Fruity Pebbles and days-old Chinese food?"

He ate at the office more often than not. Grace smuggled whatever Sean had cooked the night before into the fridge at the office and everyone knew that if they took that food, Ian would murder them.

God, his life had become a pathetic circle of sleeping, eating at his desk, and forcing himself to work out. He'd been sleepwalking through life for years because of that woman. It had to stop. If her showing up on his doorstep had taught him one thing, it was that it was time to let her go.

"I need to take a sub. That's my problem. I need someone to take care of the everyday shit and then I'll be okay. I'll tell Ryan I'm taking applications." That would do it. He'd been a pussy about his own needs for years. He needed a full-time submissive who would take care of the house, deal with the inanities of life, make sure he was fed, and see to his sexual needs. In exchange, he would offer financial support and his own unique brand of discipline.

Yes, that was what he should do. Maybe he would take two subs. He had a lot of needs.

Sean's eyes had gone wide again. "I think that would be a mistake."

"I would think you would be thrilled. I rely on Grace far too much."

Sean sighed a little, the same way he would when he

was younger and admitting something he'd done wrong. "Grace loves you. She doesn't mind. And I make extra. I know you think she's risking my wrath, but I've always known she was feeding you. As mad as I've been at you, you've always been my brother. I won't let you starve. God knows you didn't let me."

Their shared childhood sat between them. Their father had left them high and dry, and their mother had needed someone to tell her what to do. Ian had been forced to take over. He'd had to get a job and bring in money while he finished high school and made sure Sean had what he needed. There had been plenty of times during those years when there wasn't enough food, and Ian had made sure Sean went to bed full to the detriment of his own stomach. He'd had to do it. Sean was younger. Sean had needed him. He'd known that from the moment Sean had been born. "That doesn't matter now."

"You have no idea how that attitude bugs me, but I'll let it go. I'm glad you let Grace help. Kris won't take Grace's head off. I worry about what she'll do if you start auditioning subs. You have a wife. They tend to get pissy about other women taking their place."

"She's not my wife." He'd forgotten briefly that Sean had already met Charlie. They had worked together in Florida. "And her name isn't Kris."

Sean's blue eyes rolled. "I know. Sorry. Charlotte. I wish everyone would just stick to one name. I've been out of the game too long to remember everyone's fake names. My sous chef is named Hans. I don't know his last name. I don't need to. It's just Hans. One name per person, please."

His head was pounding. Hangovers sucked ass. "Good for you and Hans. I hope you'll be very happy together."

"Yeah, well, the point is you won't be happy when Charlotte starts beheading the subs at Sanctum. She seems like a nice woman, but there's a crazy bitch in there, too."

He'd seen the crazy bitch in her from the first moment. It had been right there in those crystal blue eyes. Yeah, that was kind of why he'd loved her. Wanted her. Wanted to fuck her. That was all. "She'll be gone soon."

Once she realized he wouldn't give her what she wanted, she would move on and he could forget her again.

Except he'd never managed to forget her in the first place.

"Does she know that? Because I don't think she got the memo," Sean said. "Look, why don't you tell me the story from the beginning? Where did you meet her?"

He had no intention of rehashing old history. Something was wrong. It played around in his mind. He was missing something important. "She was at a club. I fucked her. She wouldn't go away. Then she died. Story over."

"God, you're obnoxious. You married the woman. There has to be more."

What the hell was he missing? "I'm not joining your pussy-whipped men's therapy group, Sean."

Sean shot him the finger. "It's called a poker club, asshole, and we wouldn't have you."

The bacon. That was the problem. He got still, forcing himself to really listen. Someone was cooking, and it sure as hell wasn't Sean. "Did you bring Hans with you?"

Sean waved that idea off. "Nah, that's Alex."

Motherfucker. He rose to his feet, his head only threatening to crack wide open. A man couldn't simply drink himself to death quietly around here. No. His friends had to show up to watch the show. "He's supposed to be on his honeymoon."

Alex's big body was suddenly in the doorway. "Eve and I canceled. This is so much more important."

God, Alex was going to kill him. He really was going to vomit. "I don't need anyone to hold my fucking hand."

"Oh, no. You misunderstand. I wasn't talking about being here for you emotionally. I know you would never let me do that. I was talking about how much fun it's going to be to watch you deal with Kris...Charlotte. Eve and I agreed watching this shit go down is going to be way better than Hawaii."

Now he sent his best friend his happy middle finger. "Fuck you, Alex."

"Come on, man. You were always there for me. You have woman troubles. You can lean on me."

"You make it sound like I'm menstruating, Alex."

Sean nodded. "That would explain the mood swings, and so very much of my childhood."

He sent his brother a look that should have had him running. "I don't have mood swings. I just hate everything. See, that's what they mean by even tempered."

Alex just chuckled. "I think Eve would disagree, but it's good to see last night didn't change you. I worried your beloved would come back from the dead and you would be a changed man, all hearts and flowers."

"She's lucky I didn't kill her." He hadn't really even thought about it. He'd had a gun in his hand. He'd had someone who betrayed him in his sights, but no, he'd just convinced her to give him a blow job and insulted her and sent her away. Maybe Alex was right. He was totally going soft. If he didn't watch out he would be at Sean's Thursday night "poker" club which was really just an excuse to drink imported girlie beer and discuss their feelings. They played poker so they could nominally call themselves men.

He should have shot her. Then he could be in a nice comfy jail cell far away from his meddling friends.

Alex frowned a little. "I was actually surprised she wasn't still here. I thought you wanted to question her. I came over to make sure she wasn't tied up somewhere."

But if he'd tied her up, he wouldn't have been able to leave her alone. He would have spanked that juicy ass of hers and it wouldn't have been long before he shoved his cock up her tiny asshole.

God, he'd never fucked her ass. He'd been training her for it when she'd "died." That's what he should have gotten out of her. He should have gotten some nasty anal sex.

"I don't care what she has to say." He wasn't going to talk about what was going through his head. Alex didn't need to know he still had a perverse obsession with his ex's ass.

"Ian, she's smart," Alex pointed out. "If she says she has a line on Nelson, we should check it out."

"She was working for Nelson, so we can't believe her. She's also a criminal."

"I don't think she does that anymore. You didn't see her in Florida." Alex leaned against the doorjamb. "I think she's been trying to redeem herself. For you."

Getting remarried had made mush of his best friend's brain. "She's a liar. She fucked me for money and information, and that's why she's here now."

Sean whistled. "Tell me you didn't call her a whore."

Ian shrugged. He tried not to lie to his brother.

"Fuck," Sean cursed and reached into his pocket, pulling out what looked like a stack of twenties.

Alex took it with a shake of his head. "I told you." He turned to Ian. "We had a bet on how you got the shiner."

"Fuck you both. Get out of my house." He stalked

toward the bathroom. He needed a shower. He needed to get back on an even keel. Whatever Charlie was trying to do by contacting his brother, it didn't matter because it wouldn't fucking work.

"Don't feel bad. It's how he says I love you," Sean explained to Alex.

Alex laughed, shaking his head. "Breakfast is ready when you can stomach it, brother."

He slammed the door. Those two wouldn't go away. He might be able to scare Adam into leaving. Jake would follow orders. Simon didn't care enough to fuck with him, but Sean and Alex wouldn't believe him even if he threatened to shoot them both.

Maybe he needed to rethink the whole "inner circle of trust" thing. It was kind of biting him in the ass now. He should be able to wallow in his misery, but no, he had to deal with this crap.

He caught a glimpse of himself in the mirror. Damn, he looked like shit. He reached up and touched his left eye. It wasn't horrible, but it had bruised. Charlie knew how to throw a punch.

He didn't like to think about how many she'd taken. There it was again, that gnawing guilt that he wasn't going to give into.

He turned on the shower, not bothering to let the water heat up. He didn't fucking need any heat. Ice. He needed to remind himself that he had ice in his veins. He shrugged out of his slacks. He'd apparently passed out still wearing them.

What the fuck had that woman done to him? He'd lost control. He never lost control. He'd gotten drunk and blacked out. Even during all the years of mourning her loss, he always remembered every moment. Once a year, on the day she died, he would listen to that fucking song and drink Scotch and remind himself why he wouldn't let another woman in. Not once had he passed out and forgotten the majority of the evening. It was dangerous. It was stupid.

She was going to kill him in the end.

He stepped into the shower, his head still pounding. The cold blasted his system, but he welcomed it. At the very least, it shriveled up his cock some. The damn thing hadn't gone down since the moment she'd walked in.

Despite the ache in his head and his rolling gut, the minute he'd thought of Charlie, his cock had gotten hard as a rock.

It didn't matter because she was gone, and he wouldn't let her in again. If she showed up, he would call the cops. That little criminal mastermind wouldn't want to see the police. Despite what Alex said, he knew damn well she was still working some sort of con. It was just who she was.

And he was a professional with a job to do. He couldn't let Charlie get in his way.

"Coffee?" Alex held out a mug. "Holy shit. Is that cold water?"

No one left him alone. Not even when he was naked. He took the coffee, downing about half the mug before handing it back. "Yeah. It's the only way to wake up. I'll take that breakfast to go. You're going to be sorry you missed your honeymoon because all that's going to happen today is another meeting. Call and make sure everyone's at the office. I have some intelligence to check out about Eli Nelson."

"Oh, everyone's at the office already. They're in the meeting."

Ian stared at his friend. "What meeting? I didn't call a meeting, and you were supposed to be on a plane. Has

Adam decided to start a coup, because let me tell you, I'm in the mood to put someone on their ass."

"Uhm, your wife called a meeting. Seems she thinks she owns half of McKay-Taggart and she said since the boss was sleeping one off, she would take over for the day."

The cold water could no longer touch him. "She wouldn't fucking dare."

"Oh, she dares. See, totally worth missing out on vacation," Alex said with a grin.

Ian turned off the water. He wouldn't bother getting clean. It was going to be a bloody kind of day.

* * * *

"Give me one good reason why I'm sitting here." Simon Weston's clipped British accent cut through the quiet of the conference room.

"Because I'm your boss and I told you to be here." The best way to get through a rough sea was to plow straight ahead. Charlie had gotten through many a tough situation because she just acted like she owned the place.

She wondered if her asshole Master's head was aching. He'd been downing Scotch like it was going out of style the night before. She knew he kind of deserved it with all the name calling and such, but she couldn't help but wish she was there to take care of him. Sean better have done his job and taken care of his brother. They were family. It was what family did.

Or at least that was what Ian had taught her. Family didn't give up. Family kept going even when one of them was a complete nitwit jerkwad who called his wife a whore.

Simon was staring at her as though mentally fitting

her for a straightjacket. "I don't know about that."

Eve McKay set down her ever-present travel mug of coffee, a grin on her face. "Come on, Simon. You know why you're here. You're curious. Just like the rest of us."

Adam clapped his hands and tossed his body into one of the chairs. "I'm thrilled. I think Kris is going to set Ian on his ass, and I've been waiting for that."

She liked Adam, but she had to side with her Master. Despite the whole punching him in the face thing—which she would totally do again—she was trying to be a good submissive and that meant siding with her Master. It was obvious he had some difficult employees. "You should respect Ian, Adam."

Adam frowned. "I thought you would be more fun than this."

Eve leaned over. "Alex told me Ian has a black eye."

Adam fist pumped. "Fuck, yeah. You go, girl."

Serena slapped at her husband's arm. "Be polite."

Jake was on the other side of Serena, a mug of coffee in his hand. "He doesn't know how. He thinks tact is a made-up word."

Adam frowned. "Well, we all know tact just means lying about shit. How many of us cheered when we found out Kris was Ian's long lost wife? Come on."

Eve, Jake, and Serena raised their hands.

"Well, I was just pissed to find out she'd lied about her name." Jesse Murdoch was sitting beside Simon, a sour look on his face.

"I was undercover." She didn't really like Jesse. He'd totally shot her.

"So was I but I used my real name. It's confusing to keep changing names," Jesse shot back.

He was a little behind the curve, but she'd sworn to be kinder to all of God's creatures, even the slow ones.

"Sorry, Jesse. It's Charlotte. I'll try to be more clear in the future so you know the full name of the woman you're shooting and leaving horrific scars on."

She was perfectly satisfied with the way he blanched.

Simon chuckled under his breath. "She's got you there. Don't be such a fucking idiot. I'm your damn sponsor. Don't make me look bad."

"I'm only here to find out what you know about Eli Nelson." Liam O'Donnell wasn't playing around.

God, she felt like shit when she looked at him. The only way to deal with Liam was honesty. "I know I'm the reason he had the chance to blow up the apartment you were in and send your brother running with the bearer bonds. You might not believe it, but I didn't know what he was planning. He didn't let me in on it."

Liam hadn't brought his wife with him. Charlie knew this wasn't entertainment for him. This was serious. She'd betrayed more than just Ian. "Would it have changed a damn thing knowing what would happen?"

She hated the answer but had to be truthful. "No. Eli Nelson had my sister by then."

"Your sister, Chelsea Dennis. She was taken from her elementary school in North Carolina by her father, Vladimir Denisovitch, and brought to Moscow. He kidnapped her right off the playground. You were older. Did he use your sister to get you to go with him? Or were you afraid because he'd murdered your mother by then?" Adam asked, proving just how smart he was.

Charlie felt her jaw drop. She thought Chelsea had buried that information. "How do you know that?"

"Is your sister the hacker?" Adam's eyes flared as though he'd found a challenge.

Charlie nodded. "She's the best in the world."

Adam sat back. "Second best. Tell her she didn't go

far enough. No information is ever really lost. You just have to know which threads to follow and which lead to nowhere. I have amazing instincts. It's not just about talent. I'd met you. I didn't know if it was you or someone else who had covered the tracks. I made an educated guess. Can she walk? Her medical records were inconclusive."

Charlie took a deep breath. God, he'd found out far more than she'd expected. "She has a pronounced limp."

Adam's voice had a gravely tone, as though he was deeply sympathetic. "From the compound fractures of both the tibia and the fibula in each leg. I can't imagine the pain of that. She was left like that for a long period of time? I found the X-rays online. They showed a healing process. The doctors had to refracture the legs to set them. She was ten?"

The truth could only help her here. She needed these people on her side. But it was so hard to talk about. Especially with Ian's accusations running through her head. "She was ten years old. The only reason my father took her to the hospital is that I agreed to comply with his training. My father was the head of the Denisovitch syndicate. My mother ran when she was pregnant with Chelsea. She realized she didn't want her daughters being raised by a monster. She paid a man to smuggle the two of us out of the country. We lived in North Carolina for ten years. She thought he'd forgotten about us. He hadn't. He killed my mother and took my sister and me back to Russia. I was a bit rebellious, to say the least. He realized that Chelsea was his best method of controlling me so he broke her legs one day. I did what he asked after that."

"How terrible," Serena said, her eyes tearing up.

Terrible didn't begin to cover it. One day she'd been a happy junior high kid whose mom adored her. She'd had a future. She'd wanted to go to college. The next her mother was dead and her only future was with the Thieves-in-Law. "My father ran drugs and women, and Eli Nelson tried to make him out to be an arms dealer. Nelson used my love for my sister to get me to run an operation for him. He told me he would off my father if I would just spend a couple of weeks distracting a CIA operative for him."

"Ian." Eve sat forward, an encouraging look on her face. "You were trying to save your sister."

Well, at least they were giving her more room than Ian had. "Yes. I didn't know Ian then. My mission was to spend a little time with him. I didn't expect to marry him. I didn't expect to love him. He would have done the same for Sean."

"Yes," Jake said. "He would have. So why are you back?"

Grace brought in a tray of coffee and donuts. "The donut shop delivered. Why did you order ten lemon filled?"

"It's Ian's favorite."

Jake sat back. "So you love the big guy. Damn, good luck to you."

Grace looked down at the four dozen donuts Charlie had ordered. "Ian doesn't eat donuts."

Charlie waved her off. "He thinks he can't handle carbs. He loves them, trust me. Now can we get to the point of this meeting? Is anyone interested in Eli Nelson, aka Mr. Black?"

Serena sat up, a notebook in her hand. "I am."

Great. The novelist was interested in what she had to say. So all her hard-won data only meant something to the chick who would combine it with double penetration and lubricant in a literary extravaganza. "Look, this is serious.

I want everyone except members of the team out of this conference room. This is not playtime, people. Eli Nelson isn't a joke."

Grace frowned her way. "Yes, I know that. I have a metal plate in my head to prove it. You're not telling me anything we don't already know. Except that you're here without Ian. I know Serena. Serena is here because she's a member of our little family. No matter what Sean says, you haven't proven anything to me so far. So I would tread carefully or we'll call security and have you taken out."

Damn it. She'd lost Grace the minute she'd questioned Serena. So there was a "girl power" thing going. She didn't need to piss them off, but she did need to make herself clear. "I'll make my marriage license available to you."

Simon smiled, but it was a predatory thing. "We won't need to call security, love. I'll escort you out myself."

Yeah, she was sure he would escort her out in the nastiest way possible. "I'm here because I love Ian. I've already bled for this team."

"Grace, she saved Alex," Eve explained.

"She's the reason Evans's whole terrorist plot was brought down," Serena added. "I was there. I might not have been right there, but I know she was helping. They wouldn't have taken him down without her." She turned to Charlie. "I'm only here because I've been spotting lately and Jake and Adam are twelve kinds of freaked out about me losing the baby. I can wait in Adam's office if you prefer."

Yep, she was a bitch. God, life was easier when she hadn't cared about her conscience. "No. Please stay, Serena. I'm sorry. I'm trying to do something I've never done before—be professional. I want Ian to be proud of me."

"He's likely going to be mad pissed off at you," Liam pointed out, but even he was studying her with something other than complete rage.

She perked up a little, thinking of just how well Ian had spanked her in the past. He had a very strict set of rules.

"Yes, I'm totally counting on that." She sobered up. "I understand that the majority of you have zero reason to trust me. Adam, what else have you discovered about me in the last twelve hours, because I'm betting you haven't slept a wink since Alex figured out who I am."

Adam sat up straighter, his eyes lighting with enthusiasm. "I've figured it all out, honey. You're deeply interesting. Your name is Charlotte Dennis, born Charlotte Denisovitch, though I think maybe that name change wasn't completely legal."

It hadn't been, but her mother had been desperate. "Mom thought an American name would help."

"Your father was a son of a bitch. He was a brutal, violent man, and he didn't limit it to his business." His eyes softened slightly. "He didn't break you the way he did Chelsea."

She didn't like to think about those times now. "My torture was more mental than Chelsea's, but I assure you I was put through his rigorous tests. My father believed his children should be strong or they should be dead. We're lucky, Chelsea and I."

"Is the syndicate still looking for you?" Adam asked. "Is that why you've had thirty-four residences in the last five years?"

Had it been so few? It felt like a hundred. "Yes. My uncle took over after my father was killed. Uncle Mikhail took Dad's death personally. He blames me. He should. I traded my work for Eli Nelson for his assassination services. At the time, I didn't feel like I had a choice. I could work for my father and hope he didn't kill my sister or I could hope Nelson upheld his end of our bargain. He did, in the end, though he tried to take more than we'd originally bargained for."

"He wanted you to continue to work for him?" Adam asked.

Jake huffed, sitting back in his chair. "Shit. He's looking for you, too."

Charlie shrugged a little. They weren't telling her anything she didn't know. "Not personally, but he's sent plenty of assassins after me. I might have stolen a whole bunch of his money."

"I knew there was a reason I liked her," Eve said. "You know, besides the whole saving my husband's life thing."

At least she had one person on her side. "Chelsea and I have been on the run ever since. I've had one goal in life. I'm going to get my husband back. I'm going to make everything up to him and spend the rest of my life making him happy. I've done some terrible things, but I'm trying to do good now. I'm trying to make things better, and the best way I can do that is by helping you bring down Eli Nelson. Chelsea and I managed to damage him financially about a year and a half ago."

Adam's eyes went wide. "Shit. You're the reason he was dealing with the Chinese. You stole his backup money."

And just like that, she was back in the doghouse.

"Most agents keep a stash in case they get burned. Normally it's like a hundred grand or something, but not Eli. No. He was dirty as hell and it had paid well. He also liked to make certain business investments. When I took his two million, he owed a nice chunk of it to some South American gentlemen. Yeah, he had to think fast to make that up. It's probably why he went with the bearer bonds finally. I know he'd planned on keeping them for his retirement, but I forced him into the open. I'm sure you blame me for that, O'Donnell."

"I got a nice girl out of it, so we can call that one even." The Irishman was still studying her, but he'd relaxed a bit. She didn't think he had his hand on the trigger anymore.

"Where's this sister you've talked about?" Simon asked.

"I didn't know you had a sister, Kris. I mean, Charlotte." Jesse looked like someone had taken him shopping, possibly the Brit. He was in a suit and tie that he only looked slightly uncomfortable in. She had to admit, he cleaned up nicely.

"Yeah, again with the undercover thing," she replied. "I thought I would come in and see if someone shot me before I brought my sister in." That wasn't the only reason. Chelsea didn't get out much. She preferred to live her life in front of her monitor. "But I have the information she's uncovered. I thought we could talk it through before Adam does his thing."

"You know where Nelson is?" Jake asked.

"I know what he's interested in. I can't get a good line on him, but I have some ears to the ground. He's been spending a lot of time in India the last couple of months."

"India?" Simon asked. "Mumbai?"

"No, he's been seen in Goa. Southern Goa to be exact, though the reports have him running all along the western coast of India."

"Goa?" Adam asked. He had his laptop out, his

fingers already flying across the keyboard.

"It's the smallest state in India, but it's right on the coast so it's known for its tourism. Europeans flock there for holiday. I thought we could send Simon in to take a look, maybe ask a few questions. He could easily be mistaken for a tourist if someone pulled the stick out of his ass and stuffed him into some board shorts." She ignored his huff and opened the packet she'd sat up all night making for her new crew. "If you'll look at page three, you can see I have a list of businesses he's frequented in the area using one of his known aliases. Unfortunately, unlike London, these seaside towns aren't outfitted with CCTV cameras on every corner, so I'm having to rely on informants and his paper trail. You'll see that he's used several guide shops. I can't tell if he's buying products or services because he's been using cash there. He might be on to me because my informant in the area has gone silent."

"So he's dead," Jake surmised.

"Probably."

"And you want to send me in next," Simon said with a droll little grin. "How very flattering."

"Well, I expect you won't allow Nelson to catch you," she shot back.

"What's in Goa that Nelson would want?" Jake leaned forward, grabbing a donut.

She bit back a smile. She'd felt vulnerable. It was so stupid, childish, but she'd been hurt no one would eat the donuts she'd brought. She hadn't poisoned them or anything. They were just chock full of sugar and artery-hardening goodness. The fact that they had been sitting there untouched had made her feel deeply unwanted.

Once Jake reached for one, Jesse grabbed a couple and the men all started eating. Even Simon sniffed around a couple before selecting a jelly.

"I'm not sure yet, but there are a couple of scientific teams in the area, one energy project, and several billionaires. He would likely be interested in the billionaires, and I'm curious about the energy project. Mostly because I can find very little on it. It's being run by a small consortium of scientists hosted by the royalty of a small island country named Loa Mali. The island is one of the smallest countries in the world. I have no idea how it's managed to stay sovereign, but it's actually quite flush with cash. It's been a country for the last two hundred years, and the same family has been at the head of government. The king's name is Kashmir Kamdar."

"The high-tech guru?" Adam asked around his chocolate éclair. "I've heard of him. He's like a billionaire playboy."

"Or he's a terrorist working with Eli Nelson. I'm a little worried that Nelson is trying to get back into the arms market by selling to the factions in Kashmir, the region of India Kash is named for. His family has close ties with India. He's a big proponent of keeping Kashmir in Indian hands."

"And the Pakistani government wants it for its own," Simon said, neatly summing up hundreds of years of conflict. "It's perfect for a man like Nelson. So I get to go and get some sun and figure out if Nelson is trying to get that part of the world to go nuclear. Well, I'm going to need a per diem. If I'm going in as a tourist, I should definitely be a wealthy one."

"You're not going anywhere." Ian was standing in the doorframe, his big body in a pair of jeans and a T-shirt. His hair was still a little wet as though he'd run from his shower to the office. He looked big and dangerous and completely sexy. He made her mouth water just looking at

80

him.

He even looked good with a black eye. Maybe she shouldn't have hit him so hard. Well, there was only one way to get through this and that was to be brazen.

"Hello, Ian. I brought your favorite donuts. Lemon cream. Would you like some coffee? Did Sean give you ibuprofen? I told him he should get you some."

He simply walked in, reached down, and hauled her up. Without a word from him, he slung her over his broad shoulder and started carrying her out.

"All right, then, Adam, you know what to do," Charlie said, trying to hold her head up. Unlike her husband, she wasn't willing to have it out in front of his employees and friends.

"God, I wish I had a video camera. Someone make sure security doesn't erase these tapes," Adam said.

"Adam!" He could be so damn obnoxious. She had to keep him in line.

He straightened up immediately. "Yes, ma'am. I'll check into it."

A hard hand slapped at her ass, making her skin tingle. "He's not going to check into anything except getting new locks for our fucking doors."

"Mommy and Daddy are fighting, Jake. What should I do?" Adam asked.

From what she could see, they were all following her and Ian out of the conference room, snacks in hand.

Jake was watching the scene with an amused expression. "I think we figure out who's scarier."

"I'm writing this into a book," Serena said, taking notes on a small pad of paper.

"Is the meeting over?" Grace asked. "Should I clean up?"

Charlie knew exactly what was going to happen.

"He's going to say he doesn't want a donut, but he totally does. Save him three. He'll eat them before lunch and then pretend he didn't. Oh, and he likes his coffee really black, like almost espresso like."

Grace stopped. "Seriously? I've been making it medium."

"He likes really dark roast."

Another swat hit her ass. "I hate everything."

He was so annoying. "You can toss me out on my ass. I'll be back in ten minutes."

He walked out the glass doors, allowing them to slam shut behind them. "Not if I kill you you won't."

Like that was a real threat. "Sure, Superman, slay me hard, buddy."

He talked such a good game. He talked like he was the biggest badass to ever walk the face of the earth and, in some ways, he was. He could eviscerate a man who did evil and never think twice about it. He was perfectly capable of taking someone's head off.

But only if they deserved it.

She'd figured him out long ago. He would take apart the bad guys—and no one else. He would have a hard time taking out a woman, even if she did deserve it. He had his code, and he stuck to it rigidly.

Ian Taggart would undoubtedly tell her it made him vomit, but he was a hero. A real live walking and talking American hero.

He was her hero. And damn, his ass looked fine in a pair of jeans. She thought seriously about cupping those strong muscles with her palms, but decided against it. She could only push him so far before he did something he would regret.

"Or I could just send you to the street, where you belong." The elevator dinged open and he strode inside.

She took a breath, steeling herself against the close quarters. "Ian, come on."

Ian ignored her, looking toward his crew. "You guys stay the fuck in the office or you're fired."

"I won't fire anyone," she shot back. The elevator was large and elegantly appointed and empty. She'd handled it on her way up. She could take a trip down. "Except Jesse. He nearly killed me."

She heard a sad little sigh. "But I just got an apartment."

"You're not fucking fired, Jesse," Ian said, frustration evident in his tone. "This is still my company. I wanted to fire you but now I won't because I know she doesn't want you here. But if you try to follow us down, I'll kill you."

He turned so she couldn't see anything except the back of the elevator and how fine his ass was. She concentrated on that and not the fact that they were in a small, enclosed space. "He's a drama queen. He's not going to kill anyone. He's definitely not going to kill Eli Nelson because he won't find the fucker without me."

A hard smack. Yes, he was definitely coming to the end of his rope.

He slapped a hand at the buttons and the door closed. He made not a single move to let her down.

"I'm not going anywhere, Ian."

"I'll bar you from the building."

"That's going to be hard since I own half of the top floor."

A small pause. "No, you fucking don't."

It was time to point out a few irrefutable truths of his situation. "We didn't have a prenup, babe. Even if we did, this is property you bought after our nuptials. Texas is a community property state. What's yours is mine. On the happy side, I have a ten million dollar condo I'll share with you. I even bought thousand thread count sheets. I know you have sensitive skin."

He let her down with a little shove, placing distance between them. His hand shot out, pressing the button that caused the elevator to stop mid-descent. "What the fuck are you trying to pull, Charlie?"

She preferred it when he was carrying her like a sack of flour. At least there had been a connection then. Now she felt the space between them. And the tightness of the elevator. "I'm trying to make things right."

"You can't. I can't ever trust you again."

"Ian, I made a terrible mistake. I should have trusted you. I should have told you what was happening." That was her real crime. She'd thought he would help her, save her, but she hadn't risked it. From the day her father had kidnapped her until that moment when she'd taken Nelson's drug, her life had been a careful balancing act, a constant game of not tripping over the landmines of her father's world. Everyone in that world wanted something from her and they were all willing to hurt her to get it.

She hadn't known there was trust and love and softness in the world until she'd met Ian Taggart.

"I would have had you taken back to the States and placed under custody," he explained. "You did the right thing if you wanted to stay out of the rendition pool. You played me and you played me well."

"You knew something was wrong, Ian. You knew it, but you didn't do a damn thing about it because you were in love with me." If she could just get him to admit it, maybe they had a chance. Her hands were starting to shake. Just a little. She could handle it.

"I was thinking with my dick. I don't do that anymore. You cost me my job, Charlotte. How on earth do you think I would ever give you another shot? Do you want to kill me this time?"

"If I wanted to do that I wouldn't be here."

He leaned against the elevator wall, studying her through hooded eyes. "Or, the more likely scenario is you need intelligence for your boss and you think you can seduce me again. I'm not going to lie to you. I'm attracted to you. You're exactly my type. Big tits, nice hips. You're not some petite little thing I could crush. I wish it wasn't true, but I want to fuck you hard. I want to do it here and now. You might have control over my dick, but it won't change a damn thing. I'll fuck you and then I'll kick you out of this building and then I won't give you another thought."

She hated how much his words could torch her, but she'd figured out a long time ago that this was the price she had to pay. This terrible vulnerability was the price all women paid for loving a man. If she closed herself off, built up a wall between them, then she would never get back to that place where she'd been loved and safe and pure. God, loving him had made her pure, and she hadn't felt that way in such a long time.

She reached out to him, letting her fingers brush the bristly skin of his jawline. He hadn't bothered to shave. "I always think about you."

He forced her hand away. "No, Charlie. Not like that. If you want to throw down, I'll do you, but I won't listen to that shit again."

Because it wasn't shit. Because he'd loved how she'd loved him. He couldn't fool her. He could lie all he liked, but it was there in his eyes.

"Will you kiss me?" It would all be worth it if he would put his lips on hers again.

His head shook, a sharp rejection. "No. I don't kiss."

"You did." He'd kissed her so long. He'd spent what

felt like hours drugging her with kisses.

"I don't now."

"So you haven't kissed anyone since me?"

Ian's lips curled up in an evil little smile. "I've fucked probably a hundred women since you, darling."

But he hadn't kissed a single one of them. It made her heart leap. "I haven't kissed anyone either. Not in all these years."

His eyes went stony. "I don't care."

She had to find a way to make him care. "Will you just let Adam look at the data I collected?"

"I'll find my own," he replied.

"God, you are so stubborn."

"It would do you well to remember that." His phone rang. He pulled it out of his pocket and grimaced. "Speak of the devil. What is it, Adam?" He snarled into the receiver. "No, I am not fucking my fucking wife in the fucking goddamn elevator. I'm having a discussion with her. And she's not my fucking wife. And tell security I'll start the goddamn elevator when I'm good and ready. You know I can fire you, asshole, so watch it."

He slid the phone back in his pants and jabbed the button on the elevator.

"I forgot about the claustrophobia. I'll have you at the bottom in a minute." He sounded almost tender, but then seemed to remember he shouldn't do that. "When we get to the lobby, you don't have to worry about close spaces because you never have to walk into this building again."

The elevator slid down the shaft, and Ian turned away from her.

The doors opened, revealing a pretty young woman in a yellow skirt and a blouse that was at least a size too big for her. She wore glasses, and her dark hair was in a messy bun.

She'd been smiling, but she lost it once she looked at Ian. She looked like a deer in the headlights of a raging oncoming truck.

"Phoebe, you're late," Ian said in a pitch black voice.

The girl, who couldn't be much past twenty-four, blanched. "I'll just take the stairs, Mr. Taggart."

She ran as fast as her kitten heels could carry her.

"That was mean. Are you having fun scaring little girls now?"

He took her by the elbow and started hauling her out. "They seem to be the only ones I can scare anymore. I'll be shocked if she makes it up all fifteen flights. Someone's going to have to go get her. Why do I pick up fucking strays? At least you're one I can get rid of. Security!"

Two men immediately stepped up. They were dressed in almost military looking uniforms. "Mr. Taggart?"

He pointed a finger her way. "Don't let this woman back in the building."

She couldn't allow that to happen. "I will sue the holy fuck out of everyone here. He's my husband. I own half of the fifteenth floor."

Ian's jaw squared, his eyes hardening. "We're not married."

"Yes, we are and I have the documents to prove it."

Ian smirked. "And I have your death certificate. It's all framed and everything."

She pulled out her ace. "You're the only one who has it."

He stopped. "You didn't."

"Of course I did. I wasn't going to leave that hanging out there. I'm sure there are some files with MI6 and the Agency, but good luck getting those. I think you'll find they're classified." Actually Chelsea had recently erased all the pertinent info, but she let Ian believe what he wanted to. The minute she'd known the Florida operation was going to be a success, she'd put her plan into motion. "The marriage certificate is back in place as of yesterday. According to all public records, we've been living together happily for almost six years now." She smiled at the security guards. "We're trying to have a baby. The doctors told him he has sluggish sperm. It's made him really cranky."

He took a step toward her, his voice going low. "Sweetheart, I am going to settle in on that bench right over there and I'll pull up that little skirt you're wearing, pull down your underwear, and spank you until you scream and all in front of these very nice, very vanilla people. Do you want that?"

She shook her head. "I'm not wearing any underwear, Ian. You told me I wasn't allowed to. It's made packing so much easier."

He gripped her wrist and started hauling her out of the building.

He seemed to be under some kind of impression that she had dignity to protect or something. Dignity didn't mean crap to her. She planted her feet. Unfortunately, the smooth marble surface helped her to slide right along.

"Out you go, Charlie. If I see you here again, I'll call the cops. And you should understand my first call when I get back upstairs is going to be to my lawyer. If we're still married, honey, we're getting a divorce."

"I don't want a divorce, Ian."

"I don't care what you want." He used one broad shoulder to open the glass doors, letting in a blast of pure Texas heat.

Charlie stumbled a little as her feet went from marble to concrete. Ian cursed and caught her before her ass found the ground. "Ian, please. Let's talk about this. I can prove

I'm not working for Eli Nelson."

He made sure she was steady on her feet before moving away again. "No, you can't."

"There has to be something." She wasn't sure he would believe her if God came down and whacked him over his very masculine forehead with the truth. Her righteously paranoid husband would just decide that the heavenly father was a double agent sent to kill him. "Ian, you have to trust your instincts. Look at the data in front of you. Read what I've sent you. Look at it dispassionately and then form a logical conclusion. You're the smartest man I've ever met."

"Follow my instincts? I did that once. I shoved all the facts aside and followed my instincts. That's how I lost my job and I damn near lost my life. You taught me that lesson, Charlie. Good-bye."

He started to turn away, and Charlie felt her heart squeeze.

He stared for a moment, his eyes on the door, and then she saw it. A single glint off the metal handle.

"Get the fuck down!" Ian yelled, his body moving with predatory grace.

He hit her with the impact of a locomotive, and she found herself tackled and thrown to the ground just as the bullets started flying.

Chapter Four

Ian gritted his teeth hard as his shoulder hit the concrete. He rolled to the left, tucking Charlie close to his body as he tried to maneuver them to the trees that lined the walkway.

Panic was spreading. The minute the shot rang out, there were screams and shouts, and the people who had been milling around in front of the building had scattered.

He wasn't carrying. What the hell had he been thinking? Charlie had his head in a mess.

"Ian, are you all right?" At least she was calm. Most women Ian knew would be screaming by now. They would be fighting him. But Charlie had completely relaxed in his arms, making it easy for him to roll her out of harm's way. She'd trusted him to take care of her.

"I'm not hit if that's what you're asking."

"Boss?" Jacob Dean was suddenly at his side, and he hadn't forgotten his firearm.

"I thought I told you to stay upstairs." Ian brought his head up. There was a row of oleanders to his left. They were roughly four feet tall and thick. They would suit his purposes nicely. "Get us some cover. He's probably done, but I can't take the chance."

Because the minute he'd seen the glint of a scope reflecting off the window, he'd had a vision of Charlie lying in a pool of her own blood. Was this just his fate? To always see her like that?

Jake moved, his gun at the ready. He placed himself in danger so Ian didn't have to put Charlie there. "I think he's done, too, boss. The cops are already on their way. Move, now."

Ian was up on his feet, but he kept his head down and covered Charlie as he lifted her up. Three long strides and they were safely behind the bushes. Trees were at their backs. If the fucker wanted to take a shot now, he would have to get damn lucky.

"Adam's already pulling the security tapes. The cops will want them because they're going to try to identify who the intended victim is. Standard procedure. I figured we should keep Mrs. Taggart's face out of the papers since she's probably got a couple of agencies looking for her."

Fuck. He hadn't even thought about that. In the distance, he could hear sirens wailing.

"She's not Mrs. Taggart," Ian said, his teeth locked in a grind.

"I have the papers to prove it," Charlie replied.

There was no point in arguing now. They didn't have the time.

"So who's trying to kill you, Charlie?" There was no doubt in his mind this was all about her.

"Maybe someone was trying to kill you," Charlie shot back, a frown turning those gorgeous lips down. "Have you met yourself? I can think of any number of people who you've pissed off enough to try their hand at a little assassination."

She wasn't entirely wrong, but Ian knew damn well

this wasn't about him. "Charlie? The cops will be here any minute. How much do I have to lie to them?"

She shook her head. "Not at all because you don't actually know anything."

How could he go from saving her life to wanting to strangle her in less than ten seconds? "You are going to go back upstairs with Jacob because god only knows what the cops have on you. You're going to my office and you will stay there. Is that understood?"

The sweetest smile flashed across her face. "Yes, Master. I will absolutely obey that dictate. Jacob?"

Jake helped her up. "I'll take her through the back. I think I can make it without losing cover. Adam will shut down the cameras, and he's already got a call in to Brighton."

Derek Brighton was their DPD contact. He was also a Dom at Sanctum. If Ian was going to have a chance of not getting Charlie involved in this, he would need Derek.

He watched as Charlie followed behind Jake. She was calm and collected. No one would ever think she'd damn near had her head taken off by a sniper.

It wasn't sexy. Nope. It was annoying. He tried to tell himself he would like it better if she was one of those women who would scream and cry and be terrified.

He found those women to be deeply annoying.

That was it. He never really loved her. He just liked the fact that she was quiet during a shootout. Yeah. That had to be it.

Just as Charlie disappeared into the maintenance door, the cops showed up, sirens wailing, tires screeching. They couldn't be quiet during a shootout either.

But they could fuck everything up.

Ian couldn't let that happen. This had just become his op.

Two hours later, he was finally able to go back to his office, having convinced the officers that it must have been a car misfiring since there was only the one sound. People, he'd told the officers, were just too jumpy these days.

While the police were talking down frightened onlookers, Alex had already found the bullet and started his own investigation.

"I want to know where the fucker was, what he was shooting, and who he fucking works for," Ian said, walking into the conference room.

Adam was sitting in the back, his head down as he typed. Jake and Alex were staring at a bullet casing through the plastic bag it was held in.

Grace was holding Phoebe's hand as she breathed in through her inhaler. She sent Ian a dirty look. "Really, Ian? What is wrong with you? You made her walk up fifteen flights of steps?"

"I didn't make her do anything. She took one look at the elevator and ran the other way." Again, another reason to prefer Charlie. Phoebe was a pretty woman. She had curves in all the right places, though she attempted to hide them all. She pretended to be frumpy, but there was a lovely body under all those clothes. Unfortunately, she also seemed to have a ton of fucking inhibitions. If he'd told Charlie she was late, she would have shot him the finger and gotten on the elevator.

The elevator. He'd forgotten how much she hated them. She was painfully claustrophobic, but she still got on them. He would never forget the way her hands shook, but she could keep her face perfectly placid. Only the fine tremble in her hands gave away that anything was wrong.

"She's got to take a self-defense class or something," Jake said, sighing. "That is the single subbiest female I have ever met in my life. Okay, Charlie's fine. She's been on the phone with her sister."

"Did you tape the conversation?"

Grace gasped. "Tape the conversation? He wouldn't do that."

"Of course," Jake replied, ignoring her entirely. Security protocols weren't part of Grace's employment training. "I texted Alex with a 540 right before I brought her up the maintenance elevator. She was a little shaky."

Not about the shooting, but the elevator would do that to her. "Good."

"What is a 540?" Grace asked.

He should have cleared the room, but at the end of the day, Grace was family and Phoebe did a decent job. They deserved to know how McKay-Taggart operated. Though he would never tell them about a 640. It was code for what to do if they all came under fire. Grace, Eve, Phoebe, and any other women were to be protected first and foremost to the point of the men giving their lives. Every single man he employed had to agree to the protocol. Even the latest, Jesse. He'd practically jumped up and down at the prospect. That was when he'd known he would hire the little fucker. Underneath his puppy dog exterior, he was a protector. He was a Dom. "It's a code for watch and observe. Alex turned on the cameras in my office. Adam's been watching her from the moment she walked in."

"Her sister said she'd call her back, but that she thought she had a line on someone. Charlotte didn't bother to mention she'd just been shot at," Jake explained. "She told her sister to call her back and now she's waiting."

"She seems to like to smell things, boss." Adam looked up. "She's been smelling the jacket you keep in your office. She's nosy, too. She's looked through all your drawers. She also called out for pizza. She doesn't act like a woman who's terribly worried about being shot at."

"Because she's used to it." He wondered just how many times something like this had happened to her. What had the last five years really been like? If she was telling the truth and she'd walked away from both the syndicate and screwed Eli Nelson, then her every moment had to be a delicate balance of working to stay alive. The Russians alone would be hell to stay clear of, not to mention someone with Nelson's talents.

Absently, he reached over and grabbed a donut. It had been a nasty day. He needed it. He watched the monitor on Adam's computer. Charlie was sitting at his desk, her legs curled into her chest as she dropped her head back and closed her eyes. He could see the long line of her throat and how it sloped gracefully toward the curve of her breasts. Though the camera was black and white, he knew how perfect her skin was, the only thing marring it being the scars, and yet he'd always paid such attention to them. He'd kissed her scars over and over, tracing them with his tongue as though they were a roadmap to the woman and he could learn her through touch and taste.

He bit into the donut and nearly sighed. Lemon. He fucking loved lemon. Tart. Sweet. Tangy. Just like Charlie.

"Hey, I brought you some coffee. Do you want me to clear these out, Ian?" Grace held a mug of coffee in her hands and gestured to the boxes of donuts.

"Hey, I've only had one," Adam said, jumping up, his hands reaching straight for the lemons, the little fucker.

Ian batted him away. "Mine."

"Dude, there are like thirty donuts left."

"Anything else, but the lemons are mine." How long

had it been since he indulged in something as simple as a lemon-filled donut? Forever. He took a sip of the coffee Grace had handed him and his eyes closed in pleasure. "Oh, that is so good. Did you change coffee brands?"

Grace had the oddest look on her face as she stared up at him. "No, after what Charlotte said earlier, I thought I would try something new. I made it three times stronger than I normally would."

Adam shuddered. "It tastes like motor oil."

"Shut the fuck up, Adam. It tastes like heaven." Yeah, he would have Grace teach his new sub how to make his coffee. Because he was still totally doing that. Charlie had made him deeply aware that he needed an outlet. Just because she remembered he liked lemon donuts and how he wanted his coffee didn't make up for the whole screwing him over thing.

"You know what would take the motor oil taste out of my mouth?" Adam asked. "Lemon."

"Fuck you. Buy your own lemon donuts."

Grace sighed. "Also Derek Brighton is here. I put him in Alex's office. Yours was full."

He picked up what was left of the box and walked out. "Alex. Your office. Now."

"Awesome," he heard Adam say as he walked out. "I hate it when he stops using verbs. If I get scurvy it's his fault for hogging the lemons."

Alex caught up to him. "The bullet is a .30 caliber. It doesn't tell us much. Probably from a sniper rifle. Simon and Jesse are working on trajectory. They're pretty sure the shooter was roughly seven or eight stories up and to the northwest. There are two hotels that might work. Sorry. We can't be more specific without bringing out some equipment that would tip off the cops."

"I would bet you're going to find that the rifle used

was a Dragunov. It's what the Denisovitch syndicate uses. They believe in supporting Mother Russia. They also tend to work clean. Tell Simon to try to figure out what room he was in, but I would bet my life they won't find a damn thing. Our shooter's gone." He took another bite of his donut. It was the only fucking thing that had gone right all day. "Shit. She needs to leave."

"Or we need to protect her," Alex suggested.

"Or we need to let them take her out and then all my problems would be solved." He said the words and knew he would never fucking let it happen.

"Ian," Alex sighed.

He was deeply grateful to be able to push through Alex's door. He didn't want to get into it with Alex. Ever since Alex and Eve had reconnected, Alex had been all about his freaking feelings and shit. Now Alex expected him to have feelings, too. Come to think of it, that was Charlie's fault. All bad things were Charlie's fault.

All good things came from lemon cream.

"Derek, good to see you." Ian greeted the big cop who paced across the floor of Alex's office.

Derek Brighton had been on Ian's Green Beret team. Ian kept up with all his former team mates, but he'd always been close with Derek. When Ian and Alex had looked for a city to start a business in, it had been Derek who advised them to move to Texas. Derek was their liaison with the DPD, and they needed him far more often than Ian would like.

"I would love to say the same, but I'm more inclined to ask why the fuck I have two investigators downstairs who firmly believe that a possible terrorist attack was nothing more than a car backfiring."

And Derek was smarter than the average cop. Still. He had to give it a shot. He finished off his donut and took a nice swig of coffee. "Oh, that? Yeah, I was down there. Some asshole needs to get his exhaust checked. Freaked the hell out of the tourists."

Derek frowned. "Really? Just the tourists? Because I've been doing this for longer than the beat cops and I managed to notice that the shop across the street has CCTV and one of them is pointed this way. Guess what I saw?"

Mother flying fucker. He was going to crucify someone. "No idea."

"I saw you, big guy. I saw you figure out what was going to happen about two seconds before it did. What did you see? Glint off the window? Somehow I'm thinking that didn't come from a fucking exhaust problem, Tag."

He was screwed. Or maybe not. Brighton was a reasonable man. "Why aren't the cops swarming me right now?"

"Because the last thing this city needs is a terrorist threat," Brighton said, his shoulders relaxing slightly.

"I don't think it's a terrorist threat," Alex said, crossing his arms over his chest.

"So who did Ian piss off? Is the CIA finally moving past burning him to actually killing him?" Derek asked.

"I didn't get burned." Television was going to be the death of the intelligence officer. "I walked away."

He had gotten burned. Just not by the Agency. Charlie had burned the holy fuck out of him. She'd burned so hot he couldn't help but get singed.

"We have it under control," Alex said.

"I need more than a reassurance." Derek was unmoved, his square jaw tightening. "I need to know what's going on. Were they gunning for Ian? Will they try again?"

This should be the point at which he would turn

Charlie over to the DPD and let them deal with her. She would be out of his hair. He wouldn't have to see her again. She was right in his office and all he had to do was walk Derek down the hall and explain that she was very likely on several Most Wanted lists. He grabbed another donut. He was going to have to hit the gym.

"What's wrong with him?" Derek asked.

"He's thinking." Alex knew him really well. "He's plotting some shit out in his head, and I have to really, really hope that he does the right fucking thing here."

Well, he knew what Alex wanted. He sighed. He wasn't going to be rushed. Fuck, that tasted good. The combination of tart and sweet and the bitter of the excellent coffee was practically perfect.

Of course, if he gave her up, she would be taken into custody and very likely dead in the next twenty-four hours, and not in the "come back in five years" kind of way.

That was bad, how? He could let her go and find his dream sub—a hot little sub who never questioned him and cooked better than Sean and deeply enjoyed anal. He didn't know if Charlie liked anal. She probably would if he did it. He was really fucking good at it. But he wasn't going to do it.

Eli Nelson would be happy if she died. Well, Nelson would be happy if he believed Charlie's bullshit story about screwing him over. Could he totally discount it? He didn't want to ever make Nelson happy. Therefore he couldn't turn Charlie in.

Decision made.

"Eli Nelson is gunning for me."

Alex let loose a long breath of relief. "I was worried you wouldn't tell the truth."

Ian shrugged. "I'm practically George fucking

Washington. I cannot tell a lie."

Derek's eyes narrowed. "Yeah, sure. Am I looking at a sniper running around Dallas?"

Likely not. At least that he could be honest about. "You know how the pros are. They take their shot and then they dive deep. The last thing they want is a city on the edge. I'll be on guard, and Simon and Adam are already working on figuring out who Nelson hired. We'll take care of it. All you do if you bring the force into it is cause yourself and the city a mega shit ton of problems. Oh, and if you want the national media focused on every little problem the DPD has, you could call this a random sniper attack. It's not. It's about me, and that means it's going to end up being classified. Save yourself and the city a whole lot of trouble. It was a car backfiring."

Derek cursed under his breath. "Fine. But I fucking swear I will have your guts if you're lying to me and there's another attack. My ass is on the line here, Tag."

"So is mine and I can protect it better if we keep this quiet."

Derek nodded and started for the door. "I'll leave it be for now. I'm informing my CO." Derek often slipped into military lingo. "But he'll be okay with it. By the way, who's the girl?"

"The girl?" Damn it. He didn't need Derek looking into her.

"The female you protected," Derek prompted.

Alex snorted a little. "Ian took a new sub."

That motherfucker. Ian forced a grin on his face. "Hot little thing. Though I worry she might get scared off. You know, after today. She'll probably be gone tomorrow. You know how women can be. One little attempted murder and they're on to the next guy."

Alex shook his head. "Nah, she's made of sterner

stuff than that. You should meet her, Derek. She'll be at Sanctum tonight."

"All right," Derek said. "I'll look forward to seeing her tonight. I'm alone so watching the big guy get taken down by a sub might make my day worthwhile."

Alex had fucked him hard. Ian scrambled. He never fucking scrambled. "I decided to take a couple of full-time subs. She's just the first. I'm auditioning, if you know what I mean."

Derek studied him for a moment. "I do. I'm a little lonely, too. I don't think I could handle two, though. Maybe just one. Hell, maybe you're right. Maybe I should just start taking applications. I've avoided it because I know Amanda would apply. Fuck, man, couldn't you keep out the subs I have to work with? See you tonight."

Amanda was the brat bitch of Sanctum. Ian was pretty sure she was nasty to all the other subs, but no one had asked him to take care of her, so he was leaving it alone. Sometimes the subs needed to work out their own problems.

He wondered how Charlie would handle Amanda's brand of mean girl. That might be fun to see.

Derek strode out the door, and Ian turned on his best friend the minute it slammed shut. "You're a bastard."

Alex just smiled. "My parents are still happily married."

"You know what I mean. What the hell was that?"

"That was about giving you a chance despite yourself. You're not thinking about this. You need to take two fucking minutes. Your wife came back from the dead."

"No, according to everything I know she came back from St. Augustine." He didn't need this shit. Now he had to take her to Sanctum tonight. He had to dress her up in fet wear and walk beside her and pretend to be her Master.

That was Alex's fault.

Alex ran a hand across his head, obviously frustrated. "She saved me, man. She brought me back together with Eve. Why would she do that? She walked in front of a bullet. I would be dead. That bullet was headed straight for my damn heart. Give me one reason why she would do that beyond the fact that she loves you and she's trying to make her way back to you."

He couldn't even consider that. "Or you're pissed at me."

Alex's eyes rolled. "Why would I be pissed at you?"

He didn't have a really good answer for that. He actually treated Alex like gold. Alex was his brother the way Sean was his brother. One by DNA and history, the other by sacrifice and blood. "It doesn't matter now. You've set me on a path. I have to take her to Sanctum tonight. The place will probably blow up."

"I'll call Ryan and put some security protocols into place."

Security protocols wouldn't save Charlie. God only knew how many bullets would be flying her way.

Because she isn't on the move. Because she's staying here for you. She took the bullet meant for Alex for you. Why didn't she kill you before? It would have been more expedient. Why come back now?

His inner voice sucked ass. And was a little naïve.

He set down his coffee and walked to the window. Alex's office was next to his. They shared a spectacular view of the city. Was Charlie standing next door, looking out at the same set of buildings? Was there really only a wall separating them?

"Hey, I would love to know where your head's at, man." Alex stepped up. "You should know I was joking about why we stayed. We couldn't leave you. I know

you're going to think it's stupid and it would make you
vomit, but I would never leave you alone to deal with this.
You might not want my advice, but I've watched you
mourn her for five years. You loved that woman. I know
she betrayed you and if your final decision is to let her go,
then I'll make damn sure she doesn't come near you again.
But I think you need her. You either need to give it
another shot or you need closure, and you can't get that if
you don't talk to her. You might not give a shit that I'm
here, but I am here if you need me. Eve is here if you need
her. Sean is here. I know you think you're alone, but you
have a whole family around you."

He was definitely going to vomit. And he felt oddly
secure.

Would he have this weird family around him if he'd
stayed in the Agency? He doubted it. He would have
drifted further and further from them. He would have been
forced to hide so much of his life from them that being
around them would hold no meaning.

If he'd spent the last five years in the CIA, would he
even know his brothers anymore? Or would Sean and Alex
have drifted away, their lives meaningless to his plots? He
knew himself. He didn't lie. He'd enjoyed the plots, loved
pitting himself against others in a deadly little game. He'd
gotten a rush off it. He'd been a little obsessed with it.

Until he'd found something he was more obsessed
with. Charlotte. Charlie.

Had she saved him from a life that held absolutely
nothing but the game? He would never admit it but he
loved Grace. She had rapidly become the heart of his little
family. Grace and Sean and Carys. His niece. He liked the
way she looked at him, with a little bit of wonder. There
was nothing but pure love in his niece's eyes, and it had
cleansed him in a way.

Would he have held Carys in his hands if Charlie hadn't found her way into his life?

Likely not. She probably wouldn't exist because he would never have started McKay-Taggart and Sean would never have met Grace.

He didn't like the feeling that he owed Charlie anything at all. It wasn't like she meant to keep him from a family-less life.

"Do you want another donut?" Alex stared out, not looking at him. His hand was out, a sugary bit of confection sitting there.

He took the fucking bait. "I don't want to talk."

"Cool." Alex nodded. "We can just stand."

Ian stood with his best friend.

Maybe he wasn't so alone.

* * * *

Charlie let the chair twist to the left and then the right. It was a big leather chair, solid and well built, like the man it belonged to.

Was it brutally pathetic of her that it had been worth it to be nearly murdered because she'd been in his arms for a few seconds? She hadn't even thought about it, hadn't reacted herself. She'd just trusted him.

Was he about to toss her out again? Her phone rang. She looked at the incoming number before answering. "What's up, Chelsea?"

"Okay, it's official. Yuri Zhukov's in town. He's traveling under a Polish passport, but I found the fucker." Her sister sounded almost chipper, like finding out a highly paid Russian assassin had found them was a thing to celebrate. God, she was so tired. So fucking tired.

So at least she knew who was taking shots at her. "I'm

glad you found him, but you were a little late."

There was a pause on the line. "What happened? Fuck. The shooting downtown that turned out to be a car backfiring? That was about you?"

So that's how Ian had played it. She'd wondered exactly how he was going to keep the cops out of it. "It wasn't a car. I'm pretty sure it was Zhukov, but Ian took care of it."

"How did he take care of it?"

"He threw his body over mine and then handled the cops." Which was a really good idea because if he hadn't, there was every likelihood that her face would have gotten into the system and the minute that happened, she would have more than Zhukov on her ass.

"We need to move," Chelsea said.

Yes. That was the protocol. The minute they even had a hint that someone from the syndicate knew where they were, they left town. Sometimes they left the whole damn country. But she'd known the minute she'd started the St. Augustine op that she wouldn't be leaving again. She would fix the problem and get her husband back or the fuckers could take her down. She was done. That didn't mean Chelsea had to be. "I want you to go. Head to the islands for a while. You like it there."

"You want me to leave you here? That's insane. Charlotte, that man is going to get you killed."

"That man" was right behind her. Oh, he moved silently, but she had years of practice in making sure she always knew if someone was stalking her. Her teen years had been one long lesson in always knowing her surroundings, in memorizing and cataloging anything that could help her to survive. The memory of his scent had helped her to survive these last few years. He still used the same soap, clean and masculine. She breathed it in. She turned and her heart skipped a little beat. It was still amazing to be in the same room with the gorgeous bastard. Her eyes held his as she replied to her sister.

"You're probably right, but I'm going to take the chance. Chelsea, you knew this was where I was going. I never lied to you about what I wanted. I love you. Leave me a note if you're heading out." She clicked the phone off over Chelsea's vigorous protests.

She turned it off because there was no way her sister didn't call back.

"Your sister?"

Charlie nodded. "Yes. She thinks it was a man from my father's syndicate."

"Zhukov or Sobrev?"

Charlie frowned. "Zhukov. How did you know that?"

Ian shrugged a little. "Maybe I'm the one who hired him." He set the coffee down on his desk as she gave him her best stare. "Fine. I happen to know that the syndicate has two long-term assassins they use. I made a study of your father's organization after they became involved with my Irish operation."

Liar. He'd made a study of her father's syndicate after he thought they killed her. But she was going to leave him his pride. "Zhukov arrived at DFW under a Polish passport."

Ian grunted a little. It was his preferred method of communication. She'd learned to interpret his many guttural, caveman-y sounds. This one was his agreement grunt. "Not surprising. He's the senior of the two. They must really want you dead."

It was time for some more honesty. "I'm surprised. I thought they would nab me, not just kill me. I know a couple of things they would probably really like to get the lowdown on."

His eyes narrowed. "Did you steal money from the Russian fucking mafia?"

She really wished she could say she hadn't. "I thought of it as my inheritance."

"Goddamn it, Charlie." When he growled at her like that she actually felt cared for. She was so fucked up.

"I could give it back. In the years since I took it, I've made ten times that."

"Do I dare even ask how you managed that? Never mind. I don't want to know."

Because he knew her really well. Again, something that gave her hope. But she didn't mention all the information she'd sold over the last couple of years. She'd tried to do good with it, but she wasn't sure Ian would see it that way. She was absolutely certain that the world's intelligence agencies didn't see her as a force for good. She'd heard they had a code name for her—The Broker. Hopefully, Ian never had to find out about that. "Did you have a hard time with the police?"

"I have contacts. It's fine. You're in my chair." Ian frowned down at her.

She gracefully stood. "Of course, Master."

Ian tossed his big body into the chair and flipped open his laptop. "I have Simon working on who took that shot, but I need you to keep your head down. He'll try again."

So he wasn't going to toss her out. Wasn't that interesting? It would have been the easiest thing to let the police take her. Once she was in the system, it wouldn't be long before someone came calling. There were several governments who would love to get their hands on her. He wouldn't ever have to deal with her again. So he'd made his choice.

But then she'd made hers, too. She would deeply prefer to stay with Ian and that meant following protocol.

She sank to her knees. "Yes, he will try again and likely soon. Zhukov is very impatient. I guess they've decided to cut their losses and take me out."

She let her head sink onto his lap, the way she used to. He could sit for hours just petting her while he worked. It seemed to soothe him. For those hours she could let her thoughts drift because she was safe. She'd been able to daydream, and every thought had been about him.

She sighed and rubbed her cheek against his thigh and almost immediately felt his quick and sure interest.

But his whole body went utterly still, like a rattlesnake had wrapped itself around him, coiled and ready to strike. "Charlie? Would you like to tell me what you're doing?"

Getting her husband back. "You think better with a sub at your feet."

"I've never had a fucking sub at my…" Ian stopped. "You should get up now."

He'd never had a sub at his feet but he'd had a wife there. Just her. Only her. She had to remind him just how good it could be between them. She'd noticed that he'd brought the lemon donuts in with him. He needed her. He was so rigid. He didn't allow himself anything, not even comfort. She'd grown to truly understand this man. Despite the fact that he came off like a big bad take-nothing-from-no-one Dom, he was actually a service-oriented top. It was what no one at the club she'd met him at understood. Ian needed to serve his sub, to meet her needs before his own were met. It was why he hadn't taken the time to explain to Grace how he liked his coffee made. If he did that, if she changed her ways for him, he would owe her. He didn't like to owe anyone.

But he did believe in the power exchange.

"I was very scared, Mast…Ian." She didn't need to

push at this point. She just needed him in the right frame of mind. She let her eyes drift up. His hand was moving, carrying the lemon donut to his mouth. He was enjoying the treat she'd bought for him. He would enjoy this, too, if she just phrased it in the proper way. "Could I just have a few moments? It would relax me. I feel like I'm on the verge of tears, and I know how you hate them."

He groaned a little. "You don't have tear ducts, Charlie."

Not true. She'd cried more over him in the last five years than she'd cried in all the years before. He held the key to her emotions. When she'd met him, it had been years since she allowed herself the release of tears. She couldn't help herself. She rubbed her cheek against his thigh again, reveling in being so close to him.

He didn't touch her. In the past he would have petted her head, his palm stroking her softly as he worked. But there was nothing from him now.

Then again, he didn't toss her out on her ass. It was progress.

A long moment passed where she heard him sigh and tentatively relax into his chair. Even his muscles seemed to uncoil and accept the situation.

"What do you know about Eli Nelson?" There was the sound of his coffee mug scraping against the desk as he sat it down again.

A dangerous question, but one she had to answer.

"I can send you the file I have on him, but it's spotty at best. I can tell you that he's involved with my uncle."

Ian used his sarcastic grunt this time. "Does that really surprise you? You stole money from both of them. The enemy of my enemy is my friend and all that. It only made sense that they would help each other out."

She really hated her uncle. Mikhail Denisovitch had

been her father's right hand man. She had a couple of cousins who had been okay, but they were still syndicate men. She had no doubt they would kill her on sight if they had to. It wouldn't matter that they'd hung out together and laughed. Denisovitch men were loyal to the syndicate first and blood later.

"I know he's met with my uncle a few times. I'm sure he claims he found the information that I was the one who hired the assassin. He didn't do it himself, of course. I have no doubt everything looks perfect. The man knows how to set a woman up."

The tension was back in his legs. Damn. She shouldn't have mentioned that. His voice was a low rumble. "Yes, he certainly does."

She needed to get him thinking about the present. "He knows what he's doing and how to stay off the radar. Most of what I've learned is because his contacts fucked up. It's almost never him. In the beginning I got a ton of info, and when I would follow it through, he was waiting there to try to take me out."

"How do you know the Indian lead isn't the same thing?"

She'd wondered about it. "I don't, but it doesn't follow his pattern. No one can really cover every bit of his trail these days. There are too many CCTV cameras. I think that's why he left England."

"He was done in England. He was through fucking with my team. He did exactly what you said, baby. He set us up to do his dirty work so he could walk out with the prize—an already set up network of arms dealing. I managed to shut that shit down, but it took some maneuvering."

Ah, the joys of habit. He'd always called her baby. His fingers drummed along the table, a sure sign that he didn't know what to do with them. She could tell him where to put his hands, but she thought he wouldn't take suggestions kindly at this point.

"So he's looking for a new racket. I'll have Chelsea look into this Kashmir guy."

"No, I'll have Adam do it. You and Chelsea should be on a plane going somewhere that is absolutely one hundred percent not here."

She needed him to understand that leaving wasn't an option. "I am not leaving again, Ian. I'm making my stand here. I've spent five years on the run, and I'm tired. I want a life. I want it so bad, I'm willing to risk the one I have now. I want to be your wife and have some babies and be your sub. If you throw me out, I'll sleep on the street outside your house because you need me. You need me and no one else."

He pushed his chair back, seeming not to care that he jostled her. "You should go and sit with Eve. No. Phoebe. Eve would talk to you. Phoebe's scared of her own shadow."

She settled back on her heels, looking up at him. "I would rather be with you."

His jaw formed a stubborn line. "You can sit with Phoebe or leave my building. It's one or the other. I'm willing to give you some shelter because I'm not sure if you're playing me or not, yet. I can't let you go if you have information I need, but I'm not going to play the devoted lover again, so get out of my office."

Damn it, she'd pushed him. She'd always been so impatient about the things she really wanted. It was her Achilles' heel. She got to her feet with no help from him. "All right. I'll go and sit where you want me to. May I have a computer?"

Those arctic blue eyes narrowed. "So you can blow up

the world?"

He was a deep believer in hyperbole. She ignored him. "So I can make some notes about what I know."

"Just send me the file you have. I'll make my own notes."

He could be so stubborn when he wanted to be, and he almost always wanted to be. "Damn it, Ian. I can't just sit there for six hours or so until we go home."

"I'm not taking you home, Charlie. Because of Alex, we have to go to Sanctum tonight. If you don't effectively play the role of my sub, our cover with the DPD could be blown. So maybe you should sit around and think about obeying me. Go." He pointed to the door. "Don't you dare cause any trouble. I swear if I hear you even talking to someone, I'll tie you up and gag you, and not in a fun way."

He would do it. But she'd just been given the keys to the kingdom. She was going to have to make sure she sent Alex McKay a little thank you note. "Yes, Master."

"I am not your Master."

"If it walks like a Dom and delivers orders like a Dom, it's usually a Dom. If he's brutally sarcastic, he's my Dom."

Ian caught her arm, whirling her around. "I mean it, Charlie. I am never going there with you again. That part of my life is done. I might fuck you again because Alex has put us into a horrible position and we always seem to end up in bed, but it's only going to be sex. I won't allow you in again. Do you understand? I'm trying to warn you. If you let me, I'll tear you up and I'll enjoy it. I'll take everything I can and give you nothing in return except pain and regret."

But he'd already saved her life. "I understand. I'm willing to risk it."

He loomed over her. His presence sent her every nerve into overdrive. He closed in on her, forcing her back against the wall. She was suddenly so aware of her body—the way her nipples peaked, her breath picked up, her pussy ached.

"That's not very smart, Charlie." He stared down at her. If she didn't know him the way she did, she would have sworn he wasn't affected at all. His face was emotionless, his body all intimidation. But she heard the way his voice had deepened and she expected that if she just reached out a hand, she would find his cock hard and wanting.

She hesitated because touching him when he was in this state without permission would be a bad idea. Her Master needed his control back. She was going to give it to him. "I think it's the only smart thing I've ever done."

He leaned in, pressing his body against hers. Yes, he was definitely not unaffected. "Then I won't try to help you again. I'll take what you give me and I won't apologize, but this is going to go my way from now on. You're going to obey me or this whole process is done."

She nodded, not taking her eyes off him even as he pressed his cock against her belly. She couldn't help but soften against him, but she kept her hands to her sides. He wasn't ready for her affection. "All right, Ian."

"Go to the accounting office. I expect you to be sitting there in her office at five o'clock. At noon, you may get up and have lunch with Phoebe in the break room. She's the only one who doesn't eat out or in her office. You may not talk to her. I'll have someone go downstairs and get you a sandwich and a drink. You will have forty-five minutes at which time you will return to your seat. If you need a bathroom break, ask Eve or Grace to escort you."

Oh, he was going to try her limits, it seemed. She

knew she should agree, but the bratty words just flowed from her mouth. "I think I can find my way to the bathroom, Ian."

"That's ten."

She had to take a deep breath. Oh, fuck, he was going there. "I thought you weren't my Master."

His hands were on her shoulders, lightly tracing the lines of her body. His voice had softened as though he was thinking of something else, something sweeter. "I'm your Dom for now because it's the only way I can trust you to do what I tell you. You're dangerous and someone has to keep you in line. I'm viewing myself as a rattlesnake handler. We're in high protocol, Charlie. You will speak when spoken to. You will obey my every directive or you will take your punishment. If you do not follow my rules, I'll contact the Agency and let them handle you."

He wanted her in a corner with no way out. He didn't seem to understand she didn't want out. He needed to be in charge. She was willing to spend a boring day so that he got what he needed. "Yes, Master…I mean, Sir."

Master meant they had a special relationship. She'd fucked that up. A Sir could be any Dom. It was a politeness. Despite the fact that he was definitely acting like her Master, he needed to be Sir for now. She could play that way.

"I mean it, Charlie. This is all you're going to get out of me." He pressed his cock against her, bringing his forehead to hers. "I'm not the man you knew. I'm a bastard, and I won't feel a moment's regret fucking you and leaving you to your fate when I'm done. When I have what I need out of you, I'll walk away and I won't look back. I buried you a long time ago. There's nothing left but a little bit of lust and a whole lot of business between us."

But the lust was so building. She could practically feel it rolling off him. "If we're laying all our cards on the table, I should tell you that I intend to find my way into your bed and I intend to stay there. I don't care how long it takes. You loved me once. I'll make you love me again."

"I never loved you, Charlie." He breathed the words against her skin. His hands moved from her shoulders to her chest, his eyes trailing down. He let his palms rest over her mounds and sighed a little.

God, if he didn't love her, she would take the connection she felt with him anyway. "Again, a risk I'm willing to take. You want me."

He took a long step back, but his eyes remained on her chest. "Yes, but it's not the same. It's sexual chemistry. I'm willing to admit that I have it with you. I have more sexual chemistry with you than most other women. But lust is all there is between us. Show me your breasts."

Lust felt so good. She ignored his line about most other women because it was just sheer stubborn stupidity. In the last several years she'd learned to shove the bad crap aside and revel in the rare sweet times. She didn't hesitate, didn't tease and taunt him. She simply pulled the shirt over her head and tossed it aside before going to work on her bra.

Cool air hit her skin. Her nipples were still puckered from the feel of his hands on her body. She let the bra slip out of her fingers before assuming the position she was sure he wanted. Hands clasped behind her back, chest thrust out.

Ian stared. Charlie waited. He liked to spend long, agonizing moments just looking at her.

Your body belongs to me. Your breasts, your pussy, your ass are all my property. He'd said the words to her so long ago, but she could still hear his dark voice claiming her.

What do I get in return? She'd asked, her voice breathless.

I'm yours. Only yours, Charlie. Everything I am. Everything I have. Everything I will be. All yours. Past. Present. Future. I'll give them to you.

She'd screwed up the past. Needed the present. Longed for a future. So she stood there, offering him everything she had.

He reached out and placed a hand on her breast, lightly at first, his fingers skimming her skin. His eyes were down, watching the place where they connected. He traced the round disc surrounding her nipple, watching it tighten and peak for him. He brushed the nipple, making her want to beg him to tug it into his mouth. Her body was softening in all the right places. She could feel her pussy getting wet and ready. All he had to do was touch her and she was ready to spread her legs and welcome him home.

Instead, she stood perfectly still. He didn't seem to be taunting her. There was a bland look on his face, but his fingertips were tender as they explored her, running along the blue veins that crossed her chest. He skimmed the puckered scar where the bullet had gone into her shoulder, just under her clavicle bone. He spent time there, circling it with his thumb, staring as though memorizing the place.

His fingers moved again, this time to her throat. She remembered when she'd worn his collar. It had been leather at first, but he'd bought a Cartier gold collar that circled her neck, reminding her always that she was his.

"Where did it go?" Ian asked as though reading her mind.

Tears sparked against her eyes. "I don't know. It was gone when I woke up. They had taken my ring off, too."

She'd lost her collar and the platinum and diamond ring he'd bought for her. She'd felt naked for so long without them. It had taken her almost a year to stop reaching for the collar. She'd worn it for so short a period of time, but it had become a habit to touch it when she was nervous.

"It's somewhere in Scotland Yard's evidence room then. Or someone stole it." He touched the place where his collar had sat.

"I'm so sorry, Ian."

He seemed to come back to himself. "It's all right. It was only money. I made more."

She closed her eyes, blinking back tears because he was willfully misunderstanding her and there was not a damn thing she could do now to fix it. She'd known he would punish her. She hadn't known how much his distance would hurt. "All right, Ian. I'll get dressed and go sit with Phoebe."

At least it would likely be quiet in the accounting office. That Phoebe chick didn't seem like a big talker. She could think about the situation, find a way to get to him.

"You owe me ten, sub."

She thought he would forget about that. God, she was standing here with him and she was half naked and he wanted to smack her ass. Suddenly she wasn't sure she could handle it. "Ian, you don't have to discipline me. I understand. The situation is serious. I'll sit with Phoebe and I won't cause trouble."

"Twenty."

He was such a damn hardass. "Fine. Where do you want me?"

"Over my lap. You're overdressed for discipline. Take it all off and place yourself over my lap. When I'm done, you can get dressed and think about not defying me again. You'll have a whole afternoon to contemplate your new reality. If you don't like it, there's the door, sweetheart. Don't expect me to step in front of another bullet for you."

She let her fingers find the waistband of her skirt.

"Are you really not wearing underwear?" Ian asked, sitting back down in his chair. Somehow he made the functional piece of furniture seem like a throne.

She kicked off the flats she was wearing as she tugged the skirt off. "I told you. I'm not allowed to wear underwear."

"Not while you're serving me, you're not. But when we're done, you can do anything you like, Charlie. If you want to cover that pussy with plastic wrap, I won't give a shit. But while we're playing Master and sub, you'll follow my rules. Come closer. Show me your pussy. I need to make sure you meet my standards. Brighton won't believe our cover for a second if you're not groomed properly."

If she wasn't, what would he do? Very likely shave her himself. He would tell her the whole time that he didn't want to do it. He had to because it was part of their cover and he wouldn't love her but, oops, his penis slipped inside and that didn't mean anything either.

"I got lasered." She stepped in front of him.

"Spread your legs."

God, he was going to kill her. She moved her legs apart, giving him the access he wanted. His hand slipped between her legs, running across the petals of her sex, lighting her pussy up. "I'm smooth everywhere, Ian. Believe me, she was very thorough. I screamed for two days while she ran the damn thing up my labia."

His free hand smacked her ass, a sharp beat against

her flesh. "No cursing."

No cursing. No pubic hair. Nothing new there. "I'm just saying I'm perfectly smooth down there."

"I'll be the judge of that. When did you decide to get this procedure done? Did you check into the company?"

She gasped as his fingers slid into her labia, parting her and testing the skin there. God, there was no way to hide the fact that she was wet and ripe. "I got lasered about six months ago because I was tired of shaving and there were weeks when I couldn't take a bath because I was on the run. I found the shop I used on the Internet."

He moaned a little and brought his hand back out. "Not smart. You should have had them vetted and visited the facilities and gotten recommendations."

Yeah. She wasn't going to tell him she'd used a coupon. Or that the place had doubled as a nail salon. Or that the person who lasered her might or might not have been a dude. She couldn't be sure. He'd had the prettiest blonde hair that didn't match his five-o'clock shadow. "I will next time."

"Over my lap. We're on the stoplight system."

Which meant red was her safe word. Every cell in her body was suddenly awake and alive, but her brain was a little apprehensive now. Ian could be a ruthless, nasty bastard. He really could use her and toss her out like garbage. He could split her open and make her ache.

She would be safer running. She knew how to hide, knew how to disappear.

None of it meant anything without him. If he tore her up, then at least she'd have another few moments with him. Maybe hurting her would give him a sense of peace because what he didn't know, what she hadn't told him, still haunted her to this day.

She hadn't been entirely out when he'd found her

body. She'd heard his low shout, felt him lift her into his arms.

She'd felt it when his body had been wracked with sobs and she'd heard him plead to God to bring her back.

She had put him through that.

Charlie placed herself over his lap, vowing to stop being a coward. This was what she owed Ian—a chance. He would have a chance for closure with her, a shot at finding some peace. They would have a chance at being together again.

If her heart broke, then that was just what she deserved.

She filled her lungs slowly as his hand moved over the curves of her ass. Like everything Ian did, he took his own sweet time, saying absolutely nothing. Anticipation hung in the air like a mist she couldn't quite see through. She knew exactly what he was going to do and yet she lay there, her heart pounding, waiting for him.

Smack. Charlie heard the sound crack through the air before she felt the sting against her skin. Fire lashed through her. She bit back a curse because Ian wasn't warming her up. He'd gotten right to the hard stuff.

Smack. Smack. Smack. Pain flared. Tears welled. She didn't even think about stopping them. It felt too good. She'd been strong for so long. This was a release, pure and simple. She let loose, crying out as he continued his discipline.

Over and over he rained down on her willing flesh. He wanted to say she didn't have tear ducts? Yeah. She could show him. He hadn't told her she needed to be quiet, so she cried out.

He didn't say a word though she knew he would keep a perfect count. She would get every smack he'd promised her. She also knew that he would stop if she screamed out red. The word didn't even play through her head. This was what she'd longed for. Ian had taught her she needed this, taught her to not be ashamed that she was different and required a little kink to find her peace. There had been no peace before him, and no peace after him, just a deep disconnect from the world she'd grown to love.

She lost count, didn't care to know. He could go on forever and they could stay in this place. She would take the pain to feel the connection to him. While he was disciplining her, they were the only two people in the whole world. Everything else could fall away and she could be herself, the Charlie she'd discovered when she fell in love with him. The Charlie who would sacrifice herself for others, who reached out and made friends. The Charlie who was brave enough to deserve those friends.

The room went quiet. Only the sounds of her gasps and tears could be heard. Ian's hand stilled against her flesh, and she wondered for a moment if he would deny her what he would give any other sub he'd just disciplined. That might hurt most of all. She could take anything he dished out as long as she got the aftercare that completed the cycle even if it was nothing more than a few words of praise, a moment or two when she felt like she'd pleased him.

Slowly, his hand soothed against her skin, rubbing in gentle circles where he'd been so rough before. "You did well, Charlotte. But then you always did. How do you feel?"

Released. Peaceful. Just the slightest bit empty because she wouldn't be in his arms. "I'm green, Sir."

"Get up then."

She sniffled a little. Maybe it would be good to have the afternoon to think about what she was doing. She pushed herself off his lap and stood on shaky feet, turning toward where she'd left her clothes.

He frowned her way, reaching for her hand. "Where are you going? I didn't tell you to leave." He tugged her into his lap, his arms encircling her. "Have you forgotten the drill?"

She was on the verge of tears again because his cheek nestled against her forehead, the intimacy so sweet she could hardly stand it. He cuddled her close, sighing as her arms went around him.

"I do this for all the subs I discipline, Charlie."

Of course he did. He was known as the tenderest of Doms. His reputation for cuddling was world renowned. She loved him, but he was a dumbass if he thought she was buying that. She'd made a study of him before she'd met him and kept up with him since she'd died. Ian Taggart was known as a bastard who preferred to contract his sexual experiences so the women he screwed would never think that he would stay with them. Yes, she was certain he snuggled with all of them and smelled their hair, breathing them in like they were the air he needed to live. "Yes, Sir. I won't mistake it for anything but aftercare."

"See that you don't." He rocked the chair back and forth, his hand smoothing her hair back as she held on.

No matter what happened, she wouldn't let go.

Chapter Five

The overhead light shone down on the conference room table and the evidence Simon and Jesse had spent the afternoon collecting.

"Does the DPD know yet?" Ian ran a frustrated hand through his hair as he stared at the pictures Simon had taken. They showed a man, likely a businessman given the fact that he was wearing a suit, lying on the floor of his expensive hotel room. He had a startled expression on his face, but then he also had a bullet hole through his forehead so Ian could forgive the man for being startled. It was a neat, clean execution, the kind the mob specialized in. It looked like their hit man had found the perfect perch from which to shoot someone coming out of the building that housed McKay-Taggart, and he didn't really care that it was already occupied.

"No. No one's found the bloke yet." Simon was relaxed in his chair like finding dead bodies was an everyday occurrence for him. He sipped his Earl Grey. It was four o'clock. Nothing interrupted afternoon tea for the Brit. Ian was pretty sure Simon would stop in the middle of a shootout for high freaking tea. "The shooter had put the *Do Not Disturb* sign on the door. Staff won't find the body until he's supposed to check out, I would think."

And then they might start to put two and two together. Maybe. If they were smart. He needed to make things look good with Brighton or the cops would get involved and everything would go to hell.

Jesse took off the ball cap he was wearing. At least he'd had the good sense to wear a ball cap and a fairly shapeless sweat suit. The kid looked too casual for the office, but no one would remember his hair color or body type. If he slumped properly, it would take inches off his six-foot-three-inch frame. "The hotel is quiet, minimal security. Room 721 is definitely the place where the shooter was planted. We found the sniper hole. The windows don't open so he used a glass cutter to make a one-inch round hole, just enough to get the barrel through, not enough to hit the ground below and cause a ruckus. He knew he might be there for a while."

"How obvious was it?" Again, he was thinking about the cops. It might be much easier to draw a line from point A to point B if they found holes where none should be.

"I barely found it. He put it in the bottom corner of the glass. I cracked it a little so it didn't look so neat and stuffed a tissue in it. It's what I would do if I accidently broke a window," Jesse said.

It might work. It might not. "I don't suppose the fucker left casings behind?"

"No," Simon replied. "He was very neat, very clean. I managed to bribe one of the security guards. I convinced him I was a PI looking for a cheating spouse. He brought up the security cameras from the hallway at approximately the time we were looking at. A man roughly six foot or so wearing a ball cap got on the elevator carrying a briefcase at the right time. I didn't get his face, though. He was careful to keep his head down."

Ian huffed a long breath out. What a shitty day. "Well, it's good to know Denisovitch trains his people well. We can bet he'll try again. We need to come up with new protocols concerning Charlotte."

What was he supposed to do with her? If she wouldn't leave and hide, he had no idea how he was supposed to just let her run around the streets of Dallas alone. He had no doubt she could take care of herself. The question was how much chaos would she cause while she did it?

He had to keep an eye on her and that meant she would have to stay with him. *Fuck.*

He glanced over and watched her through the open blinds. She was sitting in her chair in Phoebe's office, both women quiet. Phoebe's head was down, her eyes on the computer screen while Charlie's were squarely on her hands. She stared down at her lap, and Ian wondered what she was thinking.

Plotting most likely. She always looked so pretty when she plotted.

He had to take her into the dungeon tonight. If they didn't get horrifically murdered first. Charlie would be kneeling at his feet in Sanctum, putting on a show for Derek Brighton.

Was she putting on a show for him, too?

Alex stepped into the room, holding out Ian's car keys. "I moved your car into the parking garage. I thought it would be better to take Charlie out that way than to walk into the open."

That woman was going to give him a migraine. "Thanks. I'll make sure I put her in the trunk when I leave for Sanctum."

"She'll love that. No, we're leaving your car here. We'll take mine. I doubt they're looking for mine." Alex sat down beside him, his eyes going over the photos. "Nice. So our assassin doesn't mind taking out a few civilians. What is Charlie going to want to do about her sister?"

He hadn't even thought about Chelsea, the sister Charlie had betrayed him to save. He didn't want to admit it, but he was interested in meeting Chelsea Dennis. "Send someone out to her place. Bring her to Sanctum tonight. We'll regroup there. Simon, why don't you and Jesse go and nab the girl?"

Simon's eyebrow arched. "What if the girl doesn't want to be nabbed?"

Alex shot Jesse a nasty look. "Well, I happen to know your little partner there is quite good with duct tape."

"I said I was sorry about kidnapping Eve." Jesse turned a bright red. "I'll go get the address from Charlie. Wait. I shot her. Maybe you should do it, Simon."

"You really are going to have to stop assaulting people who end up being your team members." Simon stood and Jesse followed him. "Can the girl write out the address? I understand she's on lockdown."

She was going to stay that way. The longer Charlie didn't actually talk to members of his team, the better. "Adam has it along with a phone number. He's already talked to the apparently very abrupt Miss Dennis. They're coming up with a plan to try to flush this guy out. I don't want you bugging Charlie. Charlie is thinking about all the things she's done wrong today. I'll see you at the club in two hours. Make sure this Chelsea girl has the proper clothes if she's going on the dungeon floor. If she's not, she can sit in the locker room until I'm ready to question her."

"I'm sure she'll be thrilled with the invitation," Simon muttered.

Probably not. According to Adam, she was spitting mad. Ian was really just cutting her off at the pass. If he didn't bring her in, she would show up on his doorstep and likely get a bullet to the head, and then he would have to deal with a dead girl and he couldn't explain that away to Brighton. He needed to know where the Dennis sisters were at all times. If Chelsea was anything like her sister, she could start an apocalypse without really thinking about it.

Ian pressed the *com* button on the phone. "Adam, could you join us?"

There was a slight pause, and he could have sworn he heard the fucker giggle and Serena telling him to stop. Poor Serena. She was going to have two kids soon. "Yes, of course, boss. I'll be right down."

"So Charlotte's on lockdown?" Alex asked, his eyes sliding Ian's way. There was a slight grin on his face.

"What's lockdown?" Jesse asked.

"She's not allowed to speak without permission," Simon explained.

"We can do that?"

"If only it worked that way." Simon stared out the window.

What was that grin of Alex's about? He tried not to think about it. "Yes. I thought it best to put her in high protocol. That way I don't have to listen to her. It's the one good thing about having to take her into Sanctum tonight."

"The only thing?" Again there was that smirk on Alex's face that made Ian feel like the butt of a joke.

Ian turned to his best friend. "Do you have something you want to say?"

"Nope. Just that you might want to call off the surveillance on your office. Do the subs at Sanctum know about your newfound 'cuddle every one of them' rule?" A long laugh came out of Alex's mouth.

Motherfucker. He'd practically made a porn film. And he knew exactly who would keep a copy. "Adam!"

Adam walked in with Jake, and they gave each other a look. It was the same look naughty five-year-olds slid each other's way when they'd done something stupid and couldn't help but laugh about it.

Fuck. He'd forgotten about the 540. Goddamn it. It was the kind of thing he never forgot. He'd even watched her for a while from Adam's computer, but the minute he'd gotten into the same room with her, he'd forgotten everything except the fact that he was her temporary Master. "You will turn those cameras off now."

Jake stepped in front of Adam as though he could protect his ass if Ian decided to cave his skull in. "Now, Ian, you told us to keep watch on her. Unfortunately we got to watch a whole lot more of her than we expected."

"My private life is not Adam's porno."

"Hey, Ian, don't blame him," Jake said. "He was actually working on something else. I was keeping watch. I called him over. Alex, too." Jake actually flushed a little. "And Serena might have been in the office."

Oh, this was all her fault. Charlie had turned his entire life upside down and he'd gone from being the respected head of the team to porn star. Thank god he hadn't fucked her. Because he'd really wanted to. He'd wanted to clear off his desk and spread her legs and force his cock deep. He'd wanted to make her moan and scream.

"Serena cried. She said it was really beautiful," Adam explained.

"Did she take notes?" He was not going to end up in one of Serena's pussy-ass Dom romances where the sub manipulates the hell out of the Dom.

"I believe she was too busy taking mental pictures," Jake said. "She wants Charlotte to know that she really admires her breasts. Serena actually has a deep appreciation for the human form, whether it's male or female."

Jesse frowned. "Wait, are you guys saying Charlotte got like twelve kinds of nekkid and I missed it?"

Three different hands came out, slapping him upside the head.

"Damn it." Jesse shook his head. "I don't see what the big deal is. You guys see each other nekkid all the time."

"I'm putting you in elocution lessons," Simon said, seemingly unfazed by everything except his charge's redneck speak. "Why did I get left with the backwoods version of *My Fair Lady*? It's because I'm British, isn't it?"

It was time to move past his porno. "Adam, give Simon everything you have on Chelsea Dennis. Now tell me what the plan is."

"I've left a trail for the Russian to follow. I couldn't make it too obvious or he might get suspicious," Adam explained. "I used Charlotte's credit card to book a room in a motel in Waco. I hired Karina to drive down in Charlotte's car in a blonde wig. She leaves in an hour. She's going to be passing several traffic cameras, and I told her to blow through at least one red light."

Karina Mills was a Fort Worth-based PI they worked with from time to time. She was also a submissive at Sanctum. She was tough and thorough and tended to charge out the ass. Another thing to lay at Charlie's doorstep. "So she's checking in as Charlie and waiting for Zhukov?"

"Nah, I thought you would prefer one of us to actually do the takedown. Li is with her. Jake and I are on Avery duty. Li and Karina are going to settle in at the motel. We went over procedure. They're going to keep the shades closed so he can't take them out from a distance. I checked out the surroundings. There aren't a lot of sniper positions. It's a busy motel. He's going to have to get up close and personal if he doesn't want a bunch of heat on him."

Meaning the assassin would be forced to break into the room. He would very likely try to make it look like an everyday, normal break in. He would steal some cash, maybe rape the girl. He would discover very rapidly that Liam O'Donnell didn't appreciate his person being violated.

"Liam knows I want this guy alive, right?" He wanted to know exactly who had hired him and how far Nelson's ties to the Denisovitch syndicate went.

"Alive, but fucked up, right? Because Liam apparently really wants to fuck this dude up. He claims he's gone too long without a good fight," Adam explained.

As long as the fucker was capable of talking, Ian didn't care. "Tell Li to take out his frustrations on the guy, but I want him able to answer a few questions. It's a good plan. You're still hired. Go and set it in motion and then go and erase that fucking tape."

"You know there's not really a tape per se." Adam seemed to get the gist of the nasty look Ian sent him. "I'll take care of it. Why don't you guys come with me?"

The four men walked out, all of them smiling behind their hands.

"Hey, Jesse's right, you know," Alex said quietly. "There wasn't anything on that feed that you haven't done at Sanctum a hundred times."

Oh, but there was. He didn't cuddle the subs afterward no matter what he told Charlie. Every encounter was negotiated, and the most aftercare he would give was praise for a job well done, some ointment on abrasions if he left them, and the occasional massage. Sometimes he would offer orgasms if he wanted the sub sexually.

But he didn't cuddle with them afterward and he didn't sleep beside them. He would never admit it. Not ever. He wouldn't admit that he could fool himself during sex. He could close his eyes and pretend the sub under him was Charlie, but the minute he held them, the illusion was gone and he was hollow and empty again.

They didn't smell like her, like lemons and sugar. They weren't as soft as his wife. Their skin didn't seem to sink into his. When his partners talked, they didn't have her sweet sarcasm.

They hadn't lied to him. They hadn't betrayed him.

Fuck.

"I need you and Eve to come out to the house and stay with us. If this plan works, Li will bring the asshole out to my place for the interrogation." That might solve one of his problems. Maybe if he knew Alex and Eve were there he would keep his hands off the girl.

Maybe.

Alex studied him for a moment. "All right. That should work out just fine. We're having the house we bought renovated. It was supposed to be ready when we got back from Hawaii. We were going to stay in a hotel, but your place might be so much more fun. Might I ask why? You could handle an interrogation yourself."

Well, he sure as fuck wasn't going to tell Alex he needed help keeping his hands off Charlie. Alex seemed to be morphing into Oprah, and Ian was certain all sorts of mushy advice would follow. "I want Eve to work up a full evaluation on Charlotte and her sister. She can do it better if she's watching them outside an interview."

"Are you sure you want to treat her like a suspect?

This might be the time to try to get to know her again."

Yep. Oprah was in the house.

"The only way I want to get to know that woman again is whether or not she's telling me the truth."

"That's not what it looked like on that tape, man."

"I am attracted to her," he allowed.

"You're attracted to a lot of women. You don't cuddle them and rub your cheek against their hair. You don't look peaceful when you're close to them."

He sent his best friend a hard stare. "Have you been reading Serena's books? What the fuck is wrong with you?"

Alex held his hands up in surrender. "Sorry. You're not ready to talk about this. Eve told me to take it slow, and I'm pushing you."

He had to get a few things clear. "I'm attracted to Charlotte, but I'm not going to let her play me the way she did last time. Maybe she's here for all the right reasons, but she's too late. I won't let her in again. I might fuck her because it's almost inevitable, but as soon as this plays out, I will dump her ass and I won't look back. You guys seem to be waiting for me to have some grand revelation. Well, let me tell you something, Alex. I already had it. I had it when I realized she was willing to use me, to let my team suffer the consequences so she could solve her own problems."

"She was trying to save her sister."

"I would have saved her sister," Ian nearly roared back, the betrayal so close to his surface. He forced his rage down. God, he didn't want to do this, but no one seemed willing to let him be. "She was my sub and she trusted that fucker Nelson over me. We're done."

"I hadn't thought about it like that, Ian," Alex said, his eyes grave.

Ian turned and saw Charlie looking right at him. He was pretty sure she wouldn't have been able to hear what he'd said, but she obviously hadn't missed the way he'd said it. Her face went soft as though she could offer him sympathy and peace from another room.

He felt himself go cold. Yes, that was better. Cold was infinitely better than the hot anger that threatened to overtake him. "Well, it's the only way I can think about it."

"I broke trust with Eve and we still made it."

Ian rolled his eyes, turning away from his onetime wife and back to his best friend. "No, you were stupid. You didn't listen to her and you both got hurt. Then you were stubborn for a really long time. It's different. I knew fairly soon into the relationship that Charlotte wasn't what she seemed to be, but I loved her. I knew she was in some sort of trouble, but I didn't want to push her. I loved that woman more than anything I've loved in my life. More than Sean. More than my mother. I thought we had a bond. I married her because I thought she would turn to me. I gave her every chance to trust me. Instead, she let Nelson nearly kill her. She took a drug that probably had a fifty-fifty chance of ending her instead of turning to me. No. I will not trust her again. No. I will not let her back in. I know you think I'm missing a piece of myself. You think I'm a bastard and that somehow a woman is magically going to fix me, but you're wrong. She was my shot and it didn't work. We don't all get to find our Eves. I understand if you would rather hang with the married guys. Women tend to get nervous around me."

He hated the idea of losing Alex. Really hated it, but he didn't let it show.

Alex sighed, standing up and putting a hand on his shoulder. "I'm backing off now. Not from you. You're my best friend and you have been for damn near my whole life. You can't lose me. And Eve loves you. Grace loves you. I don't know where these nervous women are because Serena really was taking notes and probably will put you in a book soon. You can rail at her and she'll just smile at you. The only woman around here who's scared of you is Phoebe, but then she screamed about a spider the size of a dime the other day. So I'm not too worried about her. I'll go talk to Eve and tell her we're sticking close to you for a couple of days to watch your back."

He relaxed a little. "I don't think you really need to watch over me. They're after Charlie."

"I don't doubt they would love to take you out, too."

"Whatever happens, you know that I don't want Eve putting herself in danger. Maybe I should rethink this." He was going in circles. He wasn't thinking of anyone but himself. How could he really put his team in danger?

"Hey, we're coming with you and that's final. Eve can handle herself. She's perfectly capable, and she knows when to duck," Alex said with a smile. "They'll be looking for your car. We'll take mine to Sanctum and then go out to your place. I can get our bags from the hotel this afternoon and be back in time to get us out to the club. Is the backyard entrance to your place passable?"

There was a reason Ian had picked that particular location for his home. He owned several acres of the land around it and had long ago put in an alternative entrance to his place. It involved some country back road driving, but he could get inside undetected when he wanted to. "It should be fine."

He would like the backup. The thought of being alone and responsible for keeping Charlie alive scared the shit out of him.

Alex winced a little. "I want you to know I'm sorry

about putting you in a bad situation with Brighton. I'll try to smooth that over, too."

He held back a sigh but realized how much he would miss Alex and Eve if they weren't in his life anymore. He was just starting to find a relationship with his brother again. Charlie was threatening to fuck all of that up. She was coming between him and the people he loved. She was forcing them to choose sides in this little war of theirs.

Maybe it was time to let her see just how hopeless this operation of hers was.

Alex walked out the door and Ian's mind started working. He strode by the office she was sitting in, her eyes following him, but he paid her no mind.

He had an evening to plan. He got to his desk and picked up his phone, dialing a familiar number. "Ryan? I'm going to need you to do a couple of things before tonight's play."

Fifteen minutes later, he had most everything in place. At least this part of his world was running efficiently.

So why was his gut in a knot again?

Chapter Six

Charlie sat down on the bench in front of the locker she'd been assigned. The locker room at Sanctum was far more plush and luxurious than any club she'd been in before. Certainly nicer than Cuffs, the rattrap she'd been stuck in for months while she was working on the op that finally brought her to Dallas. That place had barely had lockers, much less carefully crafted full-length wooden ones with hangers for clothes and drawers for anything else a sub would need.

The bathroom section of the room held several tiled showers, vanities with various expensive-looking soaps and lotions, curling irons and hair dryers.

The subs at Sanctum were treated like queens.

"The men's locker room has a row of recliners and a big screen TV. It's one big mancave. I've caught Alex and Ian hiding in there from time to time with a case of beer. They think because it's a men's locker room that I won't go in. They're wrong." Eve had the locker next to her. She adjusted the corset she was in. "That was a very nice spanking. Do you need me to lace you in?"

Ian had handed her a small stack of fet wear before

sending her into the locker room with Eve. She'd soon found herself in a cozy world where Serena sat in a comfy chair, her feet up and a computer on her lap, while Avery O'Donnell sat in an equally comfy chair beside her knitting away on what looked like a very tiny sweater.

It was weird.

"Don't mind the pregnant twins," Eve said with a smile.

"It's just not what I thought Sanctum would look like and I've been to a couple of clubs."

Serena perked up. "Did Ian take you?"

Avery looked up from her knitting. "Oh, was it in Europe? I so want to go back, but when I mention it to Liam he gets a little green and says our next vacation is going to be in an RV because nothing bad ever happens in RVs. Has he not watched horror movies?"

Eve grinned. "I think he's never seen an actual RV, honey. So, fess up, Charlotte. What clubs did Ian take you to?"

Should she answer that? Ian hadn't exactly told her she couldn't talk in the locker room. But then he'd sent her a nasty glare every time she even looked like she wanted to talk in the car.

"This is a Dom-free zone," Serena said. "Unlike Eve, they really are terrified of coming in here. When I'm late, Jake stands outside and yells in."

Avery nodded. "What happens in the locker room, stays in the locker room. This is where we plan most of our bratty behavior."

Eve leaned against her locker. "They're right, you know. We subs have to stick together. It's just the three of us since Grace started staying home with Carys. We've started getting friendly with Jillian. She runs the bar here and is married to Ryan, the Dom in Residence. She has a sister who's come in a couple of times, but she mostly just stands in the back and looks scared."

"She's not scared. She's curious," Serena said. "So have you been to The Garden?"

She shook her head. She knew about The Garden with its night-blooming flowers and its big bad Dom owner, MI6 agent Damon Knight. Knight had worked with Ian on a few cases, and he would probably very much like to haul her to London for questioning. "No. We didn't go to any clubs in London. Ian was working. We went to a club in Paris, though. The Velvet Collar. It's where I met Ian."

Serena sighed. "See, you just get the sweetest look on your face whenever you mention his name."

"It actually surprises me. He's a little intimidating," Avery admitted.

"He can be. But he can also be very sweet when we're alone. Well, he used to be. Now, he's mostly just an asshole, but he has his reasons." She looked down at the corset and micro mini. He hadn't left her shoes or undies, though she hadn't really expected those. She was going to have to make a decision. Who was she kidding? "Can you help me into this? It's been a while since I was in fet wear. I didn't have to wear it at Cuffs." She looked over at the pregnant contingent. "I didn't have a Dom there."

Serena tapped her keyboard. Multitasking seemed to be her default state. "I know. It's where you were working to find the man who nearly killed Eve. I have it mostly written here, though names have been changed to protect the innocent."

"He's going to murder you," Avery said in a singsong voice, as though she'd said it so many times it now had to be sung.

"He won't read it. Ian doesn't read anything but the newspaper and reports." Serena waved her off. "And it's not really about you and Ian. It's just about a woman who's been on the run for years and her spy husband thinks she's dead but whoops, she's not and she comes back for her man. Very little to do with you. What did they call the drug that made it look like you were dead?"

Yep, Ian was going to kill Serena, but Charlie kind of hoped she got to read that book. She definitely hoped it had a happy ending. She pulled her shirt over her head and tried not to think about how her boobs sagged a little. She wasn't usually nervous. Ian had seen them earlier and he seemed to like them. Or at least his dick had liked them. She stood up a little straighter. She wasn't a thin thing, but she was nicely curved and no one could accuse her of being fragile.

Eve was studying her carefully. "What just went on in your head?"

Honesty was the best policy, most of the time. "I was feeling self-conscious about being naked. I decided not to be."

A little smile curled up Eve's lips. "Good for you."

"Could you teach me to do that?" Serena asked. "Because I'm always self-conscious."

She didn't tell Serena that she'd learned it in the harshest of ways. She'd learned to choose because if she hadn't, she would have broken. *Never forget. You are my daughter. You are Charlotte, and no one gets to take that from you.* The last words her mother had told her.

Her father had tried. He'd beaten her. He'd denied food for a while. He could force her compliance, make her do things she normally wouldn't do, but she hadn't let him change that core piece of herself that remained Charlotte.

Only one man could do that. The one she'd chosen.

"Are you really always self-conscious? Because I've learned that most women aren't really. Serena, do you like

139

what you see in the mirror? Are you comfortable with your body when you're alone?"

She thought about it for a moment. "Yes. Actually I really am. When I'm alone, I tend to dance around half naked, so yes."

Most women were. They only started to hate themselves when other people became involved. "Sweetie, then what does it matter what anyone else thinks? You have to decide what's good enough for you. If you spend your life trying to live up to everyone else, you'll have a wasted life."

"Holy shit. I'm totally writing that down."

Avery smiled. "I like that. I like that a lot."

"My sister is quite the philosopher," a familiar voice said.

Wow. The absolute last person she thought she'd see here in Sanctum was Chelsea and yet there she stood in the doorway, a bag in hand. "Hey, Chels."

Her sister glared at her and then broke down laughing. "I should have known you would be naked somewhere. You never did have body issues like the rest of us."

"Only because I accept the whole sad package," Charlie admitted. Chelsea was definitely one of those women who was comfortable up until the moment a man walked in the room. "What are you doing here? I thought you would be in Barbados by now."

"And leave my big sis? No. I'm not going anywhere without you." She walked into the room, the only sign of her bad leg a slight limp. "If we're making a stand, then you have to know I'm standing with you. As to why I'm here in this den of iniquity, well, the British asshole and the American idiot decided I needed a little vacation from my very nice condo and they decided to bring me here. They actually got past security by claiming to be messengers. I'm complaining to management about the doorman. They were supposed to go to the fifth floor, but apparently one of them is damn good at rewiring elevators. He's also quiet or I would have taken his head off. Your Neanderthal apparently wants to keep the family together."

"He probably wants to keep an eye on both of us while the whole 'assassins trying to kill us' thing gets sorted out." She had no real idea how they were going to sort it out. She'd kind of hoped she would have some time before they caught up to her. No such luck.

"Are you really an information broker?" Serena asked.

Chelsea's eyes widened. "Did you pass out business cards?"

Charlie shrugged as Eve was working out the laces on the corset. She slipped the small band of spandex over her hips. It would barely cover her ass, but that was likely the point. She noted that someone had been a little kinder to her sister. It looked like she was holding PVC leggings and a matching tank top. "I don't lie about what we do."

Chelsea cleared her throat deliberately.

She took everything so seriously. "Well, of course I lie to the Feds. I was talking about our friends."

"You'll have to give me some time to figure out if they are our friends. Where can I get some privacy? As long as I'm here, I could use a workout. My leg is stiff. I've been sitting for days."

"There are changing rooms and showers you can use," Eve explained, gesturing toward the back of the locker room.

"Excellent." Chelsea walked back to the dressing rooms, her left leg dragging just a bit. She was probably in extreme pain, but she wouldn't show it. One of the ways she'd learned to deal with the pain was BDSM. Charlie might not have had a Dom since Ian, but she'd found several willing to help her sister out.

"So she seems oddly comfortable for a woman who was likely dragged out of her home and taken to a sex club. Arms up." Eve held out the emerald green corset, stretching it around Charlie's torso before she started in on the laces.

"She has some problems with her legs, especially her left one. A good long flogging gives her some relief. We normally had Doms come out to our place, but she's been in a few clubs as well." She took a deep breath because it would likely be her last of the evening.

The door to the locker room opened again and two women walked in. Both were blonde and looked in desperate need of a cheeseburger. One of the blondes had a nice rack and the other had a fake one. They carried in their fet wear in dress bags.

Eve groaned a little. So these girls were not friends. Eve seemed determined to ignore them.

"Hello. You must be the new girl," the blonde with fake cans said. She was dressed conservatively, though she wore a ton of makeup and had left her blouse opened far past what could be considered professional. "My Master told me you would be here tonight."

Serena looked up, frowning the blonde's way. "I didn't know you had taken a collar, Amanda."

"I didn't even know you were dating anyone," Avery said.

Eve kept working on the laces, her hands moving smoothly.

"She's had her eye on this particular Master for quite a while," the other blonde said with a nasty little laugh. She picked a locker and hung up her clothes for the night.

"We all should have known that Mandy would be the one to bring him down."

"Mandy" winked her friend's way. "You know it, Britney. It was inevitable. By the way, Serena, you look really nice today. I don't know anyone else who could quite carry off that look the way you do. I didn't know they made dresses like that anymore."

Serena shut down, looking back at her computer.

"What did you just say?" Charlie asked.

Amanda shook her blonde head. "I was just complimenting her. Subs have to stick together. Isn't that what you say, Eve? And you really have to give me the name of your moisturizer. You look so good for a woman your age."

"I'll get around to it, Amanda. I'm a little busy with my husband. We all are busy with our husbands and families." Eve had some claws, but Charlie wasn't sure she was going far enough.

Amanda glanced back at Charlie and then Eve. "Oh, honey, if you need any help getting that corset on her, I am actually really strong. Don't worry about it. I think the Master will be busy with me tonight." She leaned in. "Ryan explained it all to me. The Master needs to pretend to have something going with you so he has to have someone he's really attracted to around or he probably won't be able to pull it off. I always knew he would come back to me."

Charlie wasn't exactly sure what the blonde's Master had to do with her, but she didn't want to prolong the conversation. Amanda walked to the dressing rooms with a confidence most women didn't have.

It was a confidence Charlie was pretty sure she didn't deserve.

"Just ignore her," Eve said, putting the finishing

touches on the corset. "We all do."

Serena was looking down at her screen, but Charlie could tell she was close to tears.

That little blonde bitch had told a pregnant woman she didn't look nice. Among other things. "Is she always so nasty?"

Avery's hands moved angrily now. She could probably do some damage with those knitting needles if she wanted to. "She's hit on every one of our husbands. Even after the whole marriage thing. She also likes to tell me how pregnant I look. I can't stand her."

"She's a brat. An actual real one. She's really sweet when the men are around, but she's hateful around the women. I've tried to get Alex to kick her out, but she won't do anything to violate the rules," Eve explained.

Being nice should be a rule. "Ian doesn't care that she's mean?"

"No one really talks to him about her. He's always been standoffish. I don't understand why he would..." Serena stopped midsentence.

Everything finally fell into place. "She was talking about Ian. When she talked about her Master. That rat-fink bastard. I knew he was up to something. This is his way of showing me he doesn't care. Tell me honestly, Eve, has he ever touched her before?"

Eve turned a nice shade of pink. "Maybe once when she first came into the club, but you have to understand..."

She understood. "He screwed everything in a corset who would let him. I'm not worried about that. Tell me if they had a relationship. I want to know if he had a thing for her."

"No. He can't stand her. He's the only one who sees through her bullshit. Charlotte, he hasn't had a relationship with anyone."

Serena shook her head. "He never spends more than a couple of nights with any sub, and all of his contracts state that he isn't interested in anything permanent. The few times he's trained new subs, he didn't sleep with them."

Avery's mouth dropped open. "How do you know about his contracts?"

"Oh, I really wanted to read one and he keeps copies on Ryan's computer. Ryan never changes his password, so it was easy for Adam to grab me one. I totally used it as the basis for the contract in Sweetheart in Bloom." She flushed a little. "Now might be a really good time to remind everyone that what happens in the locker room stays in the locker room."

Eve rolled her eyes. "You are going to get in so much trouble one day."

Charlie needed them to stay on track. So he'd picked someone he couldn't stand in order to annoy her, to show her that he couldn't be won back. Well, he picked the wrong girl to pull that shit with. If he'd picked someone sweet and nice, then Charlie would have trouble dealing with it, but Ian made everything easy. "So Ian is pretending to have two subs with him tonight. Me because of the whole shooting thing and trying to keep the cops from figuring out who I am, and skinny bitch because he wants to make sure I know he's only topping me because of the shooting thing. You all let her talk to you like that?"

"She never says anything that can't be taken two ways. She's the queen of the backhanded compliment. If I called her out, she would say I took it wrong," Avery explained.

"No one ever calls her on her shit?" Charlie was really shocked.

Eve sighed. "It's the South. We all just kind of suck it up and say 'Bless your heart.'"

Blessing wasn't what Charlie was going to do with Blondie's heart. Ripping it out and forcing it down her throat sounded like a much better idea. "Okay, I am going to show you how to deal with this."

Eve's eyes widened. "I don't know if that is such a good plan."

"Are you going to kill her?" Serena asked with a little smile.

Charlie turned. "No, I'm going to be honest with her. She was honest with me about where she thought my place with the Master was. I'm going to return the favor."

She strode into the dressing rooms. A woman like Amanda got away with crap by following a very specific set of societal rules. Charlie had her own rules.

She caught sight of herself in the mirror. Amanda wanted her to think she was fat? She looked damn good. Eve had a nice hand with the laces. Her boobs looked huge.

Britney stepped out of the shower section with a towel wrapped around her skinny middle. That towel would likely barely cover Charlie's boobs, but Britney had it wrapped around her twice. "Oh, god, there's a chick in the shower with the gnarliest scar on her leg. First that Avery chick and now this one. We've become the dungeon for cripples."

Britney was easy. Charlie walked straight up to her, standing over her. "That's my sister. Would you like to call her a cripple to my face? Let me explain what will happen if you do."

"You don't have to do that." Britney swallowed twice, obviously unused to anyone calling her on her shit. "Sorry. I'm sorry."

She moved away and practically scampered out of the room.

"Wow, rude much?" Amanda asked. She was still dressed. She obviously hadn't made it back to the changing rooms yet. "You're not going to last long around here if the Master catches you doing that."

"Are you talking about Ian Taggart?"

"Yes. I'm talking about the hot hunk of Dom I've already had a couple of times. I knew he would come back to me. Look, I was trying to be nice out there, but you should understand that he's just letting you follow him around because you're some sort of job to him."

She towered over Amanda. Sometimes her height came in really handy. "I'm his wife."

Amanda's face screwed into an ugly mask. It was probably her thinking face. "He's not married."

"I have the paperwork that says otherwise, honey. I'm Charlotte Taggart and I have been for five years, so if you think I'm going to let you fuck my husband again, you're totally wrong."

Skin flushing to a mottled red, Amanda held her ground. "Well, he's been cheating on you. With everyone. Hate to be the one to tell you, but your 'husband' is kind of a manwhore."

"Oh, I think you love telling me, but you're not saying anything I didn't already know. I forgive him for the sleeping around. He didn't know he was still married. Now he does. So he's going to stop. I also forgive him for needing another sub to hide behind. He's not very self-aware. He's not good with the whole emotional thing, so I'm patient. But guess what? It's not going to be you."

"What are you talking about? Ian wants me."

"Ian is going to have to live with disappointment because you are a rude, nasty piece of work, and your reign of terror stops now."

Amanda laughed. "Who's going to stop me? It's sure

not going to be Eve. Everyone thinks she's the queen of the dungeon because she's married to Alex, but she's just an old hag. Alex married her because he feels sorry for her. And god, I don't even know what Liam and Jake were thinking when they brought those fat little mice here."

Charlie heard a gasp and realized Serena and Avery and Eve were standing in the background listening to all the crap Amanda was spewing.

It was time to take her place in the pecking order. Eve was a nice lady, but it was obvious to Charlie that she hadn't been taking care of business the way she should have. "I like Eve, but Eve is not the queen. The queen is the sub who is married to the king, and there is only one king of Sanctum."

"What are you going to do?" Amanda asked in a mocking voice. "Are you going to go to Ian and get me kicked out? It won't work. Ian thinks I'm a sweetheart. All the Doms do. There's not a lot any of you can do."

"Oh shit." Chelsea was standing in the hall that led to the showers. "You can't kill her here, sis. We don't have any acid. The showers would work. They're nice and roomy, but where would we get a couple of gallons of acid at this time of night? And I don't think even acid would work on those fake tits. We would have to bury them someplace. How are you going to explain walking around with two grade-D implants?"

Her sister was always cool in a crisis. Amanda was staring at her. It was one of those things that no one took seriously when it was said in anger, but Chelsea's cool and calm demeanor had caught Amanda's attention.

Charlie matched it. It was fairly easy to make up bullshit. They had never actually taken apart a body. Charlie had killed a couple of men, but she'd never had to bury anyone. Amanda didn't have to know that. "Chels, she's not worth killing. I mean the murder part would fun, yes, but there's all that work we would have to do afterwards. Do you remember the last time we took apart a body? The smell was horrible and we had to wear all that protective gear and it smelled bad, too."

"You're joking." Amanda's voice trembled just a bit.

"Am I? Well, like I said, you're not worth it." Charlie reached up and grabbed a handful of bottle blonde hair. "But I am going to teach you who the queen is."

Charlie started to haul Amanda out of the locker room. The girls had said that what happened in the locker room stayed in the locker room, but in this particular case, she couldn't keep her problem secret. It would likely get her in trouble, but some things were worth a spanking. And probably a lecture. And more quiet time.

"Someone help me! Get this Amazon bitch off me!" Amanda was screaming as they hit the lobby.

"Hey!" Alex was standing just outside looking awfully nice in his leathers. "What the hell is going on here?"

Amanda cried out, obviously looking for a savior. "Master Alex, please help me. She's gone crazy. Please."

"Charlotte, you will let her go this instant." Alex proved he had a damn fine Dom voice.

Yeah, he wanted to mediate, but Charlie didn't have time for that. She definitely wasn't going to allow Amanda to get him on her side. "She called Eve old and pathetic."

Alex's eyes flared. "Are you fucking with me?"

Eve was in the doorway, an amused expression on her face. "Nope. Amanda isn't the nicest girl."

"She called me fat," Serena said.

"She said my scars were ugly," Avery added. "They are, but it's not nice to point it out."

A big bouncer was standing at the front of the door.

Charlie was sure he was probably a big bad Dom, but he stared at her, obviously having no idea what to do when one sub attacked another.

"You should open the door," Charlie suggested. "Miss Amanda here has had her membership revoked."

"It's all right, Brian," Alex said. "As of this moment, Amanda is no longer a member of this establishment."

"You bastard!" Amanda yelled. Her feet moved fast or Charlie would have been dragging her skinny ass. "I'm going to sue everyone here. I'm going to let everyone know what a bunch of perverts you all are."

"Really?" a dark voice asked. Charlie looked up, and a tall man with broad shoulders was staring at the scene. "Because I think you should probably consider your other job right about now."

"Derek? Derek, don't let them kick me out. You know I can cause trouble," she threatened.

"I can murder you in a dark alley," Charlie retorted.

"And I can ignore the murder entirely. You could make it look like a mugging," the man named Derek offered before switching his stare back to Amanda. "I told you your mouth would get you in trouble. Don't forget that the chief has a membership here. I don't think that he's going to like being outed as a pervert. We'll have a talk in my office on Monday if you survive the weekend."

With that the door was opened and Charlie hoisted her outside. She tossed Amanda out and then locked the door behind her. She turned back to Eve. "See, that was very simple."

"Was it?" Ian was suddenly in the lobby, his massive body taking up most of the space. He was in his leathers, and Charlie fought hard not to actually drool.

She had just taken another one of those liberties Ian tended to object to. Sinking to her knees, she decided to play it safe. She let her head fall forward, her hair brushing the ground as she placed her palms up.

"Now you choose to obey me." Ian's boots came into view. God, even his boots were sexy. They weren't polished or new. They were lived in, with little creases here and there. "Charlie, I want to know what just happened."

She brought her eyes up. "I just took out the trash, Sir."

He was so serious for a moment that she worried she might join Amanda on the outside looking in. And then his head fell back and he laughed. "God, I've been waiting for the subs to toss her on her ass. I should have known you would be the one to do it. Derek, this is my…" he sighed before continuing. "This is my submissive, Charlotte. She's also a pain in my ass."

"All the good ones are," Derek said.

"Come on then." Ian held a hand out, helping her up. "I need a drink. Finish up in the locker room and meet us in the bar."

He turned and walked away, but she could tell by the way his head shook that he was still laughing a little.

That went better than expected.

"So have you really taken apart a body using acid?" Serena asked. "Because I would like to interview you about that. How much did you have to use? How messy does it get?"

God save her from writers. Charlie followed Eve back in to get ready for the evening.

* * * *

Ian stared out at the dungeon, trying not to think about the sub at his side. Trying not to think about just how right it felt to have her there. From his seat in the back of the bar, he could see everything that was happening, but they were far away enough that their conversation wouldn't interrupt the scenes. "Should I assign a Dom to your sister or is she all right negotiating for herself?"

He'd been surprised at how comfortable the little sister was in the dungeon. He'd kind of expected tears and recriminations from the girl. He'd expected to have her hole up in the locker room or the conference room, but all she'd requested was something that covered her legs. He'd found some PVC leggings and she'd turned and walked away from him without another word.

"Chelsea?" Charlie asked from her place on the floor. She was sitting on one of the large fluffy pillows many of the Doms used when they had their subs kneel or recline at their feet for long periods of time. From this angle, Ian could see the curves of her breasts, perfectly pushed up by the tight corset. He'd picked green, an emerald color that set off her hair. She wore far too much black. She looked pretty in greens and blues. Vibrant colors, like the woman herself.

He liked the fact that she was flustered. She'd been an Amazon queen when she'd hauled the mean girl out, but she'd seemed a bit lost ever since. Like she didn't trust anything he was doing. They had sat and talked with Derek Brighton for a good thirty minutes, or rather he'd talked to Derek while Charlie had sat at his feet and allowed him to feed her little snacks. She'd kept looking up at him like he was about to poison her. It was kind of fun. "Yes, unless you have another sister you haven't told me about."

"It's not her first time in a dungeon."

So they had been playing. That didn't sit well. "So you were lying about not taking a Dom. It shouldn't surprise me."

Her head shook. "No, I didn't have a Dom. I promise.
I haven't played in years. I just found a couple for
Chelsea. Most of the time I hired them to come out to
wherever we were living at the time, but a couple of times
we were invited to dungeons."

"I wouldn't take her for a sub. If I had to make the
determination, just glancing at her I would say she would
prefer to top someone." Chelsea Dennis wasn't an
unattractive woman. She was actually quite lovely, but she
didn't smile. There was a tightness to the way she held
herself that let Ian know she wanted to be in control.

But maybe that wasn't what she needed. Charlie had
the same tightness in her bones all those years ago until
that first week they were together. He'd watched as she'd
fought to let go, to trust him. When she had, she'd fully let
go, giving him everything she had.

Well, of her body. She'd never really trusted him or
they wouldn't be in this position. Adam was trying to track
the known assassins, but they were damn good at their
jobs. They had disappeared. There were definitely times
Ian wished Dallas had more CCTVs. They would come
after her again. The only question was when. He had to sit
back and hope one of them took the bait. So far all he'd
had was a text from Liam that all was quiet and he'd lost a
hundred bucks to Karina while playing poker.

"I can't imagine her flicking a whip." Charlie stared at
her. "But she does love the flogger. Actually, I should
probably be the one to negotiate. She's not that great with
Doms."

Up on the stage, Alex was using a four-foot whip on
Eve. He and the whip moved with the grace of long use.
The cracking sound the whip made belied what Ian knew
was nothing more than a sting along her skin followed by

a lovely warmth. Charlie used to love the whip. He'd felt like a real Dom the first time she'd subbed out while he was working on her. He felt like he finally truly understood why he'd been attracted to this life. It wasn't for the kink or because he wanted the control. It was because when she relaxed, he felt necessary. He felt like something beyond a highly paid piece of cannon fodder.

He forced himself away from dangerous thoughts.

"If she wants to find a Dom here, she's going to have to talk to him herself or I'll assign one. So she uses it as therapy? The endorphins help with the pain from her leg?" Ian asked, looking back at Chelsea.

"Yeah. She resisted at first, but after she tried it, she really saw a difference. It helps her in a way massage doesn't."

"Hidden sub?" Ian asked thoughtfully.

"I think so. I think Chelsea would be much happier if she could let go, but I doubt my sister ever will. She spent too many years without any control. She was very young when my father took us to Russia. She was barely nine. I know she remembers our mom but not like I do. My mom was wonderful. I worry Chelsea didn't get enough of her."

"I'm surprised she speaks English without an accent." It occurred to him that he didn't just have to worry about Charlie. He had to figure Chelsea out, too. Charlie had given up a lot for her sister.

"I made sure she kept up her English. When we were alone, we always spoke in English. We both speak fluent Russian though, and you wouldn't be able to tell us from native speakers when we get going. My father hated the fact that he didn't have a son, but he wasn't about to be embarrassed by ignorant daughters. My dad had it in his head that he was a czar. Czar's kids had tutors. Ours happened to be from LA. He was a really smart man, but he ran afoul of my dad's gambling organization."

"So he paid off his debt by teaching you and Chelsea."

"When he wasn't drunk, he was an excellent tutor," Charlie admitted.

He hated to think about her childhood. His father might have walked out on them, but at least he and Sean had their mother. She hadn't been the strongest woman and Ian had been forced to grow up fast, but she hadn't left them alone with drunks or tortured them to make them strong.

The world could torture a man enough. He didn't need family members to help the process along.

Chelsea left her spot at the back of the crowd and entered the lounge. She gave a fleeting nod her sister's way, but seemed to have a goal in mind. She stared at the bar for a moment.

Simon was sitting on a stool beside Jesse, both men with beers in their hands. Jillian took Simon's empty mug. She kept a stash of his favorite beer in the back and was soon returning with a pint glass. Jesse had what looked to be a Bud in his hand. Straight out of the can. God, he was going to have to work on that kid's decorum.

"This should be interesting," he murmured, his hand going to Charlie's hair. He had to keep up the illusion after all. "It looks like little sister picked a Dom for the night."

Chelsea was walking straight up to Simon. Simon was dressed in leather pants and a vest with no shirt. Most nights he didn't take a sub, preferring to spend his time in the bar, but a couple of times he'd negotiated with single subs. He seemed to prefer bondage play, where his sub was completely tied down. Simon had completed his ropes course within weeks of joining the team and now he was studying shibari with Alex.

Ian preferred more extreme play, as Charlie would soon discover.

"I would like to talk to you, Sir." Chelsea used all the right words, but there was a brattiness to her tone that made Ian frown. At least Charlie knew how to manipulate him. She'd gone right to her knees when he'd caught her tossing Amanda out on her ass.

He'd planned to use Amanda to show Charlie that she couldn't have everything her way. He should have known better. He'd picked Amanda because she was the one most likely to annoy the holy shit out of Charlie. He was a dumbass because he should have picked someone sweet, someone Charlie couldn't take on.

Or maybe he'd known what she would do. Maybe it had been there in the back of his head.

He wasn't about to tell her that he'd been waiting for someone to make a case to get rid of her. He wasn't stupid. He'd never really bought Amanda's act. Sure he'd screwed her a couple of times because she was convenient and amenable, but that didn't mean he thought she was an angel. The subs needed to stand up for themselves, so he'd backed off. He was kind of with Charlie on that one. He would have tossed her out on her ear the minute she opened her mouth, but Eve and Grace had done the Southern-lady thing.

Charlie's head had come up, and she was watching her little sister. Ian gently forced it back to his lap.

"She'll be fine."

"Do you really think Simon is the right Dom for her?" Charlie asked.

He wasn't sure the Brit was right for anyone. Simon was rigid and hid a wealth of self-consciousness under his perfect exterior. Simon had fucked up in the near past, and he wasn't over it yet. Nope. Simon likely wasn't right for anyone now. "I think it's a single encounter and he'll either handle it or he won't. Now stop talking. I can't hear them when you talk."

He knew he was being a gossipy old lady, but he kind of wanted to see how Charlie's sister handled the Brit.

Simon turned, that aristocratic eyebrow arching. "Yes? Do you need something else? I don't think those leggings are what I selected for you."

Jesse had turned, and it was obvious from the kid's expression that he was watching As the Dungeon Turns, too. His eyes went from Simon to Chelsea and back again.

"I got the clothes you gave me, but I requested something different from Master Ian." She knew all the right things to say, but somehow she put a twist on the polite words to give them a sarcastic edge.

Simon's eyes trailed across the bar, finding Ian's and narrowing. "And he gave them to you?"

Ian didn't move a muscle. Chelsea wasn't wearing a collar and she was Charlie's sister, so that put her firmly under Ian's control and protection. But just for the briefest of seconds, he thought Simon might call him out on it. Interesting.

Simon broke eye contact and went back to his beer. "What do you want?"

"I'm in need of a session." There was nothing soft or submissive about the way Chelsea spoke. She could have been walking into a department store and ordering a salesperson to bring her a shirt.

"Shit," Charlie said under her breath. "I've tried to teach her proper behavior."

Ian stroked her hair. "Hush. You can't save her from this."

"Are you asking me to play with you?" Simon asked. Even from where Ian was sitting he could see the cool appraisal in the way Simon looked Chelsea up and down.

She didn't have her sister's height. Chelsea was average, probably five foot six, and she wasn't some starved supermodel. Ian was sure a crazed bitch like Amanda would likely call Chelsea fat, but Ian just thought she looked healthy. Amanda would be happier if someone fed her. Women got mean when they didn't eat. Even Eve was much happier now that Alex was stuffing her with chocolates.

"Not at all," Chelsea returned with a brisk shake of her head. "I'm asking you to flog me. I would need roughly thirty to forty minutes of your time. I prefer a thump to a sting. I would rather use deerskin falls, and I won't be tied down."

Ian groaned a little. Most subs knew not to sound like they were ordering a burger at a fast-food place.

Charlie was trying to see again. "I told you. I need to do the negotiating. She's not good at this. She's been in front of that computer so long she's forgotten how to deal with actual human beings."

"Get up here." It was useless to not let her watch. She would wiggle and twist and probably get a crick in her neck. It was easier to pull her into his lap.

She sat herself right over his cock, and that damn little bit of spandex had already ridden up on her hips so that all that prevented penetration was his leathers. Because his cock knew what it wanted. It had been hard since the moment she'd dropped to her knees. Hell, he'd gotten aroused watching her haul Amanda out on her ass. If he didn't have his leathers on, he knew damn well his cock would be trying hard to work its way inside her. He could let her sit on his cock and watch the world go by.

"Really?" Simon was asking, his voice low and sarcastic. "You have a list of demands for me, sub?"

Chelsea shrugged a little. "No. I assumed you were intelligent enough to remember what I wanted."

Charlie buried her head in Ian's shoulder. "I don't want to see it."

But Ian totally did. Fuck, he kind of lived for this shit. It was sad, but he accepted it. He was a voyeur in all things. He liked to watch people fuck when they did it well, and he sure liked to watch people fuck up. It was funny.

Simon stood, towering over Chelsea. "What did you say, sub?"

Chelsea seemed caught on the big Brit's chest, her eyes staring at the place where his leather vest parted and showed off skin. "I was simply trying to explain what I need, Sir."

"That's so not going to work," Ian said.

Charlie was looking again, her face hopeful. "Maybe she can pull it off."

He grinned because there was no fucking way. "Wanna bet?"

Charlie shook her head and ducked in again. "No. I would lose."

Simon brought his hand to Chelsea's chin, forcing her to look up at his face, but there was a stubborn set to her eyes.

"No, Chels, come on. Soften up," Charlie was saying.

"Nah, she's about to commit assault and brattery on him. We should call Derek back," Ian said.

Charlie made a vomiting sound. "That's awful."

It was. He was full of bad puns, but they almost never came out.

If he were sitting here with Grace or Eve, they would have already pointed out how rude it was to intrude on Simon and Chelsea's conversation by listening in. Avery would already have begged him to intervene because her tender heart couldn't stand conflict. Serena would be taking notes. Only Charlie was in the moment with him. Only she understood that the dramas playing out around them might not be meant for their entertainment, but damn they were fun to watch. Other subs would just sit quietly and would likely have laughed at his terrible joke, never calling him on his bad sense of humor. Not Charlie.

Why did the one woman he was comfortable with have to turn out to be the enemy?

"Maybe I have a few demands of my own," Simon said.

Chelsea's shoulders squared. "Fine. I'm willing to listen."

"I'll use the deerskin flogger. I have a very nice one I've been wanting to break in. Thud not sting, though I think you might like a little sting if you tried it. You will be naked and tied down."

"She won't do it," Charlie whispered. "She was tied down when she had her legs broken. She can't stand it."

"All the more reason for her to face it with someone she trusts," Ian replied. "I don't think that's going to be Simon."

Chelsea's jaw clenched, and she took a moment to reply. "Loose bindings, I keep my clothes."

He looked down, and Charlie's eyes had gone wide. Looked like Chelsea had a thing for Simon.

The Brit ran his fingertips from her neck to the collar of the tank top Chelsea was wearing. "I'll give on the bindings, but no clothes."

Ah, the Brit wanted to see some skin.

"Why? Do you want to see the cripple naked?" Chelsea asked, her voice hard.

"Ouch." Charlie flinched.

"Yeah, that will get her in serious trouble," Ian allowed. Self-mockery was brutally unappealing. He would rather be around a plain woman who thought she was beautiful than a beautiful one who complained she was plain.

"No. I want to see you naked, and if you keep talking like that it's not a flogging you'll get, it's a spanking, and I promise you it will sting." Every word out of his mouth was clipped and angry.

A long moment passed where they seemed connected. Maybe he'd been wrong about Simon not being ready. The big Dom was looking down at the computer-geek cutie like he could eat her alive.

Chelsea, for her part, seemed determined to prove she didn't need to breathe.

Finally, she took a step back and turned to Jesse. "How about you?"

Simon stepped into her line of sight. "No."

"What do you mean no? He can't speak for himself?"

"Not if he wants to live he won't."

Jesse wisely kept his mouth shut.

"So if I don't do what you want, I don't get a Dom?" Chelsea's hands went to her hips.

Simon shook his head. "You don't get him no matter what you do, love. He's in training. If you want to get what you need, you'll negotiate. I'm willing to give up one of my usual demands."

"And I was willing to allow you to tie me down," she shot back. "You have no idea how hard that would be for me."

"Then I'll make it easy on you. All you have to do is take off what little clothes you're wearing and I'll take care of you. No bindings. Everything else your way."

Chelsea simply turned and started to walk away.

161

Simon watched as she left.

"Damn it." Charlie leaned back into him again. "Now she'll be in pain. She has a couple of scars. Who around here doesn't? I don't get what problem she has with being naked."

"Because you're a dreadful exhibitionist." Charlie didn't mind walking around in her own gorgeous skin. It was one of the things that attracted him. "She's more normal, you know."

He looked behind him and Alex was taking Eve off the cross, his hands moving gently across her body, their deep connection a palpable thing. Because they loved and trusted each other. Because they were in this life together until the end.

He could stroke Charlie's hair all he liked. He could sit here and play with her, but he would always be waiting for her to walk away again. He didn't like the hollow feeling it left in his gut, but there was a part of Ian that had begun pushing him to take everything from this time they had. Once the shit with Nelson shook down, he would have to let her go. But for now he could take her. He could revel in her.

"I'll ask Ryan to take care of Chelsea. He's married. He won't have any interest in seeing her naked." Ian wasn't sure why he was doing this. Typically, he would allow the sub to flounder until she properly asked for what she wanted. It was part of the process. But Charlie would be worried about her sister, and he needed her calm and collected for what he was about to do. Brighton would be watching. Despite the fact that Derek thought they were a new couple, he also had to know damn well that Ian wouldn't scene publically with someone he didn't trust.

Well, until tonight.

Derek walked up and sat back down, his face a mask

of frustration. "I just got a call from one of my men. They found a dead body at the hotel across from your office. Seventh floor."

That happened faster than he would have liked. "That's terrible. You can't even trust five-star hotels anymore."

"Cut the shit, Ian. I know I'm not telling you anything new. The seventh floor sounds just about perfect for taking a shot at you." He crossed his arms over his chest. "I'm keeping quiet for now. Give me something."

He hated sharing. Sharing was for idiots, but right now sharing information would keep the woman on his lap from a likely waterboarding. Though she did look good wet...

Charlie wiggled in his lap, reminding him which part of his anatomy was actually in charge.

"We think the guy is Russian," Ian offered. Sometimes offering up a little unimportant information could satisfy the authorities. "A man named Zhukov. He's a known assassin. He's professional, so you shouldn't expect an unnecessary body count. The man in the hotel was unfortunate. He needed that specific room. I'll try to stay off the street so he doesn't do it again. I can send you a dossier on the fucker, if you like."

"Why is he after you?" Brighton asked.

At least there was an easy answer for that. The key was not to outright lie. "I assume he's being paid."

Charlie let her head rest against his shoulder, but he could feel how tense she was. She understood the stakes, and he had no doubt that she would keep her mouth shut in this instance. She had a knack for self-preservation.

"By the man from the Fort Worth operation?" Brighton asked. "The rogue agent you've been pursuing?"

It was always better to let a person make their own

assumptions. They tended to believe themselves, to feel smart for their deductions. "His name is Eli Nelson. He's pissed at me for more than one reason. I cost him a very lucrative business deal a few months back. He knows damn well I won't stop until I've crushed him."

Not a lie in there. Just not the entire truth.

Brighton sat back, running a hand through his closely cropped hair. "I hate the spy shit. Give me a good clean murder any day of the week."

"The good news is you totally have a murder on your hands now. You're welcome."

Dark brown eyes rolled. "I can't solve that one, asshole. It's going to be on my docket, and it'll go unsolved."

An unsolved case on his docket would hurt him. "Look, when I get this figured out, I'll help you, okay? We can connect some dots and make sure this guy's family knows why he was killed."

Brighton's eyes narrowed. "Or I can take you into protective custody. It would be the right thing to do. I can't just let this guy run around. He's killed once. He could do it again."

"You could try. We'll see if you have a safe house that can handle me." Ian was well aware that his voice had gone positively frigid. "You know what will happen if you do that. This guy will disappear and he'll resurface when I least expect it. Right now I know who's coming after me. All you would do is waste months of my life, and I would lose the chance to make sure I'm right about who wants me dead."

Brighton let his head fall back. "I should call the fucking Feds in. Hell, I should call in the Agency. They should be dealing with this shit."

He couldn't let that happen. The minute the Agency

got involved, he would lose control of Charlie, and there were some places even he wasn't sure he could get into. "I'm calling in that chip you owe me, Derek. For Kandahar."

Ian had saved Derek's life in Afghanistan and covered up a very substantial flub on the former sergeant's part. It had been a messy bloody affair, and Ian had cleaned it up. He knew he was going straight for the throat. Brighton still hadn't forgiven himself for what had happened, but Ian couldn't afford to back down.

"Damn it." Brighton leaned forward. "That is so fucking unfair."

"You should know better than most that life isn't fair, Derek." Ian couldn't back down. Didn't even want to. Favors were meant to be called in, and he'd done Derek Brighton a big one.

Brighton held a hand up in surrender. "All right, but you have to keep me up to date. You should know that the minute this affects another civilian, I won't care what I owe you. I'll do my job, Ian."

He would do it because once he hadn't and that one incident had affected the rest of his life. Ian knew he should be damn happy he had that favor or Derek's duty would screw them all. "I wouldn't expect less."

Charlie relaxed a little.

Brighton turned slightly and motioned toward the bar, holding up a single finger. Jillian nodded and started to pour him a beer. "I don't think I'm in the mood to play tonight. The good news is that frees me up to drink."

Two drinks were all anyone was allowed at Sanctum if they were playing, but all of his Doms were known to treat the bar like a bar when they weren't. Derek, especially. Lately, Ian had noticed Derek didn't play much. He seemed to prefer to watch scenes and drink and go home alone.

"This one's on me." It was the least he could do and besides, Ian wasn't drinking this evening. For the scene he had planned, he wouldn't touch alcohol.

Jillian brought over a frosty mug and sat it down in front of Brighton. Ian motioned her over and quietly asked that she find her Dom and request he take care of Chelsea. Jillian, who had also witnessed the scene, nodded her assent and went to look for her husband, Ryan.

Charlie's face tilted up, and there were tears in her eyes.

"Don't," Ian said. He didn't need a crying sub. "And don't forget protocol. I've been lax. I won't be now."

There were advantages to being able to control her ability to talk. He didn't have to listen to mushy thank yous. Actually, this was kind of the dream. Charlie couldn't talk. She could only sit there and look pretty. If only there was a high protocol for not getting herself killed by assassins. He would definitely put that shit in place.

Brighton took a long sip of his beer, watching them carefully. "Are you sure it's the right time to take a sub? Don't get me wrong. I'm actually happy to see you with a sub, but aren't you a little worried she could get caught in the cross fire?"

"She's practically bulletproof." He slapped her very juicy ass. "And she's solid. She can take a lot of damage."

Charlie's mouth firmed to a stubborn line and her eyes narrowed, but she didn't say a word. She just glared at him.

Yeah, he liked high protocol.

Alex chose that moment to carry in a very happy looking Eve. She was wrapped in a blanket and cuddled in her husband's arms. Alex sat down on the couch beside Ian and Charlie. "Hey, Jillian, can you get me a beer? You want anything, baby?"

They were through with play for the evening, but Eve just shook her head and cuddled closer.

Alex grinned. "She'll be asleep in a couple of minutes. She'll be snoring away."

Eve slapped at her husband's chest affectionately. "I do not snore."

"Of course, angel." Alex mouthed a "wow" Ian's way. "So how's everything going tonight? Is Charlotte enjoying Sanctum?"

He wished he could put Alex in high protocol. "She loves it here. She's really looking forward to her first scene."

Charlie's eyes widened. He hadn't mentioned they would be playing together here. Her lips curled up and a grateful look came into her eyes. She very likely thought he was planning to spank her or flog her and then do what he used to do. Fuck her hard and long in front of an audience. Charlie didn't mind other people watching. She didn't demand it, but in a club environment, she wouldn't shy away from it either. She would give as good as she got. She wouldn't hold back for a minute.

But he didn't intend to spank her. And he wasn't going to fuck her. Probably. No. Definitely. Definitely probably not going to fuck her.

She wiggled in his lap.

Shit. He was going to fuck her.

"I saw Ryan getting the cotton ready. Are you sure about a fire play demo tonight?" Alex asked.

Charlie gasped. "Fire play?"

Fuck. Now he had to spank her, too. She was just set on getting her damn way. It wouldn't work, but it looked like he would have to prove it to her. "Over my lap. That's ten."

"Ian, we should talk about this," Charlie sputtered.

"That's twenty. Are you sure you want to go for thirty? I have set up a very nice scene to introduce you to Sanctum as my sub. Of course, you have the power, sweetheart. You can always say no and then I can find a new Dom to show you around." Maybe he wouldn't be fucking her tonight. Maybe he could wriggle his way out of Alex's trap. His life would be so much easier if she said no and he could dump her on someone else.

Simon and Jesse perhaps. They could handle close cover. Probably. Except Jesse had tried to shoot Alex and failed to hit his target. Oh, sure, Charlie had gotten in the way, but Jesse hadn't even managed to get a second shot off or anything. Ian would have to work on that problem before he cleared him to watch someone important.

And Simon didn't have a ton of field experience. Charlie could be slippery when she wanted to be.

No. He would still have to watch her.

"That's so unfair, Ian," she whispered the words, her voice breaking a little. "I'm scared. I've never seen it done before. It sounds a little extreme."

"Then you can say no. That's thirty, Charlie. Of course, if you say no, we can forget about the spanking, too. It's your choice." He was putting her in a corner, but then she'd put him in one by walking into his life. She needed to fully understand how this would work. It would be his way. All the way. Her only option was to say no and walk away and free him.

He should have known she wouldn't trust him. Deep down he had known and that was exactly why he'd planned the fire play scene. She'd resisted it before. He knew she was scared. He was a bastard, but he wasn't going to change his plans now.

Charlie stood, her legs firm on the carpet beneath her.

Her face showed no expression at all, and he was pretty sure he was about to get punched again. That would likely blow their cover with Derek.

Then she pulled up her skirt and placed herself over his lap.

Fuck. She was going to kill him. Her ass was so round and perfect and he couldn't stop himself from caressing it. He ran his hands over those plump cheeks, the skin so smooth under his palm. There was still a little pink to those cheeks from his earlier spanking.

He slapped her ass lightly. Once, twice and then ten times rapidly. He was softer this time because he didn't want her sore. Or maybe he was softer because she'd turned his fucking brain to mush. His cock was hard and pulsing with every smack to that sweet ass.

He counted in his head. It was part of letting her relax. By accepting his discipline, she was accepting the scene, and he needed her ready for it. Unless she was counting, she wouldn't know when he would stop and she could concentrate on the pure sensation.

Sure enough, he felt her start to relax, her spine softening and body melting against his lap.

He continued smacking her cheeks in a soft rhythm. Her face rubbed against his leg and he…fuck…he could smell her arousal. She responded so openly, so honestly. He never doubted that she wanted him. It had always been there. Even when she was betraying him, her pussy knew who its Master was.

He finished off the final ten slaps, each one causing her to relax further. He used long strokes to hold the heat against her flesh. Her skin was warm and pink, her whole body like butter against him.

This was what he wanted, her quiet and trusting against him. He helped her up but didn't bother to push her skirt back down. He liked the way she smelled, all tangy arousal and sweet woman. He pulled her into his lap, not giving a damn that she was wet and it would get on his leathers. It was a stain he would wear proudly. She cuddled against him, tucking her head under his chin, and he knew why he hadn't held another sub like this in all these years. Because they didn't fill his arms the way she did. They didn't fit him, like a piece of a puzzle he'd always been missing. They didn't surround him.

They didn't make him feel.

He looked up at Alex, who was cuddling Eve and sending him an encouraging look. Like he'd just joined Alex's fellowship of dipshit husbands.

Derek was staring at them, and then his eyes trailed away. He was alone and it was obvious that he was very aware of that fact.

Ian was more like Derek than Alex.

He couldn't tell Alex how much he wished he could be like him or Sean or the rest of them. Eve had never betrayed Alex. Grace had never chosen someone else over Sean. Serena had been steadfast and loyal to Jake and Adam. Avery hadn't cost Liam and his friends years of their lives.

He could admit deep inside that she was the woman for him. He'd never really denied it.

But he couldn't forgive her, and he damn straight would never forgive himself.

Feelings sucked. And Alex was right. Eve did snore.

Chapter Seven

Charlie looked out over the crowd and hoped to hell Ian knew what he was doing. It was one time she kind of hoped he'd practiced on every available sub since he was planning on setting her on freaking fire.

Fire hurt. Fire burned. Cavemen had figured that out, but Ian Taggart was behind the times.

He stood at the small stand Ryan had set up after Alex and Eve's scene. She hadn't been paying attention. She'd sort of watched Alex and Eve's scene, but mostly she'd just enjoyed being close to Ian. She'd also worried about her sister too much to get involved in anyone's scene. Now she could see plainly that her sister was getting what she needed from Sanctum's Dom in Residence who, unlike Simon Weston, didn't really want to see her naked. Chelsea was holding on to the bindings of a St. Andrew's Cross and Ryan Church was using a deerskin flogger on her back, buttocks, and hamstrings. He was very carefully working her over and Chelsea was perfectly still for the treatment. There was no passion there, just a simple exchange.

What would she have gotten from Simon? The big

Brit was standing at the back of the crowd watching the scene play out. His handsome face was stony, his eyes locked on Chelsea. He would have forced her past her comfort zone. Charlie got the feeling he also would have rewarded her for being brave.

Chelsea had gotten to the point that she couldn't give up control. Simon couldn't know how much it had cost her sister to offer to let him tie her down. Chelsea even hated seat belts. But she'd been more willing to face that fear than to take off her clothes. Was her sister so ashamed of the scars on her legs that she was willing to never take a lover? Did she honestly intend to stay a virgin for the rest of her life? Because Charlie was pretty damn sure she was. Would Chelsea spend her whole life never trusting a soul?

Charlie could spend her life like that. She could walk away from Ian and she would very likely be able to find a man who would acquiesce to her demands and she would get exactly what she said she needed.

Or she could trust Ian and discover a whole new world of what she wanted.

She tried to see exactly what was on the table. It looked like there was a large wad of cotton balls, several plastic bottles containing god only knew what, and she could see the glass pieces for a violet wand.

"Charlie?" Ian gestured to the massage table in the middle of the stage floor.

Already there were people standing around, including Serena, who gave her a wink and a little thumbs up. She was probably already writing a fire play scene in her head.

It was just a scene. Just play. Ian had never hurt her. She'd been the one to hurt him. He'd kept his end of the bargain. It was past time to keep hers.

She was afraid of fire, but then she was also afraid of elevators, and when she held his hand, she could handle them.

A deep sense of peace settled over her. Most of her life she had shoved her fear down because fear could get her killed. But it would be all right to be afraid at Sanctum. He was here. It was all right to feel afraid because nothing bad would happen to her.

She let her heart race as she walked to him.

"You're overdressed for the scene, love."

Well, of course she was. He certainly wouldn't want to set her micromini on fire and the corset was probably expensive. Surely her skin would heal.

She stepped toward him, leaving a foot or so between them. She had to tilt her head up to look at him. It was so rare for a man to truly tower over her. She was almost six feet herself and no one could call her underfed, but Ian Taggart was a mountain of a man. She let her eyes drift from his lean waist to that gorgeous line of skin shown off where his leather vest had been left open. His leathers hung low on his hips, exposing deep notches where his cut torso met strong legs. His abs were washboard perfect. His chest was big, his shoulders broad. He could pick her up and not notice her substantial weight.

And then she got to that perfectly square jaw. She wanted to kiss it, to soften it so he would smile at her. He almost never smiled, but when he did it lit up the room and he got the sweetest laugh lines. She loved the way they crinkled around his eyes. When he really smiled, when he forgot everything but his own amusement, he got the cutest dimples in his cheeks.

"Charlotte?" Ian asked. "Have I lost you again? Might I ask what's going on in your head?"

She was aware there was a crowd and they were all avidly watching the exchange, likely wondering if she was going to safe word out. Ian looked like he was wondering, too. "I was just thinking about how pretty you are, Sir."

Ian's eyes closed briefly and that straight jaw tightened as though he was holding in a laugh. He stifled it, but his eyes were warm as he stared down at her. "I'm pretty, huh? I have never once been described as pretty."

She was sure he'd been described as hot, as sexy, as intimidating. "Then they haven't looked at you, Sir, because I think you're the prettiest thing I've ever seen."

There were whispers all around and she heard some people talking about how Taggart wouldn't take "that" from a sub.

Had she fucked up again?

His hand came out, tilting her chin up. "I think we should check your eyesight, love, but I'll take it. And all the Doms out there giggling behind their hands like schoolgirls can shove it up their asses because apparently I'm prettier than all of them put together. Now show them how pretty my sub is. Let me get you out of that corset."

Warmth filled her. He was a man who could take a compliment when it was well meant. He'd taught her how to accept them, too. Before Ian there had been no compliments, no sweet words from men.

No scary fire.

She took as deep a breath as her corset allowed and lifted her arms up, ready for him to work on the laces.

Instead he held up a knife. "You won't need this for the rest of the night."

He placed the knife under the laces and lifted up as though he was moving it through butter. In an instant, she was exposed, the corset falling aside. Cool air hit her skin and her nipples puckered immediately.

Ian placed the corset and knife aside and dropped to one knee. His hands came up to her waist, pulling at the skirt and dragging it down her hips. Shivers ran along her skin everywhere he touched her and she couldn't miss the way he stopped at her pussy and took a long breath. He was such a nasty pervert and it made her spine curl, her heart soften.

He tossed the skirt aside and got back to his feet. That icy look in his eyes from earlier was completely gone, replaced with what she knew was a deep anticipation. He was looking forward to the scene. It wasn't just a punishment for her. It would bring him pleasure. It made it so much easier for her to move forward.

"Should I lie down, Sir?" She wanted to call him Master so badly.

He leaned over and picked her up with an ease that took away her breath. "I'll put you where I want you, sub. Don't worry about a thing. All you have to do is lie there and look pretty. It shouldn't be hard for you."

When he talked like that, she melted in his arms. So much of her life had been about being told where she'd failed, how she was flawed, how she needed to make up for all her shortcomings. But Ian thought she was lovely and that was all she needed. It was a miraculous thing to find the one person in the world who made all the bad things meaningless. Ian was her talisman against the dark.

He carried her to the table, laying her down on the sheet that covered it. He studied her for a moment, those hot eyes of his roaming her body. A single finger traced one of her scars absently as he inspected her. He smoothed back her hair, dragging it out of the way gently and twisting it to the side. "It's very important to make sure your sub's hair is well away from the play space. The play space, of course, is all your sub's fun parts."

He tweaked a nipple and she felt it in her pussy.

He turned away abruptly and she hated the loss of connection. When he was touching her, there was no hesitation. When he looked at her, she felt confident, peaceful. The minute he turned away, all her doubts and fears returned—that she didn't deserve him, that she'd already betrayed him so badly there was no hope.

"So I know some of you have been asking about fire play. I thought we could take this time to do a little demo. If there are enough Doms interested, I'll teach a class in the next couple of months, but you should all know damn well, there's no play until I say."

Because even among Doms he was a control freak. He would never allow a Dom to touch a sub in his club until he was sure the Dom knew what he was doing.

"Ryan is the only one here besides me with experience, so you can ask your questions of either of us. This is my personal submissive. Her name is Charlotte and this is her first fire play. I think."

She opened her eyes and sent him a look. What was it going to take to get him to believe she hadn't been gallivanting about with every Dom in the Western world? "Yes, Ian. It's a first for me. I haven't been out there setting myself on fire."

"We're having to perform a fire play scene tonight because her ass is already red from multiple spankings. She's a brat of the highest order, but we're working on the problem." His hand came out and quickly twisted her nipple, causing her to gasp. "When I need your input, I'll let you know."

"Where did you learn?" Jake was standing close, Serena at his side. "I'm sorry, but I'm very curious. I've never seen this done. I've certainly never seen you play this way."

"I learned it in England. You were too busy playing house with Serena. Li was working when he wasn't fucking our objective. Alex was mooning over Eve. So I had some free time on my hands and I have a British friend who is an expert at explosives of every kind." He seemed so confident and comfortable standing in front of this group. He usually stood in the back, watching and waiting, but this was his home. This was his club and these were his people.

God, she hoped she didn't freak out and make an idiot of herself. Was it going to hurt? Would she burn before he could put the flames out? She had to make sure she didn't scream.

"The truth of the matter is, fire play is a very effective mind fuck. If you can't tell, the sub is terrified. I would bet her mind is playing through a million scenarios of how this is going to go and some of them aren't good. Is the adrenaline flowing, love?"

Oh, yes it was. It was thrumming through her system. That was supposed to be the high of extreme play, the rush a sub got off it. She'd read some about it, but she and Ian had spent most of their time together in bed. He'd introduced her to impact play and bondage, but mostly he'd made love to her and talked to her and held her.

It was only a couple of months of her life. When she really looked at it, it was an inconsequential amount of days compared to all that had come before and after it, but those weeks had changed the course of everything. Those weeks with Ian had taught her the difference between surviving and living.

It wasn't just adrenaline flowing through her. It was hope. He was here and she was here and she would use this experience to bind them together. "Yes, Sir. I'm both scared and a little curious."

"That's exactly what I want to hear."

She heard the crack of the violet wand being turned on. She looked up, though she didn't raise her head.

Moving was a definite no no. He had attached the mushroom-shaped glass head to the violet wand. Purple light sparked from the head where he ran it over his own skin. "I like to warm the sub up a little. I thought I would use the wand on her. This is one toy she has used before."

One night in Paris. He'd introduced her to the violet wand. She'd been afraid at first and then she quickly grew to love the sensation. He had kissed her while she held the wand in her hand, sparks flaring from her tongue to his. Like they were a live wire waiting to go off.

She closed her eyes as the sound hit her first. The sound of electricity, of man-made lightning. Then the faintest whiff of ozone hit her nose. Then her skin was sparking in the most delicious way as Ian ran the wand over her torso. The sensation of bubbles playing along her flesh made her smile.

"This is on a low setting. Charlie enjoys a bite of pain, but she isn't a pain slut. If I give her too much, I'm likely to get it returned to me," Ian said with a self-deprecating laugh. "But don't let it be said I'm too kind to my subs."

She heard the change in the wand and then fought not to come off the table as he ran the damn thing over her labia. A little burn started and then the sensation intensified. He moved on to her thighs, but her pussy was definitely awake and alive now.

Charlie focused on the sensation. Ian seemed determined to not leave an inch of skin untouched. He turned the wand up so the lightest burn scraped across her. It brought her warmth where she'd been cold before.

He pulled the wand back and she missed its bite.

"The trick with flash cotton is that you have to make absolutely sure you've gotten rid of all the bunched-up pieces. You want flash cotton to be thin, spider web like. If you leave too much together, it could burn the sub. So the first thing the Dominant partner has to remember is to fully part the cotton."

His big hands went to work on the mound of flash cotton. In no time at all he had pulled it apart so it resembled a filmy spider web. He separated a piece of the cotton about the size of his palm and held it up. "This should work for our first demonstration. I like to call it mound o'fire."

Ian's friends all groaned, but Charlie was trying to figure out if he was about to place that cotton on her pussy. She breathed a quick sigh of relief as he covered her right breast with the stuff. Her skin already sensitized by the wand, she could feel every tiny movement as he adjusted the thin, filmy material.

He was really going to do it. He was going to light that cotton on fire and it was going to burn her. Right? Surely it would burn. That was what fire did. Yet she knew this was a perfectly acceptable form of play in the BDSM world. She hadn't seen a bunch of torched subs running around so it was only rational to come to the conclusion that she would be okay.

But her lizard brain was telling her to punch Ian, jump off the table and run away.

Ian looked down at her, those gorgeous lips of his curled up in a sexy smirk. "Scared?"

Asshole. "Yes."

"Good, because I'm going to light you up, baby." He held the violet wand up like it was a torch, the electric sound blotting out the murmurs around her.

Her heart was pounding, almost beating out of her chest. That was what she heard—the sound of the wand and her own loud heart.

Inside, she was shaking, but outside she kept completely still like that cotton on her breast was a spider and it would strike if she moved a single inch.

Then it started. Purple sparks flew from the wand to the cotton and she was on fire. It started at the outer edge, and red and orange flames marched a quick step across her breast, leaving a warm heat trail that fanned over her. She watched with a mix of horror and fascination as the fire flared, and then as quickly as it came, it was gone and she was left with nothing but a warm sensation and a crazy endorphin rush.

She laughed, a wild urge she couldn't contain. She'd been so afraid, and now that fear morphed into joy.

Ian looked down at her, his previous smirk softening into a smile that showed those creases on his face. "That's why they call it a mind fuck, baby." He turned back to his audience. "Now, let me show you how to form some fun patterns. You start with the flash cotton."

He talked on, but Charlie relaxed, letting his voice flow over her, finding that connection that had been missing most of her life except for those precious weeks.

She would do whatever it took to never lose it again.

Chapter Eight

Ian helped a very subby Charlie off the table. After the initial demo, she'd seemed to relax and allowed him every possible liberty with the rest of the scene. She hadn't protested once when he drew the cotton out in elaborate trails that led from between her breasts all the way down to her toes. Each time he lit her up, there was a momentary breathlessness and then a brilliant smile as the flame died out, never once harming her.

At least he thought it hadn't really touched her. It hadn't been his intention to put her into subspace, but he was pretty sure she was still there. He needed to get her out of the crowd and ensure that he hadn't burned her in any way. When Charlie was in subspace, she could take a lot more pain than normal. At least she used to be able to.

"Why don't you take her to the locker room and let her come down?" Alex asked, stepping up to start dealing with the scene clean up. "I'll take care of this. You deal with aftercare."

Charlie was in a robe Eve had brought her, her arms wrapped around her middle, but a beatific smile on her face. God, she looked so innocent it was sometimes hard to remember all the shit she pulled.

"I'll take her to the locker room for you," Eve offered.

Eve was overstepping a bit, though she couldn't really know it. Eve often took care of his subs after the play was done because they needed more than he was willing to give them. But this was different. He hadn't signed a contract with Charlie outlining what he would and wouldn't do for aftercare. No matter what he wanted, Charlie was his sub for now and he would take care of her. He swung her up into his arms and started walking away.

"Don't you think that was a little rude, Sir?" Charlie asked, but her head was already drifting to his shoulder, her arms around his neck. "Shouldn't you have said something to Eve?"

He thought he'd made himself pretty plain. "I prefer actions to words. Words can be taken different ways. Me walking away told Eve everything she needs to know."

Like to stay out of his relationship with his sub. Except it wasn't a relationship. Not really.

And maybe he'd gotten into topspace. Playing with her, having her trust him, had gotten him a little high, too. She wasn't the only one who'd been hit with a ton of adrenaline. Every time he'd touched the wand to the cotton, a thrill had flared through him as well, and he didn't pretend it would have been that way with any sub. This was his sub, the one who was attuned to his needs and desires, the one who somehow completed him. It was different with the others, and when she was gone he would mourn her all over again, but then he'd always known he would mourn her for the rest of his life.

His body was humming, a healthy lust strumming through his system. Why should he drop her off at the locker room? He'd been honest with her. He'd told her everything that would happen if she got sexual with him again. He'd explained that it wasn't a relationship and never would be. It was sex, and sex between them had always been fucking incredible.

Charlie was a big girl who knew all the rules. Why should he leave her alone? Why shouldn't he take this time and enjoy the fuck out of her body?

"Can I talk now?" Charlie asked in a low voice.

"You're not very good at the whole 'high protocol' thing. We're going to have to work on that." He carried her past the bar toward the privacy rooms. There were three in Sanctum, each nothing more than a tricked-out bedroom with hooks and eyelets in the walls and ceilings for bondage and suspension play. He would have taken his kit with him, but there was no need. This wasn't about discipline. It was about getting off. It was about letting his cock have its way.

"I get the feeling you would keep me in high protocol forever if you could." She cuddled against him, not seeming to care that everyone in the club was watching them.

Ian cared, but there wasn't a hell of a lot he could do about it. They would watch and gossip. It was a part of life. When he wasn't on the receiving end, he was usually watching and commenting, so he accepted it. "We get along better when you don't talk."

"Caveman." She slapped lightly at his chest but there was no real intent behind it. "You know you're kind of a Neanderthal."

Sometimes he envied the bastards. All they had to do to find a mate was locate a pretty female, knock her over the head and drag her away by the hair. No one thought a thing about it. The cavewoman was then expected to keep a clean cave, spit out some cro-mag babies, and make sure there was a nice sabertooth stew on when the hubby came home. He was betting cavewomen hadn't run around becoming international information brokers with assassins after them. And they were probably damn fine at high protocol.

"You're wishing we were cave people, aren't you?" Charlie asked, a little frown on her face.

She had always been damn good at reading him. "It seems like it was probably a good time to be a man."

She groaned. Again, not something he would have had to worry about with someone like Amanda. She would have agreed with everything he said and then turned around and made fun of all his female friends. Charlie, on the other hand, defended his female friends and made fun of him. Somehow, he liked Charlie's way better. Her head came off his chest as she seemed to realize something was wrong. "This doesn't look like the way to the locker room."

"You've never been here before. How do you know?"

She looked over his shoulder. "I made a quick trip around the place when you dropped me off."

Well, naturally she wouldn't stay where he put her. Again, another point for the caveman. Still, he understood what she'd been doing. "How many ways out did you find?"

She would need to know. After so many years of having to survive, Charlie had an ingrained need to know every escape route and possible point of ingress. What Ian had learned from years in the military and CIA, Charlie had learned in childhood.

"Four, but I actually feel pretty safe here. It's kind of like a fort, isn't it? There's the front door, though it's guarded. Is that bulletproof glass in the doors?"

She had a good eye. "Yes. There are only a couple of windows, but they're all tinted and bulletproof." He didn't need people off the street watching his clients and friends playing. Some of his clients included very high rollers. The CIA might have paid shit, but Sanctum made its money back in droves.

"There's the back door with the fire escape. You keep that guarded, too. I could get out the window in the storage room," Charlie said. "But I doubt many people could get in."

That little tiny thing? "It's secure, baby. I don't know that you could get out even if you could get it open."

"Trust me, I could wiggle out. I've gone through smaller places before." She shivered a little.

"Well, I think our Russian assassins probably won't try. They would get stuck and they wouldn't like what I would do to any body part that happened to be inside my building." It would be fun actually. Like that Winnie the Pooh story Sean had read to Carys, only way more bloody and with Pooh Bear screaming in agony.

"See, I always get scared when you get that look on your face."

"I was just thinking happy thoughts. What's the third weak spot?" He was curious. She had a damn better eye for weakness than anyone else he knew.

"The air ducts."

He breathed a little sigh of relief. He wondered where she'd found a spot high enough to get up and check out the air ducts. "They're my escape hatch. That's why they're so big. They're locked, too. I had them custom fitted with gates and electronically protected. The guy who built it for me thought I was fuck-all insane. I need to hire an engineer who won't look at me like I'm crazy. I need a MacGyver, but I worry I would just get another Adam."

Two of him was too much. Why were all the creative thinkers such smartasses?

"So I'll say it again. We're not going to the locker room." This time when she said it, there was a husky, seductive quality to her voice.

It went straight to his dick. He nodded as he walked past the bouncer who took care of the privacy rooms.

"Number three is open, boss," the bouncer said.

It was a busy night at Sanctum if he had to go to three. He'd seen Jesse sneaking back with a pretty brunette named Jana, who liked it rough. Ian wasn't going to mention that to Charlie, though. She'd handled the fact that he'd screwed Amanda pretty well. He wasn't going to give her a rundown of what every sub in the club liked and didn't like. "How do you know I'm not tossing you out on your lovely backside?"

Her smile was sure as she glanced up at him. "Because I was a good girl and let you set me on fire. You owe me."

He did and that was just another reason to let his dick loose. A night of orgasms was one of the ways he liked to balance the equation. The subs gave him what he needed and he gave them what they needed. Oddly enough, most of the time the sex was unsatisfactory for him, a mere biological process.

Maybe that's the way it would be this time, too. Maybe his brain was making too much of the connection to Charlie. He'd been younger, less wise. Maybe it was just the first time he'd met someone he really sparked with. Charlie was different from anyone he'd ever met. Perhaps memory was playing tricks with him and he'd fuck her and she would be just like the other women in his life.

Good luck with that, buddy. Because this is your dick talking and my memory is way longer than that piece of meat you call your brain. That is my pussy and I can't wait to get back in it, so you keep right on thinking as long as you fuck her.

Damn, even his dick had an inner monologue. That was Charlie's fault, too. It was actually a little handy to have someone around he could just blame for everything. Usually he had to spread out the guilt, but Charlie was a one-stop blame shop. Who to blame for his solitary existence? Charlotte Dennis. Why was his left side aching a little? He'd hit a rock when he'd been forced to save Charlie. Why was the price of oil so high? No idea, but he was sure Charlie was somehow behind it.

The door to three was obligingly half open. He was pretty sure the bouncers left them the slightest bit open because most Doms entered with a sub in their arms, and kicking the door open was the most expedient way to get in.

The lights were on a dimmer switch. The whole room was a low amber. He tossed Charlie on the big bed and stared down at her. Her hair looked a fiery red in the low light, her skin a silky pearl. She let the robe fall open, giving him a spectacular view of her breasts.

"Ian, are you going to make love to me?"

Yes, this was why it was so much easier when she wasn't talking. "Charlie, I thought we already discussed this. No, I am not going to make love to you because I don't love you. I am willing to fuck you because you did a good job out there."

Even in the dimness, he could see the way she flushed. "So this is just payback?"

His brain took back over. His dick wanted to lie. His dick wanted to tell her no, baby, this is all about you, wanting to be inside you, needing to take you. But she deserved the truth. "I want you. I won't lie about that, but it only goes that far. We're thrown in together until we can fix your problem, but then I do want you out of my life. I know you think you're good for me, but I consider you responsible for some of the worst events that ever happened to me."

"I can make up for them, Ian."

He shook his head. "I don't think so. But this is your choice. I'll take you back to the locker room if you would rather go there."

She got to her knees, shoving the robe off her shoulders and kneeling proudly in front of him. "I'm not willing to give up, Ian."

There was a piece deep inside him that relaxed. His dick just got harder. His eyes went straight for her bombshell body. Her breasts were a heavenly handful, her waist gracefully flowing into hips he could grip hard while he fucked into her from behind. His brain was starting to shut down, his cock hard and balls already tingling at the thought of shooting off inside her. "Then we both understand what the stakes are."

"Kiss me, Sir."

He almost reached for her, almost covered those luscious lips with his own. He wanted to taste her, to remember what it felt like to breathe with her. But he couldn't. He shook his head shortly. "No. I said no kissing. I meant it. Charlotte, you're forgetting who's in charge. I can't allow that."

He needed to be in control in the bedroom with her. It was the only way to remember that she wasn't his wife. She was the woman who had used him and left him behind to pick up her mess.

That plump bottom lip disappeared behind her teeth as she considered what he'd said. "Then may I kiss you? I won't touch your mouth, Ian. Just let me touch you. You'll still be in control. You can stop me at any time. I just want to get my hands on you so badly."

He knew it was a mistake, but his head inclined slightly and that seemed to be all Charlie needed. She moved forward, her hands pushing at the front of his leather vest, drawing it off him. Her body was so close that he could feel the heat pouring off her. Their chests bumped together, her nipples brushing against his flesh as she pulled the vest around his body with one hand. She laid it on the bed and placed her palms on his chest, her eyes closing as if she could feel his heart beating. She might be able to. It was pounding in his body, blood racing to his cock. He wouldn't be able to think with no blood left in his brain, but he was pretty sure in a minute he wouldn't give a damn about thinking or making good decisions or anything except getting inside her.

He looked down, watching the place where her breasts touched him. Her nipples were hard little nubs, the usually big areolas at their tightest point. Even with the nipples drawn in, they were still bigger than quarters. He would still have to suck hard to get them fully into his mouth.

A shudder went through him as Charlie put her mouth on his throat, her tongue coming out to trace his Adam's apple. She ran that hot little tongue all over his neck, stopping to suck and bite gently. His hands went to her hair, burying themselves in her silk.

She trailed down his chest, and he fought to stay still. He closed his eyes, letting her work her magic. This was what other subs didn't get. They allowed him to service them, but they never tried to give anything back. It wasn't to say the sex wasn't good. It was how he preferred it.

Except with her.

He growled a little when she licked at his left nipple. "Bite me, Charlie. Make me feel it."

He liked a bite of pain, too. Yeah, he didn't accept it, though, from anyone but her. Years had rolled by and he'd denied himself. He wasn't willing to do it tonight. Tonight he was going to get what he needed.

She nipped at him, the pain flaring through him, causing another kick of his favorite drug, adrenaline. She moved to the other side of his chest, giving it the same treatment.

He got a good grip on her hair, forcing her head up. "Don't you hold back on me."

She bit down harder this time and he hissed. Yeah, that would be there tomorrow, a reminder that his woman was strong enough to mark him. He was thinking dangerous thoughts, but he couldn't seem to stop himself.

She moved down his body, alternately licking and biting, making his skin come to life.

He tugged on her hair again when she moved to the floor. "Don't you fucking dare bite me there, baby. You won't like how I bite back."

There was that evil little grin that got his heart thudding. Her fingers worked the ties of his leathers, freeing him. She ran her nose along his cock. "I wouldn't dream of damaging this, Sir. I have plans for it."

She did seem to as she immediately sucked his cockhead into her mouth. He dragged air into his lungs, fighting to keep control. Sex, when done properly, was pure conflict followed by perfect symmetry. Charlie would see if she could get him to blow. He would fight her on it. He could turn the tables on her and keep her on edge for hours until she was begging him.

When the time was right, he would give in to her pleas, to the siren call of that spot between her legs where he'd found his heaven, and then they would be in perfect tune with each other.

He loved every minute of it.

He gripped her hair, knowing she liked the little sting to her scalp. He could smell her arousal, knew she was tangy and ripe, but he wanted to play for a while. He had her for the night. There was no mad rush. He wanted her begging before he gave her his cock.

Her hands were on his ass, her nails sinking into his flesh. Yeah, he fucking dug that, too.

He forced his cock in deeper. Her tongue whirled around him, encasing his dick in slick heat.

Over and over she rolled across his cock, taking him to the edge of his control. He pulled her back, his cock hard and ready to shoot off. But he wasn't playing that way this evening.

"On the bed. Spread your legs." He wanted to taste her again, to relearn how soft she was, how her cream coated his tongue.

Charlie scrambled up, her breath hitching as she moved on the bedding. The dark color of the bedspread contrasted with her skin, making her damn near glow. She was so angelic, but he loved the devil that came out when they played. She spread her legs wide, with no self-consciousness, only a deep, obvious willingness to be pleasured.

He took her ankles in his hands. Despite the fact that Charlie wasn't a tiny thing, compared to him she was practically petite. He loved the way he could circle her ankle and make a fist around it. He could master her, but it took more than mere strength to get Charlie to open up. It took trust and pleasure.

She didn't fight him when he pushed her feet up, bending her legs at the knees and making a place for himself there. She simply allowed him to move her where he wanted.

Damn but he liked the laser thing. He covered her pussy with his palm, enjoying the silky smooth feel of the skin. Though he would have preferred to select the technician, to make sure it was safe, he couldn't argue with the outcome.

He knew there was something wrong with that line of thought, but he didn't really care. His knees hit the floor and he dragged her until her ass was at the edge of the bed, her pussy right in front of his face.

So pretty. It was a flower that opened only for him. The petals were soft and moist. It was an edible flower and like all flowers, it needed love and affection. And a really good tonguing.

"You're killing me, Ian. Can't you just get on with it?" Charlie asked.

He lightly slapped at her clit. "Hush. I'm looking at my pussy. This pussy is mine for tonight, and I'll do exactly what I want to do with it. If I want to sit here and stare at it, I will."

Because he liked to look at it. He especially liked how pink and puffy her labia was, glistening from her arousal. He barely stroked a finger across it, but Charlie nearly jumped.

Keeping her on edge was fun. It was so much easier to hold himself back when he knew just how much it was killing her.

Sometimes he was a dick, but he was perfectly comfortable with that. He nosed her pussy, letting her scent fill his senses. "Was there something you wanted, baby?"

She whimpered, a sound that would have gotten him hard if he couldn't already pound nails. "You know what I want."

He reached up, sliding his fingers through her labia up

to the little jewel of her clit. That pearl was practically throbbing, but he wasn't ready to let her off the hook just yet. No way. He pinched her, a nasty little tweak to her pink parts. Charlie's body damn near came off the bed.

"Oh, god," she screamed out, a fresh pulse of arousal coating her flesh.

"That's not the way to ask for it, love."

Her legs stayed where he'd put them, but she was shaking. "Please, Ian."

Another hard twist. "What did you call me?"

"Sir. Oh, please, please, Sir."

"Master in the bedroom, Charlie. Only here." He wanted to hear the word from her lips. He'd never been anyone else's Master. Only Sir because he'd never collared another female. Never even wanted to. He would hear his title from her when they were alone and he was inside her.

She sighed, as though his words had given her the pleasure she was seeking. "Master. My Master. Please, please kiss my pussy."

He placed a very chaste peck right over her clit. "There you go."

Her head was up, her eyes narrowing. "Damn it, Ian, you know that isn't what I meant."

He flipped her over, neatly displacing her so her backside was available to him. He didn't give a shit how pink it was. If she didn't stop cursing him, it was going to be red. He laid five quick, hard slaps to the fleshiest part of her ass before flipping her back over. "Do you want me to clamp you?"

He could tie her down and force clamps on her breasts, little alligator clamps to bite down on those pretty nipples. He could place a clit clamp on her, too. He'd seen one with a little bell attached and then he would just keep her naked and he'd always know exactly where she was.

He wondered briefly if there was a piercing with a bell on it. Harder to remove. Maybe if he'd had her pierced before he wouldn't have lost her the first time. He would have just followed the sound of her jingling clit.

"Master, I promise I'll be so good. Please don't do whatever you're thinking about right now." Charlie's eyes had gone wide.

He shoved her legs open again, spreading his palms across her soft thighs. "If you don't stop misbehaving, you're in for a very long night. I had planned to fuck you a couple of times, but if you prefer, we can spend that time on discipline instead. You seem to need it."

Her head shook. "No, Master. No, please. I promise to be a very proper sub for the rest of the night."

He let his mouth hover right over her pussy, giving her his heat, letting her feel the vibration of his words. "You couldn't behave properly to save your life, pet."

Thank god for that. Otherwise, he wouldn't have the pleasure of disciplining her.

"Please, Master." Her voice was breathless, her skin flushed to a lovely shade of pink. "Please lick me. Please play with me. Please do whatever you desire. I'm yours."

She was his toy, his sweet little fuck toy. He could do anything he wanted with her, and he was pretty fucking sure he was the only one to really play with this particular toy. Pretty sure. "Tell me again how many men you've had since me. I want the truth, Charlie."

"None. Not a single one, Master. I don't blame you. You didn't know I was alive, but I knew damn well you were. I know who I belong to. I've known it for years. All this time, I've tried to follow your rules."

"Tried?" He let his nose play through her labia. He wouldn't mind waking up every morning and running his nose through her pussy so he could smell her all day.

"Yes, Master. I tried, but I masturbated a few times. I couldn't stop myself. I would get too lonely and I would think of you and I would touch myself. I pretended it was you."

He thought about her lying in bed in the dark, her fingers working in and out of her cunt, her little thumb rubbing against her clit. "Show me."

Reaching up, he grasped her left hand, pulling it down her body to cover her pussy.

Her fingers slid through the juice there, two slipping inside past her labia, the heel of her palm against her clit.

He watched as she moved against her hand, fascinated by the way her fingers drove deep and pulled back.

"Don't come yet."

She whimpered again but didn't argue with him. She kept up the pace, fucking herself with her fingers, her hips rocking with a sweet rhythm.

When he was sure she couldn't take another second, he gripped her hand, pulling it out of her cunt and to his mouth. He sucked those fingers inside. His tongue slid around gathering every bit of cream he could find. She tasted so fucking good. He'd never forgotten that taste, never lost the sweetness of it in his mind. Yeah, this part hadn't been a false memory. None of it had been false. He only ever felt this alive when he was with her.

He laid her hand back down. "Work your little clit, baby. I'll take care of the rest."

"Please come inside me, Master." She was staring at him, her eyes wide as she offered herself to him.

This seemed to be a new Charlotte, a more open Charlie. The Charlie he'd always known was right beneath her surface.

He spread her labia with his fingers and let one forage

into her pussy.

He worked one finger in, massaging her flesh. He cupped her pussy, gently fucking in and out, opening her up. He added a second finger as she relaxed and she started moving in time with his fingers. This was the one place they were always in sync.

"You have my permission. Come all over my hand. Let me hear you." He curled his fingers up, searching for that sweet spot that always got her screaming. She was panting, not holding back. She fucked his fingers with the vigor of a woman long denied.

"Yes, Master. Oh, it feels so good." She thrust down, shoving his fingers in deep as she worked her clit.

"Take your hand away." He wanted to be the only thing making her come. The minute she removed her hand, he leaned over and sucked her clit into his mouth, her unique flavor filling him.

Charlie screamed, and he felt her muscles clamping down on him as she came, juices flowing all around him.

He licked her clit as she came down and then removed his hand, finally giving himself permission to do what he'd wanted to do from the moment the door had closed behind them. He shoved his tongue up her pussy and started to make a meal of her. He licked and sucked and ate his fill.

And wondered if this was a meal he just couldn't get enough of.

* * * *

Charlie bit back another cry as Ian's tongue foraged deep inside her. So long. She'd waited so long to feel him again that this was almost a sensory overload. It was almost too much to handle, but she forced herself to lie still, to give her sweet Master everything he wanted.

He sucked at her labia, pulling first one side into his mouth and then the other before plunging deep again. His tongue seemed to dance inside her, touching her in places that hadn't been alive since the last time he'd made love to her.

And it was love. He could fight it all he wanted, but there was no way this feeling wasn't love. It was a magnificent obsession and it was the best sex ever, but it was both of those things because it was grounded in love.

The orgasm she'd just had was still thrumming through her when another started to build. Her Master seemed interested in reminding her just how well her body responded to him.

Over and over again, he tongue fucked her, spearing her in long drives before moving up to suckle her clit. When he opened his mouth, he could cover her whole pussy as though the Big Bad Wolf had come to make a feast of her. She started to shake and moan when he suddenly sat up.

"No more coming, baby. Not until I'm inside you. Now stay that way. Don't you move or I'll spank you again." He stood up.

She'd been so close and now she was cold. She was spread out for him, but the chill in the air was just another sensation to be had, one that would go away the minute he covered her again.

Ian shoved his leathers down and off, kicking his boots from his feet at the same time. His magnificent cock came into view. She'd never seen one bigger, might run if she did because he could do some damage with that massive weapon.

He stared down at her. The light from the seemingly hidden source cast him in harsh relief, making his features harder, more masculine. He was all male, and she would never completely understand what drove him. She would never be able to fathom exactly why he'd chosen her, why she was the one who could take that masculinity and soften it just enough that he wasn't always alone. She couldn't understand it, but she would fight for her rights. She was his natural mate. She'd known it from the moment he'd taken her.

That had been the first night she'd been complete. She'd been more than just Charlotte Denisovitch, victim and pawn. She'd been whole and real and someone new and shiny.

That moment couldn't have been lost forever.

It couldn't have been something he hadn't shared with her. But it did seem to be something he feared sharing again.

"Is something wrong, Master?" She kept her voice quiet, free from emotion. "Did I move? Should I present my poor backside again?"

A little smile curled his lips up. Yes, that was what she needed. "No, Charlie, for once, you're behaving. Was it hard not to come?"

Ah, the dirty talk. He craved it. He loved to force her to say dirty stuff. "Yes, Master."

He stroked his cock but made no move to cover her. He just stared down, but there was a slightly softer look on his face now. "Why was it so hard? Tell me about it."

Because he wanted to hear just how good he was. Vain man. "Because your fingers felt so good. They were big inside me, but not anywhere as big as that cock of yours."

"All these years, you just jacked off thinking about me?" There was a challenge in that question, but it was one she could match.

"I don't think I would call it jacking off. I think that's more a male thing. I masturbated thinking about you. I tried to hold off, but the dreams would get to me. I would dream and you would be there, touching me, holding me down and having your way with me. You would take me any way you wanted, anywhere you wanted, and I was helpless to do anything to stop you."

Yeah, that was doing something for him. If it was possible, she thought his cock hardened further. "Because I tied you down?"

"Because I wanted you so badly I would do anything to have you, Master. Anything to please you."

"Would you?"

"Yes." She hadn't worked her ass off for five years, dodging bullets along the way, to deny him sexually. "Anything you want, my Master."

She could make him the promise because she trusted the man with her life. He'd never brought her any pain that hadn't enhanced her pleasure. He'd never taken her to any place but pure paradise when it came to making love.

"I'm clean, Charlie. I just had a physical."

He was really going to fuck her. God, how long had she waited? "I'm perfectly clean, too. No sex since you. I swear my fingers don't have any STDs. I thought about buying a vibrator once, but I figured you might object."

She'd found one online that was just shy of his size. She'd planned on calling it Ian, but she'd been a little afraid she might end up being way too attached to an object.

"No one is using a vibrator on you but me," he said, proving her first instinct right. "I mean it. While I'm topping you, I control the orgasms. If I catch you playing with a pocket rocket, you won't come for a very long time. Now, pay attention. Are you on birth control?" The question came out of his mouth in a low growl.

It was right there on the tip of her tongue to tell him yes. She'd meant to start, but a million things had to be taken care of and she'd let that little detail slip away. She'd needed time to recuperate from her gunshot wound and then she didn't want to waste another minute before she got back to Ian. And there had been a little notion in the back of her head that everything might go better than expected and he might not want her on birth control. It had been a stupid idea, but it now left her with a choice.

She could tell him yes and he would take her without anything between them. When she'd come to him the first time, she'd known she would sleep with him, known that was her job. Before the op, she'd taken a shot promised to protect her from pregnancy for three months. He would believe her. He would think she just stayed on it all the time. If she got pregnant, he couldn't leave her behind. He would have to keep her. A child could bind them together, could make it impossible for them to really be apart.

"I'm not, Master. You should wear a condom." She couldn't lie to him. Not ever again. She owed him, and she wouldn't keep him with another set of lies.

He cursed and walked to the small wardrobe against the side of the west wall. He drew it open, revealing that there weren't clothes in this particular closet. There were boxes of toys and restraints, bottles of lube and rows of condoms. He tore one free and sheathed his dick, grabbing a bottle of lube before closing the door again.

"If we're together for any amount of time, I want you on birth control, Charlie. I won't take any chances." He lubed up his cock, his hand running along it in long, hard passes.

He wouldn't take the chance that she would get pregnant. The words shouldn't hurt. She knew it was utterly stupid to get pregnant at this point. There were way too many problems, but hearing him reject the idea made her ache. She hadn't told him that when she dreamed, yes, she dreamed of him inside her, but she also dreamed about cuddling up to him, their baby in his arms. She dreamed of a life with him.

"Anything I want, Charlie?" The challenge was back in his voice, in his arrogant stance.

"Yes, Master."

"On all fours." He indicated that she should stay on the bed.

Charlie flipped over, doing his bidding and getting to her hands and knees. He could control the penetration better this way. It was a little lie she told herself. She felt the bed move as he placed himself behind her. A long sigh came out of his mouth, and his hands ran along her spine down to her backside.

"God, you have the most beautiful ass, baby." He cupped her, groaning his appreciation before letting his hands slide up to touch her dangling breasts. "And these. These are beautiful tits."

She hated them sometimes. They were too big to fit into the pretty designer clothes women loved to wear, but when Ian looked at her and praised them, she couldn't help but feel sexy. He'd given her a confidence she never wanted to lose. "They're yours, Master. All yours. Would you like to fuck them?"

She knew exactly what dirty talk did to him.

"God, you're going to kill me," he whispered and then he was gone, rearing back to his knees. "Look up. Watch us in the mirror."

She turned her head and sure enough, the south wall was mirrored from floor to ceiling. Ian's big body loomed behind and over hers. He gripped her hips, pulling her closer to him so that her ass was right against his hips, and she couldn't tell where she ended and he began.

"You watch and tell me that I don't have the most beautiful, fuckable sub in this club." He leaned back, taking his cock in hand and placing it at her entrance. The broad head started to breach her, and she gasped at the sensation. He was so fucking big and it had been so long. Pressure built as he pressed his way in.

She watched in the mirror as he started to work his dick inside her, thrusting carefully in small motions. She could see the toll it took on him. His face was in a tight line, his every movement a testament to discipline. Over and over he foraged in, gaining ground before retreating to start again.

Charlie relaxed, giving him everything. He was so careful with her, but she prayed that soon he would let go. She could handle it. She wanted his passion.

"Fuck, you're so tight, baby." His skin flushed with the effort of holding back.

"You feel so good, Master." She wiggled her ass a little, letting him know she could handle more.

His hands gripped her hips. "You want it, don't you? You don't want me to play around. You don't care how tight you are. You want some cock, don't you, baby? You need a big stiff cock inside you."

"Yes." She was practicing his favorite word tonight.

He slapped at her ass. "Whose cock do you need?"

"Yours, Master. I only need yours." She only wanted his. In her whole life, she'd only really wanted one man.

"Then I'll give it to you. Don't you dare keep your mouth shut now. You tell me if it hurts. You tell me if it feels good." He surged in.

Pressure and tension flooded her system. She was so damn full. He was everywhere, pressing inside until she'd taken him to the root, and she wouldn't have it any other way. "I'm fine, Ian."

"That's not what I want to hear." One hand found its way around her hip, settling over her clit, his finger pressing down. He started making little circles. "I'm not moving again until you're better than fine."

He was pulsing inside her. She could feel how close to the edge he was, but he still held off because he wouldn't hurt her. Not physically.

Rubbing her clit, his hips held against her ass, Charlie watched him in the mirror. His face was so serious, his mouth turned down as he settled in to his task. He was so beautiful in the amber light that she wanted nothing more than to turn around so she could see his face, but she only had the mirror to watch him in.

A little gasp tore from her throat as pleasure started to crowd out the tension.

"Ian, Master, please," she begged. She needed him to move. She needed to feel him sliding deep inside her. The connection had been missing for so long. She couldn't go another moment without it.

He pulled on her hips, forcing himself in and then moving back out, a slow drag over her flesh. "This is definitely going to please your Master."

Charlie watched in the mirror as Ian's head fell back and he plunged deep, fucking her like she wanted to be taken, hard and rough and so possessive she could barely stand it. When he fucked her, she was the only woman in the world. Ian's hips rocked back and forth, his cock diving deep each time.

She moved in time with him, finding a perfect rhythm. Her breasts bounced, her hair going wild, but she was lost in the feeling. He thrust in and out, deep and hard, finding her sweet spot and dragging his cock over it again and again until the pleasure rocked through her system and she shouted out his name as she came.

"Ian!" Her hands curled into the bedspread because his thrusts were so powerful he could push her off the bed if she didn't hold her own.

Hearing his name seemed to break something in him. He threw an arm around her waist and hoisted her up so her back covered his front, his face in her hair. "Say it again. Tell me who you belong to, sub."

He forced her knees even wider and fucked her from behind, his cock never losing the beat.

"You. I belong to you. I belong to Ian." It was nothing less than the truth. She wanted his cock, his collar, his ring, his future.

"Damn fucking straight." He surged into her, one arm around her waist, the other cupping her breast as he shook against her. He held her tight, his cock pumping out his orgasm as he shuddered against her. His cheek moved against hers. She could feel the heat of his mouth on her face, sweet little kisses on her cheek. Just for the briefest of moments she thought he would fuse their mouths together. She turned her face up, wanting that connection again. Even as pleasure thrummed through her body, she needed more of him.

He let go and moved away from her.

Charlie dropped to her stomach, the soft bedding catching her fall as Ian hopped off the bed. He got up, stretching and shaking his head like he was clearing it from something.

She tried to catch her breath. "Ian, what's wrong?"

She watched him in the mirror, her heart falling. All that passion he'd offered her moments before was gone.

His face was expressionless as he peeled the condom off, tying it neatly. "You need to get to the locker room, shower, and get dressed. We're meeting Alex and Eve in forty-five minutes. Make sure your sister is ready, too."

She turned, pushing herself up. "Ian?"

"You need to hurry. I don't want it to get too late before we head back to my place. Apparently we have to drive by Alex's new house because the contractors fucked something up. That's what he gets for hiring the lowest bidder. I told him, but he never listens to me. So get moving." He started toward what looked to be a small bathroom.

He was talking like it was perfectly normal to fuck a girl silly and then complain about his best friend's hiring practices. He was behaving like absolutely nothing amazing had just happened. Now she was cold again.

She pulled at the robe she'd tossed aside. "Ian, what's wrong? Shouldn't we talk about it?"

She tried not to, but her eyes were filling with tears.

"Nothing's wrong, Charlie, and there's absolutely nothing to talk about. I'm just done with sex, and I have things I have to do tonight. Unfortunately you're tied to me right now so you have things to do, too. Where I go, you go, so get a move on." He walked into the bathroom.

"Why are you being so cold?" It didn't compute. She couldn't wrap her mind around it. He'd been so hot just seconds before. She'd been right there with him. Their bodies had been pressed together, and she would have sworn he felt everything she did. He'd held her so tight, like she was the most precious thing in the world and he couldn't let her go. It had been like those five years between them melted away and they were back together, back when they were just discovering each other.

He stepped back out, his hands on those sculpted hips. "I'm not being cold, Charlie. I'm done. This is how I am after I'm done with sex. I told you you wouldn't like it.

This is how it is now. You said you didn't care so I took you at your word."

"I don't understand." She pushed her hair back, looking up at him.

"You don't understand what, baby? That a guy can say and do things he doesn't really mean when he's trying to get his dick in you? I kind of thought you were more worldly than that."

She wasn't stupid. She knew that. She just didn't expect it from him. He'd always been her safe place. "So it was just sex."

He sighed. "Yeah, I think I told you that. I also mentioned that it would be my way, all my way, or we wouldn't be anything at all. So you can go to the locker room and follow my instructions or we can be done. I'll shower here. I'll meet you in the lobby."

She sat there, trying to process the words. She'd been so sure. She'd known that once they'd made love again, he would know. He would know that she was his wife and everything would be fine as long as they were together.

The world was a watery mess, and she caught a glimpse of herself in the mirror.

Her hair was messed up, her body so much bigger than what she saw in her head. It was one of those times when she knew she had to make a decision to be all right with herself, but she just couldn't when he was staring at her like she was a piece of meat. He'd told her she was hot, fuckable, but she sure didn't look that way now. Of course, he'd also admitted that he would lie to get between her legs. Just like other guys.

"I told you how it would be," he said softly. But the cold look was still in his eyes.

She pulled the robe on, closing it tightly around herself. "Yes, you did."

He'd been far more honest than she'd been when they first met. And if he was treating her like a piece of meat it was because she'd offered herself up like one. She'd been so desperate to get back to the one place she'd been happy.

What if that had been an illusion?

He stood staring at her as she started for the door. He didn't move to open it for her. She was sure he wouldn't stop it from hitting her on the ass as she left either.

Had he been an illusion, too? For years he'd been her ideal man. It wasn't that she really thought he was perfect. It was just that she loved his imperfections, too. He'd been the first man to treat her with any kindness, the first to bring her pleasure of any kind. He'd told her she was pretty and smart and she'd taken that as love.

"Charlie?"

She sniffled, not willing to face him. "Do you think any of it was real?"

He was silent.

She walked out the door. He'd given her his answer. Now she had to find her own.

Chapter Nine

Ian kept his hands steady on the wheel, his eyes on the road, but that wasn't what he was seeing. He kept seeing those tears in her eyes as she pulled the robe around her, hiding her body. Somehow he'd expected her to throw him her middle finger and walk through the club naked. He hadn't expected her to turn in on herself, to look so fucking fragile. Charlie wasn't fragile. She didn't take crap from anyone.

Except him.

"Take a right at the next stop sign." Alex sat beside him in the big SUV. "You know I wouldn't have to give you directions if you had just let me drive my own damn car."

Ian turned at the proper time. He didn't reply to Alex. It was one of those times when words were meaningless.

All three women were in the back. Charlotte didn't seem to have a problem with high protocol now. She'd been perfectly silent, her eyes on the world outside the window. Those eyes hadn't sought him out once since the moment she realized he was serious about the "just sex" thing.

Do you think any of it was real?

Her question was playing in his head. It had been real. Every fucking second had been real for him. He'd loved her. He just didn't trust himself to try it again. He couldn't put himself through losing her a second time. He couldn't trust her at all.

Could he?

Revenge should be so much fucking sweeter. He should be sitting here in Alex's dad car that barely did sixty-five on the freeway thinking about how much fun it was to show Charlie exactly how he felt. But revenge seemed hollow when all he wanted to do was hug the person he was avenging himself on until he could get her to smile again. It kind of made the whole fucking effort pointless when he felt like a shitbag because his revenge plans worked.

"Don't miss the next turnoff. It can be hard to see in the dark. Again, a good reason for me to drive," Alex said.

"Alex." Eve had a way of making her husband's name—or any name—a perfect admonition.

"I'll have you playing with your curtains in no time at all." His night vision was perfect. Alex had to be getting old if he thought he couldn't see that turnoff.

"It's not curtains. It's countertops. The contractor wants to make sure they're the right ones before they install them tomorrow," Alex explained. "The invoice says it's our soapstone, but the contractor thinks it's the wrong color."

Ian shook his head. There was no way to comprehend the changes that had come over his best friend since he'd remarried Eve. "What the fuck is soapstone? Why do you care about countertops? What is wrong with you, man? You're dragging us around in the middle of the night over home décor. When did you become Martha Stewart?"

Alex let his head fall to the side window, bashing it a couple of times before he sat back up. "Well, we all need a hobby, asshole, and you took listening to Guns N' Roses and drinking Scotch so I was left with fucking soapstone countertops, which are, according to our designer, the very latest in home design and which I can very likely manage to shove up your ass if you don't stop being an arrogant prick."

"Alex, I thought we were going to be patient with him," Eve said in a very gratingly calm voice.

Alex turned to look at his wife. "He's driving my goddamn car because he's such a control freak he can't let anyone else drive."

Eve's hand came around the headrest, resting on Alex's shoulder, and he settled down.

It sucked because Alex seemed just about ready to start a fight and that would have been so much better than the silence that descended on the SUV again. It might do him some good to pull the car over and trade some punches. Ian glanced up at the rearview mirror. It was dark, but he could get a glimpse of her face. He wasn't used to Charlie being so silent or so withdrawn. She was confident, bold, his match in most ways, but now she had gone someplace deep inside herself and he didn't like it. She was in the car, but her head was somewhere he couldn't touch her. It was perverse. He knew he'd been the one to send her to that place, but it bugged the shit out of him. He would rather she yelled at him and called him a bastard to this silent sorrow.

"It's the last house on the left," Alex explained. "Just pull in the driveway and Eve and I will run inside."

And leave him out here with Charlie? Probably not a good idea. Sure, Chelsea was here too, but he'd already proven he didn't have a lot of discretion when it came to

Charlie.

What he wouldn't tell her was he'd run to the bathroom like a scared five-year-old because his first instinct had been to lie in bed with her all night long. He'd forced her to do it doggie style because he didn't trust himself not to kiss her. Because the minute he'd gotten her naked and alone, all he'd wanted to do was get inside her and stay there for hours and hours until he was tired and he could wrap himself around her and sleep with her in his arms.

He pulled the car into the driveway. Alex and Eve's house was nice. Big. It looked like the perfect place to spit out a couple of rug rats and grow old. It was also covered with trees and shit and they were too close to the house. What was he thinking?

"Stay here." He turned off the ignition and reached for his SIG.

"What's wrong?" Alex asked, reaching for his own and checking the clip. "Eve, get your head down. All of you."

"He's worried about the trees," Charlie said in a monotone. "He thinks assassins will be hiding in the trees and they'll drop down on us, and he's wondering why you picked a place where so many people could lay in wait to kill you. I think it's pretty. I like the trees."

"The trees help cut down on electricity bills," Alex said, shaking his head. "We weren't thinking that someone would hide an army in the live oaks."

"Which just proves that you're losing it, my friend. I bet you don't even have perimeter sensors set up." He carefully opened the door, checking the trees in front of him for any movement.

"I haven't even moved in yet." Alex proved he could still move quietly. Ian heard the quiet snick of the passenger door closing and then Alex was beside him, his eyes watching their six.

They moved together like the team they'd been for the last five years. Back to back, they checked the yard.

"I can't exactly set up motion detectors and freaking laser rays. I would fry every poodle and stray cat in the neighborhood, not to mention the out-past-curfew teens."

"It would teach 'em to not be out past curfew." He didn't get what the problem was. A little laser never hurt anyone. Much.

"You're demented. And what the fuck happened to Charlotte? I thought things were looking up when you carried her off to the privacy rooms."

Ian turned, checking the ground for any signs of disturbance. Alex moved cleanly, never giving up his back.

"Charlotte is just realizing that I won't be as easy to manipulate as last time." He relaxed a little. There was nothing out in the yard. He didn't like the neighborhood they'd driven through. There were too many people, too many cars parked along the street that might or might not belong to residents. How was he supposed to properly assess risk in an area like this? He had to hope Alex had at least remembered to triple bolt the doors and install a decent security system. "I think we're clear."

Alex stepped back, shaking his head. "Well, you'll be fun at the housewarming party. Eve, come on. We're not going to be murdered in the front yard. Let's go see how much the contractors fucked up."

Eve hopped out of the SUV, straightening her skirt.

"Come on, Charlie, Chelsea. Let's go find out what the fuck soapstone looks like." He wasn't about to stand out here in the middle of the night with nothing but a SIG between him and however many Russians were trying to kill Charlie. God, he hoped Liam caught at least one of the fuckers. Maybe these assassins were like Alex and held teas to talk about each other's love lives. Then all Ian had to do was squeeze the fucker's balls until he gave up how many of them there were.

Charlie eased out of the seat, followed by her sister. She didn't look around, simply followed him as Alex unlocked the door and led them inside.

"Seriously? You have one lock?"

"You know what, buddy, when I actually move in here, I'll let you paranoid out the whole house." Alex opened the door and let Eve in.

Ian watched as Charlie walked by him. Her head was up, but there was a vacantness to her eyes that he didn't like. She was somewhere else and there was a wall between them. He couldn't see it, but he could feel that it was there. It was stupid because a wall between them was exactly what he needed, and yet it rankled. It was getting under his skin. His instincts were to tear that fucking wall down the same way he'd wanted to rip off the robe she'd worn around her like a bit of body armor. After they'd had sex, she'd stood in the doorway of the privacy room looking torn apart and fragile and he'd wanted to take away her only bit of protection from him.

It wasn't fair or reasonable, and logic seemed to have utterly fled his abilities, but then he'd never been able to think around her.

So why the hell was he carting her back to his place and where the hell did he think she was going to sleep? Was he going to shove her ass on the couch?

"I like the archways," Chelsea said as she walked through the foyer.

Eve smiled. "They used to be square, but I think the arches really open the place up."

"They left their tools out again, Eve. I swear, I'm going to fire these guys. Why is there a nail gun sitting in the middle of my kitchen? That's a concrete nail gun. Do you know what that can do to a person?" Alex asked, his irritation plain even from a room away. "It's lucky we stayed in town since the contractor looks like an idiot. We're going to have a long talk tomorrow."

Charlie glanced up, but nothing on her face changed. She just moved into the living room where Alex had turned on the lights. Eve disappeared from view, too. Chelsea didn't. She waited until everyone had moved on and then turned on Ian.

"What did you do?"

It seemed to be the question everyone was asking today. "I believe that's none of your business. If your sister wants to talk to you about her sex life, then that's up to her, but I'm not feeling chatty right now."

"You broke her, you motherfucking, son-of-a-bitch, turdwad asshole." Baby sis had a potty mouth, and she didn't mind getting in his face. Well, she would be in his face if she had another foot of height on her.

"I didn't break her. I gave her exactly what she wanted." Except she did seem a bit broken and sometimes, when she thought he wasn't watching her, he saw how lost she looked.

"She has spent five years with one goal and one goal only. Getting back to you. I told her you weren't worth it, but she wouldn't listen to me. She's in love with you. She's never been in love with anyone. Do you think I haven't thrown men at her for years trying to get her to see that you're just like the rest of them?"

He'd treated her like shit, so he probably was like the rest of them. Her father's home likely hadn't been the best place to meet a nice guy. "Do you want me to go down on bended knee and beg her forgiveness? Because that ain't going to happen."

If he went down on one knee, he'd try to get lower. He hadn't spent enough time on her pussy. God, he already wanted her again. He'd wanted her about three seconds after he'd come. Another reason he'd pulled away.

He hadn't wanted to put on that fucking piece of latex. It had been there in his brain, a little whisper that told him if he just let nature take its course, he would have to keep her. If he kept her then she would have to toe the line. She would have to give up all the criminal shit and become the woman he was sure she could be. All he had to do was let a couple of swimmers loose and he would have Charlie bound to him forever.

Or he would at least have a piece of her when she left him again because there was no way he would ever be separated from his kid. Thirty-nine years of being sure he would die childless and the thought of a kiddo with her eyes and her smile had him acting like Papa Bear.

"I want you to let her go." Chelsea kept her voice low.

"I've been trying to do that since the minute she walked back in," Ian shot back. "She doesn't seem keen on leaving."

"You know what, I should hug you for being the ass I knew you had to be. Thank you, Ian Taggart, for not being able to see how lovable she is. And know this, if you hurt her again, I know how to crucify a man in three keystrokes. You think she was the one who got you on a no-fly list? That was me. I can do way worse, and I won't hesitate. When this is over, she'll leave with me. It's my turn to take care of her and that means getting rid of you."

Chelsea turned and shuffled off.

Ian thought about strangling her. He could probably

do it with one hand. She was the reason Charlie had betrayed him in the first place.

Yep, he was so far gone, he was thinking about killing a girl who had probably seen more violence in her life than he had.

But something about her questioning his rights to Charlie really got his gut rolling.

The minute he'd seen her again, his possessive asshole had risen right back to the surface. He'd only ever felt that way about one woman. Hell, he'd been possessive of her when he'd thought she was dead. He'd kept her memory deep inside him, sharing only the smallest bits of her with his best friend and only to explain why once a year he went on a bender.

Ian followed Chelsea through the archway and into the great room. Charlie was looking at the floors saying something about the finish on them.

She was into this house shit? The way she moved, he would think she wouldn't care.

Unless she dreamed about putting down roots, about being able to pick out finishes and countertops and fucking paint for the kitchen because she wanted a house that was a home.

He hadn't picked out anything on his own except the security system. He'd just left it all the way the last owners had wanted it. He never really thought about it, but he actually didn't like it all that much. The playroom. Yeah, he'd picked out the stuff for the private playroom. So, great, his "home" was personalized with hooks and suspension gear and a really well-made spanking bench.

And he kind of liked the soapstone or whatever was on the countertop. It wasn't ugly and it looked like it was just the right height to fuck Charlie on.

She shut down the minute he came in the room, that

hint of a smile on her face gone in a flash. Well, he'd asked for it.

Chelsea was giving him the good old stink eye. She was likely trying to figure out how to fuck him up real good over the Internet.

He went to the glass doors leading out to what looked like a porch and a big backyard that hadn't been fenced in yet. Yeah, glass doors from ceiling to floor was such a great idea. If Alex was trying to invite someone to kill him, he was doing a damn good job.

A little red light flashed through the night, finding its way right over Ian's heart. Motherfucker. The invitation had been received and accepted.

"Take cover!" He dove to the left just as a high-pitched ping shattered those gorgeous glass windows Alex had probably just had installed.

Hitting the floor, he rolled past what looked like the rest of a stack of that flooring Charlie seemed to love so much. "Charlotte, get the fuck down. Get behind the counter and don't you move."

The great room separated them, and he damn near panicked that he wasn't there to cover her body with his. He took his eyes off the door just long enough to watch her pulling her sister down, taking a protective position over Chelsea.

Alex had his back flat against the wall, his gun up, right beside those glass doors. He hit the lights, sending the room into darkness, taking away the sniper's advantage. Unless he had night vision. Which he probably had if he was halfway decent. *Fuck.* He knew he should just wear a pair around his neck, but Grace had convinced him he would look like a douchebag. He was damn straight keeping a set in the car from now on. Everyone on the team would. He would make it a rule.

"How many?" Alex asked.

Eve moved quietly, not panicking at all, over to where Charlie huddled with her sister.

Ian stared out. "I don't know. One, I suspect, since that was how many little red lasers got pointed at my chest. How do you feel about lasers now, Alex? You worried about kitty cats?"

"Fine." Alex shot the word his way. "I'll install lasers and be the mean old man at the end of the block who murders everyone's pets. How are we getting the women out of here?"

"We kill the bad guys and then we can get the girls out." He really wasn't sure there was another way. Unlike the earlier attempt, this asswipe had them pretty well pinned down. If Ian was the operative, he wouldn't give up in this case. He would move positions and wait for the target to come out of hiding. He really wasn't sure how many of them there were. If he took them out the front, they would be easy targets if the fucker had a partner or was a really fine sprinter.

"Call the police," Eve said. "I'll get to my cell."

"No," Ian shot back. "We call the police and she goes on their records. No police."

"Call the police, Eve. If someone locks me up, then so be it. I'm not getting everyone else killed," Charlie said. "The sirens should scare him away for now."

What was she thinking? "Don't you dare pick up that phone. She won't just get carted off to jail. She'll go someplace where no one will see her again. Do you understand me, Eve?"

Eve nodded and didn't make another move for her purse.

Unfortunately, Charlie had her own purse. She reached in.

Now she decided to be self-sacrificing? "Charlotte Marie Dennis, I swear to god, I will make sure you never sit down again if you dial that phone."

"Ian, this is serious. I can't let other people die for me." She started to move her finger across the screen.

Chelsea reached up, grabbed her sister's phone, and before Charlie could stop her, lobbed it across the room.

"Damn it, Chelsea."

But he was on Chelsea's side this time. And he had to deal with this fucker because Charlie was his responsibility. "Give me cover fire."

"Ian?" Alex started. "What the fuck are you going to do?"

He was going to do something stupid, and he didn't have time to argue about it. The glass had shattered into neat little pieces all over Alex's brand new floors. Ian jumped over the glass and out into the yard.

He heard Alex curse and then lay out a quick pattern of gunfire. Alex's lot was at the end of the street in a sprawling, wealthy neighborhood. It looked like his closest neighbors were a quarter mile away, but the cops could still show if someone was awakened by gunfire.

He was so sick of this. Usually he only had to deal with one attempt on his life a day, but Charlie just had to raise the stakes. Given where he'd been standing and the trajectory of that red laser, the man had to be in the woods behind Alex's house.

Ian ran to the left of where he suspected the shooter had been hiding.

Sure enough, he felt something ping by his shoulder, grazing him like a near miss with a lightning bolt. Awesome, now he was bleeding. His night was turning into a clusterfuck.

He changed course, moving behind the big trees,

using them as cover. He placed his back against one and focused on the sounds around him. His sight wouldn't do him as much good as his hearing. It was a new moon, and Alex had to pick a house that didn't have street lamps.

He stilled himself, slowing his heart rate. There was no need for adrenaline here. This wasn't fun. This was a job, and he would do it quietly and efficiently. Silence. He heard the wind and someone breathing. His opponent wasn't as professional as he should be. His adrenaline was up. He was dragging air in his lungs and choosing between fight and flight.

Ian could have told him the decision had been made the minute he took that shot.

The ground underneath his feet was hard, and he had no doubt that the minute he moved, something would shift. But that meant the douchebag assassin would make some noise, too.

Ian held his position, trusting Alex to keep the women safe and Charlie in line.

No sound except the idiot's breathing, and he couldn't pinpoint exactly where that was coming from. Behind him and to his left, he couldn't be sure where to fire, so he held. It never paid to play a card before he knew he had the winning hand. Patience was the name of this game. The first one to move lost, and he didn't intend to lose.

Two minutes passed, maybe three. The woods became quiet, the world narrowing to the wait for that one sound that would tell Ian where the assassin was. Patience. Patience. Patience.

A twig snapped as the man made a run for it.

Ian pivoted out, his hand coming up. His eyes had adjusted but all he needed was that one flash of white where the man's hood had drifted back, exposing pale skin.

He squeezed the trigger in one easy move, his target in sight.

Now he heard the best sound of all. The sound of his enemy hitting the ground.

Shit. He hoped he hadn't killed the fucker.

Moving quickly, he crossed the distance between them, keeping his SIG ready in case he hadn't completely incapacitated the man who had tried to shoot him to get to Charlie.

A black-clad figure lay still on the ground, his hand on what appeared to be a sniper rifle. Ian kicked it away and the body didn't move. Shit. He needed more practice time with moving objects. He was getting rusty because he hadn't meant to hit the fucker's jugular, but it appeared he had given the amount of blood pumping out of his victim's body.

Alex was going to kill him for getting all that blood on his brand new yard. Using his boot, he turned the body over, assessing it. Six foot. Probably one ninety. He was dressed in all black, assassin chic. A black bag had fallen to the side. Ian rifled through it. Cartridges, extra pair of gloves, cell phone, passport, some cash, and a flask. Vodka. Ah, the Russians. They did like to celebrate the little victories.

He picked up the kit and started for the house. They would have to get rid of the body, but maybe something in the assassin's bag would offer up some useful intel.

He stopped just before he reached the back doors. The lights came on, nearly blinding him.

Ian jumped out of the way. Alex wouldn't have turned on the light. Gunfire cracked through the air. Fuck. There was more than one. His eyes started to adjust to the light, and he saw a man standing under the archway, a handgun pointed at Alex.

"I am looking for the girls. Give them to me and I let you and your wife live," he said in a thick Russian accent.

Alex had the man in his sights, but they were at a standoff because for some damn reason, Eve had left her safe position behind the soapstone-covered counter and was on the floor in between the two men with guns. The Russian had one upped Alex. He was two fisting, with one gun trained on Alex and the other steady at Eve's head.

He couldn't see Charlie or Chelsea.

"Somehow, I doubt that," Alex replied, his voice steady.

"I know you have them here. I was watching place. I think to take your wife and exchange for girls, but you bring them to me. You love wife? You want her to live?"

"Let my wife go and we'll talk about this. I might know where they are." It was a stalling tactic. Ian set the bag he was carrying on the ground as Alex continued. "I would be willing to make an exchange, but not until my wife is safe."

Ian chanced looking around the corner. Alex was attempting to give him time to get back to the house and surprise the fucker, but he couldn't just go in guns blazing.

Luckily, those lights were bright and Ian was covered by the gloom outside. He could see inside, but it would be difficult for anyone to see him from the circle of all that light.

The Russian had moved closer, the gun in his left hand touching Eve's head. She was turned away from the Russian. Her eyes were steady on Alex, but no panic showed there. Good girl. She wasn't feeding Alex's fear. She was calmly waiting for him to resolve the situation because she trusted her Master. Charlie could learn a few things from Eve.

"But, my friend, if I let wife go, I have nothing to

bargain with. Perhaps I take her with me." There was a nasty chuckle from the assassin as he used the barrel of his gun to play with Eve's hair. "Maybe after few hours, you will be in mood to share."

Eve wasn't feeding Alex's fear, but this fucker was damn straight going to make Alex blow, and that could be bad for everyone. He had to be precise. Ian shed his fear for Eve, his concern for Alex, and let the plan roll out in his head. Two steps toward the door. That was what he would need. It would leave him shrouded in darkness, but get him close enough that he wouldn't accidently hit Eve. Head shot. One shot straight through the brain pan and those guns would drop. The target was a little under six feet, but they weren't on level ground, so he would adjust two inches higher.

All the tension left his body and he stepped up, ready to take out his second asshole of the evening.

But Charlie popped up first. She rose from behind the counter, the nail gun the contractors had left behind firmly in her hands. She had one hand holding the thing up and the other was pulling back the safety trigger that allowed the nail gun to fire. Her pretty face showed no expression as she pulled the trigger and popped two big-ass nails into the side of the Russian's head and neck. He never saw it coming, didn't react in any way except to get a stupid expression on his face and fall to the side, dead before he hit the ground.

God, she was hot. She was a fucking warrior goddess with a damn nail gun, and he kind of wanted to do her right then and there, despite the many bodies now littering Alex's property. Eve might be really good with submissive trust, but Charlie had amazing aim and a steady hand.

Eve sat in the middle of her floor, seemingly unable to move. "Did Charlie just kill that guy with a nail gun?"

Alex was kneeling, trying to help his wife up. "Yes, thank god." He hauled her into his arms, pulling her away from the corpse. "Are you all right?"

"Is there blood on the hardwoods? Because I don't think our warranty covers that," Eve was saying.

Ian watched Charlie as she calmly put the nail gun down, but he noticed her hands were shaking, a fine tremble. Her hand went down, helping Chelsea stand. No one was there to cuddle Charlie, to wrap her up and let her know everything would be okay. He could see the sadness in her eyes, the knowledge that she was alone.

Fuck. He wanted to go and hold her and praise her for her skills with turning construction machinery into killing weapons.

"I wouldn't move if I was you, mate," a familiar voice said from right behind him. He heard the distinct sound of a safety being clicked off. "I know you're quite fast, but I'm no slouch myself, and I would really hate to kill a friend."

How had he missed it? He'd allowed someone to get his fucking back because he'd been busy worrying about Charlie's feelings. "I'm not feeling too friendly right this second, Damon."

A hand touched his shoulder. Damon Knight, MI6 agent and usually an ally, slapped him on the right shoulder. It hadn't been so long ago that he'd helped Ian with an op in London, but it looked like the cooperation ended there. "I have to ask you to drop the gun, mate."

He thought seriously about taking the chance, but Knight was hardcore. He might feel like shit about it, but he would kill Ian if he deemed it necessary to complete whatever mission Her Majesty required of him. Fuck, he was going to kill Simon if he was in on this. He would take that Brit apart limb by fucking limb and feed him to the dogs. He didn't actually own any dogs, but he would adopt the nastiest set of mutts he could just for the pleasure of feeding them Simon's body parts if he'd joined the team just to spy for Knight.

Ian dropped the SIG, hating every moment of being caught with his pants down. "What do you want, Knight?"

It was a dumb question. There was only one thing Knight could possibly want. "I want The Broker. For the last few years, MI6 has been tracking a hacker who calls herself The Broker. She's been selling information all around the world. If the Agency isn't interested in her, too, I would be shocked. I'm not trying to fuck with you, Tag. I believe Charlotte Denisovitch is The Broker. She's been causing trouble and my bosses want to have a little talk with her. She has information we need. I promise I'll watch out for her. I won't let her come to any real harm."

Just a little torture. He looked inside the house. It wouldn't be more than a minute or two before Alex got his shit together and came looking for him, but it was already too late. Damon wouldn't have come alone. "Where's Baz?"

Damon Knight and Basil Champion had been partners for years. If Knight was here, Baz would be backing him up.

"He's here." Simon walked from around the side of the house, Baz in front of him.

Baz's slender frame belied what Ian knew to be a ton of lean strength. He was wearing a black long-sleeved shirt and black slacks, looking dapper as he moved through the yard. "Hey, Damon, look who I found."

"I told you to put your fucking hands up," Simon ordered. "Do you really think I won't shoot you? I don't even bloody like you."

Ah, no dogs for the Brit. Simon was getting a raise.

"Now, seeing as I have your boy here and you have my boss, I suggest we all take a little time out and talk this through like the gentlemen I know we are," Simon said. "Or we can start shooting and see who's standing at the end."

"You've been in America too long, Weston." The gun at Ian's head disappeared as Knight sighed. "You've turned into a bloody cowboy."

No, Simon had gone from MI6 agent to Ian's man. There was no way to downplay the beauty of loyalty. Ian had taken Simon in after he'd fucked up, shown him that he didn't have to conform to MI6's rigid rules, and Simon paid him back with loyalty.

"Boss, Adam picked up this one's trail about two hours ago. I rather thought they might decide to pay you a visit. Damon, in case you're thinking about trying something tricky, you should know I have a sniper on you. Jesse? Are you in place?"

A voice came from above. "Sure as fuck am. Tell Alex his roof is totally solid. I have a great view from up here. I would have taken out the first dude, but Ian seemed to be having fun. This one, though, is all mine." A nice red dot appeared on Knight's forehead. Right between his eyes.

Yeah, he was getting to like Jesse, too.

Alex sighed from his broken patio doors. "Could we keep the body count down? As it is I have no idea what we're going to do with the sniper and the Russian Charlie used as a carpentry experiment. Why don't we all come in the house and talk this thing through? There has to be some way for Damon to get what he needs without taking Charlie to Britain's Guantanamo Bay."

Alex was a spoilsport. "Fine, but you need to think about moving, man. This is a dangerous neighborhood.

Hey, those contractors didn't happen to leave a shovel behind, did they?"

Alex's eyes went wide. "You can't bury them in my backyard. Damn it, Ian, we're putting in a swimming pool in the next couple of weeks. How am I supposed to explain that? First my French doors, then the hardwoods, and now you want to turn my backyard into a fucking body dump. It's not happening, Ian."

He walked away, muttering under his breath.

"I think that's what happens when good agents lose their brain to a pretty bird," Knight said.

At least they were in agreement on one thing.

He picked up Knight's gun and followed Alex into the house.

Chapter Ten

Charlie watched as Ian and Damon Knight sat at his kitchen table together, their faces grim as they worked out her future.

Apparently her input wasn't helpful as she'd been told to get ready for bed. He hadn't even allowed her to help bandage him up. Eve had been the one to wash the blood off his shoulder and tell him how lucky he was that the bullet had only grazed him. Ian dismissed her the minute they had gotten back to his big house in the country. Chelsea had already disappeared into the guest bedroom Ian had assigned them to. Alex and Eve took the bed in the small dungeon. Jesse and Simon were pulling guard duty while Ian had called Jake and Adam to bury the bodies until Ian was ready to offer them up to the Agency. Charlie was sure the only person who was happy with anything that had happened all night long was Serena, who would probably be taking notes.

She couldn't even think about sleeping. Not when she needed to get away. It was time to leave. Ian didn't want her and she didn't want to get anyone killed. She'd thought they would only come after her, but today had proven that her uncle was willing to hurt civilians to get to her. She'd thought she would have more time before they found her. Hell, she'd thought that maybe they had given up. She'd been in Florida for over a year working on the op that brought her back to Ian and no one had tried to kill her then. After so long without hearing from her uncle, she'd felt almost safe. Safe enough to come after her husband.

She'd been wrong and it was time to leave. After a little rest, she needed to get Chelsea and clear out of here.

The closest she'd managed to going to bed was changing into one of Ian's massive T-shirts. It would have to do for sleepwear. It hung to her knees, covering more than a lot of dresses did.

"So you're married to the big guy, huh?" Basil Champion sat down on the couch across from her, a longneck in his hand. He draped himself almost negligently across Ian's big comfy couch.

"Not really." She wasn't sure why the British agent wanted to talk about her marriage, but she wasn't getting into it with him.

"That's not what the paperwork says, love. It's just hard to believe you're here. I was there the night you died, you see. I actually got a decent look at your body. Damon and me had to get Big Tag away from the police. Our bosses thought he might suffer a bit in jail."

He likely would have been killed there. Nelson would have sent an assassin and then he wouldn't have had to worry about Ian Taggart screwing up his plans. She'd known it, but she'd still taken that pill. Maybe she didn't deserve to be forgiven. Maybe this had all been a huge mistake. "I'm sure he was grateful."

Baz took a long draw off the beer before replying. "Nah. He was too upset. I remember thinking this was supposed to be some sort of superhero. You know, he was kind of a legend even though he'd only been working for a few years. I thought I was about to meet the real shit, but he was kind of broken, know what I mean?"

She felt a little broken now, but she still didn't want to talk about her personal life with an MI6 agent. "So you're here to drag me kicking and screaming to England?"

He huffed a little, an arrogant sound. "No way. We wouldn't conduct this particular interview on British soil. Damon is being a bit of an idealist. I suspect we'll take you back to London and you won't make it out of Heathrow before the big bosses take you off of our hands and whisk you away to someplace nice and outside the confines of all those pesky human rights laws we have. Really, they're so confining when it comes to torture."

So she would be taken to some friendly government in Africa or the Middle East and they would torture her until she gave up the info. What they didn't realize was that Chelsea was the one behind most of the information brokering. Charlie was mostly muscle. The information Charlie had dealt to specific governments hadn't made them any money, but probably saved a bunch of lives. Chelsea hadn't been happy with her those times. Chelsea was the brains, but she didn't intend for that information to get out. "I haven't directly come up against MI6. Why are you coming after me now?"

He sat up, his feet hitting the floor. "Are you going to play dumb, then, love? You hacked our systems three months ago. You were polite about it. You got in, took three files, and got right back out. If we didn't have some very observant techs, we would never have known you were there at all."

Fuck. Chelsea had promised her she would stay out of MI6, the Agency, and China's MSS. They were the three countries most likely to catch her and string her up, though in this case it would be Charlie on the end of the rope. She settled in. It wasn't the first time she'd been forced to cover for her sister. "I wasn't trying to fuck with MI6. I just needed a couple of files."

"On Eli Nelson? Were you working for Taggart?"

Ah, her interrogation started now. At least she could answer those questions. "Eli Nelson is after me. I am not now nor have I ever worked for Ian or McKay-Taggart. I have, however, worked for Eli Nelson. We had a bad parting of ways."

"From what I can tell, you parted ways on your terms, not his."

He was well informed. "I never meant to work for the man on a permanent basis."

"No, you just used him to kill your father."

She shrugged a little. "It would have been difficult to do the job myself."

It wasn't like she hadn't thought about it, dreamed about it. She just hadn't figured out how to do it and save Chelsea and herself at the same time. It was why she'd taken Nelson's devil's pact.

"But you're quite effective at other work. You could be very valuable to someone like Nelson. Or someone like Taggart."

She laughed a little. "You can't imagine that I've been working for Ian all these years. He had no idea I was alive. I think that's funny since you and your partner obviously did."

An innocent look came over Baz's face. It was a handsome face, but there was something dark about the man. "Now, I'm deeply offended. I assure you if Damon had known that Ian Taggart's long lost wife was alive and well, he would have contacted the man. He's very loyal when it comes to his friends. No, we've only known you as The Broker. We started to suspect The Broker was a woman last year when a million dollars stolen from the Taliban showed up in a fund for educating women in Afghanistan."

That had totally been Charlie's idea. It had been a fun day all around. "I'm a feminist."

"You're an anarchist," Baz retorted, but there was very little judgment in his tone. "And you're playing with fire. If your 'clients' ever figured out that you play them against each other, you'll have more than your uncle and Eli Nelson out to kill you."

A girl had to have a hobby. Hers just happened to be causing chaos for some of the world's worst terrorists and criminals. It was fun. "I tend to be very careful about who I do business with."

Chelsea usually had a deft hand about not getting caught with her fingers in the cookie jar. Which was good because the cookie jar was probably rigged with explosives.

"But you really got on our radar a year ago. We had an operative in one of the terrorist cells you did some work for."

A little smile crossed her face. She'd enjoyed that little side project. "Sorry. I shut that down faster than your operative could. He was slow."

They had received information about a cell working to strike at several of Europe's public transportation systems in a coordinated effort to topple the economy. She kind of liked Europe. It was really hard to plan an operation like that when all the money disappeared.

"Our operative was working his way up the food chain. You blew the whole thing right out of the water. The cell turned on each other. Our operative watched while they accused each other of taking it. He was accused as well. He barely made it out alive."

So they had multiple reasons for disliking her. She'd upset their plans. "I wasn't in on the MI6 project. I simply saw a problem and I solved it. They were planning on releasing sarin gas into the air filtration systems of the undergrounds in London, Berlin, Paris, and Rome. They were ready to buy the gas. Your operative was too slow. I wasn't willing to risk a couple hundred thousand people and the European economy because your guy wanted to move up. I also think you'll find that I tipped off the cell's plans to the Agency."

His jaw firmed. "Yes, they didn't mind holding that over our heads. Might I ask why you didn't come directly to us?"

"I consider myself to be American." She was her mother's daughter, and her mother was from California. She'd always wanted to go home, but had settled her daughters on the East Coast in an attempt to hide from their father. He'd still found them.

"You were born in Moscow."

"But I was happy here. My mother was American. I gave up my Russian citizenship, or I would if I could actually show my face at a government office. I send bits and pieces along to the Agency from time to time and they dispense it as they see fit. But Ian has nothing to do with that. He's spent the last couple of years working strictly for himself."

Baz's eyes narrowed. "Not only for himself. He's still in good with the Agency. He wouldn't have been able to do all that work in England without having a few good contacts. Damon is high on him."

She wasn't sure she trusted Damon Knight. "He didn't seem real high on Ian back at Alex's. He seemed pretty pissed when Ian had a gun on him."

"Ian only got the drop on him because Simon was following us. Bloody bastard. Otherwise you would be on your way out of the country." He sat up, straightening his shirt. "Aren't you tired of running?"

That was a dumb question. "Of course I'm tired."

Baz sent a little look behind him, glancing into the kitchen. A laugh boomed from the neatly appointed room. At least Ian found something amusing. The British agent turned back, leaning in. "What if you didn't have to run anymore? What if you could settle down with all the money you've made and find a place where a woman of your talents could, shall we say, excel?"

"What are you trying to say?" If he was going to make an offer, she would rather he just came out and said it. Because the truth was she was tired. The thought of running again made her violently ill, but if she managed to get out of this situation, she would have to do it. She would have to take Chelsea and hide somewhere, and then they would hide somewhere else, and so on and so on until they were caught and killed or managed to make it to old age. She'd made her play for Ian and she'd lost, and she had no real idea what she should do next.

"I'm trying to say that you could do well for yourself. We're not all like the Agency. Not all organizations will use you and dump you. Some organizations would do much to be able to properly use all your talents."

Did MI6 want to torture her or hire her?

Should she listen to a proposal?

"I can't settle down. Not really. I thought I might be able to, but they found me really fast." It had been a calculated risk, allowing Adam to run traces on her identity, but she hoped her uncle had relaxed his stance. It had been years and the syndicate tended to focus on business. But she'd had no luck. Her uncle was eager to kill her, and she suspected it was because Nelson had double crossed her. Of course, she'd done the same to him, so she couldn't cry that she was innocent.

"There are always solutions to problems. Sometimes it just takes a willingness to get one's hands dirty." Baz set his empty bottle down on the table. "We all know the Agency doesn't like to get blood on its hands. It would rather farm out that work to its friends. They won't help you. They'll deny that you've ever helped them."

She'd always known that. "I didn't expect them to give me a job recommendation."

He shook his head. "You're not thinking big enough. The world is changing, and women like you can make a place for yourself."

"I think Charlie doesn't know her place at all." Ian was standing in the doorway, his broad frame dominating the space. "I asked you to go to bed."

"You told me to go to bed," she corrected. "I thought I should find out if I was going to be catching a plane tomorrow."

He frowned, shaking his head as though she'd said something a little crazy. "No. I've worked something out with Damon. I told you I would."

Damon Knight good-naturedly shoved his way past Ian, joining his partner on the couch. Unlike Baz, he had a glass of Scotch. "You're going to give me everything you have. I mean every single hard drive you own."

"What?"

Ian's face was a stony mask. "You're getting out of the business."

She let the words settle over her because they didn't make a lick of sense for a few moments. "You made this decision?"

"Yes."

The arrogance of the man astounded her. She stood, unwilling to sit while he loomed over her. "I won't do it."

She would rather go with Knight back to England and take her chances there. At least Chelsea would have some protection.

He stepped up, invading her space. "You fucking well will. Adam is going to your place to get the computers tonight."

"You can't do that." She clenched her fists, angry tears in her eyes. What the hell was he thinking? How could he do this to her? To Chelsea? "We need that information."

It was their protection, a wall against the world. It was the only thing they had.

"No, you don't. You're out of the business from now on. The money you stole or made from selling information is going to be divided between MI6 and the Agency, and it goes straight into their anti-terrorism budgets."

"What?" It came out as an angry screech. She couldn't run without money. She couldn't hide. Panic threatened to overtake her.

Ian's hand came out, gripping her arm. He looked over at the Brit crew. "We'll take this discussion to the bedroom. Chelsea is in one of the upstairs rooms. Alex and Eve are bedding down in the dungeon. You two can fight over the last bedroom. Don't hurt each other, though. It's got something called a daybed that won't actually fit either one of you. The other one can take the couch. I don't give a shit."

He started hauling her out of the living room.

"Ian, this is not happening." She wasn't going to allow him to take every bit of protection she had.

"It is. If you're worried that Adam could get hurt by

your security system, you should know he's already disabled it. He'll move the money in the morning, after the Agency has signed off on the deal."

"What fucking deal?"

He stopped, turning her toward him. "The one that keeps you out of prison. The one that just might give you something of a normal life."

"I don't get a normal life, Ian. If you take away my ability to make deals and move easily, you're sentencing me to death. It's not just the CIA and MI6 who want me. Have you cut a deal with my uncle?"

He didn't seem to have an answer for that.

"No, you haven't because he wouldn't take a deal. Not one that doesn't include my head in a box on his desk. So I have to come to the conclusion that you're really protecting your own ass and giving me up." She hated the fact that tears were running down her cheeks, but she couldn't help it. "Is this what you wanted, Ian? Do you want to know that I'm dead because you took away everything that could have protected me? Is that going to make you feel better?"

How could she have misjudged him so badly?

He took her by the shoulders. They were still in the hallway, not far from the Brits. "I'm trying to protect you, Charlotte. I'm trying to protect my people, too. Do you want a shootout? Because every single one of my people will try to protect you. They'll kill or die trying to keep you safe. Is that what you want? Because we can start a war."

With MI6 and then very likely with the Agency. She hadn't thought about anything except getting back in his arms. She hadn't thought about what it would cost them all. "No. Just let me go with them and it can be done."

"You're not going anywhere except to bed." He

started down the hall again.

She tried to dig her heels in. "Ian, stop. I'm not going to be put to bed like a five-year-old."

He simply turned and hauled her into his arms like she weighed nothing at all. "Five-year-olds have more sense than you do."

It was more than she could take. She hauled off and hit him, slapping him right across that square jaw of his. "You can't do this to me."

"Watch me." If he felt any pain, he didn't show it.

She kicked and fought, but he just kept walking. "Let me go. Fucking let me go."

His arms tightened around her. "Don't you think I want to? Damn it, Charlie, I wish I could, but you've made that impossible."

"It's easy. Put me down and turn your back and you'll never see me again."

He kicked open the door to what looked to be the master bedroom. "I can't. And I can't seem to stop trying to save you. I know you have zero interest in my protection, but you're fucking going to accept it this time. I made a mistake the first time. I gave you a choice. You don't get one now."

He set her on her feet.

She took off for the door.

An arm went around her middle, drawing her to him. "Don't make this hard on yourself, Charlie."

She kicked back, trying to get away. It was a stupid play. She knew it. There was absolutely nowhere to go. She would either end up with the Brits or Simon and Jesse, and they would all haul her back to Ian. But she couldn't stay still, couldn't submit to this.

"Calm down." Ian bit out the command, his mouth right by her ear. "They are still listening to us. I have no doubt. So you calm down right fucking now and act like an adult."

The accusation stung, but anything she said at this point would be meaningless.

His breath was warm against her ear, and despite the fact that he was a bastard son of a bitch, her body responded to him. Yeah, she hated that now, too.

"They think you're The Broker. Don't say anything. Just nod or shake your head. Chelsea's The Broker, right?"

She thought about lying to him. Just on principle. She nodded anyway.

"Did you know she's blackmailing key officials in four different governments?"

A little gasp came out. What had her sister done?

"I'll take that as a no. Your little sister is doing more damage than you suspect, and you're the one who's going to take the fall. You won't let her go down for it. I know you. So someone has to protect you. That's my name on our marriage license."

"I'll give you a divorce. Hell, I'll have Chelsea make it so the marriage never happened." It's what she should have done in the first place. She should have left well enough alone.

"It's too late for that." He kept one arm securely around her waist as he started to back up toward the bed.

Maybe reason would work. She softened her voice. "Ian, you don't want to get involved in this. Call Adam off. Tell Simon to turn his back for a couple of minutes. I'll wake up Chelsea and we'll get out of here. I won't bother you again."

"You bother me every minute of every fucking day, baby. You have since the moment I met you, and I've been fighting it. I've fought it so hard since you came back. Every good agent knows when one tactic doesn't work, it's time to try another one."

He turned her neatly so she was facing him, his arm unwinding. But before she could make a move to get away, he had both her wrists in one big hand.

And a nice length of rope in the other.

"What are you doing?"

"Trying something new." He wound the rope around her.

Charlie tried to take off. She bolted for the door, frightened not of what Ian might do, but that after all the shit he'd poured on her that she might still let him do it. She couldn't be the girl who took a guy's crap and then fucked him. She just couldn't.

He was on her in a second, pulling her down and pinning her to the plush carpet underneath them.

"Get off me," she yelled.

"I can't." He was perfectly calm. She could think this was an everyday occurrence if it hadn't been for the massive erection pressed against her.

Despite the fact that she tried her damnedest to get a knee in his crotch, he held her down and had her wrists bound together in no time at all. He tested the knots, as though he gave a shit.

"Is it too tight?" Ian asked, his voice quiet and serious.

She stayed silent, not willing to give him anything. He'd taken her world away and then expected her to submit?

"Charlie, baby, talk to me. I can't stand this. I hate that I shut you down. I don't want to. I want to be cold. I want to not care. I can't. I can't let you go."

"You're taking away my options."

"Because I gave them all to you last time and you fucking didn't choose me. You chose everyone but me. I'll fix this. I'll save you. Choose me, Charlie. Choose us. Trust me. Give me the option of being your hero."

She had, she suddenly realized. She'd chosen Chelsea over him. She'd chosen herself over him. At the time, she hadn't seen it that way. It had seemed like a clear path, and she hadn't considered once turning to him and telling him the truth. How would a man like Ian handle that? He would shut down. Ian needed to be needed and she'd trusted his worst enemy over him.

He was asking for another chance. Or was he just trying to get her to comply?

How could she know?

"Ian, just untie me and let me go to Chelsea." She had questions for her sister. If Chelsea was blackmailing politicians, they were in more trouble than she'd imagined.

His face tightened. "I can't. I can't trust you not to run."

Frustration welled. "You've made sure I don't have anywhere to run to, Ian. I have nothing to fall back on if Adam has taken those hard drives and you're going to give them my money."

She would be all alone in the world again. She would have to start over and hope she lasted long enough to make it. Her whole soul cried because he was the one who had put her here. Her love. Half her soul had banished her to death and pain.

He hauled her up, lifting her into his strong arms. "I'm giving them whatever it takes to keep you out of jail. If you give them the ten million in your accounts, and you stay out of trouble, they'll leave you be. I worked on this deal. I had to promise some very important people a couple of favors. My favors can mean dangerous things. Don't fucking tell me I'm trying to hurt you, Charlie."

Ten million? She stilled in his arms. He knew exactly

how much she had. Chelsea had told her Adam had found their bank accounts. She had almost twenty-five million in their accounts. It came from the money she'd stolen from Nelson and her uncle and the money they had made from brokering information. Tears pricked her eyes again, but for a different reason this time. Ian was trying to tell her something, but he couldn't just say it outright. Was he really trying? Was he really saving her? "You gave them the whole ten million? Ian, that's everything I have."

They could be listening. She had to be careful. Hope fluttered in her chest, a babe she'd thought was stillborn but who had just taken its first breath.

He laid her down on the massive bed, fastening her wrists to the hook at the headboard. "I did. All of it, Charlie." He winked her way.

He'd left her a security blanket. She could find new info. She could build their business again, but the money was paramount if she needed to run.

He stared down at her. "Trust me."

She closed her eyes. She loved this man and he'd hurt her. She'd hurt him. She'd cost him damn near everything, and she was threatening it again. Her uncle could take out his whole crew. So far they had handled the trouble, but they could lose one of their own.

Trust. She almost didn't understand the word.

Ian needed it. He needed her to trust him. It was like a code written into his DNA. He was the type of man who would love one woman and then be done. She was his. She was the one who could complete him but her history had fucked them both over.

She had a choice. Him or Chelsea. She'd chosen Chelsea the first time. Her sister had been so young and in need, but they were stronger now and Chelsea was almost off the radar. No one believed she had done anything wrong. Chelsea could walk away.

"So you've cleaned up *my* problems?"

His hand came out, smoothing back her hair. "Yes, thank god your sister has stayed out of trouble."

She mouthed her next question. *Why?*

He leaned over, his mouth right over her ear. "I told you. I tried. I tried to rid myself of this need, but I can't. I need you. I can't get you out of my fucking head. I haven't been able to for five fucking years."

"After today, I should walk away. It would be better for everyone in your life if I disappeared." She owed him the truth. After everything she'd done to him and his friends, she couldn't lie.

"I can't." He stood over her, his body hard and ready. "I can't let you go. You asked me a question. I didn't answer."

She asked him if what they'd had those years before was real. "Was it real? It felt real. It was real for me. I married you."

His shoulders slumped. He leaned against the wall, his eyes never leaving her. "I married you. I loved you, Charlie. With everything I had, I loved you, but you didn't reciprocate."

How could he think that? "Ian, I've spent five years trying to work my way back to you. How can you think I didn't love you?"

"You didn't need five years. You needed to trust me. You needed to trust me more than Eli Nelson. You didn't."

That was the wall between them, the chasm. She hadn't trusted him enough to tell him what was happening. She hadn't loved him enough to give him the truth.

"What would you have done, Ian?" She stared up at him. Sometimes he seemed so remote, aloof, but it was all an act. It could be hard to see past that gorgeous face and perfect body, but deep down he was just a man and she'd hurt him. "What would you have done if I had come to you? I was afraid you would kick me to the curb and then I wouldn't be able to save Chelsea. There was a tiny piece of me that was afraid you knew everything and you were playing me."

"I would have killed Eli Nelson. I would have gotten your sister."

She shook her head. He saw everything in black and white. "My dad had her. He wasn't going to let her go."

"I told you I would have gotten your sister. If anyone got in my way, I would have taken them out, and I very likely would have enjoyed killing your father."

"You were on an op."

He sighed, looking past tired. "You were more important than any op. I would have turned over the op to someone else. You were my wife. I made vows to you that I never made to another woman. I won't ever make to another woman. I would have walked away from the Agency and taken care of your problems and then I would have brought you back to the States and bought a fucking house with soapstone and shit and I would have gotten you pregnant and we would have a couple of kids by now, and then I wouldn't feel this hole inside me every single fucking day of my life. I would be some dumbass dad who takes his kid to soccer practice and bitches about the coach. I would be a husband who just likes to spend time with his wife at boring barbecues and family dinners."

The life they could have had. It played in the corners of her mind always, a dream she couldn't quite catch. "I don't know that we could ever have had that life, Ian. I think I made a mistake by coming back to you. I love you. I wish I'd made better choices, but in the end they'll always come after me."

"Can we not make decisions tonight?" Weariness had invaded his voice. "Can we just get through this crisis before we have to deal with the next one?"

Because the next crisis would come. "Yes. I'll be good. You can untie me."

He snorted a little and moved away from the wall, pulling his shirt over his head. "I think I'll keep you the way you are. That way I can sleep without having to keep one eye open."

"Ian, I promise."

"And I promise to gag you if you don't stop talking."

"God, you're such a bastard." He made her crazy. He said the sweetest things and then left her trussed up like a piece of meat on a hook. And who the hell had hooks built into his headboard?

He got down to his boxers and then the bed moved as he tossed his body on it. "Are you cold?"

"Ian, I'm tied up. I'm not worried about the cold."

His big hand came down on her belly, flattening over it possessively. "I've never had a woman in this bed."

"Yet you have hooks in the headboard."

He laid his head on her breasts, cuddling down like they were pillows. "I'm an optimist."

He was a bastard, and she still loved him. And she definitely wasn't cold.

With his arms around her, his body warming hers, she found it oddly easy to fall asleep.

Chapter Eleven

"What the fuck are you doing with my hard drives?"

Why hadn't he thought to have his bedroom soundproofed? Ian came awake to the shrill sounds of his sister-in-law fucking up his very carefully laid out plans. He'd planned on waking up and easing into Charlie's pussy before she'd really opened her eyes. He'd planned on starting the morning better than the way they had ended the evening.

"Keep your fucking voice down." Simon's low command came through loud and clear.

"Do they have to argue in front of our room?" Charlie groaned a little and turned toward him. He'd freed her after she'd fallen asleep. He'd never really meant to leave her tied up all night. It would have done terrible things to her joints and made her awfully crabby. Sleepy eyes opened, and she laid her head on his chest.

It was simple to curl his arm around her, drawing her close. He hated the fact that her referring to the room as theirs sounded so fucking right. But he wasn't going to fight it anymore. Fighting it had only made him miserable.

So he was having an affair. With his wife. He wasn't

going to look past that and keeping her alive for today.

"I swear to god if you don't give me back my hard drives, I'm going to take your balls off."

"I would love to see you try, little girl."

Charlie whined a little. "Make them go away, Master."

If only he could. He gave her a squeeze and rolled off the bed, not bothering with clothes. If they wanted to throw down outside his bedroom, they could deal with the fact that he had morning wood.

He threw the door open and Simon was standing over Chelsea, his face red. Ian could practically see the steam coming out of his ears. "You two both shut the fuck up. Where's Damon?"

Simon stood down. "He and Baz left early this morning. They're meeting us at the office in a few hours."

At least they hadn't been listening to Chelsea scream about her hard drives. "Then why the fuck are you two standing outside my door, wrecking my morning? I had a late fucking night what with all the killing and burying bodies and listening to Alex hand his balls over to Eve."

Chelsea turned, her face a stubborn mask. "I want to see my sister."

Ian wanted a lot of things that he wasn't going to get. "I want to fuck your sister but I can't because the two of you won't keep it down long enough for me to take care of business."

There was a chuckle from behind him and then Charlie's arm wound around his waist. Her body hugged his from behind. "You have no discretion at all."

Sleep seemed to have done his sub a world of good. Or maybe it was the fact that he'd stopped the macho revenge bullshit. He'd halfway expected to wake up and find her missing, but instead, she'd been wrapped around him, a little smile on her face. "Discretion is useless in this case. Now, in your sister's case, it could very likely get you killed if she keeps running around screaming about her hard drives."

"I want them back." Chelsea didn't seem to be in the same good mood as her sister. Maybe Simon should have tied her to a bed.

"Not going to happen. I traded them for your sister's freedom."

Chelsea huffed a little. "Bullshit. I could have gotten us out of that. Charlotte, you can't believe this asshole. He's one of them."

He waited for Charlie's deeply detailed defense of him, but she just put her head against his back and sighed. "No, he's not."

Neat. Succinct. To the point. He liked it.

"Charlotte, you can't let him do this to you," her sister pleaded. Her face twisted in a little frown of disgust. "Can't you put that thing away?"

His cock was tenting out of his boxers, poking its way through the fly. "I told you how to make it go away, but you're still here." Charlie chuckled behind him, her mouth on his back sending the little laughter reverberating through his skin. It did nothing to get his dick to slow down. "Besides, it looks like Simon there has wood of his own. You're not complaining about that."

Simon flushed. "God, you're a fucking bastard, Taggart. It's my deep pleasure to tell you that fucking your wife is going to have to wait. Liam's on his way in. He bagged a Russian and he managed to not kill his, so we're bringing him into the interrogation room in five."

Fuck all. He really couldn't screw his wife. Damn it. His day was already going to hell. "Fine."

"You have an interrogation room?" Charlie asked, her

voice incredulous.

"Doesn't everyone?" He wasn't going to apologize for having a proper home. Dungeon. Check. Interrogation room. Check. She didn't even know that he'd turned the shed in the back into a detention cell. Now that he thought about it, he really had made this house into a home. He just needed Charlie to pick out shit like curtains. Should he put curtains in his detention cell?

"I'll take this one off your hands." Simon had an oversized paw on Chelsea's elbow.

She pulled away from him. "Don't think this is over. Charlotte, I don't care how good he is in bed. You can't let him wreck our future."

"The future in which you blackmail high-ranking officials?" Charlie asked, finally showing some irritation. "The one where I get renditioned because you can't keep your hands out of the pie? Just tell me you haven't been hacking MSS. I don't think even Ian can work a deal with the Chinese."

Her sister flushed. "No. I stayed away from them. You have to understand that the officials I'm working over deserve it. If you only knew the kind of things they do, Charlotte."

"I don't have to know," Charlie shot back. "You shut that shit down now. We're out of the information business. If Ian can settle everything, we're going to keep our noses clean and stay off the radar."

Chelsea huffed away looking like a kid who had just had her favorite toy taken. Simon followed after her.

Ian turned to Charlie, allowing her to twist until she hugged him, his cock up against her belly, the easy intimacy comforting. "So you're on board now?"

She turned her face up. God, he loved how pretty she looked without an ounce of makeup on. "You're right. At least half of the people looking for me will go away if we give up the business, but Ian, you have to know that my uncle won't stop. I can't hide here forever."

He had no idea what he would do with her if she could stay. There was still so much between them, so much he couldn't trust about her. Still, he didn't want to fight more. He hugged her close. "We'll figure it out as we go along. Now go and take a shower and then deal with Miss Frowns A Lot. She and Simon would be so much happier if they would just get it over with and fuck."

"That's your solution to everything."

It was his solution to his massive hard-on. Now that he was kind-of, sort-of done with shoving her away, he should really be able to fuck his wife. He had five years of fucking to make up for. He pressed his cock against her, his hands finding her hair. "It's a really good solution."

He wanted to kiss her. He wanted to hold her still and explore her mouth lazily. They could start the morning right. His lips hovered right over hers.

"Ian!" Liam's voice rang out. "I caught us a nice fat fish."

There was a flurry of Russian curse words and Charlie tensed.

Fuck. He pulled her close, forgetting about his stupid, needed-more-than-it-was-going-to-get cock. "It's going to be okay, baby. I'll deal with this fucker."

"Are you going to kill him?" There wasn't an ounce of judgment in her question, just an offhand curiosity.

He'd thought about it, but he didn't really want to bury the dude in his backyard and Alex's was already full, so he was going to make another deal. "Li's going to hold him here until the Agency can pick him up. They'll take him along with the files and then it's out of our hands. I really only have a couple of hours to talk to him, so go and get cleaned up. We have to be at the office by noon."

She nodded and squeezed him one more time. "All right, Ian. I'll watch out for Chelsea and make sure she doesn't get into more trouble."

He stared down at her. "You're really going to take a shower? I expected a fight."

She shook her head. "Nope. You take care of douche-nozzle assassins and I'll make myself pretty." She sobered a bit. "I trust you, Ian. I made a mistake the first time, but I'm not making it again. I love you. I'm handing this problem over to you. Please fix it for me."

God, she couldn't know what that did to him. It made him want to wrap her up and never let the world fucking touch her again. It made him want to stand between her and anything that came her way. "I will, baby."

She walked away and after a moment, he heard the shower turn on.

"Hey, I've got the fucker in the interrogation room." Li frowned. "What are you going to do, mate? Are you going to threaten him with your dick? You should put that thing away. You're going to scare me with it."

He flipped Liam off and went to grab his pants.

Ten minutes later, he stared at Yuri Zhukov, who looked a little worse for wear. "What did you do to him? Or was his nose always three inches from the middle of his face?"

Li smiled. "Nah, that was Karina. He got a little handsy with her, and she put him in his place. She's a crazy bitch. I like her. I think she cheats at cards, though. And she broke a nail. She says that will cost you extra."

Great. Now he was paying for mani-pedis. He glanced at the mirror to the side. Alex and Eve were behind that mirror, watching everything that happened. Eve would be profiling the man, talking to Liam through a Bluetooth device. "Did he say anything in the car?"

"Beyond 'please don't lock me in the trunk' and 'don't kill me'? Some stuff in Russian, but the great news is I don't speak a lick of it. It's so much easier to kidnap people when you don't speak their language. All the crying becomes background noise."

Liam was talking out his ass, trying to get a rise out of the Russian. That much Ian got because the man he was describing was not the man sitting in the interrogation room. Zhukov was deadly silent, his face a mask of darkness.

And he damn straight spoke English. Everyone in the syndicate did. Of course, the good news was, Ian spoke Russian.

"*Dobroye utro*," It was Russian for "good morning."

A black brow rose above the assassin's eyes. "Ah, someone who has brain in head. You must be Taggart. My boss send his regards."

His boss had sent a couple of bullets his way, but at least they weren't going to have to conduct the interview in Russian. "So, you're going to drop the tough-guy act?"

"This is no act. I have been with syndicate for twenty years. Now I am dead man."

Because the syndicate didn't forgive and forget. Even if Zhukov managed to get away, they would assume he had been disloyal and kill him themselves. "The Agency will keep you safe from the syndicate for as long as you're willing to talk to them."

"Yes, I am sure their hospitality will be wonderful. I have heard so many good things from our Middle Eastern friends."

Oh, the Agency was going to want to know about

those friends. But Ian wanted to know about other friends.

He took out a picture of Eli Nelson. It was from the year before, but it was all he had. Nelson had been careful since London. "Let's have a talk. As long as you're truthful, I think you'll like my hospitality." It went without saying that if he didn't, the opposite could be true. "Is your boss involved with this man?"

"My boss is involved with many such interesting people. He is businessman."

"He is criminal." Ian pointed to the picture. It wouldn't do to give up that he was going to take out Denisovitch as well. "But my people don't tend to mess with your people. We leave that to cops. I'm interested in this man."

He studied the photo for a moment. "I know of this man. He works for a group that my boss is interested in."

"A group?" Now that was new information.

Zhukov laughed a little. "Ah, then the great Taggart does not know everything. I rather thought this was truth. You have been out of game for too long. But then again, I am merely, how do you say? I am worker bee. I probably know nothing."

Ian stared at the man.

Liam leaned over, whispering in his ear. "Eve says he's ready to deal. Something about body language and being in control. I don't know what she's talking about. I think he just looks like an asshole."

"Pass me the bottle." If the Russian was ready to deal, Ian was ready to be more hospitable.

Liam passed him a bottle of vodka and two shot glasses.

The Russian's eyes widened. "You are not barbarian after all."

Ian poured out two nice-sized shots. One didn't drink

alone in Russia. "Of course not."

Zhukov looked at the vodka. His hands were still tied in front of his body, but Ian was sure he was smart enough to know that he wasn't going to get untied. No, he was waiting for the second reason Ian was drinking this morning. To prove he wasn't trying to kill the fucker.

Ian picked up his shot glass. A toast was the way to start any important negotiation. "To your continued health."

Because if he didn't have something good, his health was in danger.

Zhukov held his up with clasped hands. "Yes, I think we could both use wishes for health."

They clinked glasses and downed the entire shot.

"It's eight in the morning. How can you drink vodka at this time of day?" Liam asked with a little shudder.

Zhukov shrugged. "Any time is time for vodka."

Ian poured out another couple of shots. "So you were talking about a group."

"Was I? Maybe there is group. Maybe there is not."

"That's interesting because just a moment ago, you sounded very sure."

He downed another shot. "I am not on inside of syndicate."

Bullshit. "You're their top assassin."

"I was favorite of old guard."

"Of Vladimir Denisovitch?" Charlie's father had run the syndicate for many years.

"He was like father to me. When his brother take over, he has his own favorite."

Yeah, Ian had probably killed his "favorite" the night before, but he wasn't going to tell Zhukov that. "So the new guard came in and you were on the outs."

"You Americans have colorful way of saying things.

Yes. I was no longer favorite."

"Yet, he trusted you to come after his number one target." There was no doubt in his head that Mikhail Denisovitch was obsessed with killing his niece.

"He did not send me alone." Something about the man's smile was off. Ian didn't need Eve to tell him he was hiding something.

"Yes, he sent at least three of you. Do you care to give me an actual number of how many he put under contract for this job?"

There was a slow shrug of the assassin's shoulder before he answered. "More than three."

Great. That told him a lot. "Why does your boss want to kill his niece while he's perfectly capable of doing business with the man who killed his brother?"

That seemed to flummox the man. His eyes tightened slightly, and he glanced back down at the photograph. "No. Charlotte killed her father."

Ian shook his head, tapping at the image of Nelson. "This is the man who killed Vladimir Denisovitch. He exchanged his services as an assassin for Charlotte's misdirection of an operative. He then used Denisovitch to cover his own criminal activities with the Agency."

"Charlotte tried to hire assassin to kill her father, but she could not find a man to take job. We discovered who killed the boss because of this man. He come to Mikhail with documents Charlotte sent him proving she was trying to hire him."

"And no one ever lied?" Why was Mikhail so ready to believe Nelson? "I happen to know that Charlotte was with me the morning Denisovitch was killed."

She'd been at their flat in London and then she'd been dead.

"It is not long flight. It is four hours from

Sheremetyevo to Heathrow. Easy flight to make when one wants to kill a man. This one has helped us in many ways since then. I think I believe man who helps over whore any day."

A hand came on his shoulder. Liam. A silent reminder to stay calm. He needed it because he really didn't like this tattooed motherfucker calling his wife a whore. He was the only one allowed to make that mistake. But he needed information from this man. He calmed himself and Liam's hand disappeared, reaching out to refill the shot glasses.

"What kind of work does he do for you?" Ian asked.

"Wouldn't you like to know."

"Yes, I would, and the Agency would like to know as well. Have you ever been waterboarded? They say it's like drowning over and over again. Just when you think it's going to be over and death will be pleasant, that's when they let you breathe again. Only for a few minutes. Just to get you ready for another round."

Liam chuckled a little. "I've heard some stories about the Agency frying a man's balls off. If they're not careful enough with the torch, the damn things go up in flames. Tell me something. How's your grooming routine, boyo?"

The man's jaw tightened and his hands suddenly threaded together as though he was finally understanding that this wouldn't be some simple stint in a comfy US jail. "He helps us with pipeline work."

What the fuck? "Are you talking about what's happening in the Samara Oblast?"

"You do not know. I thought you would know." He suddenly looked like a man who might keep his balls on his body.

"Tell me what Nelson is doing in Russia." Ian tried to come up with something. The mob tended to rule Russia. The last thing Ian heard was that Nelson was setting himself up as an arms dealer. Was he buying old weapons from the mob and selling them in Africa and the Middle East? What did that have to do with a pipeline?

"I think not. I think I keep this information for Agency or whoever shows up for me. I give this information to you and I have nothing to bargain with." He smiled a little, showing uneven teeth. "I am surprised you do not know this. I would think the whore would tell her lover."

"Ian," Li began.

But Ian was a little sick of listening to this fucker and he was pretty sure their discussion was over. If he was in the man's place, he wouldn't give up the intel to anyone except a person in power either. Ian leaned forward, trying to keep his hands on the table instead of wrapped around the man's throat. "You want to explain to me who you're talking about?"

A humorless laugh came out of the assassin, and he pointed at the picture of Nelson. "I speak of your whore wife. She knows this man well. Very well."

"Yes she does, because she hired him," Ian insisted. He really didn't like the insinuation the man was making.

"You have my computer. Maybe you should check it. We all get file on whore. I call her this because everyone in syndicate know how she stay alive so long. She fuck everything she can. Charlotte Denisovitch is called the Moscow Mare because so many of us ride her."

Ian saw red. Pure grade-A blood-red filled his brain, his sight going to a weird almost watery version of the color. Blood pounded through his system, a violent rhythm. It was funny really. He didn't even remember going over the top of the table. One minute his brain was trying to process what the man had said and the next Alex was pulling at him, shouting at him to stop because he had

Zhukov on the ground, his chair thrown back and the table kicked away. Somehow he'd been the cause of all that chaos, but it didn't matter now. He had one job to do in all the world, and he felt good about doing it.

"Ian, you're killing him," Alex yelled. "You have to stop."

But Ian didn't want to stop, not when the fucker had just started to turn blue and his eyes had begun to bulge. It wasn't time to stop yet. He squeezed a little harder. The asshole's throat was thick, but Ian easily handled it. His hands were big enough to do the job.

"Ian, stop it." Liam was getting in on the action, trying to pry his right hand back.

"Ian, we need him alive." Alex was on his left arm.

Neither man was making much progress. They didn't really need this shithead. According to him, there were several more just like him, and Ian didn't care who gave up the information. He did care about killing this motherfucker. He squeezed a little harder and managed to get his knee in the guy's crotch.

An image of Charlie underneath this shitbag nearly seared into his brain. He couldn't handle it. He couldn't be rational about it. He no longer cared about the op or the deal or anything except killing the man who might have violated his wife.

"Ian, he was lying." Eve was the only calm voice in the whole world. She knelt down, her face coming into view. "Please talk to me about this because I believe he was lying to put you in a bad position."

Ian bared his teeth, looking down at the man who was only weakly fighting now. "Who's in the bad position?"

"What's happening?" Another voice finally pulled him out of his killing zone. "Ian?"

He dropped Zhukov and turned to Charlie. She was

wearing yesterday's clothes but her hair was still damp from her shower. She wore no makeup and looked young and vulnerable.

But then she would want to, right? A good agent knew to look the part. Charlie looked the part of the sweet, innocent sub who just needed her Dom to protect her, to love her.

Fuck. He didn't want to be here. He didn't want to think about this. He couldn't talk to her right now.

"Get ready. We need to go to the office." He started to walk away.

"Ian, what did he say?" Her hand came up to stop him.

He stepped back. He couldn't touch her right now either. His head was wrong. All he could see was his wife draped around Eli Nelson. Had she lain in bed with the fucker, plotting his downfall? Had she given up all her sweetness to the man and then turned around and tossed herself in Ian's bed?

"It doesn't matter. Get ready."

"It does matter." Her eyes filled with tears. She started to walk toward him, but Liam was there, pulling her back.

"Give him a little space, darlin'. He can't talk right now. He needs to go and cool off before he speaks another word to you." The words came out of Liam's mouth like a warning and one Ian was definitely going to heed.

"Li, do you have this asshole's computer?" He'd said there was a file on Charlie. Ian wanted to read that fucking file.

Charlie was staring at him, her face pale, but she let Liam hold her back.

"Yeah. Adam's already got it. Boss, I think we shouldn't jump to conclusions," Li said.

"I want those files ready for me by the time I get to the office." He stepped away, nearly running to his room where he shut the door and tried to get the image out of his head.

* * * *

Charlie looked back in the interrogation room, her whole heart sinking. "What did he say?"

Liam shook his head. "You got to talk to Ian about that."

He wasn't going to be helpful. Charlie looked to the other woman in the room. "Eve, please."

Alex was hauling Zhukov up, forcing him to his feet. The assassin, for his part, was just trying to breathe. "Charlotte, you just need to give Ian a couple of minutes, okay? He'll come to his senses."

What did he need to come to his senses from? He'd been ready to kill Zhukov. She didn't blame Ian for that. The assassin had been one of her father's right hand men, a silent killer with evil eyes. She'd always been careful to steer clear of him.

Eve stepped forward. "Why don't we go and fix some breakfast? Maybe that will put the men in a better mood."

"Please tell me what he said," Charlie asked, hating the near begging in her voice. Ian was a professional. Ian was cool and calm when he was working. The Agency wanted to talk to Zhukov so Ian would make sure they got the chance. Except he'd been about to kill the man, which meant Zhukov had said or done something so vile that it pushed Ian out of his icy professionalism.

"I tell him how you fuck every man in the syndicate, bitch. I tell him how much we all loved fucking you." Zhukov's voice was scratchy, used, but there was no way to hide the malice there.

She gasped, the enormity of it hitting her at once.

Ian believed him. There was no other explanation for him trying to kill the man or for looking at her like she'd caught something contagious. He believed Zhukov, a man who had never spoken more than ten words to her before today. Ian believed she'd slept with him.

And…oh, god, he thought she'd whored herself out to the syndicate.

Eve took her hand. "I told him I thought Zhukov was lying."

"He didn't believe you, bitch," Zhukov choked out. "He knows truth now. Maybe he do my job for me and kill whore himself."

"Get him out of here, Alex, before I finish the job for Ian," Liam said, taking her hand and hauling her back. "I'm going to do what the boss damn well should have done. I'm going to take care of her."

He hauled her out of the line of fire, moving toward the kitchen. Charlie followed, feeling like a zombie. Her legs moved. She was still breathing, but she felt dead inside.

Liam dropped her arm when they reached the kitchen. He sighed and ran a hand through his hair before heading for the coffeepot. He poured out a mug and placed it on the big country-looking table. "Sit down and drink some coffee, love. It'll make you feel better."

She sat and placed her hands around the ceramic of the mug, warming her skin. She hadn't realized how cold she'd gotten.

"You don't know what it was like in there, so get it out of your head. Ian's a smart man. He'll figure it out." The Irishman sat down across from her, his mouth frowning.

"It sounds like he already figured it out." She felt hollow on the inside. She'd thought for a moment that they were okay. Just for one tiny moment. The whole time she'd been in the shower, she was wondering how they would make it work.

"He's being a jealous idiot. You have to give him some leeway. The man ain't been in love before."

"I slept with two men before Ian and none since." The words came out as though she simply had to defend herself, but it didn't matter. "I thought I was in love with one of them. He laughed at me after I gave him my virginity. He had a bet with some of the others that he could fuck the boss's daughter. I was looking for comfort from the other. I didn't find it. I certainly never touched Zhukov."

"How about Nelson?"

She closed her eyes. Of course it had gone there. "Never. It doesn't matter now."

Liam watched her carefully, as though searching her face for anything that would tell him she was lying. "He seemed to think he had some sort of evidence."

"It has to be doctored. I didn't sleep with Nelson. I didn't send him love notes. Nothing of the kind. I used the man to save my sister. That was all." She used Nelson and then she'd stolen his cash.

What the fuck was she going to do now?

Liam's cell phone buzzed. He looked down at it. "It's Avery. I've got to take it. She's getting her car looked at today. Thanks for helping her out last night."

So that's why he was being nice to her. She nodded as her sister walked in the room and Liam walked out. God, the last thing she needed was an "I told you so" from her sister. She stared down at the coffee, trying not to think about the way Ian had looked at her.

Chelsea slapped a hand on the table. "You can't do this, Charlotte. We need to get out of here now. Do you honestly believe they won't turn us over after they're done with us?"

Charlie looked up and her sister had a stalker. Simon leaned against the doorframe, a guard letting them know they weren't going anywhere.

"I don't know," Charlie replied.

Her sister slid into the chair beside her. "What do you mean you don't know? I thought everything was hunky dory between you and the man meat."

Her sister didn't like Ian. That much was clear. "He thinks I slept with Zhukov."

Chelsea's jaw dropped. "Eww, that's horrible. He's like five hundred years older than you."

"And Eli Nelson."

There was a low "fuck" from the doorway that let Charlie know Simon's ears worked just fine.

Chelsea frowned his way. "Go away, you pervert." She reached for Charlie's hand. "He is never going to trust you again. Can't you see that? He's not the kind of man who can forgive you. My god, he believes an assassin over you."

"Or he needs some bloody time to think about it," Simon interjected. "Did you consider that? You walked back into his life not two days ago and you expect him to keep up? You can't give him five seconds to catch his bloody breath, can you?"

Simon had a point. So did Chelsea. One was all about logic and reason and one required some modicum of faith. Faith in Ian. Faith in the fact that she loved him.

"What kind of evidence could Zhukov have on me?" Charlie asked, her eyes coming up. "Ian said something about a computer and a file on me."

Confusion crossed her sister's face. "I don't know."

"You know everything, Chelsea."

"I don't know this." Her arms crossed stubbornly. "I only know that you're going to get us killed. Why are you doing this? Can't you see it's not worth our lives? It's not worth our business."

There was part of the problem. "It wasn't supposed to be a business, Chelsea. It was supposed to be a way to stay alive. It was supposed to be protection, but you're in too deep. You've gone places that could cost us more than our lives."

"I did it for us. Information is power. We decided it a long time ago. If we couldn't get out of this world, then we had to rule it. I figured out how to do that, Charlotte. We needed power to be safe."

"We were never safe." Except she'd felt that way last night. Even this morning, she'd felt safe walking away from a problem and leaving it in Ian's hands.

"We were a hell of a lot safer than we are now. Now we have nothing and it's all because you can't keep it in your pants."

She stared at her sister. When had she become the bad guy? She'd given up Ian for Chelsea. She'd done her duty.

"That's the way you talk to your sister?" Simon said, frowning Chelsea's way. "That's the way you talk to the sister who sacrificed for you?"

"Stay out of it, Weston," Chelsea shot back. "You don't know anything."

Simon wasn't giving in. "I know enough to see a spoiled brat in front of me. I thought at first that you were just scared and on the run and that you probably needed someone to protect you, but that's not your story at all."

Chelsea sighed. "No, that's not my story. I'm a powerful woman."

"No, you're a fucking scared little brat who's willing to ship the only person who ever loved you out to a torture chamber if it means keeping your precious power. I've known men like you. They're cold inside. They're dead. Something disconnects and they can't form bonds anymore so they treat the people around them like chess pieces, and they don't tend to cry when their pawns die. They just find more."

Chelsea flushed, her fists coming down on the table. "My sister is not a chess piece."

"You're treating her like one," Simon said. "You hide behind her. You let her take the rap for the things you do and you don't tell her everything, do you? Because you're smarter than she is. You know better. She's just a woman, but you're something more. No one can touch you. Not really. You let whoever gave you those scars win. You let him turn you into a monster."

Her sister slapped Simon right across his handsome face, but the Brit didn't move an inch. "Go away. I am not telling you again."

"And I'm not leaving you alone. I think I kind of like your sister and I owe my boss the world, so I'll protect his woman when he can't. Tell her the truth. Tell her about your connections to Nelson. You didn't stop talking to him, did you?"

Betrayal bit through Charlie as Chelsea went stark white.

And said nothing.

Simon smiled, but it was a humorless thing. "It made sense. Once I started looking into The Broker, I knew it was you and not Charlotte. Charlotte did stupid shit like stopping terrorist plots and giving a million dollars to animal shelters. That was what you wanted her to think the 'business' was about."

"The fucking poodles weren't going to protect us," Chelsea bit back.

"So you contacted Nelson because he knew the business and you wanted in. Tell me, did you contact him as Charlotte?"

"Chelsea?" She waited for her sister to tell her it wasn't true. It couldn't be true. She couldn't have been working with Nelson.

A long moment passed. "He didn't want to talk to me. He always had a thing for Charlotte. She never saw it. If she hadn't fallen for that Neanderthal, Nelson would have protected us. He had power."

"What have you done?" At least she knew what kind of evidence Ian would find on her.

Chelsea stepped back. "I was just asking questions. Charlotte, I think he's bigger than he seems. I think he's connected to some very important people. I've started to see patterns that don't make sense to me, and they come back to him. If I could get something on him, if I could make him work for us again, we could maybe figure out what's happening and then we would be in such power."

Her sister had gotten in far deeper than Charlie had ever imagined and she'd dragged her along. Everything she'd sacrificed was meaningless because her sister had just ensured she could never be redeemed in Ian's eyes. And she'd placed them in a situation where Charlie couldn't start a new life.

"You're a lot like your father," Simon said.

Chelsea stopped, her body going still. "I am nothing like him."

"You ruined your sister's life over power and money. I would say you inherited a lot from him. Did you think about taking over the syndicate yourself?"

"I am nothing like him." Chelsea said it in an almost

disbelieving voice. She turned and walked away.

And Simon stayed.

"I thought you were watching over her." Charlie wanted to be alone, to let the hollowness sink in. Ian was lost. He would believe what he wanted to believe. He would believe whatever would allow him to go back into his comfortable shell and never come out again. Chelsea was lost, too. Charlie had done it to her. This was her fault. She should have insisted that her sister go to school, but she'd been so alone.

"She doesn't need watching over. I thought for a minute she did, but that one will always take care of herself. You, on the other hand, you need a keeper, love." Simon walked to the cupboard and pulled out a pot, filling it with water and placing it on the stove to heat. "Ian should be here, but he needs a minute or two."

"I think that's over, Simon." Everything was over.

"Not at all. A man doesn't nearly kill another man over a woman he doesn't love."

"What about a woman who betrayed him?"

"He's being quite the drama queen about that. I watched him last night. Oh, he looked very calm and professional, but he was desperate to get you out of that situation with MI6. If he wanted to pay you back, you would be in Europe on your way to Egypt or the UAE right now. He wants you. You just have to make sure he doesn't forget it."

"I think I've tried everything."

"How about simply staying?" Simon asked. "How about just giving him time? Just sit here and look pretty and vulnerable and don't spout shit at him. I assure you he'll come to the proper conclusions."

"And what are those?"

"That you're not capable of sleeping with the same

men who broke your sister. You're beyond that, love. You're whole in a way she isn't. I stayed up late last night looking over all your records. Yes, you took money from some corrupt bastards, but you also spread it out to women's groups and child protection agencies. You're a warrior, Charlotte. You're a protector. You're everything he needs in a partner."

She shook her head. "I betrayed him. Chelsea's right. He can't forgive me."

"Then he's an idiot and you move on. You did what you had to do to protect your sister. She was your responsibility."

"Yeah, I seem to have fucked that up, too."

"No. She's the one who chose her path. She should have followed your example. She's…a very interesting woman, but at the end of the day, she's been broken and it's made her cold. You didn't do that. Forgive yourself and move on. Forgive yourself for Ian, too, and you might have a shot at making it work." Simon stood up, brushing his dress shirt back to an unwrinkled state. "You did your penance. I'm working on mine. Let's have a cup of tea, shall we? Tea fixes almost everything, my mother used to say. A bullet tends to fix the rest."

He went about preparing tea, but Charlie just stared out the window. Nothing was going to fix this, and she wasn't sure what to do about it.

She looked out at the yard that could have been hers and wished she'd made different choices.

Chapter Twelve

Ian stared at the evidence in front of him, a series of e-mails from his lovely bride to Eli Nelson. He'd read over them three times since they had gotten into the office. There wasn't anything in those e-mails that truly damned her. They were written in a somewhat flat, intellectual tone with none of Charlie's sweet flirty nature in them. They were the correspondence of one professional to another.

Simon set his cup down on the conference room table. "My question is how did these assassins know your lovely wife would be in town now? Unless they've been here watching for her. Even then, I'm not sure how Denisovitch could be certain. She didn't fly into Dallas."

"No," Adam replied, taking the seat next to Jake. "She drove, and I couldn't find her face on any of the traffic cameras between here and Florida. If I can't find her, I doubt they could. Someone had to have very good intelligence. He wouldn't send so many men in without a relative certainty of where the target was."

Unless the target had been talking to her former lover. Unless she wasn't really the target. That red laser line hadn't shown up on Charlie's chest. It had shown up on his. Was Eli Nelson using her to take him out? He knew damn well Charlie didn't like to do her own assassinations.

So why did she take out the man last night? Think for a second. It would have been easy for her to do nothing and let it all play out. Maybe he gets you. Maybe you get him. She didn't allow that to happen.

Sometimes his dick was too logical.

"The man we caught is Zhukov. I confirmed it with the Agency and with known intelligence we have on him," Jake said.

Adam placed a file on the desk. "I busted into the feed at immigration at DFW and ran some facial recognition software and found the two we had to bury last night. I think I slipped a disc trying to toss the nail gun victim into the ground, by the way. I'm filing for workers' comp. I found at least two other known assassins who came into town in the last twenty-four hours. Do you think they got a group rate tourist fare?"

Fuck and double fuck. Why had he even gotten up this morning? "Did the Agency take Zhukov?"

He hadn't waited around. He'd come straight to the office after his shower. He hadn't done more than glance Charlie's way since then, though he wanted to. His eyes kept straying to Phoebe's office where she was sitting quietly. She hadn't asked him again. She'd simply followed him, her arms and legs moving but not in their graceful fashion. She'd been like a marionette, and he was the one pulling her strings.

God, she was killing him. He wasn't sure how much he could take.

"Yeah," Alex said, his face grim. "After a long discussion with the Brits, a man named Ten took him. Is that some sort of weird CIA name? Like Mr. Black?"

Ian felt the tiniest smile curl his lips up. He was glad he'd gotten Charlie out of there because Ten would have been all over her. Then he would have strangled his second man of the day. And he considered Ten a friend. "No, Ten doesn't play those games. He's what the Agency likes to call a maverick. Tennessee Smith. Southern born and bred. He's a good guy."

If Ian even knew what that meant anymore.

"He's a flirtatious asshole," Alex shot back.

Eve grinned. "Hey, sometimes a girl needs to know she still has it. Of course, he wasn't attractive or anything."

Liar. Ten was six foot four, two hundred twenty pounds of pure muscle. He was known for being able to get a woman to tell him anything. If Ian had been the hardass, then Ten had been the lover. He gave new meaning to the term "close cover."

There was a knock on the door, and Grace poked her head in. "I have two things. First, some flowers came for you. Yellow roses. Really pretty. No card."

Very likely it was Charlie. She'd sent him flowers before. "I don't want them. You keep them. Or you could give them to Phoebe."

That way Charlie would get the message. He wasn't a flowers and hearts kind of guy.

"All right," Grace agreed. "And Damon Knight and Basil Champion are here to see you. They said you promised to cut them in on anything you learned."

He nodded. He'd made some spectacularly shitty deals to keep Charlie with him, and now he just wanted to get away from her.

Knight walked in followed by his partner. There was a frown on the agent's face. "I thought we were supposed to be in on this meeting."

"I thought you would be on your way to DC." He'd been counting on them to follow Zhukov.

"No such luck for you, mate," Champion said, tossing himself into a chair. "We have another agent on his way. We've been assigned to work with you. Such fun."

Well, if they were working together, maybe the Brits had some information he didn't. "Zhukov was talking about Nelson possibly working for the syndicate. Have you had any luck tracking him?"

"A little." Knight pulled out a tablet, his fingers finding the files he needed. MI6 had finally gone high tech, it seemed. "There are reports of a man matching Nelson's description traveling to Novokuibyshevsk three times in the last year."

"That's in the Samara Oblast." There was a nice-sized pipeline there.

Knight nodded. "Yes, it's a city located on the western bank of the Volga. It's a refinery town. Have you heard the word *Indeitsy*?"

Ian let out a long sigh. He needed more Russian mob shit in his life. "It's a mafia term. It means Indians. They use it to refer to an organization that functions a little like the raiding parties of the Old West."

"It's not a secret that *Indeitsy* has its fingers in the oil industry rackets," Knight said.

"They don't have their fingers in it," Baz interrupted with a roll of his eyes. "They run the whole damn thing. Give them credit, mate."

Jake sat forward, his face serious. "What exactly do you mean by racket? How does it function?"

"They traffic in stolen crude," Simon explained. "They literally tap into the pipelines and steal the shit. I know about this because of my family. My uncle runs Malone Oil. They've had an enormous amount of trouble

272

in the region. All the American companies have. The mob has to have a man on the inside. The pipelines are guarded."

Baz stared at Simon. "Really? So you just happen to be connected to one of the biggest oil companies in the world? Aren't they headquartered here?"

Ian knew about Simon's connections, knew damn well it was one of the reasons he'd been willing to come to Dallas. He had an uncle and aunt and two cousins in Fort Worth, and they were loaded. But he said nothing, allowing Simon to give away what he wanted.

"Yes. I haven't tried to hide my connections. Malones and Westons have been connected for years. I spent some summers here with my cousins. Why do you ask?" Simon stared at Baz.

"I just find it interesting," Baz replied.

"Could we get back to the topic at hand?" Ian requested.

"So someone who works for the rightful oil company takes a cut for tipping off the mob. They come in, steal the crude, and get out." Alex summed up the situation nicely. "What does that have to do with Nelson? Somehow I don't see him working a pipe cutter."

"Who's the head of *Indeitsy* in the region?" Ian was pretty sure who it would come back to.

Knight turned his tablet around. "A man named Dusan Denisovitch. Mikhail's son, so that makes him your wife's cousin. He gave Dusan the territory a couple of years back."

Charlie's family was everywhere, it seemed. So Nelson was regularly visiting the same region that man controlled. Coincidence? Not likely.

"So can we absolutely connect Nelson to Mikhail?"

"I've placed Mikhail Denisovitch in Saint

Petersburg." Adam had that kind of constipated look on his face that he always got when he was about to tell him something he wouldn't like.

"Spit it out, Adam." It wasn't like he'd punched Adam for delivering bad news. Much. There was really just that one time. Adam had totally punched back. It had tickled.

He slammed a photo down. It was grainy and shot from long range. "Interpol keeps tabs on Denisovitch. I have a friend there. He sent this over."

Nelson. There he was plain as day, standing with Denisovitch in what looked to be a park overlooking a river. Saint Petersburg. He recognized the baroque buildings and canals of the famous city.

He stared at the picture for a moment, a cold hate in his gut. In all his years as an operative, his years in the Green Berets fighting some of the worst dictators and terrorists imaginable, he had never really hated anyone. He'd killed them, sure, but it had been a job done with the efficiency of a pure professional. Emotion was where Nelson tripped him up. Emotion and ego. He was honest enough to admit that to himself.

He had to think instead of react. His first instinct was to get on a plane to Russia, track down Denisovitch, and throttle the man until he told him where Nelson was. He was running on emotion and not logic. He had been since that moment when Charlie had shown up on his doorstep. Hell, maybe he'd been running on emotion where it came to Eli Nelson for much longer than that. He could still remember watching the fucker put bullets into Sean while Ian maneuvered into position. He could still hear the man taunting his brother, telling Sean all of Ian's secrets.

And he remembered feeling like he was sixteen years old all over again.

Take care of your brother. The last words his father had said to him before he'd walked out of their lives. *You take care of your brother and your mother. I can't anymore.*

Yep. He wasn't capable of thinking logically at this point. He needed a clear head.

He stared at the picture for a moment. "Adam, I need to talk to the whole team. Liam's not here, but could you bring the rest of them in? Including my sister-in-law."

This affected Grace as well. He couldn't leave her out. If he was going to put everyone in danger in order to find out the truth, they needed to have a say.

He was a long way from the Agency. He wondered if Nelson was counting on that. He wondered if his family connections would bring him down.

Adam let out a long breath as though truly happy he hadn't gotten his ass kicked. "All right then."

He turned and walked out.

"Damon, could we have a moment? This is a family matter."

Baz frowned. "We made a deal."

Knight stood up, putting a hand on his partner's shoulder to bring him up. "Of course. We'll wait in your office."

Baz was arguing his case as they walked out of the room.

Jesse walked in, looking back at the bickering agents. "What happened to them?"

"They don't ever like being left out of the loop," Ian replied.

"What are you thinking, boss?" Simon asked in that crisp accent of his.

He was thinking that it was time to finish everything, to bring down Nelson and figure out what he was going to do with his wife. "I'm wondering why we got this. The last time he surfaced, it was a coordinated effort to get us exactly where he needed us to be."

There were another couple of photos Adam had left on the table, and Jesse took one in his hand, looking down on it. "This is that rogue dude thing?"

God, he needed to put new employees through a test to make sure they didn't sound like idiots when they talked. "We prefer to use the term rogue operative, though he's been disavowed by now. Now he's just a traitor."

"He's hanging out with Kris's…Charlotte's uncle? The mob dude?" Jesse yelped a little as Simon slapped him upside the head. It was a move Ian had perfected on Adam. He knew there was a reason he liked the Brit.

"I'll do it every time you sound like a stoned surfer," Simon drawled. "You're not in the Army anymore. You have to sound like you have a brain in your head. You're not simply here to follow commands. You have to think on your feet."

Jesse frowned at his mentor and rubbed the back of his skull. "I need to learn to duck more because this really does kind of seem like another version of the Army. So your enemy is becoming friendly with Charlotte's enemy?"

"They want me to think so." But Ian's brain was working. Something didn't add up, and he wasn't sure which way to go. He could go the route that took him down logic road, or he could…find another way.

"The mob du…the Russian mob gentleman and the rogue operative traitor?" Jesse asked.

"Catch up, mate. He's moved past both of them, and he's right back to wondering if his wife isn't working him over." Simon neatly summed up what was running through his head. "It's awfully coincidental that she would show up and then suddenly Nelson is hanging out with her family. If it's really all that sudden."

"Unless he's kept an eye on her and now she's out in the open," Jesse argued. "I'm really finding it hard to believe that she would work for five years to get into a position where she could help Alex and Eve so she could get back into Ian's good graces, take a bullet to the chest from me, and it was all so maybe she could trick you again."

A flash of her still body whispered across his brain, blood staining her chest. Blood on his hands, his shirt, his everything. "Oh, but she took a bullet to trick me before."

"Yeah, she took a bullet from a man who didn't want her dead. I wasn't in on that plot. I was aiming for Alex's heart." Jesse ducked Simon's swinging hand. "Asshole. I thought he was the bad guy. Every single member of this team has smacked me for shooting my brother, but he wasn't my brother at the time and I didn't even get him. I got Charlotte. Which is kind of my point. Do you think she's madly in love with Nelson and is willing to sacrifice her life?"

It was a little bit of a conundrum. He couldn't imagine Nelson and Charlie together.

"I think Charlotte is damn good at her job. If she thought the risk was worth the reward, she would take it." But Jesse's words were worming into his head. It was a different situation. She could easily have just shown up at his place without the song and dance routine in St. Augustine. She'd put a good two years into that operation. What did she really get out of it?

"If it means anything, I believe her," Simon said. "I think she's done just about everything to protect that sister of hers. Her sister admitted that she was the one who wrote to Nelson."

Of course she would if they had gotten their stories straight. Ian had lost the opportunity to question them separately since he'd been far too angry to think rationally.

There was logic to what Charlie did to him.

He went through the photos Adam had left. Four pictures of two men Ian would deeply like to murder, and in a horribly visceral way.

How much of Charlie's story had been complete bullshit? The scars on her body were real. He'd seen the pictures of her mother's murdered body.

Was Charlotte so cold that she would work with the same syndicate that murdered her mother and tortured her for years?

Logically, he knew it could happen. She could have been indoctrinated. It had happened many times before. She could be a deeply good actress.

"What's he doing? He looks like he's going to kill someone," Jesse whispered.

Fuck. Jesse was turning into Adam 2.0. He had to shut that shit down. He narrowed his eyes and gave the new guy his most intimidating stare. "Are you volunteering? It's been a couple of hours since I killed someone and I'm starting to get the itch."

Jesse grunted a little. "See. Just like the damn Army."

"I'm bringing Sean into this. He was in Florida with Charlie and this affects him, too." Ian found the phone and dialed his brother's cell.

"This is Sean. Hans, are you trying to cook the duck or make it your bitch?"

He hated interrupting his brother at work, but he needed advice. Actually he really hated needing fucking advice. What was he? A "Dear Abby" fan? God, Charlotte had taken his dick. "Sean, it's Ian. I need to conference you in on something."

The sounds of a busy kitchen came over the line. "Sure. Give me a sec. Don't you stop stirring that sauce. I swear to god I'll murder you if it scorches."

The door opened and Adam escorted Grace inside, each taking empty seats.

"Doesn't this affect Charlotte, too?" Alex asked. "Shouldn't she be in on this?"

"She's taking a time out."

"Hey, Sean," Adam said, leaning toward the speaker phone. "You missed out yesterday. Big Tag made a porno with his wife."

Grace gasped. "Adam, you are not supposed to talk about that."

"Shut up, everyone." He was going to stop this soap opera in its tracks. "We have something serious to talk about. Sean, can you talk?"

"Yep. Adam kind of had my attention at porno," Sean's voice said over the speaker phone. "Grace, love, you don't need to be looking at big brother's junk, though I'm sure it took up most of the screen."

"He wasn't naked, Sean. Charlotte was," Grace said.

"Oh, well, that's totally different."

Ian took firm control of his temper. "Eli Nelson is working with the Denisovitch syndicate."

Thank god that got everyone quiet.

Grace picked up one of the pictures as she sat down at the conference table. "This is Russia. I thought he was supposed to be in India."

"Yes, I believe that's what Charlotte said. Charlie wants me to think he's in India, and Nelson obviously wants me to head to Russia." That was a problem for him. He just needed to figure out why it was a problem. He could go one of two ways.

Eve studied one of the pictures. "He's relaxed. He

isn't worried or tense. Do you see the slump of his shoulders?"

Yes, the fucker seemed to be having a lovely time plotting with the Russian mobster. "Yes. I see that."

"Denisovitch, the first one, Charlotte's dad, he was the Russian Nelson set up as the terrorist out to buy the uranium from the Irish mission," Adam explained. It had almost cost Liam his life, and it had certainly cost him his brother. "Or he was at least working with Denisovitch in order to make the threat credible. Did he assassinate his partner so he wouldn't have to share the money? Was Mikhail in on it?"

Ian shook his head. "I don't think so. From all the intelligence I've gathered over the years, Mikhail was deeply loyal to his brother. If he's in bed with Nelson, it's for one of two reasons. One. He doesn't know that Nelson was the assassin who killed his brother. He believes Nelson's story, which is very likely that Charlotte killed her own father and stole his money. Two. My intelligence is wrong and all three are in on it together."

It wouldn't be the first time he'd been wrong.

They all started talking at once again. It gave Ian a headache. He looked out the window that showed the office. Grace hadn't drawn the blinds up because she needed to be able to see if someone walked into the lobby, but it also gave Ian a great view of the accounting office. Phoebe had left her blinds open, too, and there sat Charlotte with her strawberry hair flowing down her back and her eyes on Phoebe. Chelsea was glum beside her sister, her eyes on the ground. He'd expected that Phoebe would be doing what she always did, focusing on her computer and nothing else, but she was talking. Animatedly. She was smiling and gesturing around.

She reached up and pulled down a bobblehead. He'd

noticed she kept a collection of bobbleheads in her office on a shelf. Harry Potter bobbleheads.

Charlie turned, her face a mask of horror as she looked out the window. Their eyes caught, and she sent him the same pleading look she used when her ass was too sore to take another single slap.

He'd thought he was punishing Charlie with silence. No. She was going to get a whole afternoon of Harry Potter talk.

Ian couldn't help it. He let his head fall back, and he laughed. It was perfect. It was beyond any punishment he could have come up with.

Charlie put a hand on the window, her lips curling into a sad little smile before she turned back and listened to her lecture.

What the hell was he going to do with her? Ask her if she'd slept with the men she claimed to be her worst enemies? The man who was his worst enemy?

Or realize that it didn't matter. That she could have slept with a thousand men and he would still fucking want her.

He could take her. He could make her submit. He could make sure she never strayed or did another damn criminal thing again. He would keep her barefoot and so fucking pregnant that she couldn't even think about running from him or building another criminal enterprise.

God, he might be going insane. He needed to think, but there never seemed to be the time. He needed advice.

"Eve, what do you think about Charlie? You spent time with her in Florida. You've been watching her since she's been here."

All eyes went to Eve. "I think she's telling you the truth. I think she loves you and she's been working to get back to you. If you want to know what I think about

Zhukov…"

He shook his head, interrupting her. He didn't want to hear that shit. He needed to make those decisions on his own. "Don't give me personal stuff. Tell me if I can trust her when it comes to giving me intelligence on Nelson."

"Yes," Eve replied. "I think she's trying to be honest, at least with you and the people you consider family. She's looking for a home. She was willing to die in order to save Alex, and it wasn't because she loved Alex. She wanted to prove herself to you. I trust her with my life."

"Sean?" He trusted Eve's opinion, but he trusted Sean's intuition.

Sean sighed. "If she only wanted to cause chaos, why not just show up?"

"Because I would have shot her."

"No, my brother, you wouldn't have. You would be in the same damn position," Sean said, his voice holding a nauseating sympathy.

Ian held up a hand. "All right then. We have some decisions to make. I didn't want to make them without talking to the whole team because we're gambling here."

"You think Nelson wants us to believe he's staying in Russia," Jake said. "He's played it this way before. He wanted us to go to England. I say we don't play into the fucker's hands. He wants us in Russia. We go to India."

Adam pointed to the picture. "He looks like he's got a tan. He sure as fuck didn't get it in Saint Petersburg. Let's go to the beach."

"You're not going to the beach, mate." Simon sat back in his chair, an almost predatory look in his eyes. Yeah, sometimes he reminded Ian why he'd hired the Brit. "I'm going. How am I going to explain the idiot? Oh, I know he'll fit in there better than I will, but we don't exactly look like gay lovers."

Jesse's eyes went wide. "Whoa. That was not part of my contract."

Simon was overthinking this thing. "Don't worry about cover yet. Let's get boots on the ground and figure out what we need. Just grab some beachwear and your kits."

"How much time do I have?" Simon asked.

"We leave as soon as the MI6 boys can get the private jet fueled. It's all I can give you. I need eyes on the ground there. Adam, I'm going to need paperwork and visas."

Adam nodded. "I keep a spare set for every one of us in case of emergency."

"I'm going to call some of my contacts at the Agency and see if I can find out if they have anything on Denisovitch." He would have to talk to Ten again to see if he was holding out on him. The Agency usually didn't give up information until it was asked for.

Alex looked over at his bride. "Hey, baby, what do you say we take that honeymoon somewhere a little colder than Hawaii?"

Sometimes Alex could read his mind. "Damn, man, I'm not asking you to do that."

"But you would feel better if I went to Russia and got us some surveillance on Charlotte's uncle. I don't like the fact that your worst enemy is potentially conspiring with hers. It could mean bad shit for two people I care about," Alex replied.

"And I've always wanted to see the Amber Room." Eve smiled steadily. "I've heard they have beautiful churches as well."

"You need visas, too." Was he really going to let them go to Russia? Alex was a brilliant agent, but he'd worked in the FBI, not the CIA. "No. This is stupid. You don't speak Russian."

Alex shrugged. "We don't need to. We're tourists."

Eve smoothed back her hair. "My grandfather was from Russia. I've always wanted to see the motherland."

"I have a friend at the consulate," Adam said.

Jake slipped a low five. "Magda. Yeah, she was a good friend."

Adam's brow furrowed. "Don't ever let Serena know."

"You're afraid your wife would be pissed about a Russian hookup?" Simon asked.

Jake groaned. "No. Magda was in good with a Ukrainian syndicate. They're in direct competition with Denisovitch. She'll help us fuck with them. Do you know what Serena would do if she found out we know real Russian mobsters? She would never stop asking questions. She would want us to take her to the Ukraine and meet with them. Can you see that meeting?"

Adam went a little green. "I have nightmares about it."

"Are you sure you want to do this? We could just stay out of his business." Grace spoke for the first time. Her hands were in her lap, tightening around each other.

He reached out to his sister-in-law because Sean wasn't here. It was something he wouldn't have even thought about doing before, but Grace was his family. He was going soft. "Grace, he won't let it lie. Those pictures are proof. He wants us to see him. He's got something in mind. We have to figure it out."

"Little one, Ian's right," Sean said, his voice low and sweet toward his wife. "He won't let this go. We've hurt him too much. He can't let up and neither can we. This is a game only one group can win. We have to make sure we take him out."

"I want to do something," Jake said.

"Take care of your wife." He wasn't about to put Jake in the field when Serena was pregnant. Adam was safe enough behind his computer. He could still do his job.

"You can't keep me out of the field forever," Jake shot back. "Serena knew what she was getting into when she married me. She knew what my job was."

Ian held out a hand. He couldn't stand the thought of that baby Serena was carrying being down a dad. "Just let me get used to it, man. I've got what I need for now. If something else comes up, I'll send you in the line of fire, okay?"

"All right. I just want to take this fucker down, you know."

"I want him dead more than anything." His eyes trailed toward Charlie's frame. Phoebe was still talking and she had a Hermione doll in her hand. Maybe he didn't want Nelson dead more than absolutely anything.

There was something he wanted so much more. He just wasn't sure he should have it.

"So we're all good?" Alex asked, getting to his feet. "Because I have some packing to do. And a camera to buy. I'm going to expense that shit."

"He's had his eye on a telephoto lens," Eve said.

So it would be an expensive op. He was willing to pay just about anything if he could get rid of the threat. If he could get rid of both Nelson and Denisovitch, he could figure out what he really wanted. He could figure out how to deal with Charlie. He could decide if he could really forgive her.

Liam walked into the room, his eyes a little wild. Something had happened and it didn't look good. "Adam, I need your help."

Ian got to his feet. "What happened?"

Liam's hands were shaking. "There was an accident.

Avery's car. It's very bad."

Ian felt his stomach twist. His day wasn't done. Not even close.

* * * *

Eli Nelson looked through the binoculars. Kashmir Kamdar was on his boat, anchored in a particularly beautiful section of Goa. His own small island nation was roughly twenty miles to the west, but King Kash, as they called him in the tabloids, didn't have to be in his kingdom to hold court. He seemed to be on a perpetual vacation.

Three buxom blondes in barely there bikinis were frolicking on the starboard side of the ridiculous yacht.

He hated the little fucker. He hadn't done a damn thing to deserve his wealth except have the very good fortune to be born well. At least Taggart had made his way in the world. Taggart had been past dirt poor before.

He wondered if Taggart knew why his father had left him behind. He'd done a study of Taggart a long time before. He wondered if Taggart knew his father had walked away and started a whole other family after he'd finally gotten off the drugs. It was a fleeting thought. He didn't really care, but it was interesting given his current surveillance. King Kash had everything handed to him while Taggart had scrapped and fought to put food in his mewling brother's mouth. Taggart had two more brothers he didn't even know existed. Apparently the Taggart DNA ran true. Despite the fact that their father was a pussy retail clerk, the twin brothers Ian didn't know about were more like him than their father. Both had joined the Navy because their papa couldn't pay for college and both were up for BUD/S training this year. Nelson had thought seriously about trying to recruit those two. It would be so much fun to have a couple of Taggarts on his side.

If only Tag had proven to be a bit more morally flexible, Nelson would have introduced him to his friends. Tag would have been an unbelievably effective agent if he hadn't had that morality. He was certain it was brought on by Tag's family.

It was better to be alone.

Not that Kash seemed to believe that. The young king seemed to think he should never be alone. The fucker was always shoving his dick into some blonde.

When he wasn't funding research Nelson's bosses wanted quashed.

Kash passed a glass of wine to his latest Swedish supermodel and then turned his face up to the sun. It was something he did often. The idiot turned his face up, his arms going out as though he was embracing the whole world.

When Nelson got the go-ahead, he would put a bullet straight through the fucker's chest.

The door to the cabin opened and one of Kash's many servants brought him a phone on a silver platter. The man was dressed in a tux and tails and bowed to the master of the boat.

God, he couldn't wait to kill him. Nelson had a plan in place. Kamdar was such an over-privileged asshole. But he was also an asshole who had information Nelson needed. He touched the earpiece in his right ear. Mostly his surveillance had consisted of listening to the king fuck a long string of blondes. The man had stamina.

"Hello?"

Nelson's whole body tightened. When the king of Loa Mali spoke English, it meant he was talking to one of his scientists.

There was a long pause on the line, and Nelson cursed

the fact that he'd only been able to bug the boat and not the king's phone. Kash was a paranoid bastard who switched his cell phones on a weekly basis. And he kept three different phones for different types of people. One for his hookups. One for his family.

And one for the people he kept on his island, paying them handsomely for what he merely called "research" in his bookkeeping accounts.

Nelson's bosses were interested in that research.

Through the binoculars, he saw Kash's smile go wide. "Are you serious?"

Another long pause and Nelson's whole body went tight with frustration. God, he needed to get more than one man in Kash's household. The only one he'd managed to blackmail spent almost all his time in the garage of the boat, and there was no reason for him to be close to the king except when he piloted him to shore. Every single person who was really close to the king, down to the dude who probably wiped his ass, were Loa Malian. He hadn't been able to bribe a one of them because Kash, like his father and his father's father, spread the fucking wealth around. First it had been about the pearl trade and the rich minerals found on the small island that was home to roughly 40,000 inhabitants. Then the fuckers found oil in their territorial waters and the Kamdars shared the wealth with the citizenry, ensuring that things like democracy and forward progress had no place on their little island.

During the '90s, the former king became fascinated with technology, buying large chunks of stock in companies that were changing the world. He also completely changed Loa Mali's infrastructure, making it one of the most high-tech countries on the planet.

Now Kash Kamdar was the king and it seemed like he wanted to change the world as well.

Too bad Nelson and his bosses were happy with the world the way it was.

"Are you serious? It holds there?" A loopy grin hit the king's face. "Are we ready to move into testing?"

Shit and double shit. He needed to hear the other end of that conversation. Or maybe not. Maybe the ridiculous look on Kamdar's face was all he needed to know. They were moving faster than he'd anticipated.

He needed to get to the oil rig where he suspected Kamdar kept his lab and start blowing shit up.

His cell buzzed, a text coming through.

Operations commenced. Expect successful termination of all players within three days. Avery O'Donnell already confirmed dead.

Poor Irishman. He'd been happy for a couple of months. Oh, well, his pain wouldn't last long. He'd be dead beside his little bride. And all the others.

Nelson went back to watching his target. It was almost time to take him out, too.

Chapter Thirteen

"The flowers are pretty." She would say just about anything to get Phoebe off her favorite subject.

"Who cares about flowers?" Chelsea asked under her breath. "I just saw the MI6 guys walk back in. Do you understand what that means?"

It meant that Ian might be rethinking his position. He might be ready to turn her over to them after all.

"It's weird that they didn't come with a note," Phoebe was saying as she looked at the bouquet of yellow roses. "Grace said they were just delivered here this morning. I've never gotten flowers but my friend bought me a first edition *Alchemist's Stone*. That was the British title for *Harry Potter and the Sorcerer's Stone*. I like the British title better. It has more mystery about it."

And Phoebe was off again. Her sister groaned beside her.

She stared at the flowers. Yellow flowers. In Russia, they were symbols of sadness. Of betrayal. If a girl in Russia got yellow flowers she knew it was the end. Maybe it was fitting.

The MI6 agents walked out of the conference room,

the doors closing behind them. They moved back toward the hallway that housed Ian's office.

Baz's eyes trailed toward her, searching hers. He gave her a grave nod and continued to follow his partner.

"Will they really take you?" Chelsea whispered.

"If Ian lets them, yes." She didn't care anymore. If they were going to take her, then it wouldn't matter that she worried about it.

This wasn't the submission she'd dreamed about when she'd planned her reunion with Ian, but it seemed that submitting to fate was the only thing left to do.

Phoebe leaned forward. "Did you really marry him?"

Charlie looked up, taking in the woman who seemed so scared of her husband. "Uhm, yes. I married him in England."

"He didn't like force you or anything, right?"

If only she could tell herself that, but no, everything that had happened between them was consensual. Everything except him throwing her out. "No. I loved him."

Phoebe shook her head. "I'm sorry. I don't understand. He's just so scary."

Charlie looked back at the conference room. He didn't look scary. He looked tired and sad. He looked like she felt. She put a hand on the window, feeling his pull.

He turned away.

If Phoebe was going to work here, she needed to learn how to deal with her boss. "Just stand up to him. He's all bark and no bite around women. Don't get me wrong, if you truly cross him, you'll pay for it, but you can't let him push you around."

Phoebe went a little white. "Oh, I can barely talk around the man. I don't think I'll be standing up to him anytime soon."

"He's just a man," Chelsea said, her tone exasperated. "I don't understand why every woman around is either afraid of him or trying to sleep with him."

"You can be both," Phoebe said, her eyes going to the conference room.

Charlie slapped a hand on Phoebe's desk, getting the girl's attention back where it should be. "If you try to sleep with him, then you won't need to be afraid of Ian. You should be afraid of me."

Phoebe's mouth dropped open. "I am. I really am right now. I'm going to go get some coffee. I'll be back."

She nearly ran out of the room.

"Way to scare the mouse, sis."

She sat in silence. She wasn't sure what she wanted to say to Chelsea. She'd failed her like she'd failed Ian.

"Can you not even look at me now?"

Charlie shook her head. Maybe Ian wasn't the only one who needed time. "I'm just sorry, Chelsea."

"For what?" Her sister got to her knees, obviously unwilling to accept the situation.

"For whatever I did wrong."

Chelsea reached for her hand. "You didn't do anything wrong. I did. I got in really deep, Charlie. I can't explain it except to say it's an obsession. But it's one that's protected us up until now."

"I should have forced you to go to school. I should have paid more attention to you. I was obsessed with Ian. I should have put it aside and dealt with you."

Chelsea squeezed her hand. "Charlotte, we can still make this right. We can get away from here. I'm not going to let them take you. I never once meant to let you take the fall for me. I love you. You're my only family. You're the only person I have in the whole world. I'm certainly not going to lose you."

Her sister was still in way too deep. "Chelsea, listen to yourself. You've been playing god for way too long. You won't be able to stop it. If those men take me there will be absolutely nothing you can do about it. I'll be gone and you won't see me again and I don't even know if you can function in the real world."

"What are you talking about?" Chelsea asked, sitting back on her heels and dropping her hand.

"You've set up your own little kingdom. Your own world and you rule it, and you don't consider what it means to anyone else."

"No one else matters."

"Everyone matters. Didn't you learn anything?"

A stubborn mask fell over Chelsea's face. "Yes, I learned that my legs break when someone takes a baseball bat to them. I learned that you either have power or you're meaningless."

"You have compassion or you're soulless, Chelsea. Momma taught us that."

"Momma let herself be used by a monster. She married him. She had kids by him."

She wished her sister could really remember. "No, she was brave. She ran. She hid."

"Not well enough, so she kind of lost that battle. You know I always thought you were the strong one, but I've had to be for the last several years. You pretend to be the leader but all your decisions are made between your legs. You forgot about me, so I've had to make sure we were safe."

Charlie turned in her chair, unable to look at Chelsea a moment longer. "What did you expect me to do? Live with you the rest of my life? Don't you want something more? Don't you want someone to love?"

A bitter laugh escaped her sister's lips. "Who's going

to love me? You might have a few scars, but you can still walk properly. You don't ache every single day. No one's going to love me, Charlotte. I'm not that girl." She finally got up and sat back down in her chair, taking a long breath. "I don't think Ian's going to love you either. I'm not trying to be a bitch. I'm realistic. He's not a forgiving man. He wants a sub, not a wife. He wants someone who will spend her whole life cooking his dinner and worshiping at his feet."

"You say that like it's a bad thing. I've spent the last couple of years pretty much doing that for you. At least he worshipped me back, and don't wrinkle your nose at the idea. Until you've had a man who wants to hold you, who wants you more than his next breath, you don't get a say in the way I feel."

Ian seemed to be talking to someone on the speaker phone. Charlie stared at the flowers. They were beautiful, just buds now, their graceful curves only starting to reveal the bloom inside. She'd been like that once. She'd been full of possibilities. She hadn't even known what those possibilities were. Ian had shown her.

She wouldn't bloom. Maybe Chelsea was right, and they had never really had a chance.

Fourteen flowers. She touched them all, a little worry sparking in the back of her brain. "Chelsea, how many flowers do you count?"

"I don't care about the flowers."

"I count fourteen. Fourteen yellow roses and no one knows who sent them."

Chelsea suddenly seemed to care about the flowers. "It could be a mistake. Maybe whoever sent them meant to send a dozen and they got fourteen by mistake. They send flowers by the dozen here in the States."

No one in Russia sent an even number of flowers to

anything except a funeral. And no one sent yellow flowers except to show their profound sadness or to mark a betrayal.

These were funeral flowers meant for a Russian daughter. For her.

"We have to get out of here." Chelsea tugged on her arm, pure fear on her face. It seemed she'd gotten the message, too. "They don't understand how far our uncle will go."

Liam strode down the hallway, a grim look on his face. He shoved his way into the conference room and immediately started talking. Everyone was facing him and then Grace started to cry.

Oh, god, what was going on? Charlie stepped to the window that separated them.

Charlie watched as the conference room seemed to tense and then Liam and Grace went running out of the room followed by a tense-looking Simon and Jesse, who was checking the clip on his SIG. Jake moved back toward his office while Adam was back at his computer, his fingers flying across the keys.

Something had happened. Something spectacularly bad.

Baz chose that moment to walk down the hallway. He stopped, looking into the conference room before poking his head into the office where Charlie was standing. "What's going on?"

"I don't know." But she needed to find out. Ian had told her to wait, but she couldn't just sit here when it looked like everything was falling apart. What had caused Grace to cry? To run out of the room like the devil was chasing her?

She looked into the lobby and Grace had her purse. Liam was escorting her out of the office, his eyes moving, searching for a threat.

"Looks serious. I better go get Damon." Baz's expression never changed. He looked back, his eyes catching on Phoebe's desk. "Nice flowers. Someone must be in love."

But those flowers weren't about love.

Ian stood up, looking at whatever Adam was doing on the computer. When his face lifted toward the door, there was a weariness to his eyes that she hated. He ran a hand across his brow, his shoulders slumping.

Alex and Eve were holding hands and suddenly Eve turned into Alex's body, his arms wrapping around her. Eve was crying.

Charlie stood up. *Fuck.* What had happened? What the hell had happened? She couldn't just sit here. Ian would just have to punish her. She moved toward the conference room door.

"Uhm, I don't think you're supposed to leave. Ian was very specific about it," Phoebe said as she walked back in the office, pushing her glasses up her nose.

Charlie ignored her, moving into the hall. She looked to her left and Grace was locking the front doors as Liam paced by the elevator. They were locking down. Her heart rate picked up, thumping through her chest.

She crossed the space between them, her hands trembling as she opened the conference room door.

"Liam, Simon, and Jesse are with her, Sean," Ian was saying. "They're taking her out the back after they get Carys from daycare. Nothing's going to happen to them, and Li might be a paranoid idiot, but I'm following his lead on this one."

"I'm leaving the restaurant right now. Have Li text me the meet spot. Not at home." There was a click and Sean's voice was gone.

"What happened?" Charlie asked. Grace couldn't go home?

Ian's eyes pinned her, making her want to squirm. "I told you to stay in your seat and you are not allowed to talk."

It was bad. Whatever had happened was really bad, and it was personal. "Please tell me."

"Why, Charlotte? Why do you need to know?"

"Because I care about these people." Because somehow through years of studying them, she'd come to love them. They had become her family.

Ian was so cold as he stood over her. All the heat that had been between them was gone, snuffed out utterly, and she could feel the vast distance that separated her from him. "Do you really? I have some questions about that."

"I didn't write those e-mails to Nelson. It was Chelsea." He might never believe her, but she would defend herself.

"And Chelsea is your sister. Your ultimate loyalty is to her. I guess at the end of the day, it all comes down to family, doesn't it? You're always going to choose your family."

But he was her family. "Please don't believe an assassin over me. Please, Ian."

"You did. You believed Nelson over me and now my family is paying the price." He looked over and nodded toward the door. Damon and Baz stood there. "We've had a setback. We're going to need to change some of our plans. How fast can we get to India?"

"I'll have the jet ready as soon as possible. Let me make a few calls." Damon stepped away, but Baz stayed, his dark eyes watching the scene playing out in front of him.

"Go back to your seat, Charlie. I can't deal with you

right now." Ian dismissed her utterly.

She couldn't accept that. "I want to help, but I can't help if I don't know what's going on."

Ian's eyes went to the door, hardening slightly, and when he looked back at her there was an icy will in them. "Avery's dead."

"What?" She didn't quite understand the words. They didn't make sense so she had to have heard him wrong. Her paranoid brain was making connections that weren't there.

"I said Avery is dead." Ian drew out each word as if giving her time to process them separately.

The air left her lungs as the meaning hit her. Liam's wife, the one who had smiled and welcomed Charlie, was gone? The one who was knitting baby clothes? Liam's pregnant wife was dead? It couldn't be true. It just couldn't. "How?"

"Her brakes were cut. She lost control of her car and the ER doc pronounced her dead an hour ago."

Charlie felt her knees go weak, but she forced herself to stand. Fourteen roses. She did a quick count and nausea rolled.

"Ian, what are you doing?" Alex asked.

Ian said something, but she didn't hear anything else. All she could see was pretty, sweet Avery. Avery had been through so much and she hadn't deserved to die.

Her uncle was coming after all of them, very likely in conjunction with Eli Nelson.

The two men who hated her most in the world were coming after her, and they were obviously playing for keeps. Fourteen yellow roses. One for each of them. They would kill everyone. They would take out Ian and his brother and their friends and wives and likely even their children.

A sob caught in her throat. They might not know about Jesse. He didn't have ties to Nelson. He'd barely been on the payroll for more than a few months. She would be surprised if they knew about him. If that fourteenth rose wasn't meant for him, then it had to be for the baby. God, there was a rose for Carys. There was a rose for Grace and Sean's baby girl. Ian's niece.

All that death would be her fault because she'd come back into his life. He would lose his family. They would all lose because Chelsea was right. She'd been selfish, thinking only of herself, of getting back to the place where she felt safe. But in doing that, she'd placed all the people she cared about in danger.

She'd never had a chance. From the moment she'd been born, her path had been set, and every time she tried to find a way out, someone died. She wouldn't get that house filled with children. She wouldn't get to wake every morning and see their little faces and know that they would carry on after she and Ian were gone.

She had always been meant to die, her painful existence erased in a single bullet.

Guilt gnawed at her gut. There was only one way to try to make things better.

She turned to the door and walked out, a calm settling inside. She'd cost Liam his wife. She couldn't cost the rest of them. Maybe her uncle would be satisfied with her. Maybe he would give up the rest. Perhaps he'd sent the flowers as a warning for her to give over to the inevitable without taking down everyone around her.

"Charlie?" Ian's voice rang out, but she couldn't listen to him now.

It would be such a simple thing. She would go and sit on the bench outside the building. It was pretty there. There were pansies of all different colors and green grass.

She could sit on the bench and wait. If she let her mind go, she wouldn't even feel it when the bullet found her heart or her head or wherever they decided to aim.

It would be fitting to let them take her outside his office. She'd gotten close. So close.

"Charlotte!"

She got to the outer doors of the office, opening them. Except they didn't open. She pulled at them again, trying to stay calm. She had to stay calm. She had to be calm in order to do what she needed to do. She couldn't lose it. She had to get to the stairs and out of the building.

The doors stuck, despite using all her strength. She needed to get out and the doors were fucking locked, and Grace was somewhere out there and they would get to her. If she didn't do what she needed to do the others would die.

A little hysteria started to churn inside her. She kicked at the doors. She had to get out. Couldn't they see she had to get the fuck out of here?

"Charlie, you can't go out there." Ian wrapped those big arms of his around her, pulling her away from her goal.

She kicked back, completely losing it. "Let me go!"

It no longer mattered that her dignity was gone. All that mattered was stopping what was about to happen.

"No." If he even felt her puny attempts to get out of his arms, he didn't show it. "You're safer here. I told you I won't let you run again."

"She's not trying to get away from you." Chelsea had tears running down her face. It was the first time she'd seen her sister cry since that awful day she'd nearly lost her legs. "She's going to go down and offer herself up. She's going to let them kill her. Can't you see that? She would rather die than be the reason you lose someone else."

Charlie looked at her baby sister. She loved her so much. For so many years, Chelsea had been the only thing that kept her going. Protecting Chelsea had been her whole life, the only thing she'd managed to do right until it had all gone wrong. "We can't escape fate, but we gave it a good try, didn't we, sister?"

Chelsea choked back a sob and nodded. "We did. Let me go with you. I can sit with you. I would rather go with you."

"Nobody's going anywhere, damn it." Ian hauled her up, ignoring her protests. He looked back at the crew gathered around them. "That door stays locked, Alex. You tell Simon and Jesse to secure the women and then get their asses back here. Li, Jake, and Adam can handle them. I need extra eyes on her."

"Ian?" Alex's face was flush with emotion, the question meaning something she didn't understand.

"I'm going to take care of her. Make sure I can. Watch that one. She doesn't get to play the martyr either." He started to walk down the hall, carrying her easily.

She was trapped in his arms. She had to make him see reason. "You have to let me go, Ian. Did you see the roses? My uncle sent them. It had to be him. Yellow roses. An even number of yellow roses."

"It means someone thinks we're going to be planning a funeral." He seemed to understand, but he didn't stop. He just walked toward his destination.

"There are fourteen of them. Ian, there are fourteen of us if you include Carys. He's going to kill the baby. He's going to kill the wives. He's going to eradicate everyone you love if you don't let me go. If I make it easy for him, maybe he'll be satisfied with that."

"He won't. His path is set. He knows damn well that I

will come after him. I won't stop until he's dead. We're all on a path now."

She'd set them there. "You can get off. Please, Ian. Please, let me go."

He walked into his office and set her down on the sofa. He put his hand over her mouth. "Don't move." His voice lowered to a growly whisper. "Charlie, trust me."

She looked up at him as he stalked back and shut the door. He grabbed what looked like a walkie-talkie and turned it on, looking at the screen. He walked through the room, staring at the screen and fine-tuning it.

He was looking for bugs?

He finally turned it off and shoved it back in his desk before turning to her, a grave look on his face. He walked her way and she stood up. Now he had to listen to her.

"Ian, Avery's already gone," she said. "We can't lose someone else. Please let me go."

Her whole world tipped upside down as he got to his knees and wrapped his arms around her waist. "Forgive me."

"Ian, what are you talking about?" She couldn't seem to catch her breath. Without even really thinking about it, her hands found his hair. God, she wanted this. To hold him one last time. She sank her hands into his thick sandy hair.

"Forgive me. I can't trust anyone. Not anyone outside of our family. Please forgive me, baby."

Had he used the word "our"? "There's nothing to forgive, Master. I love you, but you have to let me go and face them."

"I can't. Forgive me for lying to you but they were watching. It's too important. I'm trying to protect all of us. They were in the room. I had to lie."

"Lie?"

"Avery's alive, but it was a close thing. She managed to get the car to stop, but she collided with another vehicle. They took her to the hospital. She and the baby are fine, but Liam thinks it was an attempt on her, and the assassins from last night at Alex and Eve's weren't there for you."

Pieces of the puzzle fell into place. "They were trying to get Alex and Eve."

"I just found a device on Alex's cell. Someone is listening in. We decided to fake Avery's death. Adam hacked the hospital system and had her pronounced dead. Liam is taking the rest of our women to a safe place. He and Jake and Adam will protect them. Sean will run with his family. They won't come back out until I tell them it's safe."

"Fourteen yellow roses, Ian. They want to kill you all and it's my fault."

His head shook slightly. "It doesn't matter now. All that matters is that you have to keep the secret, too. I don't want either of the MI6 agents to know Avery's alive. I'm pissed that they know we've already killed two of them."

At least he trusted her this much. "I won't tell them a thing. Chelsea doesn't need to know, either." She was making her choice. She loved her sister, but her final loyalty had to be to Ian. "But they can't stay in hiding forever. My uncle won't stop trying to kill me. Let me go and maybe he'll forget about the rest of you."

His arms tightened around her. "I'm so sorry, but you have to understand that I will never allow you to walk out that door and let them take you. I don't care if you could make a deal with them that saved us all. I won't let it happen."

Confusion swamped her. "Ian, I don't understand. You were mad at me. You think I slept with Nelson."

His face turned up, and there was no way to miss the

torture there. He was usually so shut down, but every aching emotion was playing across those normally arctic eyes, and it kicked Charlie in the gut. "I don't count anything that happened while you were with your father against you. You have to know that I never would do that. But I should care if you slept with Nelson. Goddamn it, Charlie, I should care about that. That's the problem. I think it doesn't fucking matter. I think I would still want you. That's the insane thing, Charlie. I still fucking want you. I still crave you."

Nothing had changed. Not really. He didn't trust her.

Simon's words came back. *How about just giving him time?*

She'd been willing to give him everything else. He was likely right. Her uncle had put them on a path. So what if he didn't believe her now? How could she change that if she left?

If there was no way out of this war her uncle had started, then she should fight on the right side, and that meant standing up, not sitting on a bench and waiting for the inevitable. And that meant giving her Master what he needed.

He'd just discovered that his world was on a timer set to explode. Everyone he cared about was in danger, and he couldn't trust anyone around him. They would all look to him to lead, and he had no one to lean on.

No one except her.

He might only be willing to say he wanted her, but he needed her. Her ego didn't mean a thing in the face of what he needed.

She dropped to her knees, wrapping her arms around him, offering him everything she had. "All right, Ian. I'll do whatever you need me to do. I want to stand by you, but if you can't trust me then I'll go wherever you want me to go and I'll stay there. I promise. I'll give you the rest of the money and I won't allow Chelsea to touch a computer. I'll wait, Ian. I'll wait until you do what you need to do. When you're done, if you still want me, I will be there."

His hands found her hair, pulling her back, forcing her to look into his eyes. That little tug lit up her skin. "You want me to shut you away? You think that will prove something to me? Maybe it would be the best thing to do, but I can't. Do you want to know why?"

He was so close it was hard to even process the words he was saying. Her head was reeling. She'd gone from complete desperation to pure desire. "You think I would run?"

"No, I would make sure you can't run. If I shut you away, I can't fuck you, Charlie. I can't think about anything but getting inside you again." His mouth hovered over hers, tempting her, teasing her. So close to heaven, but she wanted a kiss from him to be more than a way to control her. "I can't think about anything except you. I nearly killed that man today."

"Ian..." she began, wanting to explain.

"No." He shook his head, a hard negative. "I don't want to talk about it. I told you. I don't give a fuck. I just want you. I can't help it. You're an obsession. I can't let you go. I can't let you walk away, and I sure as fuck can't let them have you."

She wanted to be more than an obsession. She needed it, but now wasn't the time to talk about her needs.

Now was the time to give to him. To be what he needed.

"Then don't, Master. I'll stay with you as long as you want me."

Another tug on her hair. He seemed to be in a

ferocious mood, and he was willing to take it out on her. His world was out of control. Her heart skipped a couple of beats because she knew what he would need. If he couldn't control the outside world, then he would control her. He would dominate her.

"You'll stay?" The words came out of his mouth in a hard grind. "Will you stay when I tell you that what I want more than anything is to fuck your ass? Tell me how many men have been inside your ass."

She shook her head, nearly shivering at the thought. How many nights had she dreamed about having him in every way there was to have a man? She'd been a good sub. She'd prepared for him. "None. Absolutely no one. I only want you."

"Show me."

Charlie stood up and prepared to serve her love.

Chapter Fourteen

A savage need flooded Ian's system. To take her. To brand her. To ensure that she never looked at another man. He could keep her so satisfied that she couldn't open her eyes to look at one.

It pounded through his veins and nothing else mattered. Something had switched on inside him when he'd realized what she was trying to do. She'd tried to offer herself up, to give herself away because the guilt was too much for her to bear.

And he remembered her body cold and dead in his arms.

She was fucking alive now and he was going to make sure it never happened again.

They were all his responsibility. Sean and Grace and Carys. Jake and Adam and Liam and their wives. Alex and Eve. Even Simon and Jesse were his responsibility now. He had to ensure their safety.

But she was his. Only his. He didn't have to share her with anyone, not if he chose to keep her. His submissive. His wife.

He wanted a piece of her no one had ever had before.

"Take off your clothes." At least he'd turned off the cameras in his office this time. Not that it would stop him now. He needed to burn off the knot in his gut. He needed to take all his guilt and the resounding fear that he was going to fail them all and burn it away in her body.

She pulled at her shirt, fumbling a little as she tossed it away. He hadn't even gotten her clothes from her place. He'd forced her to wear what she'd worn yesterday. He wasn't taking care of her the way he should. He had to shove his anger down and take care of her because she belonged to him and he was starting to think that he couldn't change that. He was fooling himself if he thought he could fuck her out of his soul, but right now he meant to try.

While she worked on her clothes, he walked to the small closet at the back of his office. He kept extras there. Extra guns. Extra ammo. Bulletproof vest. The tiniest bit of C-4. And an extra kit complete with lube and a still-packaged anal plug.

Just the basics. What every man needed to survive the apocalypse. Grace had been horrified, but Ian liked to be prepared.

He pulled out the kit and laid it on the coffee table in the sitting portion of his office. He wasn't sure why he needed a fucking sitting room, but the couch had come in handy when he needed a nap. It also looked to be just the right height for what he wanted to do.

He glanced over and Charlie was naked, her gorgeous body flush with desire. Her eyes had already taken on the sleepy look he associated with her subspace. She subbed so fast, sometimes even without a single slap of his hand. Sometimes all she needed was a deepening of his voice as though the minute he opened the door, she fled inside and tried to lock herself away from the rest of the world.

"Is that how you start a session?" He wouldn't call it what it was. It was lovemaking. It was need. It was the very air he breathed.

She dropped to her knees, her head falling forward, strawberry hair caressing her breasts and shoulders like a canopy concealing her secrets. He loved her hair. It didn't matter what color it was as long as there was a lot of it. As long as he woke up covered in the stuff, a web he'd been caught in and didn't want to get out of.

Her hands were placed on her thighs, palms up as he'd taught her. She didn't make him ask twice about the placement of her knees. They were wide open, her pussy on display and he could already tell his sub was getting hot. Her pussy was a pearly pink, her nipples tight.

She was waiting for him. Calm and patient. Trusting.

Fuck. He couldn't do what he wanted to do. He was too fucking big. He would hurt her. He'd never thought he would rue his big cock, but the day was here. A tightness formed in his chest. "Get dressed, Charlotte. I have to get you some clothes before we leave here."

His cock was screaming at him, promising him it would be very good and patient if he would only give it a chance at fucking that sweet little asshole.

His cock was shit out of luck.

Charlie's head came up, the sleepy look vanishing and in its place a near panic. "What did I do wrong?"

He held on to his temper. He wanted to roar and scream and fuck her anyway, but she was his. His. He couldn't hurt her any more than he already had. Revenge had sucked when it came to Charlie. His words came out on a shaky breath as he tried to calm his cock. "You didn't do anything wrong. I never take a lover without preparing her first. I could hurt you. You remember when we were married, I was training you then. That's why I made you wear the plug every day."

She flushed again. "Ian, what I am about to tell you might sound weird and creepy at first, but I want you to remember that you gave me orders and even though you thought I was dead, I knew I was married and had a Master and I wanted to be an obedient sub."

What the hell was she trying to say? "You're rarely obedient, Charlie. I suppose I should have written it into a contract that you weren't allowed to fake your own death or start up a criminal enterprise that would have three countries after your head."

"Sometimes I just need guidelines, Master." Her eyes came up, wide and innocent. God, he loved watching those eyes widen when he worked his cock in. It was one more thing he hadn't liked about fucking her in the club. He wanted to be face to face. He wanted to watch her up close, see every expression as he took her.

"Your guidelines are to go and get ready. We've got a long flight ahead of us." At least twenty-four hours where his cock would be in hell.

"But I followed your instructions," she said quickly.

He stared at her, trying to understand. And yes, he thought it was weird. And kind of hot if he was right about what she was saying. "You plugged yourself?"

She flushed, though now he could have sworn there was embarrassment in there. Her eyes found the floor. "Yes. Not every day, but at least once a week. Usually more. You told me to. I found comfort in following your directions. I know the vanilla world would think it perverse, but I pretended it was you."

She was completely and utterly fuck-all crazy. She'd plugged herself for five years? It was ridiculous. His cock was jumping in his jeans again.

"Back in position and stay there." He walked out of

his office and down the hall, not giving a shit that he was carrying an extra-large butt plug and a container of toy cleaner in his hands. The world was falling apart around him, but it didn't matter because he had a toy to clean. All that mattered was getting ready because one way or another, he was going to find out if she was lying.

He stalked into the bathroom, his brain buzzing. She could be lying again. It could be her way of covering up the fact that she'd had a bunch of men in every way.

Or she could be telling the truth and she was a faithful wife for years, finding comfort in even the oddest of his rituals. His heart clenched a little at the thought of her trying to plug herself for the first time. She would have felt awkward and alone. It was a game between lovers, but she'd been on the run and by herself. Had she done it in the dark? The way he yanked his own dick and thought about her?

He knew he should back off. He should send her into hiding. He should separate her from the others and task Simon with making sure she stayed alive.

And he wasn't going to do it because he couldn't stand the thought of her not being with him. Now that he'd seen her again, touched her, fucked her, the idea of Charlie being out of his sight, his control, was unacceptable.

He cleaned the plug, dried it off and then turned to go back to the office where she would be waiting. She would be in position, waiting for him. It made him a bastard, caveman pig but he liked knowing she wasn't thinking about anything but him, but what he was going to do to her, with her.

Damon Knight was walking down the hall, his big body taking up most of the space. They couldn't actually get through the hall without brushing against each other because they were so broad. He should have thought about extra-large halls since he seemed to only hire or work with men built like Mack trucks. "Excellent, I was just looking for you. The jet will be ready at four. I've been informed that we have to take an extra passenger along."

"Ten." He'd known the minute he made that deal that the Agency would want an observer. It was a testament to Ian's stubbornness that Ten wasn't taking over the game.

"Yes. We've been given leave to support you in any fashion you choose. You have influential friends, mate."

He'd done favors for a lot of powerful men. And now he owed a few more. "I'm going to kill Nelson."

"I'm going to look the other way when you do. I'm perfectly certain it will be in self-defense." Thank god it was Damon they had sent and not someone else. He mostly trusted Damon. He just didn't know his partner well enough. "So we'll refuel in Frankfurt and then Mumbai and we should be in Goa in roughly twenty-four hours. That's as fast as we can get there. Do you know you're carrying around an anal plug? Is this how you deal with office discipline?"

He started back to his office, not bothering to look back. "It's how I deal with my sub. If anyone asks, I'm unavailable until we're ready to head to the airport, and tell Adam he better have our papers ready or I'll use this on him."

He walked back through his door and there she was, a vision of submission waiting for him. God, he should be prepping for the operation, but all he wanted to do was lose himself in her. He wanted to lock the office door and never come out. For the first time, he thought seriously about running with her. He knew how to hide. No one would find them. They could be anonymous. They could give up everything and just find an island and never leave it.

And never see his brother again. Never know how Carys would look as a sassy teenager giving Sean hell. Never have kids of his own because they would be a weakness.

Life had been so much easier before she'd walked back in, but he knew in a moment that he didn't want easy.

"Show me." He stood in front of her, his cock twitching insistently, but he wanted to see it.

She nodded slightly, taking the plug in her hand. "I need some lube. I always use lube."

As she should. He passed it to her, forcing his hand not to find her hair. When he was in a room with her, it was hard not to touch her, and when he wasn't in a room with her, it was hard not to find whatever room she was in and be there, too.

She very carefully lubed up the plug. He'd picked the one that was just shy of being his size, but she didn't seem intimidated by it. She simply ran her hands over it, covering the hard plastic plug generously.

There was no hesitation, no worry in her movement. It seemed almost like a loving ritual, one she'd performed often.

He'd told her he would spend weeks preparing her for anal sex. He'd explained that she would have to wear the plug regularly to stretch her so he didn't hurt her.

Had she really spent five fucking years preparing herself for him?

"May I move to the couch, Master? I usually do this on a bed."

He didn't correct her anymore. He was her Master. He always had been. He'd never allowed anyone to call him that on a personal basis. He was Master Ian at Sanctum, but Sir when playing. Because as much as she belonged to him, he knew in his heart that he belonged to her. Forever.

He just wasn't sure it could work. "Yes. Do what you always do. I want to watch."

She rose, grace in her every movement. She'd only started to practice when she'd left him, but her ease now spoke of years of rising from the submissive position, years of lowering herself down. She was a well-trained sub.

Had she done that herself? Had she done all of it while thinking of him, planning to come home to him?

Had this woman truly ached for him the way he'd ached for her?

He watched, his cock throbbing as she knelt on the couch, her backside to him. She spread her knees wide and allowed her torso to lay flat so that her ass was in the air, stretched by the position of her knees. She gave him the most delicious view of her asshole, all rosy and pink. Her hand held the plug, moving from underneath to place the flesh colored plug right against that gorgeous hole. Her rosette was tight, small. It didn't look for a second like it could handle the monster she'd placed against it.

Her back was supple, all her muscles relaxed. She let out a long sigh as she pressed the plug to her ass, twisted it, opening the right side first so she could slip the plug in.

One smooth move and she was plugged, only the flat base in sight.

Other women might offer him a home-cooked meal or ask to hold his hand as a romantic gesture, but his wife understood him.

She plugged herself like a pro, and it was the most fucking romantic thing he'd ever seen.

He moved forward, placing a hand on that gloriously round ass, loving the little mewling sigh that came from her throat the minute he touched her. "How long do you usually keep it in?"

"I like to sleep with it."

She didn't say anything more, but he heard everything she didn't say. She slept with it because it was like sleeping with him buried deep inside her. Because in those moments, she could close her eyes and pretend he was still with her.

God, he wanted to believe her. He wanted it more than anything in his life.

He lightly touched the base of the plug. Her muscles contracted around it, a pleasure reflex. "Do you like it?"

"I didn't at first. It was weird. I did it because you wanted me to. I thought it would be something I would endure because it would bring you pleasure."

"And now?"

"I dream about it, Master. I dream about you fucking my asshole and taking what's yours."

She was going to make him come with nothing but sweet words.

There was no question about it. He could fuck her and she would love it. He would love it.

All he had to do was take out that plug and shove his cock in. He could get off fast and then maybe he would be able to think. He could take what he needed and retreat again.

"Turn over." He couldn't handle using her the way he had before. He might not know what to do with her outside of the bedroom, but he was going to be her true Master in it. A Master took care of his sub first.

She carefully lowered herself to the couch and rolled over. Her eyes stared up at him warily. Did she think he would dismiss her now? Maybe laugh at her for years of service?

"Thank you, love." He picked up her right foot, bringing it to his lips and kissing her toes. They were ticklish. He could torture her for hours by playing with her feet. What he'd never told her was he hadn't done it because he wanted to punish her. He just loved to hear her laugh.

"You don't think it's weird?"

He bit gently at her toes and she practically jumped. "I think it's entirely weird, and you're the most perverted woman I've ever met. Lucky for you I have a thing for perverts."

"Ian, don't." She tried to wiggle her foot away.

He tightened his grip. "You don't tell me what to do when we're in the bedroom."

She whimpered a little. "You know I hate that, Master."

"But I love it." Most subs hated the whip or being caned, but not his Charlie. She hated having her feet tickled. Unfortunately for her, he loved to do it.

He ran his tongue over the soul of her foot.

Charlie let out a strangled scream, squirming on the couch, and then he heard it, that low, gorgeous sound. It rang through the whole room and made his soul feel lighter. Yes, he was going to take her. He was going to fill her with his come until she couldn't see straight, but god, he loved her laugh.

"Oh, my love, is it hard to keep that plug in while you're laughing?" The worries he had were floating away. This was what he needed. Whatever happened hours from now could happen, but in this moment he was safe and happy and making his sub laugh.

Her face was pink, her smile wide as she glared up at him, a ridiculously stubborn look in her eyes. "I can keep this plug in all day long. Do your worst, Master."

He picked up her other foot, adoring how he circled her ankle with his hand. She wasn't petite, his wife, but he could top her easily. He put all five of her toes into his mouth, scraping his teeth along her sole.

"Oh, god!" She was lost to a fit of giggles. Her whole body shook, her breasts bouncing beautifully, her hips swaying. "You're a sadist."

He put her feet against both his cheeks, admiring her perfect pussy. "I'm not a sadist."

Her mouth came open as he ran his nose from her heel to her toes. "Evil. You certainly are. You love to make me scream. You love to whip my ass and torture me."

And she loved the way he did it. But she didn't exactly understand him—or herself. "It's not sadism if the partner loves the pain, pet. Sadists want to hurt their partners. You love what I do to you."

Her hands came up, a brilliant smile crossing her face as she laughed. "Yes, I do. I do, but if you're not a sadist, what do you call yourself?"

He knew exactly who he was when he was with her. It got cloudy, uncertain, when she was gone, but, oh, when she was close, he knew who he was. "I'm the man who gives you what you need."

He dropped her feet, making sure they were spread wide. He wasn't going to turn her over. No. He wanted to look into her eyes, to see her as he loved her, to take her fully and without restraint. He wasn't going to pull that bullshit "pushing her away" crap afterward. He was going to sink into her and take what he needed and give her something back. He couldn't promise her anything past this moment, but he would be here with her in the now.

He got onto the couch with her, shifting her so he could move with her body. She gasped a little as he shoved her to the opposite side of the couch, the crown of her head hitting the arm. "Sorry, love."

"What are you going to do?" Her voice was sultry, her

legs spread wide. She didn't care about anything but the fact that he was here with her, and that made his heart swell.

"I'm going to give you what you need." He lowered his mouth down, the heat of her pussy damn near killing him.

He placed a soft kiss on her clitoris, breathing in her scent. She'd managed to calm him, to take away his violent tendencies. Her submission had quelled his need to go fast and hard, softening him to the point that he could take his time with her. He pulled her labial lips apart and sucked each one inside his mouth as she gasped and moaned. He ate her pussy, her tangy taste filling his mouth and sharpening his senses until all he wanted and needed was to be surrounded by her.

Her little asshole was clutching the plug like a favorite toy it wasn't going to give up. He spread her knees wide, but she didn't let the plug slip.

His sweet sub deserved a treat before he took his prize. He laid the flat of his thumb right on her clit, pressing down with firm intent. He speared her with his tongue, fucking her in long passes as he rubbed the pearl of her clit.

She went off like a rocket. Cream coated his tongue as she screamed out his name and clamped down around him.

She was still shaking as he got to his knees and tore at the opening of his jeans. He'd given her everything she needed. It was his turn. His cock sprang free, and he pulled the plug from her ass, watching her rosette clench around it.

Fuck, that was about to be his dick.

"Let me turn over." She reached up, caressing his chest, her words lazy and satiated.

"No." He tossed the plug away and briefly wondered

if the janitorial staff would quit en masse, but he didn't give a fuck. Five years he'd longed for her. Five years he'd been half a man. He grabbed the lube and started working it over his straining cock. "We'll do this my way."

"I thought I would be on my knees."

Because she'd never had anal sex before. Because she didn't understand how creative he could be when he wanted something the way he wanted this. "You thought wrong. I'll show you about a hundred different ways to do this. But today, I want to watch you. Trust me."

"I do, Ian. I won't make the same mistake twice. Show me what you want, Master." She lifted her hips when he offered her a pillow.

Carefully placing it under her backside, the pillow lifted her pelvis and gave him easy access to her ass.

He joined her on the couch, lifting her ankles and making a place for himself between her legs. Reclining Lotus, as the Kama Sutra would call it. "Keep your feet on my thighs, knees out."

The position opened her completely to him. He could take her pussy or her ass, and she was utterly vulnerable.

"You look so fucking soft, baby. Do you how vulnerable and pretty you look? You're just lying there for me, offering me everything. You're a sweet little sub." He lined his cock up to her tight rosette. "Do you know who I am?"

"My Master." Her breathy answer was accompanied by a little smile.

He pressed against her, his cockhead fighting to get inside. "Oh, baby, I'm the nasty, dirty man who's about to ram his filthy cock up your asshole. Yeah. Do you feel it?"

A little gasp told him she did.

Back and forth he worked, the head of his dick

beginning to disappear inside. He stared down at the lovely sight. Her delicate hole couldn't hold out on him. No. He was a fucking Viking and he was going raiding. "I won't let you keep me out. Don't you even try. You let my cock in. You let your Master fuck your ass."

Her eyes had widened, her mouth coming open in a little *O* as he forced his cock inside. "I don't think I used a big enough plug."

He held his weight off her with one hand and with the other he tweaked her nipple as he continued to thrust inside. "No more plugs for you. I think you like them too much. From now on you only get my cock in this sweet hole. Fuck, you feel good, Charlie."

So tight. He could barely breathe. Her ass gripped him like nothing before, the heat so different from her pussy. He loved them both equally and promised not to favor one over the other. He would fuck her pussy and her ass and her mouth. He would fuck just about anything on her body that he could push his dick inside because that body belonged to him. *His. His. His.*

He pushed in, feeling savage again. She might have been able to erase some of his worries, but she couldn't take away his raging possessiveness. Whatever had happened before, he had her now and he had zero intention of allowing her to leave again.

Charlie took a shaky breath. "I'm so full."

"Not quite yet." He wasn't granting mercy. She would take every inch of him inside.

She groaned as he worked his way in inch by inch. Her beautiful face flushed pink. "I don't think I can take more."

But he still had so much more to give. "Yes, you can. You'll take your Master. You'll welcome me inside. Say it, Charlie. Tell me to give you my cock. Tell me you want it."

"I want it. You know I want it."

A low groan came from his chest as he finally managed to tunnel into her. She'd taken him to the root, and he held himself steady there, letting her get used to him. "Tell me how it feels."

"Like my anus is going to explode, Ian. Seriously." But there was a smile on her face as she panted, obviously trying to adapt.

He let his eyes close briefly, sinking into the sensation of being balls deep in her ass. "It only feels like I'm going to split you in two. It won't really happen. Tell me, baby, did you fuck yourself with that plug?"

"I don't understand. I plugged myself."

He loved how out of breath she was. And that she didn't seem to understand. He looked back down at her. "So you didn't move it in and out? You didn't fuck the plug."

"No, Master. You only told me to plug myself. Ian, please. Please, I want to give you what you need but this is killing me. What's happening?"

No. She hadn't fucked the plug. She thought this was all there was. She didn't understand a damn thing. A sweet little virgin and he was going to show her how nasty and dirty and glorious anal sex could be.

"Are you ready, baby? Are you ready for me to fuck you?"

She gritted her teeth. "I kind of thought you already were. Ian, if you have anything left that isn't already inside me, we need to talk."

A laugh bubbled up. She was the only one who could do that to him, who could take him from raging passion to laughter in a second. "No need to talk. Just feel."

He dragged his dick out in a slow pass.

Charlie's eyes flared as she caught her breath. "Oh, Master."

A long, slow thrust back in. "There's a reason women let us do this to them, baby. Tell me you love it."

Her hands came up, tightening on his shoulders. "I love it."

This time when he pulled out almost to the tip, her ass tightened around him, trying to keep him in. "Tell me you love it when I fuck your ass."

She groaned, biting her bottom lip as he thrust harder this time. "I love it when you fuck my ass. Please, Master. Please fuck my ass."

"Now that is a polite request and one I'll honor." He gave up the dirty talk. It was time to let his cock do all the communicating. Heat poured through him, his every muscle clamoring for release, but he didn't want to stop.

Over and over he moved inside her, his eyes watching the place where his dick disappeared inside, where he dominated her. Over and over. In and out. That tight asshole fought him as he thrust inside and then greedily clamped down on him as he pulled back. Every inch of his cock was pressed and squeezed inside her.

Then her asshole spasmed around his dick as she came, her nails biting into his shoulders.

He couldn't hold out another second. His balls drew up tight. His spine tingled. His vision narrowed down to one thing only—her. The orgasm flared through him like a wildfire and he came in long passes, giving her everything he had. He thrust deep, holding himself hard against her, spreading her even further so there wasn't an inch of space between them.

Pleasure made his eyes cross, his brain flare, and finally a calm sense of peace settled on him as he slipped from her ass and let her take his weight. Pressing her into the couch, he laid his head on her breast.

Her hands found his hair, stroking him softly.

Ian closed his eyes and hoped that time could slow down so he never had to make the decision he was going to be forced to make.

Chapter Fifteen

Charlie looked around the well-appointed jet and decided that Damon Knight must be the shit back at MI6. It wasn't a massive jetliner, but it more than made up for size with luxury.

There were twelve leather seats in the cabin and they didn't look anything like the tiny coach seats she'd flown in before. This sucker reclined fully and looked to have been built for two.

Or just really oversized men. Ian took up all of his seat. He sat beside her, looking down at reports as they waited for the others to board.

Of course even the comfiest of seats couldn't make up for the soreness she was feeling. Damn plug never made her sore. It also hadn't made her come like the world was ending. She squirmed a little, trying to find a comfy position.

Ian's head turned, a devilish grin lighting his face. "Do you need help, love? Is there something making you uncomfortable?"

She would take a little soreness to see him smile like that. If he thought he was embarrassing her, he was so wrong. Embarrassment was for people who had nothing better to do. "Yes, I am because someone decided to shove a very large item up my poor backside and now that same person is making me take a twenty-four hour flight."

His smiled broadened and he leaned over, brushing her hand with his. "Your Master is a horrible man. He obviously thinks only of himself and about just how good your ass felt."

"Oh, my god, please stop," Chelsea said from her seat behind Charlie. "I can't tell you how gross that is."

Ian winked at Charlie. "Your sister is a prude. Are you really in pain? I'm sure they have something you can take for it."

She rather liked the ache. It was a reminder that he was still here with her. She squeezed his hand, adoring the intimacy. "I'll just have a glass of wine. I'll be fine."

He nodded and turned back to his files, the ones she'd given him. Small steps. She couldn't ask for anything more.

Well, she could hope that they were all still alive tomorrow, but that was about it. She wouldn't put it past her uncle to have a couple of surface-to-air missiles at his disposal.

The cabin door opened and Simon and Jesse entered. Simon looked dapper in his three-piece suit, as though he hadn't been up all night. Charlie watched as Simon's blue eyes found Chelsea's before moving past her. Jesse was carrying a briefcase and had gotten a haircut. He looked deeply uncomfortable in his dress shirt and slacks, but it looked like Simon was forcing him to take the job seriously.

Simon stopped at their aisle, looking to Ian. "Everything is in place."

"And the office?"

"Is closed for the week. I sent Phoebe home, and she's going to work from there until we decide it's safe."

"She probably threw a party," Ian muttered.

"She cried. She cries a lot," Simon said with a sigh.

Jesse frowned as he took a seat at the back. "She's just a little sensitive. You should try being nicer to her."

"So everyone is off then?" A new voice filled the space, and Charlie turned to see a large man with golden brown hair and green eyes standing in the aisle. He was wearing jeans and a black T-shirt that molded to his broad shoulders and muscular chest.

Ian glanced up at the newcomer. "Everyone who's alive."

He'd asked her to keep up the illusion that Avery was gone.

The newcomer shrugged a little. He leaned forward, moving in close to Ian. "I'll believe that when I see it." Had she not been sitting so near, she wouldn't have heard him. "I know Adam's work when I see it. If you need anything, I'm here for you."

Ian's eyes tightened. "I'll let the Agency know. Ten, this is Charlotte Dennis. Charlie, this is Tennessee Smith. I hope you're still using your real name. Has the Agency forced you to join the color scheme of aliases yet?"

An "aw shucks" grin came over the man's face. "Naw, you know I think those Agency names are a little silly. I know we're supposed to hide our real names, but I'll just kill anyone I need to and it'll be fine." He reached out for her hand, drawing it up to his lips in a gallant gesture. "Not that I'm a killer, darlin'. I'm really more of a lover. Charlie, is it?"

Ian reached over and grabbed her hand out of Ten's. "Not to you. She's Mrs. Taggart to you."

He pulled her hand back, but didn't let it go. She

threaded her fingers through his.

Ten's handsome jaw dropped open. "The dead one?"

A shit-eating grin lit Ian's face, and he brought her hand to his lips, brushing them across her knuckles. "Guess you don't know everything, do you? And if I hear you calling her Charlie, I'll strangle you."

Ten sat down across from Ian, his big body taking up the chair. "Well, I like my natural coloring. Zhukov still looks blue, by the way. He's also become decidedly chatty."

Charlie could imagine what had loosened his lips. His time with Ian would almost certainly have warmed him up. "Did he admit that I wasn't supposed to be his only victim?"

"He's already admitted that the entire McKay-Taggart team was on the list. Though they had left off the new kid. He was real disappointed about that. Apparently not being on a hit list makes him feel like he's not on the team."

"It's rude," Jesse said from the back. "I'm just as dangerous as the rest of you."

"I'll kill you myself if it makes you feel better." Simon took his seat.

Jesse shrugged. "I just think it was rude for them not to include me, that's all."

Ten frowned, his grin disappearing. "The fourteen people on that list included your niece."

Ian's hand tightened slightly on her own, the only acknowledgment that he'd heard what Ten said. "What does the Agency know about Nelson's recent activities?"

Ten crossed his arms over his chest. "We've placed him in Russia and a couple of places in India. Since you shut down his last enterprise, he's been moving quite a bit."

"What are his ties to the Denisovitch syndicate?"

Ten hesitated, his eyes looking around the cabin.

Ian shook his head. "We made a deal, Ten."

"Is she really The Broker?"

"I don't know what you're talking about," Ian replied.

How much had he given up to keep her out of the Agency's hands?

She kept her mouth shut. There was no way she was going to push him. Her ass was already sore.

Damon Knight walked out of the cockpit. "You know who she is and you also know that he's not going to admit to anything, so you might as well not try. I'll be honest, I suspect the younger one, too, but he put her in the deal so we can't have either one of them."

He'd protected her sister? Even Chelsea turned, staring at Ian for a moment.

"The Broker is done," Ian said with a grim finality. "You don't have to worry about that particular problem again. Now, part of my deal with the big bosses was that you would give me full disclosure on Nelson, so start talking." He dropped her hand, his body closing off from her.

Nelson was still between them. She fought to keep a smile on her face. No matter how close they seemed when he was making love to her, there was still a gulf there, keeping them apart.

Patience. It had always been her downfall, but she was determined to remain patient this time.

"Fine," Ten finally said. "From what we can tell, Nelson's ties to Mikhail Denisovitch go back four and a half years. We have a man in a friendly syndicate. As friendly as syndicates can be. He says Nelson started meeting with the heads of the syndicates after he claimed to have evidence against your wife in the murder of her father."

Charlie shrugged at that. "Of course he had evidence. He's the one I hired to kill the bastard. I'm sure he didn't mention that to my uncle."

"No, I'm sure he left that bit out," Knight said. "So the question becomes what is Nelson doing in India? I understand why he would spend so much time in Russia. He's doing some of the syndicate's dirty work."

Ten looked up at the MI6 agent. "Why would he be working with Dusan? Tell me something, Charlotte, what does your cousin do and why would he need someone of Nelson's talents?"

Charlie shrugged a little. "He wouldn't unless a whole lot has changed. Dusan wasn't my father's favorite. He put up with him because he was his brother's kid, but he thought Dusan wasn't loyal enough. He wanted to go to college. My dad wasn't big on the whole scholarship thing when it came to his soldiers."

"He liked them dumb and loyal, huh?" Knight asked.

Charlie nodded. "Yes." Dusan was actually one of the only cousins she could stand to be around for more than three minutes. "He didn't have a high profile when I was living in Russia. My uncle must have put him in charge of a group after I got out. You said he was working the pipeline?"

Ian nodded. "That's what we've figured out. They steal crude straight from the pipeline."

She knew how the scam worked. "But they would need a finger man. Uhm, a man who works for the oil company who can tell them when the coast is clear, so to speak. The government has been trying to crack down on that kind of thing. Most of the oil companies take security seriously, so he would have to have someone on the inside or he would have to be negotiating with someone who was already there. It's how they dealt with all the hijacking stuff."

Chelsea popped up over Charlie's seatback. "Our father particularly enjoyed hijacking aid and relief packages. He stole everything from antimalarials to AIDS drugs to vaccines for babies. He would sell them on the black market. Such a lovely man."

Baz was suddenly behind Knight. "We've got the go-ahead. If we're all here, I'm ready to take off."

Knight nodded, turning away.

"Give it another minute or two. We have one more passenger." Simon glanced out the window to his right. "Here he comes now."

Ian stood. "What the hell? Did the Agency send someone else?"

"Nope. I have no idea who it is." Ten held his hands up. "As far as I know, I'm on my own."

"You might be, but Tag is not," Simon said as a shadow fell over the front of the plane.

A man entered, the sun behind him making it hard to see him for a moment.

Sean Taggart had a duffel bag in one hand and a ball cap on his head. "I have my knife kit. If it gets taken by some security fuckers, you're buying me a new one, brother."

Sean had come for his brother. She couldn't help but love him for it. The fact that Ian would have backup that he absolutely, one hundred percent trusted warmed her.

"What the hell are you doing here?" Ian sent a terrific frown his brother's way. "You're supposed to be watching out for Grace and your daughter."

Sean sobered. "Grace and Carys are perfectly safe and you know it." He was tight-lipped as he looked around the cabin. He obviously wasn't going to talk freely until he and his brother were alone. "And someone has to watch out for you."

"In the back. Now." Ian looked down at her. "Don't you move."

She glanced around the small cabin. "Where would I go?"

"We leave in five minutes, Taggart. You should get your family situation sorted," Baz said before disappearing back into the cockpit.

Ian stalked off followed by his brother. Charlie was left with Ten.

"Now, darlin'," he said, switching to sit next to her. "Whatever are we going to do on this very long flight?"

"Tag is going to kill you," Knight said with a shake of his head as he left to join his partner.

Gorgeous lips turned down in a sulky frown. Tennessee Smith likely wouldn't have to kill often. He would just seduce the information out of his victims. "It might be worth it. Besides, I'm not so bad myself. Don't discount me just because the packaging is so damn pretty. Maybe I can take Tag down. I'm just wondering why he would hide such a lovely wife. I wouldn't hide you, honey. You were obviously meant to be shown off."

"Ian didn't hide me. I faked my own death and then spent the next five years working my way back to him. He's my Master and my husband, and if you think I won't shoot your balls off if you try to touch me, then you haven't worked up a proper profile on me." She gave him a smile and couldn't miss the fact that Simon was covering a laugh.

Ten might be gorgeous, but he had nothing on Ian.

"You can't blame a guy for trying. It's a long flight and I don't read magazines." He turned his chair around. "How about you, sweetheart? Why don't you come sit on old Ten's lap and we can talk about all the things we can do at thirty thousand feet."

"Touch her and I'll kill you," Simon said. "If you need some relief, Yank, I suggest you have a wank in the loo."

Chelsea faced forward in her seat, her shoulders up around her ears.

Ten glanced Charlie's way, sitting back in his chair and giving her a little wink.

Yes, it was going to be a very long flight.

* * * *

"What the hell is going on, Sean?" Ian closed the small curtain that separated the cabin from the kitchen.

If Sean was intimidated by his very dark voice, he didn't show it. It sucked because it was the same voice he used to use on his kid brother to get him to do his damn homework. No one was intimidated by him anymore.

"It's time to kill Nelson. I'm coming with you." Sean set down his bag. "Everyone has scattered. Li and Avery are going to our safe house on the East Coast and Jake and Adam are taking Serena, Grace, and Carys to the west. Alex and Eve are headed to Canada."

Sean was smart enough to not say more. Ian didn't care that Ten had watched his back on multiple occasions or that Damon Knight had been one of his mentors when he first started working. No one needed to know the locations of his team. No one. Alex and Eve were making their way to Toronto where they would fly to Saint Petersburg on Canadian passports and visas that allowed them to sight-see. They would report back on Denisovitch's movements.

But he'd meant to keep his brother out of this. "You can't come with me. You have a kid."

"And you have a wife. I don't see what the problem is, brother. Grace has always known that if you went after Nelson, I would go with you."

"She's not my wife. Not really." But the words sounded stubborn and dumb even to him.

His baby brother's eyes rolled in frustration. "You can keep saying it but I hope like hell you wake up before all this is over. Nothing you say is going to get me off this plane. Adam worked up my visa and I managed to get a bunch of shots. What's up with that? Can't Nelson pick a country with less contagions?"

He didn't have time for Sean's complaints. "I can have you hauled off this plane."

"You could try. You might even succeed, but I'll hop the next flight to India and I'll be on your doorstep a couple of hours after you get there. Don't think I can't find out where you've set up shop. Adam might be afraid of you, but Serena craves my enchiladas. Who do you think wins that war, big brother?"

Ian's fists clenched in frustration. "I don't want you hurt, Sean."

"And I don't want you dead." He stepped up, leaving very little space between them. "I know you are always going to see me as your snot-nosed kid brother. I know that deep down you'll think you're responsible for me until the day you die. And I know that I haven't done the one thing I should have done for all those years you treated me like a brat kid and bossed me around."

Fuck, he didn't want to have it out with his brother. He'd spent the last year and a half trying to make up for choosing Sean over Grace when his brother had asked him to protect the woman he loved. Sean couldn't know how much the distance bothered him, how much he missed his brother. "What is that, Sean?"

Sean put a hand on his shoulder, his face grave. "Thank you, brother. You didn't have to take over after Dad left. You could have watched out for yourself but you took over and made sure I had what I needed. Don't think for a second I don't know who bought my birthday presents or made sure I had school supplies."

Ian looked down at the man he'd raised. There was six years between them. It didn't seem like much now, but when their father walked out on them, Sean had only been ten and then it was a chasm. Their mother had been depressed and barely functional. He'd had to grow up at sixteen. He'd had to take control. He remembered that first night when he sat waiting and hoping that his father would come home. And then he'd gotten up the next morning, begged his mother to get out of bed so she could go to work. She'd stayed in bed for a month. He'd gotten a job working after school until midnight at the local grocery. His childhood had been over. "It's not a big deal, Sean."

Sean shook his head. "It's a big fucking deal, Ian. I know our relationship has been strained, but I'm done with that. I love you. I admire you. If anything happens to me and Grace, you should know that we've left Carys in your care."

That shocked the fuck out of him. "I thought you would leave her to Alex and Eve."

"No. It was never even a thought in our heads. You're her uncle and I happen to know that you're damn good at raising a kid. I hope like hell you get your head out of your ass and start raising some with that crazy bitch in there because she is your match, man. Charlie is everything you need."

Somehow he didn't mind his brother calling her Charlie. It bugged him when other people did it. Charlie was his name for her, but when Sean called her that it was an acceptance, a brotherly front. But he didn't want to think about this right now. He wanted to live in the damn moment for once in his life. "I'm not kicking her out."

"Ian, you can't honestly believe she's here to hurt you. What does your gut tell you?"

"My gut was wrong before."

"No, it wasn't. You said you knew something was wrong with her. What does your gut say now?"

"My gut isn't in control. My cock is and my cock doesn't give a shit. Do you understand, Sean? My cock doesn't care that she could have slept with Nelson. She could roll out of his bed and into mine and my cock would be ready to go. I don't care that she might have slept with half the syndicate, that she had her father killed, that she nearly got me and Li killed. I don't care. I just want to get inside her again. If you told me this had all been a lie, that she was walking me into a trap, I would probably go into it willingly because I don't know that I can survive losing her again."

A smile crept over Sean's face. "I think we call that love."

Yep, the vomit was right there at the back of his throat. "It's stupidity, Sean."

"You say potato, I say true love. I know you. I know you've played through every horrible scenario in your head. I know you've gone through all the ways she could be tricking you and everything she would gain by betraying you, but have you thought through the fact that she just loves you and wants to be your wife?"

The plane jumped a little. He was out of time to get his brother away unless he wanted to toss him on the tarmac. "That's not the likely scenario."

"You can't play this on percentages and chances, Ian. Did you read Eve's work-up on her? Did you read about the way she behaved, the things she did when you weren't around?"

He glanced into the cabin. Charlie was looking out the window while Ten seemed to be staring down her shirt. And he was sitting in Ian's fucking seat. What did she really do when no one was watching?

Ten reached out and put a hand on her arm, pointing at something outside the window. Ian felt a low growl start to build in his chest. But then Charlie frowned at him, removed his arm, and seemed to give him a good talking to.

The raging jealousy that had been inside him since the moment she'd walked back in eased a little. Charlie wasn't interested in Ten. As far as he could tell she hadn't looked at another man, and Eve had said she was perfectly celibate in Florida. It had been her reputation there.

Why was he believing a pathetic piece of trash assassin over her?

"You know she sent a bunch of information to the Agency? She stopped a couple of terrorist plots in their tracks. That wasn't Chelsea. That was Charlie. When I sat down with the Agency, they didn't want to torture her."

"They wanted to hire her," Sean surmised.

"I didn't tell her that." He didn't want that life for her. He was allowing her to believe that he'd saved her from torture when he might be keeping her from a job she would love.

"She wouldn't go. She is right where she wants to be and that means you have some decisions to make." His brother slapped him on the back, a manly gesture of affection.

He might have to choose between her and Sean because she would still be wanted, still be under the syndicate's kill order. "Sean, if I run with her…"

"Slip me a postcard every now and then. Let us know you're okay. You should always know that we're here if you need us. You have to choose her now. If you love her then you have to pick her over me, like I picked Grace. Let's finish this and then you run with her. Your job is done. I'm fine. Better than fine. We're all happy, Ian. You played a part in all of us finding what we need. Your little family is set. So you can run and know that we'll be fine. You have a new family now."

Charlie's eyes came up, finding his. She gave him a smile and mouthed the words "save me" and pointed at her erstwhile suitor.

Save her. It was all he'd wanted to do back then.

Knight's voice came over the system. "This is your pilot. We're about to take off. If you want to keep your ball bag in the right place, you'll sit down and buckle up."

So he was set. He was going to meet with Eli Nelson and his brother was at his back.

And he kind of wanted to keep his ball bag where it belonged, but Ten might lose his. He strode down the aisle. He wasn't going to fight with Ten. He didn't need to.

He took the seat across from Ten. "Charlie?"

She didn't need more than that. She unbuckled and immediately moved to sit beside him without a backward glance.

Sean settled in across from Charlie, a smirk on his face.

"Buckle up, baby," Ian said.

It might be a long flight, but at least he liked the company.

Most of it.

* * * *

The sun beat down on Nelson's head, the heat nearly unbearable, but he stayed in position, watching the massive yacht in the distance.

He was getting too old for this shit. He was starting to envy the king and his carefree world. Kamdar didn't have to hustle, didn't have to worry that every day might be his last.

He was a little naïve to not worry about that last bit since Nelson's job was to make sure the king didn't have a good many days left.

The king was lying back on a chaise as his harem lounged around him. Beautiful women in bikinis that barely covered anything at all. They were all there awaiting the king's pleasure. Including the new blonde he'd picked up when he'd refueled yesterday.

It had been the simplest thing for Nelson to get his own pretty blonde on board. His attempts at getting close to the king himself had met with failure. The king, he'd been told, was on vacation and not meeting anyone for business.

It would be so simple if he could just murder the fucker, but until he figured out where the research documents were stored, Kash Kamdar had to be kept alive. The last thing his bosses wanted was the research being made public. He needed every copy either in his hands or destroyed.

Hopefully Olga would do her work and do it well. She simply needed to get into the king's bed and then wait until he made a mistake.

Or if he took too long, then Olga was not only magnificent in bed, she was also a well-trained torturer. She could lick a man's balls and then make him wish he'd never been born with them.

He just wished she would get on with it. The shit in Russia was getting to be a pain in his ass. His employers didn't understand that the pipeline raids were a delicate balance. He had to keep both the syndicate and the insider he'd placed at Malone Oil happy. The young engineer he'd found spied for him and let him know when security was weak, and then Nelson let Denisovitch know where to strike. All his bosses wanted was more profit. They didn't understand that the minute Malone Oil found his spy, they would likely find him and figure out that rival oil companies were using the mob to weaken their competitors.

The world was changing. Governments controlled very little now. Oh, they made a good show of it, but they no longer had real power. Nelson had seen it coming a long time ago. The Agency paid shit, and they weren't known for their loving care of retired employees. So when The Collective had first recruited him, it had been a godsend. The Collective understood how the world worked. They also knew how to keep an employee happy. Money. Profit. That was what The Collective traded in. He'd found his place.

Until fucking Taggart had ruined everything.

He'd been valuable to The Collective when he had CIA entrée. Now he had to hustle like the rest of them and hope he satisfied the men in power.

Corporations were the new kings, and they liked their warfare waged quietly.

He just sometimes had to convince them to be patient.

His cell rang—the private one he always had to answer. He put down his binoculars just as the king started in on a pretty Asian woman. It looked like he was branching out from his usual blondes.

"Yes." No need for "hello" or "this is." They knew

exactly who he was and they didn't care for pleasantries.

"Why was the Agency and MI6 swarming Dallas?"

Fuck. He hadn't exactly explained to his contact that a round of assassinations had been part of his deal with the syndicate, but then he was awfully good at deflecting blame. "Denisovitch found his niece. I'm afraid I wasn't able to convince him of her worth."

Like he would try. He wanted the bitch dead, too.

"I explained to you that The Collective believes she could be an asset."

"I brought your concerns to the syndicate, but I'm afraid they believe in revenge more."

His contact's frustration was clear in the tightness of his tone. "Try harder. We want the girl brought to us. She's proven to be smart and capable and willing to get her hands dirty."

They didn't understand Charlotte Denisovitch the way he did. "Then why did she tip off the Agency about Al-Qaeda plots?"

There was a small chuckle over the line. "The fact that she knew about those plots at all makes us interested in her. We're not terrorists, Mr. Nelson. We're capitalists. There was no money to be made off anarchist plots. We stood to lose billions if the Euro dropped, so in our minds she's quite the hero. We expect you to keep the syndicate in line."

Yeah, because that was an easy job. "Denisovitch can be unreasonable."

"Then maybe he shouldn't be the head of the family anymore."

Fuck. He was going to have to off another mobster. He'd been lucky last time. If he got caught, it wasn't like The Collective would send the cavalry in. They would just find another agent to take his place and move on.

"Finish the job in India. If you can kill the project and bring us all the research, there will be a rather large bonus in it for you. Then you can handle the Russian problem and we can discuss your retirement from the field. We think it might be time to move you to management."

Those were the magic words that kept him dangling on a string. Oh, he knew he would never really be out of The Collective, but he could move out of the field. He could move into recruitment and training and stay for months on his island.

He would be able to enjoy it because Taggart would be dead. He could always claim that Denisovitch wouldn't listen. Everyone knew the man was insane. He would let the syndicate do his dirty work and then get rid of the head and install someone more reasonable.

It could work out for everyone.

"Of course. I've placed a spy inside the king's household."

Another chuckle. "You mean you put a whore in his bed. That man has the stamina of a rutting bull. Don't let her kill him until we have that research. Is the site rigged?"

At least he'd managed to do one thing right. "I have more than one spy. I managed to find one of his employees with a gambling problem. I think I'm almost ready to move. And yes, the research site is rigged to explode when I choose. I have to make sure I get the research out of there before I blow it if I can't get Kamdar's copy."

"It might be easier to take it from the king than to get it from the site. Make sure the scientists are inside when you pull the trigger. We have our own who can continue the research or quash it, whatever we decide."

Because The Collective ran the world and they didn't

like anyone else interfering. Technology, research, innovation had to come from The Collective and no one else. Whether they bought it or stole it, all knowledge would come from them.

"Absolutely. Perhaps the next king won't be so disagreeable." The Collective would likely make sure of it. Nelson already had several candidates in mind. After all, it was always in their best interests to install their own leaders.

"We shall see, Mr. Nelson. Now, listen closely. I have it on good authority that you have some visitors on the way."

His whole body tightened with dread. "Who?"

"Well, let's just say your old friends aren't in Dallas anymore. Good luck to you. You know what happens if you fail." The line went dead.

If he failed he would very likely find himself answering questions he didn't want to answer. And his retirement might be from life and not the field.

How had that fucker found him?

Unless sweet Charlotte had been keeping tabs on him and wanted to please her dipshit husband. Otherwise, Taggart would have taken his bait and been looking for him in Russia.

He should have known assassins couldn't take down Taggart himself. Now Tag would want revenge for more than Grace's near death during their first real meeting.

He had to move fast. It might be time to call in a few friends and take the boat over himself. He picked up his binoculars again and prayed the king decided to go back to blondes.

Chapter Sixteen

The sound of the beach eased Charlie out of a deep sleep. The rolling waves had soothed her all night, forming a rhythm she'd eased into. After the long flight and then the drive from the airport, she had fallen into bed after barely getting a glimpse of the beach huts they had taken out.

Soft light filled the room, and she could see the ceiling above her and a large, slowly rotating ceiling fan. The salty smell of the ocean wafted over her and then she smelled coffee, dark and rich.

She rolled over and sighed as she realized the other half of the bed was still neat as a pin.

Ian hadn't come to bed. Though he'd been kind and had taken care of her during the long trip, he had pulled back into himself after a few hours. He was right back where they'd been before. Undecided. She reached out and touched the place where his head should have laid.

Patience.

She just needed patience. She was here with him and not stuck in a safe house with Liam frowning at her, and that was a plus.

It had been her mantra on the long flight to Mumbai and then the shorter hop to the Goa airport in Vasco da Gama. Two cars had been waiting for them and she'd sat beside Ian as he drove the winding coastal road. She'd tried to pretend everything was all right as she'd taken in the natural beauty of the sea on one side and the rice terraces and coconut groves on the other. She spent so much of her time in cities that it was easy to forget how beautiful the world could be.

But there was a hollowness to it all because he was so far from her.

"Charlie?"

She turned and he was sitting in a rattan chair, his eyes thoughtful. She wondered if he'd been watching her sleep. "Hi. Is everyone already up?"

He nodded. "Yes, they've got some crazy-ass plan to go and meet this king. Ten and Damon really believe in subterfuge. They're coming up with all these plots to get us on his boat. Apparently today is the day he brings his yacht in and restocks his liquor cabinets or something."

She yawned behind her hand and wondered if she would be stuck here while Ian worked. She would worry about him every single minute. "Yes. He's quite the party boy. According to the tabloids, he seems to love fast boats and gorgeous women."

"According to your research, he also likes science."

Charlie got out of bed, not bothering with the robe that was laid out at the end of the mattress. She'd put on one of Ian's T-shirts and it hung down to her knees. She looked out the window of the small, but likely wretchedly expensive "hut" they had checked into. Agonda Beach looked out on the Arabian Sea, the waves gentle, the water seeming never to end. White sand stretched out in either direction. There was peace here. Quiet. Tranquility. She wished they were here to be alone. "Yes, he's spent a lot of money on research. He funds all kinds of studies."

"I've been thinking. Why would Nelson be interested in the king of Loa Mali? All reports have Kamdar as a humanitarian, a great ruler. The US has pushed him for elections, but there's no doubt his people love him. From what I can tell, he's not corrupt. He shares the wealth. Yes, they have oil, but Nelson's already getting oil from Russia. Unless, he's not really interested in the money from the oil."

She turned back to Ian. "How could he not be interested in the money?"

"Because it's petty cash. He has to share it with the syndicate. You have to know how your relatives pay." Ian stood up and stretched. "It doesn't make sense. I've been trying to study the man, but he's shown me what he wants me to see. I need to study his actions. The truth is there. Why did he try to steal the drone plans for the Chinese and then turn around and get into arms shipments? Now he's interested in oil. There's too much jumping around."

"I didn't look at it that way." Now that she really thought about it, it didn't make sense. It was nearly impossible to shift so much in so few years. His contacts would have to be far and wide, running across many countries, many sectors. Agents in the CIA tended to have a territory. They tended to work in one part of the world. Ian and Nelson had both worked in Europe. So why was he working for the Chinese and now in India? Unless he wasn't dealing in money. Not really. It would come back to money, but that wasn't the first goal.

His eyes were dark as he stared at her. "How did you contact him the first time?"

So he was finally going to get into it. A little shiver went through her. This was the conversation they should have had five years ago. "I didn't. He contacted me."

"So you weren't looking for an assassin?"

She felt pinned by him, unable to do much more than answer his questions. "I was, but I was doing it quietly. I had reached out to another syndicate, one in the US. They had problems with my father. They were both fighting over some territory. My father wanted to expand out of Russia."

"What kind of territory?" His tone was flat, the same as he probably used on everyone he interviewed.

"Drugs. They were just trying to get into the pharmaceutical business, and the States was the best place to do it."

Ian nodded. "They were bilking Medicare and Medicaid?"

It was a common practice for the syndicate. They took money from government programs. "Yes. They would buy doctors who would write prescriptions for patients. OxyContin mostly. He didn't care if the patients took the drugs or went and sold them. The patients worked for the syndicate."

Ian held up a hand. "I understand how it works. So let me get this straight, you reach out to a rival syndicate, but Nelson replies. You reach out to a syndicate that is making money off pharmaceuticals. Nelson was supposed to be working in Europe at the time, but he wasn't in Russia according to what I could find out. He sees a way to get the ten million in bearer bonds that I'm going to use in my operation, but he has to get rid of me to do it. So he sends you in. An exchange of services, so to speak."

God, he could make her feel like a prostitute, but then again, she'd put herself here. "Yes."

"And he used your father as a scapegoat. He convinced the Agency that your father was the likely suspect for claiming to have the uranium we were attempting to buy. Once he was dead and there was no further evidence, the case was closed. He couldn't use the bonds for years so everything quieted down. The Agency was too busy dealing with me. I suppose I should be happy they bothered with me at all. They could have burned me and let me rot in a London jail."

He wouldn't have lasted long. When she looked at the evidence from Ian's perspective, there was no way to find her innocent. "I didn't understand what was going on at the time. I only knew I had to get out or my father was going to eventually kill my sister. Nelson offered me a way to run. He offered me money and a chance to be free of my father."

"What else did he offer you? Did he offer you comfort?"

She shivered at the thought. "No. He offered me a job."

"Now that I find interesting. What did it involve?"

She had to shrug. "He just gave me money and told me to get to the States and he would contact me."

"What do you know about his finances?"

She hated the cold, flat tone he was using on her. "Chelsea knows more than I do."

"I don't want to talk to Chelsea. I want to talk to you."

He wanted to torture her, but she owed him answers. "Fine. I know he's got accounts all over the place, but I was surprised to find out he doesn't have a ton of liquid. In the last year, I've connected him to several mafia jobs and a couple of terrorist groups."

"Why would he be working with terrorists…Charlie, baby, what did the terrorism involve?"

Fuck, how could she have not seen it? "Oil fields. They were destroying equipment in oil fields. The groups do it to protest American involvement in the Middle East."

Ian stood up, stretching. "Yeah, well, I don't think Nelson gives a crap about the Middle East. But he does seem to care deeply about oil."

A few pieces to the puzzle fell into place. "He's working for an oil company."

"That would be my guess at this point. If we take everything we know, we can probably figure out what company it is. He's freelancing, but it isn't for other governments. He's freelancing for corporations. A terrorist for hire, so to speak. It makes a man wonder. I heard a rumor a couple of months back about some ex-Special Forces aiding in the civil wars in certain African countries that have a high level of diamond mines. They were getting paid by diamond merchants to keep the war going because the minute the war ends, the market will be glutted with diamonds and the price will go down. What if Nelson is trying to manipulate the price of crude?"

She thought about everything she knew about the king of Loa Mali. "The rumor is Kamdar is working on an energy project."

He walked up to her, his expression softening a little. He reached down, touching the pad of his index finger to her nose. "Smart girl. Keep quiet. The other rumor was that the man brokering the deal with the mercenaries was an intelligence operative."

She didn't like the suspicion in his voice. "You don't think it's Ten, do you?"

He was suddenly invading her space, pressing his body to hers. It seemed the interrogation was over. "Don't let Ten's idiot bongo beach boy attitude fool you. He's deadly, Charlie. He's been with the Agency since he was a kid. They recruited him straight out of college. He's smart, fast, and he has no ties to anyone. He grew up in foster care. Do you know why he's named Tennessee?"

She could only guess. "His mom loved Tennessee Williams?"

"His loving mother dumped him in a trash bin with his umbilical cord still attached. They named him Tennessee because the diner he was left in was close to the state line. Another couple of miles and he would have been named Kentucky. He was raised in foster care and kind of fell through the cracks. By the time he was nine, he'd been in seven different homes, and when he was thirteen he was running away, getting in trouble. But he scored a perfect score on his SATs and showed an aptitude for moral flexibility the Agency likes. His last foster parent worked for intelligence. He knew what to do with Ten. Think of Ten as a very charming version of Dexter."

Somehow she couldn't see it. He was so laid back, so flirty, but she believed Ian. "All right. So you think he might be working with Nelson?"

"I don't know. I don't want to believe it about him or the MI6 agents, but we're going to keep our mouths shut and our eyes open." His hands found her hair, tangling in it. "He wants you."

She rolled her eyes. "He seems to want anything with the proper female parts."

"Not like that, baby. He wants to hire you. He wants to take you back to DC with him and install The Broker at Langley. It would be a coup for him."

That was an easy decision. "I'll pass."

A long sigh came from his chest as he let her go. "All right, then. I thought I should tell you. You need to get dressed. We have to go and listen to whatever plan they've come up with."

"Ian." She couldn't stand it, couldn't stand the way he kept turning away from her. "Do I even have a shot at this? I know I should be patient and I will be. I'll give you all the time in the world if you'll just tell me I have a shot at making this right."

"You can't make it right."

Her skin flushed with emotion. "Never? You can never forgive me?"

"I don't know. Maybe I can forgive, but I don't know that I can forget." He looked back at her, his eyes weary. "And I don't know if it matters. I want you every minute of the day and I don't think that's ever going to stop, but what are we going to do, Charlie? Are we going to give up the game and buy a little house like Alex and Eve? I don't think we get to do that. So the question becomes what do we do about it? I'm tired of fighting it. I don't care if you slept with Nelson. I don't care if you did everything that fucker said you did."

She shook her head, tears forming. "No. I didn't, Ian."

He held a hand out, silencing her. "It doesn't matter."

"It does." She couldn't lose him to a pack of lies.

"Do you love me, Charlie?"

An easy question to answer. "Yes. God, yes."

"Then promise me something." He came over and stood above her, his eyes looking down into hers.

"Anything."

He took her hand and placed it in the middle of his chest where she could feel the heat of his body through the cotton T-shirt he wore. "If you betray me this time, shoot me. Straight through the heart. Make sure I'm dead because I don't want to live in a world where you betray me twice. Promise me."

She shook her head. She needed him to understand. "Ian, I'm not going to betray you."

"Promise me." His mouth hung over hers. So close. He was so close.

She shook her head. "I don't have to."

His hand tightened on hers. "Promise."

"I promise." Her heart ached as she said it. How could she make him believe?

His mouth took hers, lips forcing hers open under his dominance. Arms wrapped around her, drawing her up to his chest.

She clung to him, her tongue meeting his and gliding in a silky dance. Five years she'd waited for that kiss. Five long years of aching and praying and hoping to make it back to him. His mouth covered hers, blanketing her in heat and desire and something so much sweeter. Adoration, worship was in his kiss. Love was in that kiss and though she didn't have everything she wanted, she could hope because his lips were on hers. She let him lead her, turning her head one way and then the other as he explored her again, reminding her of the long nights he would spend kissing her. He could kiss for hours, his hands skimming her skin and driving her crazy. She would beg him to move on, but he would be content with his tongue tasting hers.

He drugged her with kisses, making all her fears go away and replacing them with the certainty that this was the right man and it was finally the right time.

When he came up for air, he laid his forehead against hers. "I can't fight you anymore, Charlie. I want you too badly. I don't care what you've done in the past, but you're mine now and you're going to behave. Do you understand what I mean?"

He was keeping her? "Ian, I want to be good. It's all I've ever wanted. I want to be your wife. I want you to be proud of me."

"Do you understand what I'll do if I catch you on a computer doing anything but playing solitaire or spending too much money on clothes?"

A little hope lit through her. Oh, she wanted a life where he bitched at her for how much she spent on clothes and shoes and then made her make up for it in his arms. "I suspect my ass will be red."

"You have to trust me, Charlie." His words were a passionate plea. "I want that above everything else. If you can't trust me then you should think about Ten's offer. The Agency could protect you."

She didn't want that. "You'll protect me."

He picked her up, hugging her tight. "I will. When we're done here, we'll leave and figure out what to do."

She stilled in his arms. "Ian, what are you saying?"

"I'm saying I'll go with you."

Now she started to push him away. "You can't. You can't leave your family."

"You're my family now. I tried to fight it, but I can't."

It was everything she wanted and so bittersweet it nearly broke her heart. "I never meant to do this to you. I thought I could hide with you. I thought that maybe my uncle had moved on to bigger things. It was stupid, but I honestly thought I could make this work. It had been over a year since my uncle had sent someone after me."

"Yet he found you so quickly after you came to me. Nelson had me watched. He'll always have me watched if I'm out in the open. I think the people he's working with will do the same as long as they need your uncle's cooperation. They'll watch us."

Maybe she should consider working with the Agency. How could she ask Ian to give everyone up?

He reached down, drawing her chin up so she had to look at him. "I wouldn't like what's going through your head, would I?"

Very likely not since she was thinking of running.

"You can't leave your home."

His arms tightened around her. "My home is with you now. Trust me. Choose me this time."

She searched his face.

Choose him. Choose to rise or fall with him. Choose to run with him, to make a home with him wherever they could. Choose to face everything that was coming with him by her side.

She'd promised him. She'd taken vows. He knew exactly what he was doing. He wasn't the type of man who would walk into this situation without thinking everything through. It was what he'd been doing on the plane, while he was driving, while he sat up all night watching over her. He'd been making his decision.

He was offering himself to her. If she tried to play the martyr, she would be rejecting him.

"I love you. I know I should walk away."

His head shook. "Then put a bullet in me when you go. Charlie, my decision is made. Honor it. Choose me even over your need to sacrifice yourself. God, you've been fucking doing that all your life. You could have gotten out, but you stayed in because of your sister. You sacrificed for her. You were ready to die so the rest of my team could live. Don't you see that this is your pattern? Break it for me. Choose me. Choose to fight to be with me. Even if it means we go down. Because if we go down, we're going down together. Make me the one thing you don't ever sacrifice."

He wanted to be the one thing she was selfish about. It might not be right, but she could give him that. And she knew what was at the heart of it all. Trust. If she stayed, she was trusting him to know his heart, to protect them, to put her first, to never leave her. God, he was practically begging her to not leave him.

"Never, Master." She laid her head over his heart. Though his face might be blank, his heart was thundering in his chest. "I'll never sacrifice us. I love you, Ian."

"I love you, too, Charlie." His head rested against hers. "I love you, wife. No matter what happens, I love you." He kissed her again, his tongue plunging deep. "God, I love the way you taste."

"And I love the way you kiss me. I love the way I feel when I'm with you. I love the me I am when I'm with you."

His lips played on hers. "I think I would be like Ten if you hadn't saved me."

"I didn't save you." It was the opposite.

"Yes, you did. I might never admit it again, wife, so drink it in now, but I think I would have sunk into my job. I would have become nothing more than a weapon for them to use. I knew I couldn't be that after I married you. You were the reason I got out, the reason I have any family at all."

His hands pulled at the shirt, leaving her naked in an instant. The windows were slightly open, letting in the early morning breeze. It played on her skin, puckering her nipples.

Long, trailing kisses made their way down her throat, stopping at her shoulders, his tongue tasting her skin. She stayed still for him, knowing what he wanted. He wanted to relearn her, this time with kindness and love. He dropped to his knees in front of her, drawing her back to his mouth.

She let her head fall back, giving over to him as he tongued her nipples, one after another. His hands clasped the cheeks of her ass, molding and massaging them.

"Tell me you're mine." He bit gently down on one nipple.

"I'm yours." She'd been his from the moment she'd met him, maybe longer. Maybe she'd been his since the moment she'd been born. Maybe he was the gift the universe had given her for everything she'd suffered. Maybe he was a happy coincidence. It didn't matter because she'd found him and her soul had settled into place. Finally. Completely.

"Always, Charlie. You're always mine. And I'm always your Master. Your husband." He latched onto the nipple and sucked hard, the sensation going straight to her pussy. "Get wet for me. Get ready for me."

She already was. She didn't need him to do anything but walk into a room for her to be ready for him. Her body was tuned to his. "Yes, Master."

He bit her other nipple, making her eyes widen and her heart skip a beat. "I'm going to clamp you, baby. I want to see your tits in clamps, and when we can, I'm going to have them pierced so I can run a chain through them and lead you around by the nipples. I'm going to look at those hoops and know that your breasts are mine and always will be."

The very thought caused a fresh rush of arousal to flood her system. He moved away from her, grabbing the duffel bag he'd packed. Opening it, he placed a few items on the dresser, a couple of guns, some lube and condoms. He held up a pair of clamps. She should have known he would fill his luggage with guns and ammo and sex toys. Her Master liked to be prepared.

"Do you know how pretty you'll look in these?" A sweetly sadistic light was in his eyes.

There was a knock on the door and a masculine voice broke through their solitude. "Yo, Tag, we need you out here for the op brief. How are you going to know what to do if we don't tell you? Get your lazy ass out here. And your brother made breakfast. He's a hell of a guy."

Damn, damn, damn. Frustration threatened to stop her heart. She hated Tennessee Smith in that moment. She didn't want the world to intrude.

Ian didn't make a sound, but suddenly the nipple clamps weren't the only things in his hand. He opened the door slightly, not so much that she could see out or anyone could see in, and pointed his big SIG Sauer at anyone who was standing on the other side of that door.

There was a pause and then a low chuckle. "Well, then, I can see you're busy. I'll just let everyone know that you'll come on out here and join us when you're ready."

Ian slammed the door. "I am going to take the head off the next fucker who tries to stop me from fucking my wife. It's goddamn rude. Now hold those breasts in place for me. I want to play, Charlie. I want to play with my sub. What are you right now?"

Oh, if he wanted to play she could play so dirty. "I'm my Master's toy. I'm Master's little fuck toy."

Sure enough his cock was nearly straining out of his pants. He kissed her again, a carnal joining of mouths and tongues. "You're my toy and my joy, Charlie. Always."

God, she'd forgotten how sweet he could be. He could take the most perverted acts and make them loving. He could say the filthiest things, get her so hot she couldn't stand it, and then remind her that she was loved. "Always, Ian."

She held her breasts up for him, her nipples hard and ready for what he was about to do.

"I think my toy needs some jewelry." He held two clover clamps in his hand. Little devices that would torture her tits and make her come so much harder. They were silver, joined together by a silver chain. After adjusting them, he pinched at her right nipple before slipping the clamp on. It bit into her, sensitizing her and making her shiver at the feeling. Before she could take another breath, he'd attached the second and stepped back to look at her. "Fuck, that's pretty. Your nipples get ruby red, like fucking raspberries I want to gorge myself on. Show me your pussy. Get on that bed and spread your legs and let me look at it. It belongs to me, too."

Her Master was in a possessive mood. The men waiting for them might want to get comfortable because she had the feeling he was going to take his sweet time.

Nothing mattered while they were together. Nothing except the two of them. When he looked at her with that supernova heat in his eyes, she could easily let the rest of the world slip away. She could believe that they could be together forever.

And it could be the most romantic thing in the world for her Master to want to look at her pussy.

She fell back on the low bed, the sounds of the surf and ocean winds behind her while her Master's eyes took in every inch of her. Every inch she moved jostled the clamps, allowing her to feel the bite. She let her legs fall open, knowing what her Master would want.

"You're so fucking beautiful. Wider," he commanded.

Such a gorgeous pervert. She spread her legs wide, pulling her knees up and giving him a view of everything she had.

"Touch yourself." He pulled his shirt over his head, letting her see that cut chest and the muscular arms that nearly made her drool.

She let her finger run over her labia, skimming the sensitive flesh and spreading the arousal she found there. It was humming through her, desire for him, desire for the life they could have.

Desire for a future she'd been dreaming of from the

moment she'd met him.

Ian shoved his jeans off his hips and tossed them aside. His weariness had fled, drowned out by obvious desire. His cock sprang up, his heavy balls already drawn up. "Fuck yourself with your finger. Only one. You're not allowed to come. I just want you ready."

She groaned. He was going to torture her, but she gave him what he wanted. With a little sigh, she stroked her finger deep inside her channel, slowly, so he couldn't miss an inch of the penetration. She let her finger fuck all the way to the base of her hand before pulling it back out.

"Let me taste." He grabbed her hand, bringing it to his mouth. Instead of sucking it inside, his tongue came out, starting at the tip and licking every centimeter, rolling around and enjoying her flavor. Finally he sucked it inside, the pressure causing her spine to tingle.

His hand came out, touching the chain that ran between her breasts. All it took was the slightest tug to send pleasurable fire running in her veins. The tug bit into her tender nipples and sensitized her skin.

"Ian, you're killing me." Need rode her. She couldn't stand being apart from him. She needed to feel him inside her, filling her completely.

He tugged again, harder this time and she couldn't help the cry that came from her throat. "Baby, do you know what that throaty little shout does for me?"

And he said he wasn't a sadist? Still, every inch of discomfort he gave her heightened her pleasure. If he was a sadist then her masochism perfectly matched him. Just enough. Just enough to take her to another level, to show her another world.

"I'll scream for you, Master." She wasn't worried. His little tortures never truly made her cry. He played with her and she played back, dirty little games that fed their desire for each other. "I'll take your clamps and your rings and your hand and your crop. I'll take anything you think to give me."

Her vision was suddenly taken up with the sight of his cock in hand. "And what if I want to give you this?"

"Oh, I can take that, Master. I can take every inch of it." She'd taken it in her pussy and her mouth and her ass. She was his match in every way.

"I know you can. You can take everything I give you. You can handle it all." He touched her throat, a single finger tracing a line around it. "I want you to wear my collar again."

"I wish I'd never lost it." She thought about that gold chain every day, had thought about replacing it, buying another and wearing it so she felt close to him. But it had to be his hand that placed it around her throat or it was meaningless.

"I'll buy another one and I'll spank the hell out of you if you lose it again." The last was said with a little smile.

Her Master would find any excuse to spank her. She knew he loved to see her ass a pretty pink and he delighted in making her squirm. Oh, she couldn't wait to have his collar around her throat again. But there was one other piece of jewelry she'd lost. "I want my wedding ring back, Master."

"You'll have it, but don't expect another grand wedding."

"I didn't get the first one," she grumbled. "I got married at a courthouse."

It had taken roughly half an hour. They'd gotten caught in the rain and her pretty wrap dress had been drenched, her hair plastered to her head. He'd kissed her so sweetly she hadn't cared.

"It was a British courthouse." He crowded her back as

he climbed on the bed. "Do you know what hoops I had to jump through?"

"Probably not very many. You had friends in high places."

He shrugged a little, his body covering hers, his legs forcing hers open to make a place for himself. "I did. Someone had to jump through hoops. It's not easy for two noncitizens to get married there, but I managed it. Still, I don't want to go through all that white wedding crap Alex and Eve went through. A simple collaring ceremony followed by some righteously nasty sex should do the trick."

All he wasn't saying was there in his eyes. They might have a collaring ceremony, but it wouldn't be at Sanctum. Even if they took out Eli Nelson, they wouldn't be able to go home. They would be on the run.

"Hey." He tugged on her chain. "Come back to me. Don't go there."

"It's hard not to." Guilt still bubbled up.

"I'll take care of it. I have no intention of being on the run forever, Charlie. I'm not going to allow anyone to keep us from our home, so stop worrying. I'll take care of you. I'll always take care of you. Now shh. I can't leave the clamps on for too long." He suddenly frowned. "Unless you've been clamping your own tits for the last five years."

Laughter lightened her. "No, Master. Just the plug. I've stayed away from all other toys."

"Well, then, this is going to hurt, baby." He released the clamp on her left nipple. Pain flared but before she could scream, the wounded flesh was in his mouth, his tongue soothing the ache as blood flooded her nipple again. She was tender, raw, and she suspected that was exactly how he wanted her.

The pain flared again when he moved to her left breast, giving her the same treatment as before. He was her Master, giver of pain and pleasure and love and security and joy. He was the man who soothed her aches and understood her needs. He was the man who taught her to laugh though he was often so grave himself.

Her soul's mate.

"Look at how pretty they are," he ordered.

She looked down and her nipples were a ruby red, deeper and more colorful than the normal rosy brown. Ian played with them, running his face along the soft skin of her breasts, his five-o'clock shadow bristling and making her skin the faintest pink.

Her hands found his sandy hair, holding him to her breast, letting her legs wind around him. "Please, Master. I need you."

Playtime was fun, but this wasn't play. This was reconnection. This felt sacred.

His head came up and he stared down, their eyes connecting, holding. "Charlie, you talked about your fate. I think you're mine. There's no fighting fate, baby."

He lined his cock up.

God, he wasn't wearing a condom. She gasped a little.

"Fate, Charlie." He pressed in hard. No playing this time, just one long push of his body into hers. Her Master was taking what was his, giving her the promise she'd always longed for.

Nothing between them. The past behind them. And the promise of a future in his arms.

With an eager cry, she wrapped herself around him, holding him close as he completed the union.

"I love you, wife." The words were a benediction. He might say he couldn't forgive her, but she felt it in those words.

"I love you." He was her everything.

He stroked into her, resting his body on hers, pressing her into the mattress. His cock never stopped moving even as he kissed her breathless, fusing their mouths together. His hands tangled in her hair, holding her for his passionate exploration.

She was pinned by him, surrounded by him, deliciously crushed by his weight, and this was where she'd longed to be. For the first time in years, she felt free.

"Take me, baby. Take everything I have." He kissed her over and over as though he couldn't get enough, couldn't stand for any part of him to not be touching a part of her.

He twisted his hips, hitting her clit with every stroke, building the tension until she was a live wire waiting to go off. One more deep stroke and the orgasm crashed through her.

He halted her cry, drinking it down. "That's what I want from you."

Then he gave her what she wanted. He pressed deep, holding himself inside her as he gave up his come, his gorgeous face tightening as he came.

His body relaxed, lowering to her, his muscles losing their tension and sweet peace showing on his face. She'd given him that, and he'd given her a future.

"I would have done it, too, Charlie." His cock was still inside her, and he made no move to roll off. He kissed her again, but this was a lazy, satiated seduction. "I would have chosen Sean."

She squeezed him so tight. "You forgive me?"

"For choosing Chelsea? No. There's nothing to forgive there. For not trusting me? Yes. There wasn't enough time. But there is now. We have to choose each other. We have to pick each other. I trust you, Charlie. I'm sorry for even thinking about what that fucker said about you. You're my wife. I believe you."

That meant something to Ian Taggart. "I'll put you above everyone, Ian. I'm yours now. Yours and no one else's. I love my sister and I hope I can help her, but at the end of this life, I want to be beside you."

A little smile curled up his lips. He thrust his hips again, proving he was already recovering. "And I want to be inside you. Three times a day, baby."

His mouth took hers and he proceeded to prove his point.

Chapter Seventeen

The perpetual buzzing in his ear was starting to get to him.

"All right, that's Kamdar's boat pulling up on the beach," Damon said through the communications device they were using.

"Thanks, I couldn't tell that was a boat," Ian shot back.

Damon seemed to think he needed a running commentary. The MI6 boys, Ten, and Simon had taken a perch high above the beach at the Cabo de Rama Fort. The fort was nothing but an interesting set of ruins surrounded by fruit trees and monkeys. It did, however, give them a good view of the beach and the exchange about to take place.

Jesse had been relegated to babysitting the brat and making sure she didn't find a handy Internet connection. Chelsea seemed to have gone quiet, turning in on herself. He'd expected her to argue with him, but she'd simply nodded and gone back to watching the palm trees outside the hut. Hopefully she wouldn't give Jesse too much trouble. Of course, he was also supposed to be watching

Charlie, but Ian had other plans for his gorgeous wife.

He wasn't leaving her behind with anyone. But the boys up at the fort didn't need to know that until the time came.

Sean huffed a little as he sat back, his feet in the sand and the rest of him on a low-slung lounger. He was dressed formally for the beach in khakis and a polo, a camera bag by his side. "Do they think we can't read?"

His brother's voice dripped sarcasm. There was only one lightweight speedboat plowing up the sand, and it had an elaborately painted name on the side that read *Little Kash*.

Ian assumed that the massive yacht in the distance was *Big Kash*. The king obviously didn't have self-esteem problems.

"Stop with the whining and listen up." Baz's voice came through this time. "According to everything we've been able to dig up in a short period of time, you should be safe. Kamdar's security has always been tight with the exception of the women he sleeps with. However, they apparently don't wear a lot of clothing so if you see a bird coming at you with an Uzi, you should duck."

Yes, he needed humor right now. He was already in a bad position because he was running out of time. This was a calculated play on his part. Kamdar's men were said to be terrifically loyal, and according to MI6 they had all been with the king for a long period of time.

This was his shot. The boat was larger, but contained. As long as the king's guard was loyal, Charlie would likely be safer on that boat than she was out in the open.

A large man with a poorly concealed pistol in his pocket parked the boat and motioned toward the road. Immediately a group of men started hauling crates of what looked like liquor and food from a truck parked up on the road that ran along the beach.

King Kash didn't have to pull into port. Port came to him. Men immediately went to work, loading down the speedboat with crates.

Ian waited. His timing had to be perfect. Too soon and there would be too many men around. Too late and he would miss the boat. Literally.

Sean yawned a little, watching the workers scurrying around the tourists. "You seem happier today. Is that because we're going to get to kill Nelson or do you have other reasons? You seemed determined to sleep in this morning."

Yep, this was his life now. This was why real Agency men didn't bring their brothers out into the field. So they didn't have to have relationship talks in the middle of an op. "I took your advice. Let's leave it at that."

But Sean didn't. A grin spread across his brother's face. "Are you kidding me? You finally listened? Shit. I owe Adam some cash. I said you would stay stubborn to the end. Hey, big brother, you want to spot me a couple hundred?"

He was so not paying for his brother's bad habit of betting on his love life. He had a love life. The thought of putting the words love and life together didn't make him want to vomit. Though he would never say that out loud. Yeah, he bet Sean would have lost a bundle if he'd bet on that.

He was saved from having to reply by Damon's voice coming over the transmitter in his ear. "All right, mates. So it's almost time. From what I can tell, he only has a small dedicated security team with him, but you can bet the crew on board that yacht is likely trained as well. We've vetted them as much as we can. They all look like loyal Loa Mali citizens. We think he's got roughly three women with him right now. We have no names on them. Remember your cover. You have to convince this man that you're reporters who have a meeting to interview the king about his upcoming appearance at the United Nations next month."

Baz's voice came through next. "Your man Adam says he's managed to break into the king's secretary's system so when he looks at the calendar, it will tell him he's scheduled to pick you up here."

With the liquor. Nice.

"Do you boys have your credentials? Now don't tell me you got all lazy and left them in the car. You wouldn't want to disappoint the nice folks who stayed up all night making sure your cover looks good." The question came out on a lazy drawl, but Ian was pretty sure Ten thought this was his op.

He was about to find out otherwise.

"I have them," Ian replied. They had gone to a whole lot of trouble to dummy up very respectable-looking credentials. He was supposed to be some reporter named Brian Klein from *Newsweek*. Sean was his photographer. It was an elaborate plan, the kind agencies like the CIA and MI6 loved to come up with. Ian would swear that most operatives really needed to be writing fiction. They could be so damn overdramatic. He and Sean were supposed to infiltrate the king of Loa Mali's yacht under the guise of reporters getting a scoop and figure out if Kash knew anything without telling him what they were up to.

It was a stupid plan and it very likely wouldn't work. Simplicity was really the way to go here. He needed to get the king's attention. The king wasn't known for liking reporters. But Ian knew what the man did like.

"So where's our stowaway?" Sean asked. He'd

wholeheartedly agreed to the change of plans, and Simon was up at the fort to make sure no one decided to run down in time to mess things up.

Ian couldn't help but grin a little as he looked down the beach. Charlie had hopped into their Jeep after the rest had headed up to the fort. She'd kept her head down as they drove a couple of miles down Palolem Road. Now she made her way to them wearing exactly what Ian had asked her to wear. He'd had the bikini delivered along with her other clothes before they left the US. *Thank god for personal shoppers.* His breath nearly caught as he looked at her. Despite the bikini, she looked innocent, damn near angelic with all that hair and her soft eyes. She didn't look at him as she approached, merely wandered down to the beach as if she didn't have a care in the world. She could be so obedient when she wanted to be. "Here she comes. Do you think she'll do?"

"Ian, we have trouble," Damon said, his voice rising with urgency. "It looks like your girl got away from the nest. Good god. I think she's trying to get your attention, mate. This could be very bad. I don't think you spank her often enough."

Oh, she had every bit of his attention. His wife. His sub. His. Just his. Fuck, he was in love with her and it felt damn good. It felt so fucking good to just let go of all the shit between them. They weren't exactly starting over again. He didn't want that. He didn't want to let go of a minute with her, even the bad stuff. The bad stuff was still theirs. But they did have a clean slate.

She walked toward him wearing a ridiculously small white bikini that showed off her every luscious curve. The beach was full of lovely women, many much more slender and fashionable than his baby, but she reeked of sex to him. Charlie walked with the confidence of a woman who was comfortable in her own skin, and that had every man with eyes following her with their stares.

Sean shook his head a little. "Damn. Yes, I believe she'll do the job. What is wrong with you? You said she was wearing a bathing suit, not pasties and a thong. If I caught Grace wearing that little clothing outside a club, I would slap her ass red."

When had his brother become such a prude?

"I'm not worried." He winked at her as she started to walk by them. Her strawberry blonde hair caught the light as it swung down her back. She was never cutting that hair if he had a say. It nearly reached her ass. It was perfect for holding onto and controlling her during sex. He was getting a hard-on just watching that juicy ass sway as she strolled along. "They can look all they like. I'm confident I can kill anyone who touches her."

He didn't mind them looking. He understood it. Charlie's sex appeal came from far more than her curvy body. There wasn't any self-consciousness in her movements. She'd accepted herself a long time before. He'd gotten to be the one to usher her into that beautiful state. When he'd first met her, she was gorgeous but shut down. Like a tightly budded flower that just needed a little light to bloom.

She glowed now. She glowed because she loved him.

Something calm had settled in his soul. Some piece of him that had always banged around in his head had finally stopped, finding its natural place because she was here.

"Ian, you need to stop her," Damon said, his voice tense now. "She's going to ruin the plan."

Ian stood up. He was dressed somewhat like his brother. It was comfortable and he had no real intention of swimming this afternoon, so he'd gone along with it. "Plan's changed, my friends."

He and Sean made their way across the sand. Following in Charlie's wake, no one really took notice of them.

"I think that dude is drooling," Sean pointed out. "You were totally right. They don't even check the women. What is he thinking?"

"He's thinking he wants to get laid." He'd made a quick study of Kamdar. He was known for inviting beautiful women onto his boat. He would find one, likely from watching the shoreline like a Peeping Tom pervert, and then send his men out to bring her to him. But men getting on the boat would likely go through rigorous checks.

The king's errand boy was, in fact, drooling. He had gotten out of the boat to push it back toward the water, but he'd stopped the minute he'd gotten sight of Charlie.

"So you're coming from that big yacht out there? Wow, that's really impressive." Charlie sounded so sweet and slightly dumb as she pointed out to the mega yacht. So very different from the way she sounded when she was giving him hell. Oddly, he thought she was way sexier when she was mouthing off.

"Yes," the man replied, his chest puffing out. "This is the boat of my king. It is one of the largest yachts in the world. It is almost one hundred meters in length and has everything you could want. So much luxury. King Kashmir is the greatest king in the world."

Charlie laughed, a giggly sound. She would make such a naughty schoolgirl. Just put a little skirt on her, put that hair up in pigtails, and he could go to town. "He must be really rich."

"So very rich. I am very close to the king. Perhaps you would enjoy seeing the boat, meeting him? I could arrange this."

Yeah, Ian could just bet what that would cost Charlie. The man had stepped up to her, almost touching her. Luckily her husband was here to back her sweet ass up.

He put his arm around his girl as his brother eased behind the man, shoving his SIG in the fucker's back.

The driver's eyes widened, but he didn't scream. "I view the girl as I would a sister. I was only trying to make sure she was safe. So many bad elements around here, you know."

Yeah, Ian wasn't buying that, but he was impressed with the man's calm demeanor. It looked like the king trained his employees properly. "Look, buddy, here's what's going to go down. You're going to float us out to your king, and we're going to have a nice long talk with him about the fact that his freaking intelligence department is full of idiots."

The man shook his head. "I do not know what you are talking about, sir. I work for a Hollywood star. Very big star. Sleeps with many women. Likely has many diseases. You do not want to go there. Very bad. That boat is a floating venereal disease."

Ian nearly rolled his eyes. "Look, I know that's not George Clooney out there, so let's drop the BS. That's the king of Loa Mali and there are CIA operatives and MI6 agents watching him from the fort. If he wants to find out why, you'll have to take us all there. I like to tell heads of state how fucked they are in person."

"You're a bloody bastard, Taggart." Damon Knight was not impressed with his maneuver, that was for sure. His voice had turned rough and angry in Ian's ear. "If you fuck this up, our deal's off. Do you understand me?"

Ian pulled his earpiece out. He didn't need to hear from the peanut gallery. He shoved it into his pocket though he really wanted to toss it away. He might need the damn thing later. "Yep, they're pissed as shit at me right now, but I think your king and I can come to some solution without having to involve those busybodies."

Sean winced a little. He couldn't pull his earphone out yet. It looked like he was getting the brunt of their frustration. "They're on their way, brother. Or at least they're going to try to get down here before we can leave."

"See, if we don't head out now, your poor king's party is going to be swarming with nosy assholes. Does he really want that? We're kind of the good guys here." He nodded to Sean who shoved the SIG back in his pocket and let the guy go. "See, that was just to get your attention. Let your boss know that we'll surrender our weapons when we get to the boat. We just want to talk. He's in danger from several fronts. If he talks to us, it can be a quiet chat. If he waits for them, well, the government gets involved and that can be a shit storm."

There was a crackle as the radio in the boat came to life. "Bring them, Taral. You might want to hurry. I am watching the fort and they are certainly right about the level of activity up there. And, Taral, don't leave the woman behind. I am so looking forward to meeting her."

The king of Loa Mali would find out that Ian could pull off royal balls just as fast as he could common ones. He helped Charlie into the boat and hopped in after her. Sean and Taral shoved the boat back into the surf. Sean leapt in and Taral hauled himself up with a practiced hand. Now that he had his boss's permission, it seemed he was all smiles.

"Welcome on board. My king wishes to see you. Thank you so much for coming with us and for not shooting me in the kidneys. I have heard this is very painful."

He turned on the motor and started to ease the boat

around.

Sean pulled his earpiece out and pocketed it. "Brother, Ten was just explaining all the ways he's going to roast your ass. He seems to be very creative when it comes to hot pokers. You should watch your backside. I don't think he intends to use any lubricant, if you know what I mean. He's also pissed about the monkeys. According to Simon, they're as sexually aggressive as Ten himself."

Charlie smiled slightly. "It sounds like they have as much discrimination as Ten, too."

Ian turned back, looking at the beach. It was still calm and peaceful. Once Damon and the others realized there was no way to stop him, they would slow down and try to keep their eyes on the ship. He didn't give a shit that the Agency would be pissed. This was his op. His wife was at risk, his people, and he wouldn't let Ten or anyone else tell him how to handle it. He needed this man to trust him, and he wouldn't get that by lying. He had one shot and one shot only at getting King Kash on his side.

Charlie was standing at the front of the boat, her hair whipping behind her. He moved in. Since he'd realized that he was being a stubborn prick, he wanted to touch her all the time, wanted to be close. He didn't fight the urge. Not anymore. She was his. If she didn't like the fact that his hands were always on her, then she shouldn't have chosen him.

When he wrapped his arms around her, she immediately leaned back, her body fitting into his.

"Ian, do you think he's watching?" She had to raise her voice to combat the sounds of the speedboat as it hit the waves, bringing them closer and closer to the yacht.

Nelson. She wanted to know if Nelson was watching her, probably getting ready to jack off at the sight of her. God, he was going to kill the fucker for making her feel self-conscious. She should always feel safe, always secure knowing that her husband would take care of her. He cuddled her close. God, how had he lived without this feeling? "Don't worry about it. I'm going to handle him."

He would have to because he knew damn well Nelson was watching. Now he knew they were here. It would force his hand, and Ian had to be ready. Nelson would come at him and he would come hard. The minute he could, he was going to make sure Charlie was someplace safe. They would talk to the king and then he would hide her away with Sean.

Then he could be the bait.

Her hands came up, covering his, holding him close. "I know you will, Master."

This time she was trusting him with her life, with her sister's life. With everything that was important to her. She wasn't running away from him or trying to control things. She'd trusted him, the way he would trust her when it came to the Russian mob. She was smart and her instincts were good. He would lean on her, but he so needed her to lean on him.

He put his mouth right by her ear. "Do you know how much I love you?"

It was so easy to say now. He loved her with everything he had.

He felt her smile against his cheek. "As much as I love you. God, Ian, I love you so much."

"And you look ungodly hot in that suit." He squeezed her tight as the boat pulled up to the yacht.

A group of well-armed security men were waiting above on the lower deck as Taral expertly parked the speedboat. It was tiny compared to the massive yacht. He had the faintest moment of worry in his brain, but Sean was at his back. Sean knew what to do. He turned back to his brother and a long look passed between them. He kissed the top of his wife's head.

Sean nodded, obviously understanding that Charlie came first. Her life was more important than Ian's. Sean slapped his brother in a show of affection. They had learned a lot. The brotherly bond they shared now included their wives and children and those precious beings came before everything else.

"Surrender your weapons!" a large guard with a semiautomatic weapon ordered in heavily accented English.

Ian moved Charlie behind him. If they were going to have a heavy finger on the trigger, they would have to go through him, but he doubted they would open fire.

He would never have put his wife in the man's way if he thought for a second Kamdar would hurt her. No, the king of Loa Mali had a thing for women. All of them. He'd enacted laws against domestic violence that would make the West look misogynistic. He encouraged the women of his country to go to college, to seek high-level jobs.

The king had a reputation as a lover, not a fighter. He routinely ditched his security detail in favor of chasing after a woman.

Ian handed up his SIG, but didn't bother to mention the knives he had on his body or the small pistol he'd hidden in his boot. He wasn't going to give up everything.

Sean handed his primary weapon up as well, but then his brother was deadly with knives and he had them all over his person.

"Let the woman come up now," the guard said.

He shook his head. He couldn't let Charlie up until he was sure he would be on that boat with her. No way. No how. "I come up first."

The big guy frowned down at him. "I said hand up the female."

"Stand down, Kaj." A softer voice called out. "He's protecting his lady. It's a good thing. It makes me believe he's here for the reasons he's stated. I've found spies don't tend to care much about their partners. Come. Come."

The king of Loa Mali pushed his way to the front of the small crowd. There was no way to mistake him. He dominated the other men, though he kept his voice quiet. That man was a Dom and a confident one. He might not be trained, might not even really know what he was, but Ian did. He met Ian's eyes and a long look passed between them.

"She will be safe. You have safe passage. Please come on board. I wish to hear why the Americans and Brits are so interested in me."

Ian stepped forward first, allowing himself to be pulled on board. He immediately turned and put his hand down for his wife, hauling her up and back into his arms. He stepped back, keeping her close as Sean climbed on board.

Charlie remained behind him, her hands clasping his waist, letting him know she was there.

King Kash Kamdar stepped toward him. He was a large man, roughly six foot four with a well-defined body and a face that most women would die for. His skin was a golden caramel and perfectly white teeth shone from his smile. "Welcome, Mr...?"

"Taggart. Ian Taggart."

"Mr. Taggart, you've brought a beautiful woman with you. I don't suppose that she is for me? Perhaps the Agency has changed their tactics and actually figured out that I respond much better to the fairer sex?"

Ian wasn't surprised that the king had dealt with the

Agency before. They really were nosy busybodies. "She's my wife. She goes where I go. If you want to understand what's happening, you have to make sure she never leaves my sight."

The king reached forward, grasping her hand and bringing it to his lips in a gallant kiss. "Mrs. Taggart, it is a pleasure to make your acquaintance. Your husband is an interesting man. McKay-Taggart is a private security firm, known for its ex-Special Forces employees."

So Kamdar did have some smart people working for him. "Facial recognition?"

He shrugged. "I leave that to the intelligent men. I find them deeply annoying. They are sarcastic and unruly. I often think I should let the sharks take them, but they provide good service, do you know what I mean?"

He did. Adam was a pain in his ass, but he got the job done. "They also work quickly."

"Yes, but then I take it seriously when someone shoves a gun in my employee's back. I knew your name within moments. I merely wanted to see if you would lie to me. You'll have to forgive me. Taral's family has worked for mine for many years. I take all my employees' safety very seriously. It's why I have them watched when they leave the boat. The world can be a dangerous place. Please follow me. There is a luncheon laid out on the deck. You can see all my pretty ladies." He held out a hand gesturing them to move toward the stairs that led to the upper deck. "You are his brother? Sean?"

Sean nodded. "Yes. I'm just along to watch my brother's back, Your Highness. I'm not in the business anymore."

"You both have exemplary service records," the king said. "But I suspect Mr. Taggart has spent some time with the Agency. Well, my obnoxious computer guru suspects this. When did the world turn upside down? Now we are all held hostage by the geeks."

A thin young man with studious glasses frowned at the king and spoke in rapid-fire Hindi, his entire body spouting sarcasm. He switched to English, which he spoke with a near-perfect British accent. "If my king paid as much attention to security as he does female body parts, we would all be much safer. We should run checks on everyone twice a year. We should check their accounts, see where they are going, who they are meeting with."

The king shook his head. This was obviously a familiar argument. "I am not spying on my employees, Chapal. We have been over this."

The young man with glasses threw his hands up in the air and walked off, muttering in Hindi again. Yep, it was good to know Adam had a clone on every continent.

The king rolled his eyes. "He is also my cousin. I am not allowed to execute him. My mother would kill me. Sometimes I long for the old days when a man had his harem and absolute power."

Unfortunately, Ian was going to have to go with Chapal on this one. The king was being naïve.

Ian reached the upper deck and took a quick inventory. The damn boat was bigger than his house. The king steered them toward the aft of the ship where there was a large outdoor living space complete with couches and chaise lounges. There was a huge buffet to the side that looked to have been recently laid out. Fruit and vibrant greens were on display along with the lovely smell of a curry.

Three beautiful women lay out on the deck, sunning themselves. They all giggled as the king walked by. Two of them weren't wearing anything but bikini bottoms. The third was a gorgeous Asian woman wearing a sleek one piece, her pitch black hair in a bun. He caught a glimpse of her face, but turned before she could see his.

Damn. He hoped his wife was still all about forgiveness for his past transgressions. He kind of hoped he didn't have to play that card.

The king gestured them to sit as the yacht began moving again. The boat was so big, Ian barely felt the movement. A tuxedoed servant brought four crystal glasses and a bottle of what appeared to be dark liquor.

"Is that what I think it is?" Sean asked, a little smile on his face.

The king poured liquor into the glasses. "Old Monk. The best rum in the world." He took a long sniff. "It's made in India. They do not advertise. I'm surprised you know it. You must have traveled extensively."

Sean waited until the king had taken a long drink before sampling. Ian was glad his brother wasn't completely out of practice. "I have a couple of line cooks I work with. They bring bottles back with them when they go home. We can't get this in Texas."

Ian took a sip, the rich, almost vanilla-like flavor coating his tongue. But he wasn't here to drink. "So do you know that you're being targeted by an ex-CIA agent who I believe now works freelance for various employers?"

The king sat back, his face not showing a moment's surprise. "Mr. Taggart, I am the king of a small country almost no one knows about. We're one of the smallest countries in the world."

"With very important resources," Charlie pointed out.

"But limited compared to others," the king argued. "There is no reason to target me. Yes, we have oil, but if you added up the barrels we produce, it's a drop in the bucket. We have moved to biodiesel on our island. The oil is a nice income, but nothing anyone would fight a war over. Most of our income now comes from tourism. Do you honestly see anyone invading the Arabian Sea equivalent of Hawaii?"

Yes, he could see that plainly. All he would need was one sub, three black ops teams, and a nice quantity of C-4. After he took over the country's communications systems, the airports, and its central city, he could easily install himself as the new king of Loa Mali. Luckily, he didn't want a crown. "I think you're not giving men enough credit or maybe your view of wealth is skewed. The hundreds of millions your oil brings in is certainly enough to start a couple of wars."

The king waved him off. "Bah, I play the game. I deal with OPEC and the US. They have no reason to come after me. You sound very much like my mother. She keeps begging me to settle down and start producing heirs so the line is secure, but I have a very fine nephew who can take over if they get to me."

"I don't think this is about a political coup."

The king toyed with his glass, his fingers running around the rim. "The Agency would love for me to do something that might bring down the wrath of the democratic world on me, wouldn't they? Fine. Perhaps they do want my oil. So does India. You have to know they would love to swallow up my little island. So much drama over a resource that will be gone in a hundred years. Perhaps less."

"You're worried about peak oil?" It was a term the media and economists used to describe the tipping point, when the world's supply of oil was consumed to past the fifty percent mark. It was argued that the planet was already there.

The king leaned forward, his face turning serious.

"Everyone should be worried about it. The world is run by companies now. If I were, say, to prove to be a horrible dictator, do you know who would be the first in line to petition your government to protect my people from human rights violations? The oil companies. They are likely more dangerous to me than any government."

The special interest groups didn't care about the citizens of Loa Mali. They cared that the oil industry was nationalized there. But at least now he and the king were on the same page. "I believe this man is possibly working for an oil company. Can you think of any reason why he would be targeting you if killing you wouldn't change the state of politics in your country?"

"I have several projects going," the king admitted. "But I think you're being overly pessimistic, Mr. Taggart. There is nothing out of the ordinary. If someone is watching me, that is normal. It's nothing my security team can't handle."

He'd only seen a couple of men with guns. Nelson wouldn't barge onto the ship all by himself.

Fuck. Nelson would send someone to distract the king. Like he'd done before. Chapal was about to get his wish. He was going to do a whole lot of spying in very little time because there was no way Nelson didn't have a team here.

"How well do you vet your women?"

The king frowned. "What do you mean?"

Apparently the king had one massive weakness. "I'm talking about your sexual partners. The women on this boat have been through a security check, correct?"

The king sighed. "You sound like my guards. These are beautiful women. They are models and actresses. They are completely sweet and harmless to everything except my stamina. Come here, little flower."

The Asian woman stepped up, a smile on her face. She was graceful and willowy, and Ian remembered just how good she was with a stiletto, and he wasn't thinking about shoes. She also had awesome aim with a semi, and he had the scar to prove it. "Your Majesty?"

She suddenly turned and looked at Ian, her eyes going hard. She cursed in Mandarin under her breath.

"My parents were married when I was born," he shot back. She understood English perfectly well. She'd been able to curse him in at least three different languages.

Charlie sat up beside him, obviously feeling the shift in the woman's mood. Her eyes narrowed. Yeah, his wife didn't miss much. "Really, Ian?"

"I had a colorful life before I met you, love."

Sean coughed but there was no way to mistake the word. "Manwhore."

"She is nothing to be afraid of. Beautiful women need protection. There are so many men out there who would take advantage of them." The king brought her hand to his lips. "Lin, please say hello to our guests."

Ian sent her a frown. She was one of the most intelligent operatives he'd ever tangled with, and now she was playing a supermodel and screwing royalty? How the mighty had fallen. Of course, she'd probably gotten her ass demoted because he'd gotten away with the prize. "Lin? Really? And they made you a supermodel? I thought the last time we talked you said all models were idiots without a brain in their heads." He looked back at the king. "If you had run a deep check on that little flower, you would have discovered that she's MSS, Chinese intelligence. Her name is Jiang Kun. She's one of their deadliest operatives, but I suspect she's here on a gathering mission rather than a hunting one."

Kun sent him a scowl as a security guard came up

behind her. "After everything I did for you, Taggart?"

His wife tensed, an offended huff coming out of her mouth.

"You shot me," Ian replied. "I don't think that qualifies as tender treatment."

Sean snorted beside him. "You let her shoot you?"

He sent his brother his middle finger and looked at the MSS agent. "You're not here to kill the king, right?"

"Of course not. If I was, he would be dead by now." Her voice was all arrogance now. "Like you should have been. And yes, I consider leaving you alive at the end of our encounter to be tender treatment."

The king finally looked a little confused. "Wait. She's not a supermodel? But she had a portfolio."

Ian ignored him. He had some questions for the operative. "What do you know about Eli Nelson?"

The faintest grin curled her lips up. "I know he's a bigger problem than you think."

No help there. He thought Nelson was a pretty big fucking problem. "What are the Chinese interested in?"

She shook her head. "I'm not answering your questions, Tag. You should know that by now. The king won't let you torture me so you should just let me go and we'll call it a day."

"Torture?" The king stood. "You lied to me?"

Dark brown eyes rolled. "Of course I lied. Although not about everything. You actually were quite a pleasant assignment, Your Highness. I didn't even have to fake it. And just so you know, I'm certainly not the only one. I think Nelson got his own girl on board, but I haven't figured out who yet. If I were him, I would have bought a couple of guards, too."

"Why do you think he already has people on board?" She'd been an operative long enough that if she said she wasn't the only one, Ian would keep looking. She also wouldn't want someone else to succeed where she'd failed.

"Someone's been trying to get into the king's private office," Kun explained. "It's the only room that isn't keycarded. It's got a really sturdy lock and he has the only key. Check the door. Someone's been trying to pick that lock. I should know. I was there for the same thing, but someone had beaten me to it. He keeps five women with him most of the time. He sent two home yesterday. I can't be certain one of them wasn't Nelson's girl. The Swedish blonde is new. The American blonde has been here around two weeks. Either one of them could be on Nelson's payroll."

One of the guards started to haul her away.

The king ran a hand through his hair. "I can't believe it. I thought she was so sweet. And she was so very good at fellatio. If that isn't a sign of a generous spirit, I don't know what else is. Damn it. Chapal will never allow me to live this down. He will gloat for the rest of our days."

So the king was a little naïve about women. He couldn't afford to be that way any longer. "You need to have your team dig deep on every woman on board this boat."

"What do you keep in your private office?" Sean asked.

The king took a long swig of his Old Monk as he watched the guard take away his former lover. "The usual things. Paperwork. My computer."

Now they were getting somewhere. "That computer has your work on it?"

"It has all the research from my latest project. It is a very secret project, you have to understand. I've put a lot of money into it. Only the head of the project and myself keep the documents. I have one set with me and he has the other at the project site. I don't want it to leak until I'm ready to make a big announcement."

So that was why Nelson hadn't made a move yet. He wanted those documents. "It's already leaked. Your Highness, I have to ask you. What is your project?"

"I can't talk about it." But Ian could see he was wavering.

"She's not the only one on board your ship, and I know the man who's watching you. He won't hesitate to use anyone and anything he can to get what he wants." It was time to manipulate the king a little. What the king wouldn't tell another man, he might give up to a feminine plea. "Charlie, tell him."

She put a hand in his as she stood. "He tried to divert us by sending assassins after me and my whole family. He was willing to do just about anything to make sure we didn't stop him. He put Sean's daughter on a contract. She's just a baby. He's willing to kill women and children to get that research. Is it really so important that it stays a secret, Your Highness? I think it's only a secret to the people who want to help you."

The king bowed slightly to her and then made his decision. "I have been working with a very smart scientist. He trained in England and the US. When he came home to Loa Mali, he requested an audience with me. He said he wanted to do something for the world. Something to change everything. This, I was interested in. For the last seven years, I've been funding him and giving him a space to work in secret. We're close to a working prototype."

The hair on the back of his arms started to stand up. This was it. This was what Nelson wanted. "How are you going to change the world, Your Highness?"

"We've found a way to run a combustion engine on

salt water."

Bingo. Fuck. Yes, that would certainly be worth going to war over. And this was bigger than Ian had thought. "Your Highness, we're going to need to get you to a secure location."

"What?" King Kash held his hands up as if trying to force the world to slow down. "What are you talking about? I am perfectly safe here. This is my boat. I have my security guards around me. I don't see how I would be safer somewhere else."

A massive boom sounded through the air, a crash of sound that could be felt against the skin and the sea. This time the boat rocked as large waves started pounding it.

Ian grabbed his earpiece. It was time for backup again. "Simon, what do you see?"

"Not much. There's a ton of smoke coming from the west. But it's too far to see what's on fire. Wait, Knight says there's news on the radio. A big explosion. Some oil rig off the coast of Loa Mali."

Fuck. Fuck. And mega fuck. He turned to the king. "Tell me the research wasn't being done on your oil rig."

The king's mouth dropped open. "I thought no one would know we were working there. I had special rooms built."

Sean cursed. He'd put his earpiece back in as well. "Your rig is gone."

If Nelson blew the rig, then he was planning on taking the boat. He would have to get those documents. Either he already had them or he was about to assault the yacht.

"I have more bad news, boss," Simon said, his voice low. "You've got company. Off the starboard. Looks like two fast-moving boats. They're coming from the west. The same direction as that explosion. I don't think they're coming for tea, Tag."

Ian ran to the right side of the ship, away from the shoreline. Sure enough, there were two boats moving toward them, and there was no way for him to mistake them for anything but what they were.

Somali pirates. He could just bet who was playing the pirate king today.

Chapter Eighteen

Charlie felt her heart nearly stop as Ian took her hand. Everything had gone wrong, and she wasn't even sure what the hell had happened. One minute the world was fairly calm and the next it was all going to Hell in a hand basket. Around her people were rushing either toward the stairs or to the side of the boat where they could watch the damage about to happen.

"We have to get you someplace safe, baby. I don't want him to know you're here." He started leading her down the steps to the lower decks. He pulled her hard, forcing her to look away from the water view where she could plainly see ships coming toward the starboard side of the yacht. She'd counted two medium-sized ships, all with full crews and, she suspected, full armaments.

"He already knows I'm here. Can't we outrun them?"

The king shook his head. "We're too big. These are Somali pirates. They're quick and efficient in these waters. They'll be on us in a minute." He barked out orders in Hindi, and four armed guards showed up.

They stepped up to the side of the boat and began to fire, raining down bullets on the incoming boats.

The world became a cacophony of gunfire as the guards began to defend the yacht. Ian dropped down, hauling her with him and covering her body with his.

The king was on one knee beside them. Chaos seemed to have taken over the boat. Feminine screams were punctuated by volleys of staccato gunfire. She managed to peek out from under Ian's arm and saw one of the guards being peppered with bullets, his gun falling, arms flying back before he dropped to the deck and the blood began to flow.

Nelson was here. God, he was here and this time he wouldn't pretend to kill her. This time he would try to kill them all.

"We need to get to the speedboat," Ian said, his voice the only calm thing in the world, it seemed to Charlie.

The king shook his head. "No. I must get the research. All will be lost if I don't get my computer. If he's taken out the rig, then this is all we have left. I have Internet on the boat. I can at least send it out. I have to do this. This kind of technology could save the world."

She could feel how tense Ian was. He turned to the king as he spoke. "I don't care about saving the fucking world right now or giving it a freaking gift. I care about getting my wife off this floating tomb."

Sean had a P90 in his hand. He'd grabbed it from the fallen guard. "I'll take him. You get Charlie off the boat."

"Sean," Ian started.

A world of willpower was plain on Sean Taggart's face. "No. I'm taking Nelson out. I'm doing it for my wife and my daughter, and you can't stop me, brother. There are other ways off this boat and I'll find one. Go."

The king nodded. "I have another small boat for emergencies. We will do this and then attempt to leave ourselves. You take her. Taral shouldn't have gotten to the garage yet. The speedboat should still be on the port side. Get her to Taral. I trust him. His family has served mine for generations. He will take care of this. I swear it. Tell him his king commands this."

Ian cursed heartily and touched the device in his ear. "Simon, are you there?"

She was close enough that she could just barely hear the reply. "It's Knight, Tag. Simon's already on his way if he didn't break his neck getting to the water. I hope he can swim as well as he thinks he can. Ten is on his way to the beach, and I'm in communications with Indian authorities. You'll have backup soon."

"Is the speedboat on the port side of the ship ready to go?" Ian asked.

"That appears to be an affirmative. The minute the gunfire started, the driver fired up the boat again. He seems to be waiting for someone, probably the king."

"Charlie's coming in. Tell Ten to commandeer the boat when it hits the beach and get his ass out here if he can." Ian stood, helping her up. "We have to hurry. They're closing in. Keep your head down, baby. Sean, I'll come back for you. Stay alive."

"I don't intend to be any other way." Sean was already moving toward the interior of the yacht. "Come on, Your Highness. Let's go grab our only bargaining chip."

Sean disappeared down the stairs with the king following him.

Ian was moving to the port side of the boat where they'd first boarded.

A woman rushed by them, screaming as she ran for the cabins.

Jumping to the lower deck, Ian turned back and held his arms up. Without a single hesitation, she leapt into them. The speedboat was still in the water with Taral standing at the helm.

"I need you to get her out of here," Ian said.

"Where is the king?" Taral asked, looking at the decks above.

"He's taking care of business. Just get her to shore so I can take care of mine." He started to push her toward the boat.

"You're not coming with me?" It was a stupid question. She'd known it the minute the words came out of her mouth.

"Baby, I don't even have a gun right now. I can't protect you while I try to find one. Please."

He couldn't leave his brother behind. She understood that. Sean had come here to back him up. Sean had a kid. Ian felt responsible for Sean. He wasn't picking Sean over her. He simply couldn't help his brother while she was in danger. He was just being Ian Taggart.

She had to love him for who he was.

She kissed him, throwing her arms around his neck. "I love you. Stay safe."

"The king is staying?" Taral asked. "He is remaining on board?"

Ian stared down at her, but he spoke to Taral. "Get her out of here and I'll go protect your king. He told me to tell you he commands this."

Taral nodded and held a hand out to help her on board. He gunned the engine.

Charlie watched as Ian began making his way back to the upper decks. His body moved with a predatory grace as he made swift work of the stairs. He disappeared into the main deck cabins.

She needed to get to the shore, get to Simon. They would find a way to help Ian and Sean.

The speedboat was damn fast when Taral opened it up.

Which he wasn't. He eased the boat out and then made a swinging turn away from the beach.

"What are you doing?"

He shook his head sadly even as he pulled out a Taser. "What I have to do, pretty one, though I wish the king was here as well. I love my king, but I love my head on my body, too."

Panic threatened to seize her. They were going the wrong way. They were going toward the pirates and the gunfire was slowing. That really wasn't a good thing because she was pretty sure it meant that most of the guards on the boat were dead and all the pirates had to do was jump on board and start slaughtering people.

She had to make a move and fast. She had to hope that fucking Taser's darts didn't have much reach. Turning, she began to jump and then a shock hit her.

Her teeth clenched, her body shook. Out of control. No stop to the pain. It raced along, screaming against her every nerve.

She hit the deck of the boat, trying to get some control over anything as electricity made her body a vessel of pain.

The boat kept moving. With the darts attached to her back, it seemed like Taral didn't feel the need to guard her. From her vantage point, she could see the big driver turning the boat toward the very man she'd been trying to get away from.

Tears squeezed out of her eyes as the pain began to fade. She was limp, her muscles drained and unmoving.

And couldn't her husband have included a freaking cover-up with the ensemble? It was stupid, but it went through her head. God, she didn't want to become a

392

prisoner in a white, barely could be called a bikini.

The gunfire was sporadic now, little volleys and small explosions. She could hear shouting in several different languages.

The sun shined down on her. The beach would have been a good place to have a honeymoon. They hadn't had a honeymoon.

She'd been too busy dying.

The boat stopped moving, and there was a soft thud as though they were brushing against something. Then the boat listed to one side and settled back into place.

A shadow fell across her and she blinked. She couldn't see who was looking down.

"Hello, my dear," Eli Nelson said, his voice a familiar nightmare. "I see you've met my friend. He's got a bit of a gambling problem, and unfortunately he can't play in the reputable establishments anymore. A couple of months ago, he lost a hundred thousand to one of your uncle's casinos. It's such a small world really."

His hand came out, brushing against the flesh of her chest. His fingertips circled the scar that was left from the gunshot wound he'd given her. "This is beautiful, dear. I always wanted to see it on you. Such lovely scars. I can give you more. I know what you want now. You want pain. Consider me your new best friend. Now, what do you say we go kill that husband of yours?"

Charlie tried to scream as he picked her up. Nothing came out but a strangled cry.

* * * *

The feel of metal in his hand was a welcome sensation. Ian checked the cartridge on his SIG and carefully sidestepped the dead bodies on the deck. He'd managed to collect a couple of handguns, including both his and Sean's and he'd strapped a dropped P90 around his chest.

He moved toward the stairs to the lower decks where Sean and the king had disappeared.

Or he could take up a sniper position and end everything. Sure the percentages would play out badly for him, but if he could take out Nelson first, one threat would be handled.

And his wife would be alone. Sean couldn't run with her, couldn't hide her. He might try and then the syndicate would come down on all their heads.

Fuck. He had a weakness now. He didn't like the feeling. It was easier when all that mattered was the kill, when all he wanted was Nelson's head on a platter, but he'd found something he needed so much more.

A future with her, and he had to stay alive to have that.

Where the hell was the office?

"Lay down your weapons, Mr. Taggart."

Fuck. He turned and saw one of the bathing beauties from earlier. She was a tall blonde, and she'd managed to find her top. Not that she needed a bra. Those fake tits weren't going anywhere. The king had terrible taste in women. Especially since this one was working for Nelson. "Easy there."

She held a pistol on him, her legs in a wide stance, both hands on the grip. "I would shoot you here, but I believe my employer would rather do this himself. Poor King Kashmir. He cannot tell a Swedish accent from a Russian one. He is not as smart as he thinks."

Nope. The king was a dumbass who thought with his dick, and his dick was an idiot. But it looked like Ian was the one who would pay the price.

Where was Charlie now? Had she made it to the shore? God, he hoped she was on the beach and Ten was moving her completely out of harm's way.

Would she forgive him for staying on the boat? Would she see that he had to take care of this or Nelson would never stop?

He tossed down the SIG and held both hands up, a sign of defeat he didn't feel. All he needed was a second of her guard being let down. This wasn't the way he wanted to go to Nelson since the fucker, if he had a brain in his head, would just shoot his ass, but he would figure his way out of anything because he wasn't about to die now and leave his wife behind. If he died, she wouldn't be very far behind. Even if he took out Nelson, if Ian didn't survive, Charlie would still be at risk. He had to fucking find a way to stay alive.

"Come out here, Mr. Taggart." How could anyone mistake that accent? "My employer is about to board the yacht. I'm sure he will pay me handsomely for having taken you to him."

He estimated the distance he would need to swat that gun out of her hand. He saw it play out in his head. He would move forward, pretending to be ready to do what she asked. His head would be down, but at the last minute, he would swivel, bringing his foot up, catching her in the gut. It would throw her off and the gun would fall, and he would be quicker than her.

"I'm coming out."

"Take that gun from around your neck," she commanded.

Before he could move there was the ping of a pistol, and he felt something fly by him, nearly burning the flesh on his left bicep.

The tall blonde's fake tits couldn't stop a bullet. She

should have thought about that when she upgraded. Ian could see it. Fake tits that protected the chest from bullets. It could be the next big thing in spy plastic surgery. Nevertheless, the Russian discovered that silicone couldn't save her. A bright red spot bloomed on her chest, and she fell forward with a look on her face no model should ever have.

Ian turned, looking for Sean. He found Jiang Kun, a smirk on her lips.

"You so owe me, Tag. Pick up that damn SIG." She suddenly sounded like she was straight off the streets of New York. "Don't you dare shoot me. Talk to Ten. There's a reason I didn't kill you just now. I'm a double. Let's play nice."

He grabbed the SIG, wondering what all Ten wasn't telling him. "What happened to your guard?"

"He's taking a nice nap." She stepped to the stairs. "Get down here, Tag. Nelson's coming on board, and we need to ambush him if we have a shot at this."

"Why should I trust you?" Why the hell would she work with him? Why wouldn't she just kill him and take the prize? Nelson might think she was just one of the king's playthings and leave her alone.

"I told you. I'm Agency. My twin sister was MSS. Our mother smuggled me out at birth rather than abort me, but she kept in touch with my American family. When I found out my sister had been recruited, I joined the Agency to try to get her out. I found her and tried to bring her with me to the States. She told me everything. She never wanted this life, but they forced it on her. Her escape went wrong and she died in my arms and I took her place. I'm spying for Ten on the inside of MSS now. He doesn't know I'm on board, though, or he might have contacted me to tell me to look for you." She smiled a little. "She liked you, Tag. My sister said she didn't have to fake it with you."

If she wasn't lying through her teeth, then that was a hell of a story. "She still shot my ass."

"She shot your chest, Tag." Jiang Kun, or whatever her name was, winked. "Now let's get this thing done. And you need to tell Ten that he has a leak. That's the only way they're here right now. Nelson doesn't have the research. He should have waited until the blonde bitch did her job. Only one thing changed and that's your arrival. This is about you. He knew you were coming. Get your ass moving. I have to protect my cover, Tag. I owe it to my handler and my sister. This is the one shot you get at me helping you out, and I'll shoot if you open that gorgeous mouth."

He grabbed the SIG and followed her down the stairs. If she'd wanted his ass dead, she would have taken him out while his back was turned. It proved her loyalty more than any words could say. Well, more than any words except one. "What's Ten's middle name?"

She sighed. "Alistair. There, I've said the secret password. Let's go."

Ten didn't have a middle name. Alistair was a code that let Ian know she really was one of Ten's operatives. "Where's my brother and how do we get off this shithole?"

Her eyes rolled. "This is a mega yacht. It's not a shithole, but we need to make our way to the other end of the ship. There's a dive port with equipment. Getting under the water is going to be better than taking one of the tenders. They'll just shoot those."

She was probably right, and he turned with her, noting the position of the guard she'd sent "napping." He stepped over the body and continued along the narrow corridor. He could hear the sound of feet slamming on the deck above him.

"They're on board." He kept his voice just above a whisper.

"They'll secure the top deck before they move down. We have a few minutes. It's a big-ass boat." She pressed her back against the wall as she got closer to the middle of the boat. "So you've figured out the whole 'no-oil automobile' thing?"

"The king mentioned it."

"We need those plans."

He knew exactly what would happen if the Agency got the plans. "So we can hide them because the oil lobby would bury the idea?"

She frowned. "We wouldn't do that."

Fuck yeah they would. "Let's just get what we need to get and slide on out of here."

He needed to get to Charlie. He needed to hold her in his arms again, but he had some work to do first. Part of that was making sure Sean was okay. As for the rest of it, he would prefer that the king dealt with the whole save the world shit. The save the whole world shit should come from a person who cared, and that wouldn't be him or his government or the apparently naïve double agent.

"The office is this way," she said. "We have to get through the living area first. Keep your head down."

He moved through the large living space, keeping his head down, his body low to the ground. The starboard side of the living room was a row of windows that looked out to the sea. Now it showed the boots of the pirates Nelson had hired as they boarded the yacht. How many were on boat? Twenty? He hoped less. Luckily it was a big boat and it looked like they had split into pairs to search it. Two pairs of boots crossed his line of sight and then disappeared as they turned the corner for the door.

"Stop," Kun said, her voice a whisper. "They'll see us. Hide. You take one and I'll take the other. Quietly."

She disappeared behind a large lounge chair, and Ian put his back to the sofa. They wouldn't immediately see him, but if they came far enough into the room, there would be nowhere to hide.

A firefight would bring more of them down here. Ian eased the knife out of his boot, his adrenaline pumping.

There was the sound of boots on the deck and the two spoke to each other in Somali as they rushed into the room.

Out of the corner of his eye he could see that they were carrying AK-47s, the long barrels pointed outward as they moved through the room. It was a big gun, so much easier to pry away because there was more of it to catch.

Ian heard the familiar crunching sound of a man's neck being twisted and broken. Before he even had a thought about how disturbing it was that the sound was so familiar, a booted foot came into view and Ian struck. Before the man could do more than shout, Ian reached up, grabbed the body of the gun and hauled the man down. The pirate hit the floor, and Ian had his blade in his neck before he could pull the trigger.

Nice. Quiet. Really messy. Blood was already spilling across the pristine white carpet. He hated wet work. Unfortunately, he was really good at it.

"Let's go before they find these bodies." Kun was already moving.

Ian got to his feet, pulling the blade back. He wouldn't leave it behind. If he could take out a few more quietly, he would.

He had his chance, sneaking up on another pirate who seemed to be looking for the king. He was coming from the opposite direction, but had stopped, looking into another room. Ian slit his throat easily and dumped the body in what looked like a secondary bedroom. Three down.

How many more to go? How many more until he got to Nelson?

Kun moved with deadly grace as she made her way to the other side of the boat. Ian followed, keeping his steps as light as possible. Gunfire could be heard above him as the pirates seemed to be sweeping the decks one at a time. They would be moving in soon, and the minute they found the bodies, they would be searching for him in earnest.

They came to a door with a high-tech keypad next to it. Kun placed her thumb on it, looking back as the door slid open. "What can I say? He really liked me. His office is back here in the private section. Only the king, his personal servant, and two of his women have access. The other girl is harmless. Seriously, not a brain in her head. Get in. It will slow them down for a bit."

He stepped in and the door slid closed again, locking with a tiny snick.

Sean appeared, slinking along the wall as he exited what had to be the office. He tensed for a moment, pointing his SIG right at Kun's head.

"Don't shoot her. She's a friendly," Ian said, his voice tight. "Is the king with you? Does he have cameras on this ship?"

The king was standing behind Sean, wrapping a long black lanyard around his neck. Before it disappeared under his shirt, Ian saw a small thumb drive attached. "I only have them in the nookie rooms, but they are not attached to any network. I turn them on and off based on whether my partner likes to be taped."

Even in the middle of all the tension, he had to shake

his head. "Nookie rooms?"

His cousin Chapal was behind him, a laptop in hand and a disapproving frown on his face. "My cousin is a perverted man."

The king stared at him, but Chapal held his ground.

Kun rolled her eyes. "I didn't even think of that. We can try it, but if the crew talks, we're screwed. Move it, Tag."

He was standing beside an ornately decorated wall. It looked like it had been fashioned out of beaten silver. It was a lovely work of art. It also was a hidden door, as Kun proved when she ran her hand down the side and it slid open.

Thank god. He had a place to stash the king until he could figure out how to get him out of here because the halls had to be teeming with guys with guns at this point.

The king frowned at Jiang Kun. "I thought she was on the bad side."

The king needed to stay out of the intelligence world. It moved mighty fast for him. "She's working with us now."

A smile came over the king's face and he sent the double agent a suggestive wink. "See, I told you she was a delicate flower."

Apparently the king could think about sex even when the world was falling apart. "Get in here, Your Highness. Did you do what you had to?"

The king shook his head. "He's jamming the Internet. I couldn't get it out. I downloaded the research to a thumb drive."

Chapal held his computer over his chest as though it would prove a good defense. "I have the whole thing set to send the moment we have a connection. If we even have a few seconds, it will go out to several addresses."

"I can't lose it," the king said. "It was my researcher's whole life. I cannot have his death be meaningless."

"You don't know he's dead," Ian said. "But you're going to be if you don't hide. Unless you know a secret way off this boat."

"You should get down to the garage," the king said.

"Garage?" He wasn't a big yachter.

"It's where we stow the jet skis and small boats. The speedboat would have been in the garage if we hadn't been anchored," the king explained. "It's on the lower deck, the one just below this one. There's scuba equipment if you're thinking of slipping out underwater."

He wasn't thinking at all. He was running on instinct. "Is that door the only way out of here?"

The king shook his head. "No, there is one in the back as well. It leads to stairs that go directly to the garage."

That was better. "Stay here with your cousin, Your Highness. Wait until we've cleared the garage and then one of us will come get you. Do you understand? Don't make a sound."

He started toward the back of the magnificent suite of rooms. Chapal followed him. "I can reprogram the security to give you access. Our system doesn't run off Internet. It should work." His hand touched the keypad, typing in numbers. The screen next to it glowed. "Place your thumb over it."

Ian put his thumb on the keypad and it blinked twice.

"Now you have access. I will keep trying to get into the system." Chapal turned and walked back to the nookie room, his head held high.

"Kun, watch them," Ian ordered.

"I should come with you," she returned.

"Watch the asset for me. Shoot anything that comes his way. They'll get through the door eventually." He could already hear them on the other side of the suite, trying to get it to open.

She snarled a little his way. "You owe me, Tag."

"Are you sure about her?" Sean asked.

As sure as he could be. "She didn't kill me, and she knew Ten's middle name. She works for him. She'll keep the king safe. Well, as safe as he can be since we have pirates on board."

"Any idea how many?" Sean followed him, closing the door behind.

The stairs were ornate, like the rest of the boat. Ian started down them, keeping his step light. "No idea. I've had to keep my head down." He touched his earphone. "Any count on how many hostiles we're dealing with?"

Knight's voice came over the line. "Tag, it's bloody good to know you're alive. We didn't want to make contact in case it could be overheard. There are two boats off the yacht. You're dealing with at least twenty armed men. Pirates, from the look of them. They're likely hired hands. One of the boats is hidden by the yacht. I can't see how many people are still on it."

It didn't matter. He just needed a rough number to know how to proceed. He reached the door that hopefully led to the garage.

"Can you see the garage?"

"That's an affirmative, Tag."

"How many?"

"I can't see inside, but the boat that's parked on the port side let two out before parking. It's open to the sea. Are you going to attempt to swim out?"

"I'm going to see if we can get the king out that way. He says there's scuba gear. If we can go deep, we will. What's the ETA on the Coast Guard?"

"The commandant said they're on their way," Knight

explained. "Fifteen minutes out."

"Understood. Tell Ten I expect my wife to be unmolested when this is over."

There was a long pause on the line.

"Tell me my wife is on the beach, Knight." Every muscle in his body tensed. Charlie was safe. She had to be safe.

Knight's voice was very calm as it came over the line. "I think Nelson had a mole on the yacht. The boat you put her on turned and went around to the other side of the boat. I haven't seen it since. Your wife was on board."

Ian heard Sean curse behind him. At least he didn't have to fill his brother in.

His wife was in Nelson's hands, and he'd left his only bargaining chip behind.

"Hey, calm down, brother. We can handle this. Let's get our assets in order. Let's take the garage and then we can go from there. He said there were two, maybe three? We can handle that." Sean was cool and collected, which was good because Ian felt like running screaming through the fucking boat.

Sean took over the conversation. "Knight, we copy you and we're going silent."

He cut off the feed.

Ice. Charlie needed him to be the ice man. And Sean was right. From the garage they could move into the water if they had to.

The garage might offer a few distractions.

He would need them if Knight was correct and Charlie was in Nelson's hands. Shoving his panic down, he put a hand on the door. As quietly as he could, he pushed it open no more than a half an inch. He caught sight of two men moving at the water's edge and another walking up the side.

Without looking back, he held up three fingers, then gestured to show his brother where they would be.

They would have seconds. Surprise would be their only real advantage.

Ian shoved the door open and used the P90 to lay out a line of suppressive fire. The air cracked around him, a symphony of bullets and low shouts that was so familiar to Ian he'd almost missed it.

Cover. He'd taken down one, hitting him squarely in the chest, but now the others were returning fire and he needed cover. He ducked, throwing himself behind a row of jet skis.

To his right, Sean took up position behind the door, only the barrel of his gun sticking out. His brother proved he hadn't lost a beat as he placed a bullet neatly in a pirate's forehead.

But that left one, and he'd taken position behind a small boat, tied up on the side of the garage just at the water's edge. Ian fired but the boat looked solid. His opponent simply shoved his gun over the top and fired, not giving Ian a target.

But he didn't need one because his backup was on the way. He saw a figure surface, his head coming briefly out of the water before he took a silent breath and went under again.

There was a strangled scream and the sound of a body hitting the water and then silence.

Sean stepped out. "What the fuck just happened? Tell me that guy didn't get pulled in by a shark."

He should never have let his brother watch *Jaws* when he was a kid. Sean could stare down just about anything but still had a fear of sharks.

Luckily, this shark had a British accent.

Simon hauled himself onto the ramp, standing

gracefully and straightening his tie. The fucker even swam in a tie. He slicked back his hair and sounded as though he'd come for tea instead of just drowned a man. "Sorry I'm late."

Ian pointed at him. "You I like. Now we have a problem. Nelson has my wife."

Simon simply took the gun Sean was holding out for him. "Then we shall have to get her back."

"Mr. Taggart?" A familiar voice came over the overhead speakers. "I hear you're already at work."

Shit. They'd found the bodies, and it sounded like Nelson was already on the bridge. Or they might have heard all the shit that had just gone down.

"We never had to play it this way, you know," Nelson continued. "We could have worked together. Alas, you had all the skills but lacked that special something I require in a partner."

Yep, Ian had a conscience. Oh, it was a flexible conscience, but it was there. He also had a certain loyalty to his country that Nelson would find offensive. Fucker.

"Luckily, I managed to find a couple of friends to help me out along the way. They'll be the ones who kill you if you don't surrender right now and bring me the king of Loa Mali. I'll need his computer as well. You see, I bombed his testing site so I really am going to need that computer. I'll just have to kill his employees until he brings it to me."

Thank god for soundproofing or the king would likely be martyring himself.

"Or maybe I'll just start with the pretty lady in the white bikini."

Ian's body went cold.

A nasty chuckle came across the speakers. "You dressed her nicely for me, Tag. I'm going to enjoy her before I kill her. Or I could always reunite you. I have a soft spot for lovers. Especially when I was such a good matchmaker. Your choice, Tag. Your wife has five minutes before I slit her throat."

"Stay calm," Sean said.

"I am calm." He was deadly calm. His focus had narrowed to one point in the world. Saving his wife. He laid out his options, shitty as they were, and came up with a plan.

"Do we have what he wants?" Simon asked.

Ian shook his head.

"We can always get the computer," Sean said. "We have a copy so if we need to hand the computer over, I don't think Kash would argue. He was horribly torn up about his guards. He won't want Charlie's death on his conscience."

Ian nodded. "I'll get it. I'll do the trade."

"You think he won't just kill you on sight?" Sean asked.

That would be the smart play on Nelson's part. It was what Ian would do if their roles were reversed. "I'll password protect it. He doesn't get the password until I have my wife. Then he'll try to kill both of us."

"I'm thinking that's not a smashing plan, boss." Simon shook his head.

"That's because you don't know what your part is yet. Get those bodies and some rope. What we need is a little chaos." And a little time. The minute the Coast Guard showed up, all bets would be off.

His team leaned in and Ian told them the plan.

Chapter Nineteen

Charlie stood on the bridge, watching as Nelson's men boarded the boat. She kept her eyes on the outside. It was better than seeing what Nelson had done to the crew.

They were lying in heaps of dead flesh, their corpses cooling. He'd just put out that he wouldn't kill the rest of the king's people if the king gave him what he wanted, but Charlie knew the truth. He would kill everyone. No matter how fast he got the data.

She'd seen what one of his men had attached to the side of the boat just under the water's surface. He might have thought she wasn't looking at the time, or maybe he didn't care, but she knew damn well he intended to blow the yacht sky high. She'd also watched as he put the bomb's trigger device in his pocket.

She had to get that device.

Unfortunately there were four guards watching over the bastard. The pirates were dressed in a mixture of camo and jeans and tank tops. They looked dirty and mean and very comfortable with AK-47s.

"Do you think he's panicking, dear?" He put a hand on her shoulder.

She shivered and tried to step away. She was steady on her feet again, but her hands were still shaky.

His hold tightened. "Don't. I wouldn't want to be forced to make a point, Charlotte. I think Taggart will be more inclined to be helpful if you're in one piece, so be a good girl and don't flinch when I touch you." His hand stroked her shoulder, but she couldn't forget that he had a gun pressed to her side. "You might make me think you don't want me, sweetheart."

Nothing could make her mouth stop though. "I thought I made that plain when I turned down your first offer, Eli."

"Or you could have just been playing hard to get." He took a step back. "You know I understand the value of not giving in too soon. Sometimes you have to make a man work for it, don't you? Charlotte, you're a smart girl. We could use you. You have to know that Taggart is a bad bet at this point. Why else would you have contacted me?"

"I didn't. It was my sister." The last thing she needed was to play out the creep's sexual fantasies. She was going to have such a long talk with her sister. If she survived this, Chelsea was getting off the information-gathering wagon forever. That kind of power had become a dangerous addiction for her.

He frowned and stepped over the captain's body. "I should have known. Well, that's a shame. I mean I'll still try to recruit her because obviously she got all the brains in the family, but I was hoping for a fuck buddy, too. I'll have to take a pass on her. You got the looks. She got the brains. Taggart is going to lose his balls over a woman. I kind of love that. I wish the others were here to witness it. I've had to be in his shadow for years. I was an operative before he was old enough to join the Army. Then one day they recruit him out of black ops and put him on some fucking pedestal. Well, I showed them."

She'd always known his problems with Ian weren't strictly professional. "Yes, you showed them that he was human and that you're a traitor."

He waved that off. "Traitor? I'm more American than any of those fuckers. They still think we're some sort of democracy. We left that long ago. You know what took down your father's precious USSR? It sure as fuck wasn't a thirst for freedom. Hell, no. It was capitalism. The world doesn't run on democracy. It runs on capitalism, and I'm a capitalist."

As long as he was talking, he wasn't shooting her full of electricity. "So you're going to take the plans for the engine and sell them to the highest bidder."

"No. I'm going to hand them over to the oil company that's paying me and let them sit on it. There's still money to be made in oil. A lot of it. Until such time as that changes, there's no place for technology like this. Do you really think some bumfuck beach bum from Loa Mali is the first scientist to think this up? No. This is just the latest, and we'll take this down, too. When the company is ready, they'll roll out their own version and the money will stay in the right hands."

Ian had been right. This wasn't about selling secrets to other governments. "So you work for companies that want you to steal technology for them. Or hurt other companies. That's why you're working with my uncle on the pipeline."

Nelson shrugged a little, like a small boy who had been caught cheating at Monopoly. "Malone Oil doesn't belong to my employers. If you aren't in with the big boys, then you're fair game. The Collective watches out for their membership."

"The Collective? They have a name for themselves?

Oh, god, I hate the Illuminati crap. So I'm supposed to believe that a bunch of CEOs have gotten together and they hire you to what? Steal some plans? What the hell can you really do?"

A nasty little smile lit Nelson's features. "Well, let's see. Let me give you an example. Let's say my latest assignment is for a pharmaceutical company whose top-selling pain reliever is being beaten out by new-blood competition. New drug research takes years and millions of dollars. It's so much easier to simply herd the public where we think they should go."

She got a chill as she remembered what had happened a little over a month before. Someone had coated the caplets of a certain brand of ibuprofen with a cyanide paste. It was clear and undetectable to the human eye. Fifteen people in five states had died.

The company's stock had plummeted while the rival company had seen its shares and its products purchased at higher quantities than ever before.

They had called it a terrorist attack. For Nelson, it seemed it was just good business. "You're a terrorist for hire."

"I'm just a lowly employee, Charlotte, looking to make his pension. Like a lot of other people in my line of business. The Collective finds it easy to recruit from Western intelligence agencies. They pay crap. The Collective offers an alternative. Did you wonder how I knew to be here at this particular time?"

She had wondered about it. And come up with some unsavory answers. "You're saying one of the agents is working for you?"

"Maybe more than one, but certainly you have a viper in your little nest." He picked up the microphone again and pressed the button on the side before speaking into it.

411

His voice filled the air around her. "Mr. Taggart, you're down to one minute. Has the bloom worn off the rose so quickly? Well, then you won't mind when I try her out myself."

"I'm here."

Charlie's whole body went electric with the sound of his rough-as-gravel voice. Fear crept along her spine as her husband stepped on the bridge and every gun in the room pointed his way. Four AK-47s that could tear him apart in an instant.

He shouldn't have come. He should have found a way off the boat. She wasn't worth his life, not after everything she'd done.

"Hey, baby." He held a laptop computer in one hand, his eyes on her.

Two more pirates came up behind him, surrounding him with death.

God, she couldn't lose him.

"Mr. Taggart, so nice to see you again." Eli Nelson sounded perfectly content, but then he did have the upper hand. "Did you bring me my data?"

Ian tapped the computer with his left hand. "It's password protected. I'll give you the laptop, but you don't get the password until Charlie and I are off the ship."

A low chuckle came out of Nelson's mouth. "Really? You think this is a negotiation?"

If Ian was bothered by all those guns pointed at him, he didn't show it. He stood tall, his shoulders squared, his stance firm. "I think I have something you want and you definitely have something that belongs to me."

"I wish we had more time," Nelson said, sighing with regret. "I really do. I would honestly find it fascinating to peel back your layers, Tag. I mean that literally. I would love to take you with me and skin your hide. But I would also try to understand how you fell for a woman I hired to fuck you. I'll be honest. I thought I had a fifty-fifty shot at it working."

"Whatever you paid, you should have doubled it because she's really good," Ian replied.

"Ian!" It was good to know his sarcasm didn't fade just because they were about to die.

Ian sent a slow, infinitely sexy smile her way. "Hey, baby, it's true. I like to acknowledge great work, and you have the sweetest pussy in the whole world. It's totally worth a man's downfall."

Why was he so damn calm?

He obviously had a plan and it didn't involve giving Eli Nelson everything he wanted.

One of the pirates, a large man with scars covering his face, leaned in, speaking in broken English about some boat being sighted.

Nelson frowned. "We'll be faster than the fucking Coast Guard. What the hell did I hire you for if you can't handle a couple of Coast Guard boats? Get my boat ready. We leave in a few minutes."

The pirate jogged off, ducking down the stairs.

Only five guns now. What was Ian planning? And how was she going to get that remote device off Nelson?

She glanced down at the water. It was fairly calm. She knew roughly where they had placed the bomb.

If she couldn't get the remote, maybe she could get the damn bomb. Maybe she could turn it all around. How far was it to the water? She just had to get out the side door and over the railing, but she would have to jump out or she would hit the larger main deck instead of the water. She didn't need a couple of broken legs.

Nelson pointed his own gun Ian's way. "Give me the laptop."

Ian didn't move. "Give me my girl."

Nelson grabbed her arm, hauling her to his side. "I'm going to give you your girl the same way I did before if you don't hand me that laptop."

"It's useless without the password. The system has been encrypted to erase the hard drive if you put the wrong password in more than three times. I hope you're good at guessing, Nelson." He handed the laptop over to one of the pirates.

"All right. I'll need the password then. If I have to, I'll take you with me and I'll have fun torturing it out of you. Or you could just watch me rape your little whore here. I've always had a thing for her." His hand moved up her torso, nearly to her breast, but she remained still because that gun was oh so close to her brain. "Yes, I think torturing her will be a more effective way to get you to talk. Or maybe I could get two for the price of one. Tell me something, Tag. Where's that snot-nosed baby brother of yours? I know he's on the boat. Did you hide him away?"

A smirk lit Ian's face. "No, I'm distracting you so he can get away."

There was the sound of an engine gunning and then out of the corner of her eye, she saw something jet out of the yacht's garage moving at a high speed. She turned and a jet ski was skimming along the surface of the water in a straight line.

"Fuck." Nelson turned, his attention going to the bow of the boat. "Open fire. Stop that jackass. I want him dead."

Ian's hands moved faster than she could track. He bent over and when he came back up, a knife was flying across the room, finding a place in one of the pirates' neck. The man's hand was on his gun, and as he fell his finger spasmed, sending a line of bullets into the man beside him.

Both fell, dead, on the floor.

Three left. And very little time. Ian didn't know about the bomb. He didn't know that Nelson could still take them all down.

He kicked out as the bullets started to fly.

Charlie brought her elbow forward and then back, catching Nelson in the chest. He groaned and stumbled, giving her just enough time to make it out the side door. Complete chaos rained down on them. From the bridge, the sound of gunfire racked the room.

She glanced back and saw blood staining Ian's left leg, but he'd gotten a gun and he was moving down the stairs.

Jumping over the railing, she took only a second to judge the distance between her and the water.

Then fire lit her and sent her careening over the edge. At the last minute before she fell, she managed to kick off the railing and gain the momentum she needed. She tried to control the dive, but the pain in her arm was burning.

A bullet. She'd taken a bullet.

She hit the water with a whoosh and the world above went quiet. Light filtered down into the water, a lamp by which to see. Something started to cloud the liquid around her.

Blood. Her blood. How bad was it? It didn't matter. She gritted her teeth because she had to find that bomb.

Above, the sounds of battle were muffled as though they were so far away, but she knew every moment counted. Nelson and Ian were trying to kill each other. She had to get back on the yacht and help her husband.

She forced herself to move, though her lungs were already burning. She moved from the light into the shadows where the pirate ship touched the yacht. Instinct told her to move away. The boats were so close together they formed a tight little space. Too tight. But she had to force herself to stay calm.

Surfacing, the sounds of battle rushed back to her, but she had to take the chance that Ian was keeping Nelson occupied. In between the two boats, they might not even see her. She was tiny compared to the two boats that bobbed around her.

Her arm ached and bled, but it looked like a through and through. The white surface of the yacht's hull was in front of her, the only thing marring it a large cake of C-4 that had been attached by one of Nelson's hired goons.

She forced herself to swim between the boats. So tight. The space seemed too small, but she turned her face upward and breathed in. She could do this.

She'd thought to send it to the bottom of the ocean, but a much better plan occurred to her.

The cake pried off in her hand. She turned to the pirate boat. It was a simple thing to toss the explosive up and over the side. There was a little *thunk* as it hit the deck. She prayed no one was watching, that everyone was on board the yacht.

Suddenly, the pirate ship shifted as a wave hit them. Charlie was caught between the two and sent headfirst into the yacht's hull.

Pain bloomed in her skull and then she could see the water all around her. It was quiet again and she was floating. The pain seemed to be gone. She knew her lungs were trying to work, but it seemed far off and darkness was just on the outer edge of her consciousness.

The first time she'd died, all she could think about was what she would miss, all the things she hadn't done. Regret had blanketed her. Death had been a cold, dark place.

It was different now. As the world started to go dark, all she could see was him. Her Master. All she could feel was the way he'd cared for her, how vibrant and beautiful the world had been in the end.

This time when she died, she realized another truth. At the end, there was love. Love for him. Love for her.

Death was so much easier the second time around.

* * * *

Ian cursed as Charlie went over the side of the yacht, but there was very little he could do about it because he was pinned down on the main deck. He'd managed to jump down from the bridge and take up a tactical position, but Nelson still had him caught and he'd called for reinforcements.

And he had the fucking laptop. Ian had lied about the security. There hadn't been time to do anything beyond getting the king and his cousin to the garage. Jiang Kun was fitting them with scuba gear to get them the fuck off this coffin.

Luckily all the furniture on the boat was nailed down. Ian was behind a large chaise where the king probably did his little harem on a regular basis. It was sturdy enough for two and provided decent cover.

Anxiety knotted his gut as he popped up and laid out another round of fire. It was immediately met, and he took a slug across his shoulder. It burned but the bullet hadn't done more than broken the skin. The bullet in his thigh was another matter. It was buried deep and bleeding like a motherfucker.

He wasn't sure he'd be able to swim very far.

"Cease fire." The command came over the loud

speaker. "Get to the boat. Follow the plan. We have what we need and you will be paid."

Fuck. What had happened?

He touched his earpiece. He'd been silent for a long time and had to hope Knight was still in position. "What's going on?"

"The Coast Guard," Knight said. "I just caught sight of them. They're probably ten minutes away."

"Do you see my wife?"

"That's a negative, Tag. I don't have a visual on her, but your brother and Simon are making their way along the port side, heading for you."

His brother's voice came over the device. "I'll be there in 60, brother."

One minute. He wasn't sure Charlie had a minute. If Nelson got on his boat and saw her in the water, he would shoot her out of sheer spite.

He stood up, firing toward the stairs that led to the main deck.

Unfortunately, there was no one left to kill.

"I left you a present, Tag." This time the sound was coming from the starboard side of the ship. Ian moved his ass, trying to get to the fucker before he got away. "Sorry to leave so very quickly, but I think our little game is over now. It would have been nice to have the tech, but in the end as long as I've destroyed it, it doesn't matter. I've rigged the ship to explode so you won't be able to play anymore. It's okay since your little whore is floating. You'll join her as soon as I get enough distance between us."

"Tag!"

He heard his brother shout as the boat Nelson was on began to pull away.

He pulled the trigger in frustration, trying to spray the

boat. He'd already lost sight of Nelson.

And then he saw something that made his heart stop.

A body floating in the water, face down, her hair around her like a halo.

"Ian, we have to go," his brother said as he ran up to him. He looked out and then pulled at Ian's shirt. "Ian, no."

But he wasn't listening. He tossed the gun aside and dove in, bad leg, aching shoulder and all.

Suck it up, Taggart. She's alive. She's fucking alive because she can't be dead.

Pain flared through his system but he swam to her, forcing her body over, her face up to the sun.

"Come on, baby." He started to swim back, trying not to think about the fact that she wasn't breathing. Her chest wasn't moving up and down. Her body was dead weight in his arms.

Not fucking dead. Not dead.

It became his mantra as he swam back, the rhythm that kept his limbs moving, his heart pumping.

Not fucking dead.

Charlie wasn't dead. Charlie couldn't be dead. He'd just found her again and he'd wasted time being mad at her. He should have just laid down in front of her and thanked the fucking universe for a second chance. Because the anger he'd felt was nothing compared to the love. He loved her. She was his in that stupid Hollywood way that made a man think dumbass things about the future.

"Give her to me." Sean leaned over, reaching for her and hauling her up.

Simon pulled Ian on to the deck.

Sean held her, but there was no strength in her body, just useless limbs hanging down. Everything that was Charlie seemed gone. "We need to go. It won't be long before he detonates that bomb. They left the second boat. Not enough men left to crew it. Let's go."

Charlie wouldn't last long enough to get to the boat.

"Lay her down," he commanded.

Sean laid her on the deck. "I'm so sorry, brother."

"Go. Both of you." Dropping to his knees, he ignored the pain that was screaming along his nerves. It was easy since the panic in his head was shouting down everything else. He was sure his face was passive, a trick from years of training, but he was fighting for control. Fighting the need to scream.

He moved to her mouth, tilting her head back. A kiss. It was like a kiss. He could trick his brain into believing it was just another kiss with his wife. He should have kissed her more. All the time.

One breath in and then another.

Methodically, he found her xiphoid process. It was there at the base of her breastbone. He moved the flat of his palm to her chest and pumped. One. Two. Three. Four. Five.

His brother was still here. If his brother died, Grace would feel this ache. She would feel the blinding pain of having half her fucking soul ripped away from her. She would understand what it meant to sit up at night and wonder where the hell her husband had gone. She'd already been through it once. She couldn't again. Not while Ian could stop it. "Get him out, Simon. That's an order. If you have any loyalty to me at all, do it."

He bent over and breathed into Charlie's sweet mouth again as Sean started to argue. There was a thud and when he moved back to chest compressions, Simon was picking up Sean's unconscious body and hauling it over his shoulder.

His deep blue eyes found Ian's. "Good luck, boss.

And thank you."

"Take care of my crew." One. Two. Three. Four. Five.

His body was on autopilot. He couldn't seem to stop. Part of him said to just give up, hold her in his arms and wait for the world to explode because wherever she was, that was where he wanted to be. He'd meant it. He didn't want to live in a world where he lost her twice.

Fuck. His vision was blurry. Something splashed and hit Charlie's cheek.

He was crying. He didn't fucking cry.

"You don't get to leave me!" A violent anger raged inside him. She didn't get to die. Not twice. Not now. If he was going out, then he wanted her looking into his eyes when it happened, he wanted them connected so he could hold on to her. So he didn't lose her.

He struck her chest, a deep thud causing her body to jerk. "Wake up. You wake up, bitch, because I'm not doing this without you."

There was no going back to a half-life of Scotch and songs no one else wanted to listen to and pretending he wasn't dead inside.

He struck again and her eyes flared, her mouth opening as water bubbled out of her lungs.

"Oh, shit." Ian thrust his good arm under her neck, turning her to the side as she vomited up what had to be a gallon of pure Arabian Sea.

"What did you do to me?" Charlie asked, her voice raw and so gorgeous to him. "I think a Mack truck hit my chest."

He didn't have time to argue about his CPR methods. Now that she was back, all he wanted to do was live. With a low groan, he got to his feet. They needed to get in the water, swim as far as they could. Just a chance. He would carry her as far as he could and then take whatever fate she suffered.

Live or die, he would do it with her.

He hauled her up even as she protested. "Ian, put me down. It hurts."

Limping, he started for the port side. He would do whatever it took. Getting her out of here was the most important thing in the world. "Can't, baby. We have to get out of here. Nelson is going to blow the ship."

She shook her head. "No. Not ours."

"Maybe he's lying, but I can't take the chance." God, he hoped the bastard was lying because their time had to be up.

"Ian, we're fine. Watch his boat. Watch his. Got into the water to do it."

Her words hit him with a flash of hope. His wife was smart and kind of really fucking mean, and it would totally occur to her to hand Nelson back his surprise. He turned to the boat that was speeding away from the yacht. He could have sworn he saw Nelson standing at the bow, watching. He seemed to be holding something in his hand. Nelson waved. The asshole.

And then Nelson's motherfucking boat exploded.

Ian stood strong as the concussive wave hit the yacht and made it list back and forth. His arms tightened around his wife and despite all the pain, he threw back his head and laughed.

Eli Nelson had just gotten taken down by a girl. A woman. Ian Taggart's woman. It was surprisingly better than taking the fucker down himself.

The yacht continued to move, and Ian stumbled to the chaise. He laid his wife down, her gorgeous body barely covered. She had a wound on her arm, but it didn't look serious. Dropping to his knee, he could hear the sound of

Nelson's boat hitting the water again after flying apart through the air. He would bet there were a whole lot of body parts flying around, like the best fireworks ever.

Charlie was still pale, her hand on her chest, rubbing it like it pained her. He hoped he hadn't broken anything. "So it was a good wedding present? I didn't get you one the first time."

She was alive. He breathed her in. She was alive. His wife was still with him, his future right in his arms. "Best present ever."

He kissed her as the Coast Guard started shouting in Hindi and the world was complete chaos around them.

"Tag?" Knight's voice came over the line again. "Tag? Do you want to explain what the bloody hell just happened?"

Ian took out the earpiece and tossed it over the side of the boat.

And got back to kissing his wife.

Chapter Twenty

Saint Petersburg, Russia
Two Weeks Later

Ian moved alongside the tourists, blending in as they crowded into the packed Peter and Paul Fortress. It was a rare sunny day in Saint Petersburg, and it looked like the citizens were out in droves. It seemed to him that the minute the sun came out in Russia, all its citizens dropped whatever they were doing and found a patch of grass to lie on.

Unfortunately, he couldn't be lazy today. Today was the day he gave his wife her life back.

After today, everyone got to go home. Even his brother, who was back in the States at the safe house with his small family and Adam and Jake's. Avery was staying with them while the rest of the team took care of business. Chelsea had chosen to return to the States with Sean. Damn, but he hoped she was there when he and Charlie got back.

His brother had only punched him once. Sean even waited until after the doctors had pulled the slug out of

Ian's leg to do it. Simon had taken a worse thrashing, but seemed to have given as well as he got. Sean had been pissed as hell that Ian had ordered him out, but they were already back on speaking terms.

All in all, it had been a damn fine op.

He walked through the bricked archway that led to the fortress as the tour guide spoke in her heavily Russian-accented English.

"The Peter and Paul Fortress was built in 1703 by Peter the Great. He feared attacks from Sweden so he decided that this island at the delta of the Neva River would be the best defense. The fortress was founded on May 27th and this is now considered the birthdate of the city of Saint Petersburg. If you will all follow me, we will go to the cathedral."

That was Ian's cue to break from the herd.

He walked toward the right hand side of the fortress, cobblestones at his feet. Damn cobblestones were all over the city. He had no idea how a person was supposed to run on the things. At times like this he was happy to be an American where the streets were usually even. If he had to run down his prey here, he might break a leg.

And since his thigh still ached from the bullet he'd taken, he wanted to avoid it if he could. He wanted his prey nice and contained.

Above his head the sky was a brilliant blue with puffy white clouds. To his right, the Peter and Paul Cathedral rose from the cobblestoned ground around it, an angel and a gold cross at the very top of its spire.

To his left was his destination, though not the final one. A building made of light-brown, almost gold-colored bricks housed the still-working mint. Dusan Denisovitch stood outside wearing very Western looking jeans, a T-shirt, and Ray Bans. It was fitting he'd chosen the mint as their meet-up spot since Ian was about to make the young man a whole lot of money.

Or he was about to get murdered in front of a bunch of tourists. It was a risk Ian was willing to take because he wanted it all. He wanted his wife and his family. He wanted a home.

"*Dobroye utro*, Mr. Taggart." Dusan said good morning with an almost formal tip of his head. The man was roughly Charlie's age. He pegged him at thirty or so. A ripe age to want to move ahead in the world.

"*Zdravstvujtye.*" A simple hello, or as simple as Russian ever got.

Dusan smiled. "Your accent is good."

He shrugged, taking in the four men surrounding Dusan. The young man's muscle was out in force. At least Ian knew Charlie's cousin was taking the meeting seriously. Or he was about to get jumped. His wife kept chiding him for his wretched pessimism, but until he actually pulled this off, he would just wait to see if someone was going to pull a gun.

"He's already in the cathedral," said a voice in his ear.

Luckily, Ian had backup of his own. Alex was in position outside the cathedral watching their prey. He'd spotted Liam as they'd walked in, ready to come to his aid should the second in command of the Denisovitch syndicate become unruly.

Of course, if he didn't, he just might become the first in command.

"So you are the man who married my pretty cousin," Dusan said. "I always like Charlotte and Chelsea. On the rare occasions my uncle would allow me to see them, they were nice girls. Smart girls. I did not like the way he treat them, you understand."

Charlie's cousin spoke fairly good English, though it

was easy to tell it wasn't something that came naturally to him. He spoke slowly and some of his words seemed broken, though he was easy to understand.

"Your father doesn't feel the same way."

Dusan shrugged, looking off in the distance. "My father believe that blood is all that matters, but I know blood can hurt blood. I have been my father's son for far too long to not understand this."

So his intelligence was right. He was making this gamble because he'd learned there was a fissure in the family that ran deep. Dusan was trusted by his father, but still treated as a child. It was time to be bold. The watch on his hand read eleven forty-nine. His time was running out. "If you suddenly found yourself at the head of the syndicate, would you feel the need to continue your father's mission?"

A slow smile cross the younger man's face. "Our mission should be to make money, Mr. Taggart. My father, he take too much time pursuing vengeance for a man who everyone agrees was monster. If my cousin is satisfied with her life and will no longer play games with us, then we will no longer play games with her. Besides, I hear she has new place to live now."

Ian laughed a little because he was pretty sure Dusan wasn't talking about Dallas. "I think we'll have to keep the Loa Mali property strictly as a vacation place."

The king had been very grateful. He also felt more than guilty about his servant turning on Charlie. He'd gifted them with a gorgeous piece of beach property. Once Ian got over the whole nearly being killed by Somali pirates thing, it would make a great getaway spot.

And the king was searching for a new man to take over his research. Both the Agency and MI6 believed the research had been destroyed. What they didn't know wouldn't hurt them.

"Like I say," Dusan continued. "I hope Charlotte is happy."

She seemed happy. He was going to make it his new mission to ensure that she always was. "I'll take care of her."

Dusan lit a cigarette, taking a long drag. "See that you do or I may have to pay visit to America myself. When I was fifteen, I get very sick. My father and uncle left me to rot because they had other things to do. My cousins, they nursed me back. No. I will not pursue vengeance against my family. Nor will anyone in power. It is time for a new power in this house. But I might be persuaded to avenge my little cousins should anything bad happen to them."

The men around him nodded gravely.

"All right, then." He turned toward the cathedral. God, his freaking in-laws were Russian mob. At least this once it came in handy.

"Mr. Taggart, since you do me favor, why don't I do one for you?"

"Yes?" he asked, keeping his eyes on the church.

"The men Nelson worked for, they have more people in their employ, people who still seem to work for their nations but who truly owe their loyalty to The Collective. I worry this will be bad for my business. Tell your friends to watch their backs. They never will know when a partner will turn on them. Rather like family. Now go. It's almost noon. If you miss this chance, we have to wait another week, and I have plans for celebrating tonight."

Dusan wasn't telling him anything he didn't already know. Someone had tipped off Nelson. There was a mole, and he wasn't sure who to trust anymore.

Which was a good reason to be happy he wasn't in that life anymore. He could trust his crew and no one else.

Damn, but he hoped Ten hadn't gotten into anything bad. Under all that charm was a cold son of a bitch. Could he really be that mercenary?

He let the thought go because all that mattered was the job in front of him.

"He's inside making the rounds. He doesn't have his normal guard with him. It looks like Charlie's cousin pulled through. Apparently his usual guard had a terrible car accident yesterday. Doesn't look like he'll live," Alex said over the Bluetooth.

Ian made his way through the massive wrought iron gates that led to the Peter and Paul Cathedral steps, the tops adorned with gold tips. He walked up the steps, surrounded by tourists. Most of them followed guides carrying numbers and walking frantically about trying to fit everything in. Many had small devices in their ears to hear the guide better in the crowded, noisy tourist spots of the city.

No one would think twice of a tall man walking though the cathedral. Hell, he fit in well in Northern Europe. Just last night his wife had claimed he was a Viking come to plunder her.

Yeah, he'd done that up right.

"So this asshole visits churches because he's so religious, but he's killed like a million people? I don't get it, man. My religion and his do not even exist on the same planet." Alex was always chatty when they were working.

Ian stepped into the ornate cathedral, the sunlight of the day giving way to a subdued light. Massive crystal chandeliers ran down the center of the space. There were no pews. No one sat in an orthodox Russian church. There was even a space left, a remnant of czarist Russia. It sat before the altar, a place swathed in rich cloth that led up to a gold covering. It was where the czar would stand.

All around him were white marble coffins with gold crosses, the final resting place of Russia's leaders.

They were about to get a new friend. Mikhail Denisovitch claimed he was a czar. He could join them.

"That's because you don't understand European religions, boyo. Your religion is what, two hundred years old?" Liam got in on the discussion. "Call me back when it's properly aged."

Liam stepped by him, winking as he went. He nodded toward the right side of the church. "I think you'll find what you're looking fer over there, mate."

Ian stopped looking at the green and white ceiling overhead. Every inch of the cathedral was painted or gilded. But he wasn't looking for beauty.

He turned to the right and spotted his prey.

Mikhail Denisovitch stood in front of a velvet rope looking into a room off the main floor.

"This is the resting place of the Romanovs," a tour guide was saying. "Hopefully we can get closer."

Denisovitch turned and the tour guide paled.

"We come back later. Come along. It is almost time for our lunch."

The gaggle of tourists flocked away. Denisovitch stared ahead, looking at the tombs of the Romanov family, slaughtered that day by the Bolsheviks at their Winter Palace. They had finally found their way here.

Ian glanced at his watch. Ten seconds if he was properly synced.

Liam flanked him, Alex coming up on the right.

The guard who was standing slightly behind Denisovitch tipped his hat and walked away, likely to join Dusan outside. Their prey was left with no one to watch over him.

Ian slipped the knife from where he'd hidden it in his

sleeve. It slid into his gloved hand.

Then the world seemed to explode. The building shook. The ground beneath them reverberated with the sound.

The cannons from the Naryshkin Bastion went off every day at noon. And every day at noon the tourists screamed and turned and, just for a moment, were afraid.

That was the moment Ian Taggart struck.

He pushed his knife in precisely under Denisovitch's ribs and into the man's heart. There was a small gasp and the jerk of a body as it fought briefly for life.

"For Charlotte." It didn't matter if Denisovitch heard him. All that mattered was the job was complete and his wife no longer had to fear for her life. He eased the man down behind the velvet rope and off to the side, left the knife in, and turned and walked away.

He and Charlie were free to live the way they wanted to—together.

The sun was bright on Ian's face as he turned toward the river and made his way out of the enclosure. With Alex and Liam behind him, they made their way to the edge of the fort and down the steps to the rocky shore where Simon and Jesse and Eve waited at the water's edge with a boat.

Then she turned and he caught sight of her. His Charlie had her face to the sun, soaking in the day.

The sun had nothing on her.

"Are we ready to head home, then?" Liam asked.

"Yes, we are," Ian replied, walking toward the boat.

It didn't matter, though. Home had ceased to be a place for Ian Taggart. He hopped on the boat, the waters of the Neva rocking them as Simon fired the engine and they pulled away.

"Hello, my Master," Charlie said to him, her wedding

ring sparkling in the light as she put her arms around his neck and held her face up for a kiss.

"Hello, my love." He looked down at the collar he'd placed around her neck before taking her mouth with his.

"Newlyweds," Eve said, grinning. "They can't keep their hands off each other."

Alex took that as a cue to kiss his wife silly. Ian couldn't let his best friend have all the fun. He kissed his Charlie again, the wind whipping through their hair as Simon started toward the Palace Bridge.

No. He didn't need to go anywhere to be home. He was already there.

* * * *

Kensington
London, England

The Garden was quiet at this time of day, and Damon Knight preferred working here to dragging himself into the gloom of MI6. Everyone was always rushing about, doing very important things. Everything was important at MI6. The Garden was his own personal kingdom, and he missed it when he was on assignment. He tried to stay in his own quiet office as much as possible when he was in England.

He stared at the e-mail he'd just received. It looked like there was a new head of the Denisovitch syndicate. His operative in Russia announced that Denisovitch had been found dead at the Peter and Paul Cathedral just an hour before. He claimed that Dusan Denisovitch was already moving to consolidate power.

Good for Taggart. Knight had offered his own services in bringing down the man who was threatening McKay-Taggart, but he'd been quite forcibly turned down.

That had actually hurt a bit more than he would have thought. He couldn't take it too personally. After all, Taggart had told Tennessee Smith to go to hell as well.

It just wasn't every day that he had a man he considered a friend suspect him of being a traitor.

And it wasn't every bloody day that he had to conclude that his partner was the real traitor.

Fuck him. The evidence was right there in front of him, a long string of coincidences that led to one conclusion—Baz was working with Nelson before he'd died.

Damon shoved a hand through his hair and cursed.

Baz had been his best mate for years. How could he not have bloody well seen it?

The door to his office opened. At this time of day, there were usually a few submissives working, cleaning the club and preparing for the night's scenes. He'd asked Jane, a sweet sub he'd been playing with lately, to bring him tea. And Scotch. He would need it to make the call he was about to make. He had to talk to the higher ups about arresting the man who had been by his side for years.

Was he really going to make that call? Or was he going to try to deal with it on his own. Maybe Baz had gotten in trouble. He could be impulsive. Maybe he should check into it further.

"Come in, pet." He turned toward the door.

And stopped. It looked like he wouldn't get a chance to make that decision about his friend.

Baz stood there, a Ruger in his hand. "Sorry, mate. Jane is, shall we say, unable to perform at the moment. Well, she's dead, so not likely she'll be performing anytime soon."

Before Damon could get out of his seat, Baz pulled the trigger and pain slammed into Damon's system. His chest. He had a bullet in his chest. Damon fell back, his hand coming up to cover the place where the bullet had gone in. He fell forward, hitting his desk.

He couldn't breathe. He tried to suck air in but somehow his lungs weren't working. He could hear a wheezing sound, like a balloon slowly losing its air.

"Sorry, mate. I couldn't let you make that call. I've been watching you. I know you figured it out. Couldn't have been too hard after the way Nelson fucked everything up. I need to thank the Taggarts for killing him. I just got promoted." He unplugged Damon's laptop.

From Damon's vantage he could only see his old friend's waist as he retreated with the laptop and his cell phone.

"You should have come with me, Damon. It's far more fun to work on the dark side, so to speak. But you just liked to play at being a Dominant. I'm the real thing. See you in Hell, brother."

The sounds of footsteps retreated, though everything seemed to be retreating. Sound, vision, feeling.

Everything except one.

Rage filled him.

As the darkness threatened to take him, Damon Knight knew one thing. Revenge would get him through.

Damon Knight and the McKay-Taggart crew will return in 2014 with *Dungeon Royale*.

Dungeon Royale

Masters and Mercenaries, Book 6
By Lexi Blake
Coming 2014!

Broken by betrayal, one woman holds the secret to his redemption…

An agent broken

MI6 agent Damon Knight prided himself on always being in control. His missions were executed with cold, calculating precision. His club, The Garden, was run with an equally ordered and detached decadence. But his perfect world was shattered by one bullet, fired from the gun of his former partner. That betrayal almost cost him his life and ruined his career. His handlers want him to retire, threatening to revoke his license to kill if he doesn't drop his obsession with a shadowy organization called The Collective. To earn their trust, he has to prove himself on a unique assignment with an equally unusual partner.

A woman tempted

Penelope Cash has spent her whole life wanting more. More passion. More adventure. But duty has forced her to live a quiet life. Her only excitement is watching the agents of MI6 as they save England and the world. Despite her training, she's only an analyst. The closest she is allowed to danger and intrigue is in her dreams, which are often filled with one Damon Knight. But everything changes when the woman assigned to pose as Damon's submissive on his latest mission is incapacitated. Penny is suddenly faced with a decision. Stay in her safe little world or risk her life and her heart for Queen and country.

An enemy revealed

With the McKay-Taggart team at their side, Damon and Penny hunt an international terrorist across the great cities of Northern Europe. Playing the part of her Master, Damon begins to learn that under Penny's mousy exterior is a passionate submissive, one who just might lay claim to his cold heart. But when Damon's true enemy is brought out of the shadows, it might be Penny who pays the ultimate price.

Steal the Day

Thieves, Book 2
By Lexi Blake
Coming October 22, 2013!

The world's most unusual thief faces her greatest challenge—stealing a soul from the depths of Hell...

When a member of her crew is dragged to Hell by a demon, Zoey plans the most dangerous heist of her career. With her team at her side, Zoey intends to sneak onto the Hell plane and steal Sarah back.

The job seems impossible until a new client makes them an offer too good to refuse. If she can find an ancient artifact called The Revelation, she can use it to locate an angel who holds Sarah's redemption in his hands.

Surrounded by warring angels and demons, the greatest threat may come from one of her own. Torn between her Fae lover and the vampire who has always held her heart, Zoey finds that she and Dev are trapped in Daniel's web of secrets, and it may be Zoey who has to pay the ultimate price.

* * * *

Chapter One

I stretched as I rolled out of bed, trying not to wake

the man next to me. I caught sight of Devinshea Quinn and couldn't help but stare. His tan skin made a stark contrast to the white sheets. His dark hair was mussed from our activities, and though his face was relaxed, there was no way to soften that perfectly shaped jawline. The sheet was around his waist leaving most of his lean, muscular body on display. Everything about Dev Quinn was perfect, from his washboard abs to his cut chest, to those ridiculously sensual lips. I felt a smile cross my face as I sat there and just watched him sleep.

He shifted, rolling over in bed, and I decided it was time to go. As much as I liked to look at him, I really didn't want the argument that was sure to come when he realized where I was going.

I stood up and was finally able to get out of the Christian Louboutin's Dev had gifted me with earlier in the evening. I flexed my feet. The shoes were ridiculously gorgeous. My eyes had widened when I opened the box, and my heart had fluttered. It hadn't taken Dev long before he had me in the shoes and nothing else. Those shoes were exciting and sexy, and just the slightest bit uncomfortable. They were a little like my relationship with Dev. The sex was incredible, and while I was in bed with Dev, I didn't think about anything but him. The minute I rolled out of bed, I wanted to get out of those shoes and put on a pair of Converse. That was our problem.

Well, that and my husband.

I walked through the grotto, collecting stray clothes along the way. Dev's apartment was at the top of a building he owned in the middle of downtown Dallas. The bottom of the building housed his club, Ether, the hottest club of its kind. But it wasn't the kind of club that showed up on the "Best of Dallas" lists since I'm one of the only humans to be permitted entrance.

Ether was the place where the supernaturals of the world went to mix and mingle and do a little business. It was an official place of peace, despite my last year's best effort to burn it down. I hadn't meant to, but then I never do. Trouble just follows me. That had been my first date with Dev. At the time, I wasn't married. It didn't take me long to remedy that.

I slowed, unable to rush through. Dev's "condo" took up the whole top floor of the building and was the most decadent space I'd ever seen. The first time Dev had taken me up the private elevator from his office in Ether to his penthouse, the doors had opened and I'd gasped. I called the whole place "the grotto." It was something like an indoor forest, complete with a brook that ran through the various rooms of the apartment. When the sun was out, the whole place was lit with soft, natural light. In the dead of night, moonbeams streamed through the overhead windows, shining down and making the room seem magical.

It's odd for a faery to live year round in the city. They don't like the feeling of being enclosed. It goes against their nature, but Dev was mortal. He was the only one of his mother's children who had not taken after her, and because of his mortality, he'd chosen to leave the *sithein* and cut off ties to his family. Since the day we'd met, I could remember two conversations we'd had about his family.

This place made me think he missed them.

I walked into the bathroom and turned on the shower. The bathroom was bigger than my entire living room. The splendor of Dev's home put in stark contrast our relative differences. Dev had money and a lot of it. I had recently finished a job that gave me enough money to buy a little fixer-upper in the country, but I was starting to hurt for cash. My account was down to the low four digits, and I didn't have more money coming in.

I would have given up all the money I had made on my last job if I could have changed the outcome of it. Some jobs aren't worth the payday.

I tossed my clothes on the sink and stepped under the rainfall of deliciously hot water. The water stroked over my skin, and I stretched again. Sex with Dev was inventive and exciting, and required a certain level of flexibility. I could see yoga classes in my future.

Suddenly two big hands came from behind and cupped my breasts. I sighed for two reasons—one because it felt so good, and two because there would be no getting out of a fight. I let my head fall back against his chest, his body nestling against mine. If we were going to fight, I might as well enjoy the first part.

"Zoey," Dev breathed in my ear, his voice the sweetest of seductions. "I sincerely apologize. I have treated you poorly."

I smiled because I knew what was coming next. "I disagree, Dev. I was treated incredibly well. At least three times."

One hand stayed at my breast, plucking at my nipple, pinching and lighting it up. Another clever hand made its way lower. His fingers slid over my clit, and that was all it took. I was warm and wet again. "If I had done my job properly, you would have passed out. The fact that you can move means I have more work to do. I didn't even get to the part where I tie you up and we play."

Dev liked to play. He liked to play with handcuffs and toys. He had a whole closet full of naughty little devices, like an FAO Schwarz for kink. With a low growl, he shifted, turning me toward him. His mouth took mine in a deep, luxurious kiss. This was what Dev and I did best.

He lifted me up, settling me on the ledge of the shower. I was sure the contractors who had built the place thought the wide shelf was to store shampoo and soap, but I knew better. Dev had designed it with sex in mind. He moved between my legs, the ledge placing my pussy at the perfect height for him.

"I can't get enough of you. I fucking crave you." He'd come prepared. He slipped a condom on and worked his way in. It wasn't long before my back was up against the natural rock of the shower and I was screaming out number four.

"Let's dry off and go back to bed," he whispered as he held me up because my legs weren't quite working yet. It wasn't easy keeping up with a man whose grandfather had been a fertility god. "I'll tell Albert to send up breakfast for two in the morning."

I hugged him close to me, hoping that my affection would make the next few minutes easier. "I can't. I have to go. I have a meeting with a client."

Dev stopped, his whole face lighting up. I suspected one of the reasons he liked me was my unusual job. I was a thief who specialized in procuring objects of an arcane nature. Stealing from supernaturals made my job one of the riskier fields. It was thrilling when the job ran well, and completely terrifying when anything went wrong. Dev had run one job with me and had been bugging me ever since to let him go again. He'd gotten off on the adrenaline rush.

He winked down at me. "That's great, sweetheart. I'll get dressed and go with you. I promise to keep my mouth

441

shut and be good eye candy. Should I take the Ruger or the Glock?"

I pulled away from him because no amount of affection was going to fix this. "Sorry, but I have to go alone."

His deep green eyes formed suspicious slits. "Alone? You never go alone. That's your first rule." He took a step back, his mouth turning down. "So if you're not going alone, you're going with Daniel."

And there it was, the one word that could wreck our day. "He is my partner."

"He's your husband." Dev spat the word out as though it was poison. He stalked out of the shower, leaving me with an incredible view of his preternaturally glorious ass.

I picked up a bottle of something Dev liked the smell of and then put it back down in favor of plain old soap. I told myself it was because I needed to be professional. I didn't want to go into a client meeting smelling like a woman who had just had sex four times. If I was honest with myself, and I tried not to be, I didn't want to hurt Daniel.

I finished up in the shower and turned it off, wrapping a warm towel around my body. Dev was sitting on the sink when I went to retrieve my clothes. He'd slipped into silk boxers and looked at me with a sad smile.

"Sorry," he said. "I know I'm being an ass. I'm just jealous."

"You have nothing to be jealous of." It sounded like a reassuring lie even to my ears. "If I could get a divorce, I would."

I'd come to accept the marriage I had been tricked into. It wasn't like I had much of a choice. Tricked is a harsh word. Daniel had been trying to protect me at the time. It was his excuse for everything. I didn't resent the protection. I resented the fact that he'd left me ignorant. I had to find out from a demon that we were married. There'd been no vows of love and devotion, no white dress or fabulous reception. There had been blood and sex and a transfer of ownership between Daniel and myself.

And there was no divorce when you were married to a vampire.

Wicked and Dangerous, featuring Wicked All Night

Wicked Lovers, Book 7.5
By Shayla Black
Available October 1, 2013

A sweet school teacher who changed towns, jobs, and lives after her divorce decides to take a lover. She hooks up with a bodyguard whose talents under the sheets make her melt. Until she learns that his motives are just as dangerous as they are wicked…

* * * *

Excerpt:

Rachel Linden fixed her gaze across the room at the man staring her way, standing between the two suits. Her jaw dropped before she forcibly snapped it shut. *Holy cow!* Between the alcohol and the press of bodies, she was overheated. But he made her shiver.

Military-short black hair capped off his angled face, covered by a healthy two days' growth of beard. His eyes remained hidden behind a pair of aviators that rested on top of chiseled cheekbones. His black shirt nearly busted at the shoulder seams. Under the short sleeves, his biceps bulged. The soft cotton clung to every valley and ridge of his pectorals and abdominals.

He was a man with a capital M, the sort who made a woman swallow her tongue. The kind her mother had warned her about. The type who'd starred in her fantasies. And the one she wanted sliding against her skin-to-skin now. Dark and bad, yes . . . but those big hands and muscled forearms alone said he'd be oh so good.

Just looking at him, Rachel had trouble breathing. Every inch of him was hard. If she'd had a fantasy in the flesh, he'd be it.

A tattoo—Asian writing maybe—drifted down his veined forearm. Dog tags hung from his neck. The little smile curling his lips was somewhere between an invitation and a challenge. And he was staring directly at her.

The bottom fell out of her stomach. Normally, she'd shy away from such a man. Aaron, the fifth grade social studies teacher, had asked her out a few weeks ago. He was polite and had kind brown eyes. He'd mentioned a local theater production that sounded interesting. That was her speed. This man in front of her . . .

"He looks good enough to eat. And to lick, slurp, suck . . . Damn, girl!" Shonda, one of the art teachers, murmured in her ear.

If you're going to dive into a meal after starving, why not start with the juiciest one you can find?

She glanced at Shonda's dark skin gleaming under the dim house lights and faintly flashing colored strobes. "Is it my imagination or is he staring at me?"

"Right at you, like he thinks you're a tasty snack. Go on now. Talk to him."

And say what? Hi, I haven't had sex since I divorced my ex over a year ago, and I've never had it as down and dirty and sweaty as I'll bet you could give it to me.

"Maybe he thinks I work here."

Shonda snorted. "Maybe you're insane. Jarelle is an

445

awesome fiancé with enough freak in bed to keep me smiling, but hell . . . If I were single, I'd be all over him like paste on wallpaper."

Rachel laughed. Leave it to Shonda to tell it like it was. And to be right. Rachel had to admit that she'd never know what could be if she didn't try to talk to Mr. Tall, Dark, and Hot.

She turned back toward him, a welcoming smile in place. But he was already leaving behind his two friends, wearing insanely expensive suits, and walking her way. No, "walking" was the wrong word. "Approaching" was too weak. "Looming" maybe? Still not right. "Prowling," yes. "Stalking" sounded even more like it.

He tore off his sunglasses to reveal a stark pair of blue eyes, unabashedly roaming over her body with a heat that made her swallow. He kept coming at her, invading her personal space without compunction. Reflexively, she retreated. He smiled, then did it again and again—until her back hit the wall.

"Hi, beautiful."

Mercy, the low rumble of his voice was sexy. Her knees quaked.

"Hi." She breathed the word as if she couldn't quite catch her breath.

He looked her up and down, obviously scoping her out. "Hmm, you with all those curves, and me here with no breaks . . . Damn!"

OMG, was that some sort of pick-up line?

"Um . . ."

If he'd intended to flatter her, he was headed in the wrong direction. She'd write him off, except . . . The black skirt Shonda had insisted she wear tonight had seemed stupidly tight—until she saw the appreciation in his gaze.

446

That and his line, no matter how terrible, made her think that, maybe, he actually found her sexy. And she wasn't interested in him for his conversational skills.

"Too much, huh?" he asked with a frown. "How about, there must be something wrong with my eyes because I can't take them off you."

He was trying to pick her up—badly—but out of a bar full of pretty girls, he'd zeroed in on her. Would wonders never cease?

Maybe if she stopped focusing on her ex-husband's litany of critical comments and started to believe that some men might like her as she was, curves and all, it wouldn't seem so weird.

"Definitely too much." She gave him a smile that she hoped looked sophisticated and wry, rather than giggly and excited.

"Oh, you like subtle. I got it." He leaned closer and leered. "Hey, baby, you come here often?"

The most obvious pick-up line ever, and when he delivered it with a grin, she laughed. If this was his idea of starting a conversation, she wasn't sure whether she should be annoyed or charmed against her will. But she was definitely leaning toward the latter.

"Never. This is my first time," she admitted. "You?"

"Same. I was thinking that I hated places like this until I saw you. You're better than a broom because you swept me off my feet."

Rachel couldn't help but laugh. "Right . . ."

"No lie, beautiful." He winked at her. "Tell me, what's your sign?"

Yield. If she were holding a sign, that's probably what it would say because that's kind of what she wanted to do for him. Oh, but she guessed that wasn't what he meant.

"Libra," she said finally. "Today is my birthday. And I'll only keep talking to you if you stop with the pick-up lines."

"Happy birthday! You mean I can't ask you for a Band-Aid?"

She frowned. How had they gone from pick-up lines to Band-Aids? "I'm sorry?"

"I need one because I scraped my knees falling for you."

Rachel tossed her hands up, shaking her head, and giggled. "Does this sort of thing usually work for you?"

He shrugged. "Don't know. I never tried. You wanna tell me come morning?"

About Lexi Blake

Lexi Blake lives in North Texas with her husband, three kids, and the laziest rescue dog in the world. She began writing at a young age, concentrating on plays and journalism. It wasn't until she started writing romance that she found success. She likes to find humor in the strangest places. Lexi believes in happy endings no matter how odd the couple, threesome or foursome may seem. She also writes contemporary western ménage as Sophie Oak.

Connect with Lexi online:

Facebook: Lexi Blake
Twitter: www.twitter.com/@authorlexiblake
Website: www.LexiBlake.net

Other Books by Lexi Blake:

EROTIC ROMANCE

Masters And Mercenaries
The Dom Who Loved Me
The Men With The Golden Cuffs
A Dom Is Forever
On Her Master's Secret Service
Sanctum: A Masters and Mercenaries Novella
Love and Let Die
Coming Soon:
Dungeon Games: A Masters and Mercenaries Novella
Dungeon Royale

Masters of Ménage by Shayla Black and Lexi Blake
Their Virgin Captive
Their Virgin's Secret
Their Virgin Concubine
Their Virgin Princess
Their Virgin Hostage
Coming Soon:
Their Virgin Secretary

CONTEMPORARY WESTERN ROMANCE

Wild Western Nights
Leaving Camelot, *Coming Soon*

URBAN FANTASY

Thieves
Steal the Light
Steal the Day, *Coming October 2013*
Steal the Moon, *Coming 2014*
Steal the Sun, *Coming 2014*
Steal the Night, *Coming 2014*

CPSIA information can be obtained
at www.ICGtesting.com
Printed in the USA
FSOW02n2106290917
39362FS